PENGUIN BOOKS

WRITERS FROM THE OTHER EUROPE
General Editor: Philip Roth

A DREAMBOOK FOR OUR TIME

Tadeusz Konwicki was born into a worker's family in 1926 near Vilna, in Lithuania. He attended a high school run secretly under the Nazi occupation and, after the Nazi defeat, joined a guerrilla unit fighting Russian troops. Later, his native region having been absorbed into the Soviet Union, he moved to Poland. His novels have established him as one of the leading writers in the Polish language. He is also an eminent screenwriter and the director of several highly personal and imaginative feature films. Three of Mr. Konwicki's other books have appeared in English: a children's book, *Anthropos-Specter-Beast,* and the novels *The Polish Complex,* which is also published by Penguin Books, and *A Minor Apocalypse*.

Leszek Kołakowski was born in Radom, Poland, in 1927. He was professor of the history of philosophy at the University of Warsaw until March 1968, when he was expelled for political reasons. Since then, he has held visiting professorships at McGill University in Montreal and at the University of California in Berkeley. He is currently professor of philosophy at Yale University.

A DREAMBOOK FOR OUR TIME

TADEUSZ KONWICKI

Translated by
David Welsh

Introduction by Leszek Kołakowski

PENGUIN BOOKS

Penguin Books Ltd, Harmondsworth,
Middlesex, England
Penguin Books, 40 West 23rd Street,
New York, New York 10010, U.S.A.
Penguin Books Australia Ltd, Ringwood,
Victoria, Australia
Penguin Books Canada Limited, 2801 John Street,
Markham, Ontario, Canada L3R 1B4
Penguin Books (N.Z.) Ltd, 182–190 Wairau Road,
Auckland 10, New Zealand

First published in Poland under the title
Sennik Współczesny by Iskry 1963
First published in the United States of America by
The M.I.T. Press 1969
Published in Penguin Books 1976
Reprinted 1983

LIBRARY OF CONGRESS CATALOGING IN PUBLICATION DATA
Konwicki, Tadeusz.
  A dreambook for our time.
  (Writers from the other Europe)
  Translation of: Sennik współczesny.
I. Title. II. Series.
PG7158.K6513S43 1984   891.8'537   83-13361
ISBN 0 14 00.4115 X

Printed in the United States of America by
R.R. Donnelley & Sons Company, Harrisonburg, Virginia
Set in Fototronic Baskerville (CRT)

WRITERS FROM THE OTHER EUROPE

The purpose of this paperback series is to bring together outstanding and influential works of fiction by Eastern European writers. In many instances they will be writers who, though recognized as powerful forces in their own cultures, are virtually unknown in the West. It is hoped that by reprinting selected Eastern European writers in this format and with introductions that place each work in its literary and historical context, the literature that has evolved in "the other Europe," particularly during the postwar decades, will be made more accessible to a new readership.

PHILIP ROTH

OTHER TITLES IN THIS SERIES

*Available in Great Britain

INTRODUCTION

An American reader unfamiliar with modern Polish history may have trouble decoding all of the dreams in Tadeusz Konwicki's novel and in setting the events in the proper historical context. Thus, a brief explanation may be useful.

A Dreambook for Our Time, published in Warsaw in 1963, tells of the inconspicuous events that took place in a tiny Polish village in the early 1960s. Time and again, the narrator remembers the cruel and traumatic war years 1944–1945, when wounds were inflicted from which Poland has never entirely recovered. These flashbacks reveal much about the author's own life, but, not surprisingly, a "dream-book" blurs these autobiographical details.

As in previous books, Konwicki is concerned with simple, ill-educated people—in this case, ordinary townsfolk whose lives have been torn asunder by war and who are trying to piece together their shattered existence. Some of them, including the narrator (and the author), came from the Vilna region, the northeastern corner of pre-1939 Poland (now in the Soviet Union), which has played an enormous part in Polish history, legend, and literature.

Poland was abandoned by her allies when the German occupation took place in September 1939 and suffered partition as a result of the Soviet-German nonaggression pact. A Polish government, exiled in London after the fall of France and recognized by the vast majority of Poles as the legitimate ruler of the country, provided leadership to the Home Army, a nationalist underground guerrilla force that struggled against the Nazis and the Red Army troops. Polish Communists formed a small guerrilla underground of their own. Although they fought the Germans alongside the Home Army and also perished on the battlefield, in concentration camps, and in Gestapo torture chambers, they organized no single anti-Nazi front with the Polish nationalists. Indeed, hostility between the two factions was particularly evident in the eastern region of Poland, where the Soviets had ruled for two years before the Nazis' spectacular eastward run, culminating in the invasion of the Soviet Union, in June 1941.

By August 1944, eastern and central Poland had been retaken as far as the Vistula River by the Soviet Army and by Polish troops mobilized in the Soviet Union. At this time almost half of Poland's prewar territory enlarged Stalin's empire, and the foundation was laid for a new, Communist-dominated Polish government. Non-Communist and anti-Communist underground forces were now systematically crushed by the Red Army, to whom they were "fascist bandits." When a group of Polish underground leaders was invited to negotiate with Soviet military authorities, they were arrested on the spot and imprisoned. Not all of them survived. Underground guerrilla fighters were also captured and sent to Soviet prison camps or simply liquidated.

The Warsaw Uprising began on August 1, 1944. For two months the Soviet Army stood watchful, but inactive, along the eastern bank of the Vistula as German troops conducted the massacre within the Polish capital. Although this battle rendered the Home Army nearly helpless, some in the underground forces refused to disarm and surrender. This opened a new chapter in what was rapidly evolving into a civil war. The fighting continued, but not with the Germans. Now Poles shot Poles—both sides unfortunately believing they were acting in good faith. Konwicki's narrator, who joined the Home Army as a teenager during the occupation, was among those who continued the hopeless war.

There are two ways of looking at the development of Communism in Poland. It was, of course, imported by the Soviet Army and forced upon the overwhelming majority of the population, but the Soviet Army nevertheless replaced what all Poland had known as the ultimate evil—Nazi occupation. During German rule a moral vacuum existed; the Poles lived with an enemy who wanted only to annihilate them. There were a few Polish collaborators, but there was no pervasive ideology of collaboration as there had been in France. The Germans themselves did not even try to organize the collaborators into an important political movement. Communism, although imposed by another foreign power, was not without indigenous roots and could not simply be seen as another "occupation."

For the first three years after the war, independent political parties operated legally in Poland, and university and cultural life, though controlled, was not yet subject to the devastations of Stalinism. The country was in ruin, and it was the Communists in power who undertook the immense task of its restoration. Moreover, Communist ideology itself bore traces of rationalism as well as the prewar radicalism that had attracted many intellectuals by providing an alternative to the deeply conservative strains in Polish culture. Thus many intellectuals and writers in the postwar period found themselves in the Communist party, and although most of them sooner or later dropped out of it—Konwicki himself left the party in 1966—they often experienced confused guilt as a result of their own changing allegiances during this period of political and moral ambiguity.

In the years 1944–1947 Polish literature frequently expressed the confusion and ambiguity that marked the tragic events of this quasi-civil-war period. Jerzy Andrzejewski's novel *Ashes and Diamonds,* published in 1948 before hard-line Stalinist cultural policy was consolidated in Poland and better known in the West than other Polish novels because of Andrzej Wajda's 1958 film, grew out of the hope that a bridge would be built one day over the torrent of blood that had been shed in fratricidal fighting. If such a bridge has never been built, it is because it would require truth about these events to be spoken aloud by all sides—and to this day such plain speaking is impossible.

It is not surprising that the horrors of a war that destroyed one fifth of Poland's population have continued to fascinate Polish writers in the postwar decades. The German occupation of September 1939, the partisan war and its conspiratorial struggles, the German prisons and concentration camps, the ghettoes, the massacres, the fate of the Polish Army in the west—these events and themes out of Polish history recur again and again in recent Polish literature. The physical and moral atrocities and the suffering and heroism of these years are reflected in the writings of Zofia Nałkowska, Jerzy Andrzejewski, Adolf Rudnicki, Tadeusz Borowski, Kazimierz Brandys, Jerzy Pytlakowski, Melchior Wańkowicz, Tadeusz Nowakowski, Jerzy Putrament, and Bohdan Czeszko. Other significant aspects of the war—the fate of Poles in eastern territories under the Soviet occupation, life in Soviet labor camps and prisons and in Siberian exile—were, of course, forbidden subjects in Communist Poland. Polish literature written in exile made up partly for this lacuna; among the works dealing with these themes, one of the most outstanding is Gustaw Herling-Grudziński's novel *The Other World.*

Even in the latter part of the 1950s and early 1960s, despite a relaxation of political censorship, these sensitive topics generally remained taboo. In light of such censorship the publication of Konwicki's novel in Poland is exceptional.

It is important to stress, however, that the destructive impact of Stalinism on Polish literature was less damaging than in other Soviet-dominated countries. Since the late 1950s there has been relatively little fiction written according to the requirements of the official ideology. Novels tend now to be realistic and, for that very reason, objectionable to the political authorities. Hence the increasing number of works which cannot pass through the needle's eye of censorship. In the last few years novels by Andrzejewski, Marek Nowakowski, and others have been denied publication. Some authors, at great risk, manage to publish their books abroad, either pseudonymously or under their own names.

A Dreambook for Our Time would seem to be the most "political" of Konwicki's many novels. Yet even that adjective lends an improper emphasis. All his novels, whether childhood reminiscences or tales of contemporary Poland, have a dreamlike quality to them. The events rarely follow each other in natural or motivational succession, and the characters often seem half real. Well located though they are in space and time, Konwicki's stories tend in style and method to be lyrical and expressive rather than descriptive or historical.

In this "dreambook" Konwicki attempts to find a meaning and, one might say, a logic in an incoherent, often strangely distorted, mass of images as they loom up from memory. Do we perceive a meaning? Not with any certainty. There is nothing unambiguous to be said of the human and political struggles about which Konwicki has written —except to say that in looking back at the sides that clashed in Poland's civil war, we can condemn no one. Moreover, the survivors of both sides, as they appear in *A Dreambook for Our Time,* are now wrecks, their lives given over to joyless lovemaking, futile recollections, and the drinking of vodka. Even the landscape that they inhabit in the novel is about to perish forever beneath an artificial lake, thus sealing the future to the past.

Still, this is not a book about the futility of life. Although the narrator has gone over from one fighting side to another in his country's bloody struggle, his commandment remains: "Thou shalt not betray!" His loyalty to his past is contained in the very act of questioning his past. Is such a haunted self-interrogation possible? The answer is that it has to be possible lest he fall apart irreparably.

LESZEK KOŁAKOWSKI

A DREAMBOOK
FOR OUR TIME

I didn't open my eyes, and, like a man awakened from an afternoon doze, I did not know where or who I was. The venomous taste of bile burned my mouth, the ticklish centipede of a pulse ran across my temples. I was lying in a ponderous sack of pain and sweat.

"Look, everyone, he's moving!" cried a woman's voice.

"Aha, he doesn't like the taste, for sure," declared a man. "He scowled like a squealing pig."

"He threw up the entire substance," declared a familiar baritone. "When I couldn't reach with my right hand, I used my prosthesis. I stuck it in up to his gullet, as far as my elbow. But the nickel jarred against his teeth. I could have stroked his pancreas."

"Ah, back home in the East, mister, people were sensitive," sighed the woman. "I remember one such government clerk in Snipiszki, God rest his soul, who had a very delicate constitution. One time, mister, he lost his temper at work or maybe at home, with his nasty wife; anyway he took a drink of wood alcohol and on top of that he went and shot himself in the head with a government pistol, mister. But d'you think that was the end of him, mister? He was so agitated he ran all the way to the railroad station, and that was four miles, and he threw himself under a train. In those days, mister, back in the East, people took life easier, and the train went through only two, maybe three times a day, so he was lucky to catch it."

"Here we're chattering," interrupted the baritone, but the other man's voice interrupted:

"Shhh, quiet, he's waking up."

I raised my eyelids slowly. In front of the bed stood Miss Malvina Korsak in tears, her brother Ildefons beside her, as usual without a jacket, in an old-fashioned shirt buttoned at the neck, while a little to one side was the partisan, wiping his artificial arm on a towel.

"Where am I?"

"You've come back from a business trip," said the partisan and threw the towel down on my bed.

"Was that a nice thing to do?" whispered Miss Malvina. "Old enough to know better, gray hairs on your head, and to go against God's laws so . . ."

"What happened?" I asked uncertainly.

"Come, don't be foolish, mister," said Mr. Korsak, sternly and snorted into his greenish whiskers. "Maybe people will forget, but not the Lord God."

Behind them was an oil painting, the kind that hangs in all old houses; with snow, the track of a sleigh, bare birch trees, and a red sunset.

I turned my face to the wall: "I must have eaten something."

"I already know what harmed you," said the partisan. "Lucky the Korsaks heard you."

"Oh mister, how he was snoring! Not like a human being at all," Miss Malvina shuddered. "I knew right away it was no ordinary sleep."

"I've seen the very same at the Front, back in '17," Korsak added. "Only in those days they let off gas, mustard gas. You're young, so maybe you don't remember."

"We've seen all sorts of things, grandad," said the partisan.

I rose on my elbow, then let my feet down to the floor. Warmed by the sun, the rectangular window swayed violently in front of me. I tried to stand up. All at once a slimy chill gripped my skull. I took a few uncertain steps toward the door and then suddenly the ground slid away, I reeled backward, my head banged on the cherrywood planks.

When I came to, Korsak and the partisan were dragging me back to bed. I felt the chill of his prosthesis under my armpit.

"Easy, he'll throw up," Miss Malvina warned them.

"With what, O ministering angel? You'd better give him some sour milk."

They poured something sour and salty into my mouth. Korsak smoothed a quilt over me. It was hot and associated with disease. The partisan was vigorously working his prosthesis.

Then Romus arrived. He didn't really arrive but had been standing in the room for a very long time. His movements were so lazy and slow that one could analyze their separate phases to one's heart's content. Every one of his exceedingly slack and incomplete steps was emphasized by a rotation of his hips. When in some imperceptible manner he completed his process of conquering space and halted at the door, he waveringly raised a hand, then reluctantly rubbed his enormous and sleepy mop of hair.

"They're coming," he said.

"All you're good for is to fetch the undertaker," said Miss Malvina, but hastily clapped her outstretched fingers to her mouth, "Goodness, what am I saying . . . !"

"Maybe we should call a doctor too?" suggested the partisan.

"What for, mister, who needs that?" Miss Korsak replied. "I'm sixty-five years old and never needed a doctor in all my life, thank God. If he's doomed to survive, he will. These days, mister, doctors only drive a man quicker to his coffin. Back home in the East, we had a different kind of medicine."

"I've heard that, back home in your East, they used foot-clouts made of warmed flannel most of the time," said the partisan.

Miss Malvina was somewhat taken aback, not being sure what the partisan meant. "Well, for sure, keeping warm is the main thing when you're sick," she replied evasively.

Romus scratched his back against the door frame and slowly removed himself from the room like a figure in a dream. Then I saw him through the window, as he gathered graying burdock leaves and like a lunatic lay down on their pulp, turning his face toward the sunlight that was pouring down in a dense, autumnal glow. A horse fly, intrigued by his motionless recumbent body, began circling around his head, until he sent it away with feeble puffs through numb lips, without opening his eyes.

"Well now, you son of the Party," asked the partisan, "do you feel any better?"

"I don't know. I suppose so."

"You used to look hale and hearty, a real buck. What suddenly took a hold of you?"

I was silent.

"Ah, looks don't mean anything," Miss Korsak put in. "Back home in the East, I remember. . . ."

I swallowed gluey saliva, "I want to be left alone."

"He's getting fussy," said Korsak with an understanding smile.

At this moment the railroad man Debicki came in. He put his stick in one corner and took off his railroad cap, from which dust poured into an oblique sunray: "What's up?"

"We saved him, Mr. Dobas."

The railroad man looked at her somberly: "My name is Debicki."

"Yes, yes, we know. But the old ways are always handier. Habit is second nature," she explained in confusion.

"Police been?"

"What do we want the police for?" Korsak was surprised.

"Mister Railroad Man likes curing people by other means," said the partisan ambiguously.

"What sort of a hint is that?"

"What do you mean 'hint'? I was just talking. In this heat, this stuffiness, a man sometimes says a thing that's neither here nor there, but you right away . . . 'hints.' "

"Very well, I know what's on your mind."

A tactful knocking was heard at the door: "May I come in?"

The enormously long face of Count Pac, overgrown with sparse yellow hair, appeared in the doorway. He kissed Miss Malvina's hand with a great show of gallantry and then politely greeted the others present. Finally he approached my bed: "O *pardon,* that's to say, I mean 'excuse me,' " he said, stammering, after taking one look at me.

"Please go away. I want to be left alone," I said quietly.

"Oh, he's whining again," declared Korsak.

"Very well, but he didn't do this of his own accord," said the railroad man.

"Out of some class motives?" the partisan put in, soothingly.

"Don't you provoke me." The railroad man shot him an unfriendly glance. "I'm not asking you."

"There's nothing wrong with me," I said with difficulty. "Go away, go away, God damn all of you. Don't you see I'm sick?"

"Sick," the partisan emphasized. "Talk."

"Who's known him the longest?" asked the railroad man.

He eyed them all intently. Everyone was silent. First to give in was Miss Malvina:

"Mr. Dobas . . ."

"Debicki."

"Debicki . . . He came and asked for a room. He looked respectable, with a tie and briefcase. My brother and me, we're just plain folks, so we rented it to him. Who could have known?"

"There's no law against renting a room," Korsak added.

"Maybe we ought to leave all the same?" Count Pac interposed.

"How come you're so susceptible?" the railroad man glanced at him earnestly.

"Me susceptible?" the count was alarmed.

"Who else?"

"Son of a bitch," Pac swore fervently.

The partisan clanged his prosthesis on the metal bedrail: "He's odd, that he is."

"You s-s-speaking of m-m-me?" groaned the count.

"Begone, you vestige of history, you," said the partisan, "and don't force yourself on the forbearance of the people's authority. As for the wood alcohol, no one knows anything about that, I'm sure."

I raised myself on my elbows: "Gentlemen, get out of here. I'll croak. Let me alone, all of you."

"He's making a fuss, he's just fussing," Korsak smiled indulgently.

At this moment something crashed on the veranda and everyone looked in that direction. Sergeant Glowko had tripped on the slippery threshold, his official equipment emitting various kinds of thuds and clanks. He used a strong word and saluted. "Is he still alive?" he inquired.

"Glowko, you're always last," said the railroad man.

"I can't be everywhere at once, excuse me."

He stood there a moment, gazing at me with official attention: "He's moving his eyes."

"He can even talk," Miss Malvina warned him.

"So why did Romus send for me?" He began fastening his leather bag and straightening his elaborate accoutrements.

"I wasn't born yesterday," interposed Korsak, snuffling into his greenish whiskers, "and I know what has to be done in such cases. No matter who is in authority, if someone raises a hand against himself, then a police officer, a gendarme, or (shameful to say) a cop is always sent for."

"People, I can't stand any more of it," I groaned. "Mr. Glowko, please get them out, my head is splitting."

"Well yes, pardon me," the sergeant clicked his heels, disconcerted.

"Do your duty, Glowko," said the railroad man sharply.

"What am I supposed to do? The man is registered according to regulations, pardon me. He has his identity papers, speaks sensibly, and can move his limbs."

"Maybe we should leave, all the same," Count Pac murmured.

"What's your hurry?"

"Heaven forbid, Mr. D-D-Debicki."

All at once I felt faint. With a sudden gurgle I hid my head between the pillow and the cool wall.

"Aha," remarked Korsak laconically.

"But a while ago he was snoring his head off like a beast."

"Are you going to do your duty, Glowko?" asked the railroad man.

"What am I supposed to do? Haven't had a bite to eat all day.

My wife told me to be home by four, but what time is it now?"

"Quarter to seven," the count informed him.

"Merci," said Glowko.

Count Pac shuddered: "What does th-th-that mean?"

"What?

"We-we-well, that *'merci'?"*

"Habit. I was in a concentration camp with some Frenchmen, your excellency."

"I p-p-protest. I'm Ko-Kowalski, from a poor family."

"Oh, you're like kids, the whole lot of you," the railway man sighed.

I raised myself up in bed. For a moment I gasped for breath, looking with hatred at the people gathered around my bed: "All of you, I won't answer for myself. . . . All of you, I'm sick, I'm in pain all over. Damn the whole lot of you!"

Korsak smiled benevolently and raised one finger: "Now then. He's being fussy."

"Well, what's to be done?" asked the railroad man, put out.

They were silent, caught up in an uncertain situation. Finally Miss Malvina brightened, touched by a saving thought: "We might have a bite to eat."

"So we might," said Sergeant Glowko timidly. "I haven't had a bite to eat all day, excuse the expression."

The Korsaks bustled eagerly about their apartment; the dust was blown off their old radio which had long since lost any features of an industrial product. Pickles were brought, floating in a liquid full of caraway seeds, a piece of unboiled, well-smoked ham with a beautiful bone sticking like a fist out of fine, cherry-pink meat, and pigs' knuckles with a layer of white fat as thick as a man's finger, a potato cake browned on all sides and larded with pieces of home-cooked salt bacon, not to mention home-baked bread laid out on fresh maple leaves. All this was placed on the deformed radio cabinet. The railroad man found a knife and began scraping the golden leaves from the loaf. The more particular among those present, such as for instance Miss Malvina, began protesting, stopping up their sensitive and delicate ears. The railroad man laughed jovially and made various gestures with the knife which ill became the sacrosanct custom of cutting bread.

The sight of this food and the eager bustling around it made me feel worse. I turned heavily to the wall: "I'm feeling bad."

Ildefons Korsak, half a pickle drenched in tasty sauce in his mouth, at once approached my bed: "Maybe the patient will take a bite, eh?"

I was silent. "It happened, it's gone, forget it," he said sternly. "It won't do to coddle yourself."

The partisan cleared his throat several times and at last said, discontentedly: "We're eating, we're eating, and that's all."

A sudden silence fell, full of concentration, of intense mental activity.

"Oh goodness, what am I thinking of!" Miss Malvina clapped a hand to her forehead. "I completely forgot."

No sooner had she hurried out than she returned with a dark green bottle covered with dust.

"Aha," the partisan greeted her.

"It isn't like it used to be. Back home in the East, in Ejszyszki I used to keep the real thing," Miss Malvina excused herself hypocritically.

"Let's try it and see," said the partisan.

"What can I uncork it with? I sealed it up properly."

A pocket-knife was sought, a hum of polite banter broke out, which was interrupted by the partisan's powerful baritone voice: "Let me. I've got this."

He struck the bottom of the bottle with his prosthesis, the cork flew up to the ceiling, a few drops splashed on the railroad man's jacket and seeped in bright drops through the honorable material of his uniform: "No harm done, no harm done, better on me than on the children."

"For Heaven's sake, there aren't any children here!"

"It was a manner of speaking, to liven things up."

"We don't have any tumblers, because we older people . . ."

"Shot-glasses will do, it's healthier to drink up at one go than to sip little by little."

They fell silent, gazing at the dense liquid in which the red light of the setting sun was quivering.

"Well, what about it?" the partisan said irritably.

The railroad man blinked and murmured: "Here's how."

There was a gurgling. Friendly snufflings were heard; Miss Malvina coughed, as ancient tradition requires.

"Oh, ambrosia," the partisan exclaimed.

"Back home in the East . . ." Miss Korsak began again, but the railroad man interrupted her instantly: "Let's not remember the past. What used to be, but is no more, don't count. We must live in the present."

"I meant no harm. Excuse me. At times old persons say things out of turn. We read the papers, to be sure, we know that present times aren't the same as they used to be."

"Well, what about it?" said the partisan again, impatiently.

I was feeling weak and sick. I must have groaned, for suddenly everyone fell silent.

"Let him groan," said Miss Malvina, looking attentively in my direction. "Please don't stand on any ceremony. I'll clear away later."

"Here's to him," said the railroad man. "He who falls from a hangman's rope makes a fine hole in the water. Here's how."

The count tittered nervously.

"And what are you baring your fangs for?" the railroad man asked stormily, removing the glass from his lips.

"Nothing at all, my dear sir. I myself don't know how it happened."

"These days everyone is as good as the next. You may have graduated from five universities, but when I squeeze, I squeeze."

"What do you mean, you squeeze? I don't understand," the partisan interposed.

"I know you, Krupa," the railroad man replied somberly. "Mind what you say."

"Gentlemen, gentlemen," interposed Miss Malvina, "why get started on politics? Isn't it better just to eat and drink up?"

They drank up, they puffed.

"*Merci,*" said Sergeant Glowko and reached for the enormous chunk of the potato cake.

> *On a kolkhoz the life is just great,*
> *One does the reaping while eight others sleep.*
> *But when the sun scorches*
> *He too runs away . . .*

Ildefons Korsak suddenly burst out singing in his thin, little voice; then he sank to the floor. His sister, as though prepared for this turn of events, seized him adroitly under the arms and propped him up against the wall.

"What's that he's singing?" asked the railroad man, wiping sauce from his chin.

Miss Malvina briskly squeezed her brother against the window-frame: "Oh some nonsense, not worth mentioning."

"I've never heard that song before," the railroad man persisted.

"He's feeble as a baby, my dear, he himself don't know what he's singing. All he needs is one little glass, and he starts uttering

Russian words and even blasphemies. That's still from the first war, when he was in Siberia."

"You've always told us he served under Kaiser Wilhelm in '14."

"God's truth, so help me. Only at first, in 1905, he fought for the Tsar against the Japanese, and then he went to Germany to find work, because there was poverty everywhere. Then the Germans drafted him and he was taken prisoner. It was the Cossacks that sent him all the way to Siberia. There, with all due respect, my dear, it was nothing but famine and misery. But our Ildefons is an honorable man, and terribly proud. So he says: 'When there's naught to eat, then out with my innards.' And he went to a doctor and told him — I'm ashamed to say — to take out his stomach."

"Come, Miss Korsak, don't put such ignorance to us," protested Sergeant Glowko.

"May the Holy Virgin be my witness that it was so. And here Mr. Jasiu Krupa don't have his hand, but he's alive."

"Where's the comparison? What's a hand to a belly?"

"Keep my hand out of this," the partisan snarled.

"No one means to do you any injustice," said Glowko with dignity. "We're talking about scientific matters, if you'll excuse the expression. Well tell me, Count, did you ever hear anything like it?"

"I do-do-don't know, Baron," replied the count, and he blushed.

"I'm not humiliating you," Sergeant Glowko raised his voice.

"Nor I you."

"You used that word."

"Shut up, you county aristocracy," the partisan interposed. "The vodka's already warm, and here they go, making scientific observations."

"For Heaven's sake, don't give Ildek any more. It takes several hours for vodka to get to the legs of an ordinary man. But he's only a chick; no sooner does he take a few sips than he gets weak and unwell."

Blue sea, red steamer,
I'll board and travel to the Orient.
In the Orient cannons boom,
White officers lie dead . . .

Ildefons Korsak burst out singing again and his knees shook, but his sister's powerful hands prevented him from toppling.

"Lay him on the bed, miss, alongside the patient, and we'll have some peace and quiet," advised Sergeant Glowko.

I felt a sort of weight on my feet, someone struggled desperately for a moment, but then calmed down by Miss Malvina's whisper: "Well, don't coddle yourself, lie quiet, else you'll only be ashamed of yourself."

Clearly his sister's words acted soothingly, for Ildefons Korsak quietened down and all I could feel was his damp breath on my feet.

The railroad man tried to reach for his glass, but his uncertain hand faltered all of a sudden, upsetting a plate of pigs' knuckles.

"Hm, what was I going to say?" he asked, abashed.

"Never mind, it'll bring good luck," Miss Malvina eagerly caught up.

"But I don't know whose health to drink. Whose day is it today?"

"Well, it's his day," said Sergeant Glowko, pointing a finger at me.

"Whose?"

"His."

The railroad man approached me and gazed attentively for a while. On his face there could be discerned an enormous attempt to snatch at one of many rapidly passing thoughts. Finally he threw up his hands in resignation and said: "Here's to us."

Count Pac unexpectedly giggled. The railroad man turned toward him and rested a fixed gaze upon him.

"M-m-mister director, it's his s-s-second christening, for sure."

Again the railroad man waved his free hand. And, without lowering his gaze from the count, he touched the glass with his lips. Then he put it down, relishing a drop of the liquid left on his lips with his tongue, and said, "Obviously, you're not doing so badly if you can keep your head filled with such nonsense. If you had to slave until your ass shook, then everything would taste better to you. . . . Here's to us."

He gulped down the vodka and puffed: "To get anybody to work, you have to invite him as if he were gentry. And don't offend anyone, or he'll be writing about you in the newspapers. He does you a favor by just working. I'd like to take you to an old soup kitchen. To remind you how it used to be . . ."

"Shame on you, it's not proper to pollute Marxist doctrines in barroom company," said the partisan.

The railroad man was embarrassed. He bit off a piece of pickle and munched it laboriously. "I know you well, Krupa," he said without conviction.

Ildefons Korsak stirred at the foot of the bed, belched, and shifted angrily, struggling with a nightmare. Finally he began scrambling toward me.

"It's all very well for you," Glowko sighed, "but I've got a wife waiting for me. I was to have been home by four. Oh what a life!"

Korsak uttered a groan and slumped beside me, seeking the pillow with his gray pate. With an enormous effort, I turned over. In front of me, in the thickening twilight, I could see the floor cut across with broad cracks, a pickle in a half-circle of scattered pips. This floor looked extremely cool and comfortable to me. I thrust myself up with one elbow and fell on my knees. Overcoming giddiness, I slowly rose to my feet. Beyond the veranda door I could see clumps of lilac bushes and a red strip of sky lit by the sun already hidden below the horizon. Holding on to the walls, I crossed the room and reached a garden house, reminiscent of a crazy gardener's hotbed. I caught the hot smell of ripe chestnuts.

I felt very sick. And I wanted it to stop. My wandering gaze desperately sought a place and a method of shortening my sufferings.

I caught sight of the fence, baring its teeth hostilely against a background of bright sky. Staggering, I set off in that direction. I longed to retain these seconds stretching into infinity, in order to know how the end looks. That's the ultimate fragment of knowledge, which is never any use afterwards.

I stumbled in the dry grass and slumped to the ground with the useless thought that it was cool on the earth, a coolness smelling of the river.

Regina came into the doorway, blinking her eyes in the sunlight. She was tall, buxom, dressed as people dress out there in the world. Her excessive makeup and fine wrinkles at the corner of her lips proved, however, that she bore within her a ceaseless dread. She swayed a while on the threshold without opening her eyes. She looked as though she was afraid of waking up.

"Good morning," said Miss Malvina Korsak, "the sun is so hot it's terrible. Not even the oldest of us can remember a fall like this."

Regina raised eyelids heavy with mascara; at this instant her movements adopted a flirtatious softness. Rustling her petticoat, she ran down the two stone steps and stopped in the middle of the yard. Shifting the weight of her body to her left leg, she swayed her right hip, which gave her skirt a rounded shape.

"Good morning, good morning," said she, "it's really a lovely fall."

"Nothing to be glad of. The apple trees are in blossom again, any amount of strawberries in the forest, the birds that flew away are coming back again. It isn't good. There will be some misfortune or other from it all."

"Do you believe the end of the world is coming, miss? People are always spreading rumors."

"People talk until they've had their say. But do you think that when the end comes, it'll be all of a sudden, with thunderbolts and the earth opening up? Perhaps it will all come little by little, gradual. Have you heard of all the misfortunes that beset the world — the wars, conflagrations, catastrophes? God alone knows how close the end is."

"Oh, I never think of what tomorrow will bring."

By the gate Romus came to a very slow halt. He leaned his elbows heavily on the toothed railings and stared into the yard.

"There's nothing too difficult for the young," said Miss Korsak, indulgently.

Regina moved her hips vigorously, listening to the glassy rustle of her petticoat. By the fence, Romus noisily swallowed spittle and shifted his weight from one foot to the other.

"And what are you idling for, there by the fence?" the old lady scolded. "Get yourself some work and don't offend God."

"I'm bored," Romus replied; slowly he removed his elbows from the fence and took one almost imperceptible step, then another, in the direction of the railroad tracks, beyond which meadows tousled with clumps of alder sloped down to the river Sola.

"Yesterday I heard something going on in your room."

"Not worth mentioning," Miss Korsak whispered.

"I had come home late from a party, because I was in Podjelniaki. Oh, it's real nice there, lots of young people, you can't keep the boys away, I nearly danced my feet off, so I come home and here in the next room there was shouting, laughing, singing. It's always so quiet in your room. Was it someone's birthday, excuse me, I didn't know . . .."

"Not worth mentioning," the old lady repeated. "Our lodger, Mister Paul, was taken ill."

"That gloomy one?"

"Shhh, he's lying right here."

And she pointed to me, hidden in the shade of over-ripe sunflowers. I wanted to feign sleep, but it was useless. I could hear the flirtatious refrain of her petticoat above me.

"Here we are living under the same roof, and we don't know one another at all."

"Mh," I groaned.

"You do look poorly. What do you mean by getting sick in such lovely weather?"

"He ate something indigestible, no doubt," said Miss Korsak, hurriedly.

"But his forehead is all black and blue."

"He fell down, poor thing, from weakness."

Ildefons Korsak had appeared in the yard. He was gazing to one side, pretending he didn't see us. He hurried with an uncertain step between the tool sheds, hastily puffing into his mournfully drooping whiskers.

"Surely I know you?"

I smiled crookedly.

"Didn't you once live in Bogatynia?"

"I've lived in many towns, but not Bogatynia."

"Did you come here to be ill?" she glanced coquettishly at me.

"Things do happen."

"Did you ever meet my husband, Mr. Dabrowski? He was a director in lots of places, he's a very well-known person."

"Never heard of him."

"I divorced him three years ago. A good man, no denying it, but coarse. And he hadn't the faintest idea at all how to approach a woman. Your pillow is going to fall, please don't move, there you are. Just one moment and I'll straighten it for you."

"Thank you, miss."

"Pray don't thank me. When you're better, I'll take you to a party. People around here talk of 'a little evening,' that's comical, isn't it?"

"Thank you."

"Is that all you can say? But you look as though you're from the capital. Oh dear, we've been talking away, and there's the store waiting for me. These days everyone must have some place to cling to, even if he is destined for something different."

She turned on her heel, leaped to the gate and then, once out in the street, did she adopt a studied walk: careless, curvaceous, emphasizing the qualities of her charms.

"Yes, yes," Miss Malvina sighed, "she must have been asking about you a hundred times. Where's he from, who is he, what sort of education does he have, why is he working on the railroad with ordinary folk? Once she examined one of your shirts hanging on the line and shook her head. She said there was some foreign writing on the label."

"I bought it in a used clothes' market."

"I don't pry into other people's business."

She was silent a moment, scraping dried petals off a sunflower big as a washbowl. Somewhere in a thicket of greenery smelling like heated watercress, grasshoppers were raising a hullabaloo.

"It's not my business, and it's better to forget," she said quietly. "But you're still young, your life's before you. Who knows what's in store for you? Maybe some unusual destiny, maybe great happiness, maybe a reward from mankind. God alone knows. Now and then a time comes when life becomes horrible. Then a year passes, and a person laughs to remember what a fool he was. Maybe various notions come into everyone's head at some time or other. But are we the only people in the world? It's the same for everyone."

I gazed into the sky overhead, so intensely blue and so at variance with this faded earth and these blackened trees. A white braid was growing overhead, woven by an invisible jet aircraft which, hidden in the blue, was indefatigably moving north.

"I know that," I said, quietly, "I know that, and many other things besides."

"Excuse me for talking bluntly, what's my understanding compared to yours? But I've seen my fill of everything in life. Maybe that's why I didn't choose happiness. . . . You ought to go and see Mr. Joseph Car some day; he's a wise and holy man, he knows how to advise people and administer the sacraments."

"The Baptist?"

"Goodness, what are you saying, what Baptist? He's a true angel, who understands ordinary folk. He takes no money from anyone, doesn't demand anything, nor does he deceive people with trickery."

"The one who lives down by the river?"

"That's him. He came here some three years ago. And there must have been something in that, because folk really needed him. Here, mister, we're a mixture of people from all over, you can count the locals on the fingers of one hand. Life has brought each person from a different locality."

"Is he a quack doctor?"

"Don't blaspheme, please. Am I a fool, to believe in quacks and magicians? You'll talk to him, you'll see for yourself."

Tiny bits of swallows were sweeping under the sky cut across

with the white trail of smoke. Long strands of gossamer were gliding above the sunflowers. A little forked streamer caught my hand
on a pine stump which was bleeding resin.

"You must go to him. Obviously this is why you were fated to
come here."

I was silent.

"People say he's even met with Huniady in the forest."

I glanced at her swiftly. She raised a hand as though to cross
herself.

"And who may he be?"

"An unfortunate man, a bandit, the likes of which God's earth
never did see. Since the war he's been murdering people, mostly
Communists, but he's despatched others too. He wiped out so
many that he didn't even come under the amnesties. His confed-
erates gradually came out of the forest, paid the penalty, and now
they're living in freedom, but he's hiding in the Solec forest to this
day. Nothing has been heard of him lately; maybe he did away
with himself somewhere."

"Huniady? What sort of odd pseudonym is that?"

"Gypsies nicknamed him that. He had a different name once,
partisan fashion."

Ildefons Korsak emerged from somewhere on the premises. He
glanced mournfully at us, nodded his head and froze motionless.

"You bother him," said Miss Malvina. "Yesterday was bad for
him. For he, you know, in Siberia . . ."

"I know, I heard."

"In what army didn't he serve, mister, poor dear, what uniform
didn't he wear. . . . The Tsar, God rest his soul, and the Germans, and the Bolsheviks, and his own folk, the Poles."

Old Korsak brought out an ax, spat into his dry and brownish
hands, and began chopping up a forked spruce branch.

"Yes, yes," said Miss Malvina, "as long as we live, there'll always be work."

"I want to sleep," I said.

"So go to sleep. May it do you good."

She walked away toward the porch. There she paused a while
to gaze at her brother chopping wood and breathing heavily.
Then she stepped into the cool darkness of the house.

Our house stood on an almost imperceptible mound on a ta-
pering cliff, or rather on the ancient bank of the once powerful
river, which had carved out a spacious valley before nature made
it a modest stream not marked on all maps. Lying in the sloping
garden, I could see the fields rising up steeply toward the sun as it

moved low over the black spruces. An old monastery, amidst golden maples, stood surrounded by these fields, clinging tightly to the cliff. It was tranquil and neglected, rotting, with innumerable sidebuildings, its plaster crumbling, and red with the bricks underneath creeping into the daylight, fresh as though made today, and with its huge shapeless rocks brought up from the bottom of the old river. But I knew that four aged monks dwelled in this ruin, that the youngest of them, deformed and with the face of a sick child, sometimes came out to the township, as the messenger linking them with a world whose shapes they'd forgotten. I also knew they'd turned one of the monastery cells into a museum, an absurd panopticon of exhibits that had strayed into these parts by some strange accident. That minerals to which the local earth never gave birth lay in glass cases, that starfish and dried fishes from tropical oceans lay on the tables. No one knew why the monks collected these secular oddities from distant countries rather than the remains of the history of the locality and the local faith, though they agreed with this anomaly, assuredly seeing in it a sort of expression of monastic yearning for lost temporality.

In the opposite direction, beyond the railroad, beyond the meadows and the Sola River, was a similar slope, but steeper; above it the sun hung in summer, red and preparing to set. The Solec forest, which had once been a wilderness, started there with an exuberant oak wood. Our township, cut across by sandy little streets without names, lay in the center of the valley, along the railroad tracks. It had no market place and no particular architectural order. But this doesn't mean that it had no traditions or history; it was generally known that the place had been settled by people of varying religions and languages, that it had been destroyed and burned many times, without ever having had the opportunity to take root as a meaningful urbanistic organism.

I gazed at Ildefons Korsak chopping branches of dry spruce. He was working in an automatic rhythm, apparently without effort, although I felt his senile body was operating on the principle of inertia and that it could be thrust out of movement forever at any given moment. His brownish skin was wrinkled over his heavy bones, here and there a serpentine muscle showed for a moment, his ribs worked like the spasmodically gaping gills of a lamprey. Watching his work, I had the impression of watching the death throes of a clock, whose pendulum was imperceptibly dying after exhausting its accumulated energy.

Unable to endure the sight, I turned over. Now I could see dry blades of tall grasses, already dead and deprived of all sap. Strands of gossamer, anchored in the grass, shifted like microscopic gliders in imperceptible breaths of wind. However, I could still hear the thud of Korsak's ax, like an intrusive pang of conscience.

So I got up from my makeshift bed, found a juniper stick used to support the gate and went out into the sandy little street bordered by pepper plants. I set out along the main street of the township, parallel to the railroad tracks. It seemed to me I could perceive the outlines of faces in the windows of houses, which gleamed with the blueness of sky, and that inquisitive eyes were accompanying me down this sun-baked street. A little old woman, bent under the weight of a yoke with buckets of water, stopped for a moment and then spat over her shoulder in fright.

I speeded up my pace, but soon felt an overwhelming weariness, so I stopped under a chestnut tree. There was dense shade here, with coniferous fruit shamelessly burst open lying on the ground, revealing unusually meaty insides, tempting and delicately brown. I wanted to proceed when I suddenly heard a kind of uproar inside the store; I saw the partisan Jasiu Krupa running out of the dark interior, which smelled of soap and flour, into the street. Here he stopped, straightened the frayed cuff on his shiny prosthesis, smoothed his hair and after a moment of hesitation, turned back.

"No," I heard Regina's voice.

The partisan was explaining something in an insistent tone.

"No," said Regina, again.

A jar of some kind crashed, her petticoat rustled: "Be off with you, d'you hear?"

"I've changed my mind, I'm not leaving."

"What's got into him, just look at him. . . . Better men than you have come here."

"We can leave together, if you want."

"And where to, pray?"

"I've friends in Warsaw. In important jobs, in the government."

"Thank God I'm still young and not bad looking. I don't have to go with just anybody."

Something thumped in the dark interior so the window panes shook.

"And don't you bang your stump at me. A suitor has turned up!"

It was quiet for a moment, then the partisan murmured something.

"Anyone would think I'm scared. I said 'No,' and that's final. Be off with you; if a customer should come in there'd be nothing but shame."

The vespers bell rang in the monastery. Its tiny rounded notes rolled down into the township like beads.

"No?" asked the partisan.

"No."

"Just so you don't regret it afterward."

"Why should I regret not going into the bushes with a drunken bum?"

"Do you know why I drink?"

"I don't know, and I don't want to know."

Another tense silence.

"Well?" insisted the partisan, "will you give me an answer?"

"Eighty-three plus forty-six makes a hundred and twenty-nine, and add twenty-seven . . ."

"Little princess of the county grocery cooperative!"

I heard a thump, a stifled shriek and something resembling the rapid patting of dough. The partisan appeared on the threshold of the store, copiously bespattered with flour. He shook himself like a dog after a bath and pondered a long while, staring helplessly ahead. Then he banged his prosthesis on the store shutter and came out into the road.

It seemed to me he would go his own way, but clearly he was aware of my presence, since he suddenly turned into the dense shade of the tree.

"Did you hear?" he asked anxiously.

I kept silence.

"Surely you must have heard?"

"I'm aching all over, I'm almost dead," I said quietly.

"Just think: What did she come here for? To trap a sucker. Her husband dumped her. He took off with some high-school girl, they still don't have a divorce. But look what airs she puts on. Every evening she flies around the neighborhood settlements and villages, looking for an opportunity. She always sits by herself, putting on an expression as though an ordinary Pole wouldn't have a chance. She's on duty. Waiting for happiness."

"I have to go now. Excuse me."

"Where in the world are you off to, respected sir? You've only just got back, thanks to people's help, from a long journey."

I was staring at bare feet plunged in sand warm as ashes. A

flock of sparrows was scuffling in the middle of a friable rut not far off. The vespers bell fell silent, but its echo still wandered in the oak thicket on the other side of the river.

The partisan raised his flour-sprinkled prosthesis.

"Take a look. Fifteen years ago they'd stand me vodka on account of this, they gave me hospitality in any home, girls fidgeted their legs if I'd only look kindly at them. In those days this was a treasure. A magic wand. A relic, you might say."

I dug up the sand with one foot and began to sketch something clumsy with my big toe.

"Well, take a good look, unknown passer-by," said the partisan, shoving his leather fist under my nose. "Don't look away like they all do. I'm used to it. It doesn't bother me. I've learned to pay the price for my fine disfigurement."

"Don't talk that way," I said, with difficulty.

"D'you think I'm tipsy? It's on account of that bitch. If I were going to her myself, if I paid court . . . But it's her. She won't come across unless she twists her ass, she won't look unless she lies with her gaze."

A cart was moving along the road. The horse kept flicking its tail to drive away the flies accompanying its sleepy journey. The driver, in his sheepskin cap, was asleep on his load of pea stalks and pods, and beside him sat a child with huge eyes full of light.

"Did you hear about Huniady?" I asked suddenly.

"Huniady?"

Now he was staring at the ground, at the crooked drawing in front of me: "Huniady? I've heard of him. Who hasn't? He came here from the East. There was a time when he ruled the county."

"Where did that strange pseudonym come from?"

"Apparently it's a Hungarian word, maybe Gipsy. What do you want to know for?"

I found a cigarette, at length, and carefully struck a match: "I myself don't know."

"Formerly people hated him, now they've stopped. He hasn't shown himself lately, but they say he lives in the Solec forest. He'd be better off with no arms or legs. Ah well, we've outlived our time. . . ."

He thumped the tree trunk with his prosthesis and went off down the middle of the road, raising clouds of dust. I waited until yet another chestnut dropped with a dull thud. I dragged myself toward the railroad tracks.

A man was standing on the balcony of the building in which the Party committee had its office. Dressed only in a shirt untidily open at the chest, he was gazing somberly at the quiet township dead in stillness. I knew his name was Szafir.

I could feel his gaze as I crossed the rusty tracks along which no trains had run for years, since the war. Between the dried-up oil deposits discolored with soot, exuberant herbs and dry, overblown cornflowers were growing.

I passed several scattered little houses, which might be regarded as a suburb; I passed a building with its windows boarded up and dead, a monument-building, a reproach to the conscience. Before the war it had belonged to a wealthy Jewish family which later perished at the hands of the Germans. Then it was bought by certain traders who were shot by partisan bullets. After the war troops were quartered in it. Then it was bought by someone whose wife shortly died. So he went abroad, as they said, the house was left without an owner; it became an institutional object of memories, warnings, and aphorisms defining the essence of life.

On a hillock not far from the river, amidst shrubs, a large building was hunched under its huge roof. A tall sorb tree, all red with berries, was growing beside it.

I was walking down a road made of coarse river sand, leading to the banks of the Sola, to a bridge which had never been completed. Transparent smoke was lying over the mouldering peat bog on my left. I could hear the monotonous chatter of the river already.

It was flowing through a deep ravine, hemmed in by rows of alders. Under the mirror of water I could see the interminably long beards of water weeds and green stones polished by the current.

On the other side someone was trying to get down to the water, but he slithered in the wet mud and now, breaking shrubs, slid down to the river. He fell in up to his neck, spattering rainbow splashes, remained a while as though taking a health bath, then suddenly broke away and began to conquer the rapid current with unusual vitality.

Completely drenched, Romus scrambled up my bank. He jumped up and down on his left leg, trying to eject the water out of his ear: "Oh, you puffed up with plankton, may the dogs drink you up," he swore at the innocent river.

Then he caught sight of me.

"Are you all right now?"

"As you see."

"And here was I, God damn it, hurrying with news. Well, this is what you get for being good to people. There will be a time when we'll be blowing our noses with river fish."

He squeezed water out of his trouser-legs and looked at me suspiciously: "Aren't you interested?"

"I don't know, my head aches."

"They're going to cut down the Solec forest."

"Such a big forest?"

"No, only this part, from the river on. Surveyors are measuring it today, the head forester has already arrived."

"What sort of news is that?"

"Obviously you're still weak. They're going to cut it because the Sola will be dammed here, the water will rise and flood this piece they're going to cut out of it."

"Mh."

"Oh, you're still in bad shape. On the other side there'll be forest, but on our side? . . . Understand now, mister? Maybe it doesn't matter about the forest. It's an accursed place filled with graves, some from the first war, but most from the last one. For the Germans were secretly building something in there, something important was to be here. They brought the tracks, laid roads, built bunkers in the forest. But they didn't have time. When the Russians were approaching, one night they killed all the men working here and buried them in ditches. Maybe it would be better if this forest was done away with. But it's too bad about our township. It'll be too bad for everyone."

I was gazing at the water which carried a reflection of the sky and the trees along its banks. Now and then a fish snapped at a fly, briefly arousing fine rings of water.

"You don't belong here," said Romus ill-naturedly. "It seems to be all the same to you."

He spat out a green water plant and almost imperceptibly began moving away in the direction of the township.

The river was rumbling between black roots that clung to the bank with the last of their strength. Shoals of minute fish, motivated by unknown impulses, swam in a zigzag course along the shallows, stopping here for a moment, then rushing to one side with a violent impetus. Single maple leaves, veined with redness, swirled in the restless current.

All at once I caught sight of something like a knife blade, gleaming with a pale glow among the water plants. I gazed at this scrap of light and something tempted me to extricate the unknown fragment from the water. Finally I yielded to my strange curiosity and, holding on to an alder with one hand I began to poke with the other, using a juniper branch, into the dense, hair-like water plants. At last I brought out on the bank a small object with a gleaming, metallic edge, thickly overgrown with rust or slime.

It was a cross, somewhat Ruthenian in shape, with a rounded rosette at the arm joints, and in it I could see the outline of an engraved head of Christ with huge Byzantine eyes. Some inscriptions showed on both arms, and the date 1863, enclosed in a frame.

I gathered some sand and cleaned the cross. Only then did I see the words printed in Cyrillic letters: *Gospodi spasi ludi tvoja* (O Lord, save Thy people).

It seemed to me as though someone repeated these words after me. I turned around hastily, and a strange chill clung to my back.

On the summit of the unfinished road scattered with river sand there stood a tall, swarthy man with very dark eyes. He was smiling, but only with his lips. He stared persistently from deeply sunken eyes, and I could feel my hands trembling and something pressing my temples with the utmost force.

I knew this face very well, I'd remembered it for years, I dreamed of it nights, when wind and rain roared outside the window, when nightmares pursued me.

"That's an 1863 insurrectionist medal," he said. "The Cossacks once broke up the last unit here. The last party, as they called it in those days. Before the insurrectionists died, they threw everything they wanted to hide from the enemy into the Sola. Sometimes people find bullets in the water, scraps of weapons, primitive printing matrices, pieces of harness, even ordinary army buttons."

"Good morning," I bowed clumsily, "I suppose I should introduce myself."

"I know you. I expect you've heard of me."

I was standing in deep, moist shade. I could see him high above me, red sunlight lying across his head and stooping shoulders.

I stopped myself with difficulty from telling him that I knew him, I remembered him, I couldn't free myself from him.

"So this is you," he said.

"I'm sick. I feel very bad," I replied softly.

"But after all I don't want anything from you," he again smiled with his lips. "Over there, beyond the peat bog is the insurrectionists' grave mound. You see what our earth is like: No matter where you tread, there are graves everywhere."

I was silent.

"Have you come to stay with us for long?" he asked after a moment's silence.

"I don't know. I myself don't know, I'm sick."

"Yes, so I heard."

"What did you hear?" I asked, my heart beating.

He considered a moment: "That you're feeling bad."

"People talk a lot of nonsense. As it is, in a small town . . ."

"Yes, when people are having a hard time, they find consolation in other people's misfortunes."

A leaf dropped from a tree above me. It glided a long time, twisting on its axis, until it finally settled on the water and floated into the dark abyss of the ravine. We watched it.

"If you ever get bored, please visit us. We live not far from here."

"Thank you very much. I'll remember."

I wondered at the plural in which he clothed the invitation.

Suddenly he turned away and disappeared behind the yellow hump of the unfinished road. Only now did I realize I was clutching the cross, dripping with water, in both hands. I put it inside my shirt and began scrambling up the bank on all fours, under cover of the vegetation that was suffocating with the smell of mint.

I caught sight of him climbing the path up the hillock where the house with the huge roof was, and by it was the red sorb tree, like a permanent mark of its owner's friendly intentions.

The slender figure of a woman came out from between the rusting shrubs to meet him. He put his arm around her, and thus linked in an embrace they went into the house.

When in the evening Miss Malvina came out in front of the porch, I was lying in the garden and gazing at the sky as it turned cold. She was dressed in her best, her eyes filled with concentration and solemnity: "Aren't you coming to pray with us?" she asked.

"You know I don't pray, miss."

"We don't force anybody. But you are in need of prayer."

Ildefons Korsak stopped on the threshold. He too was ready for the journey. In his hands, symbolizing the meaning of his existence, he held a worn school exercise book.

"Well, time to get going," she said.

They set off along the road in the direction of the railroad, accompanied by the fragile sound of the vespers bell resounding in the monastery. The monks were bidding farewell to the day.

I rose too. I left the empty house behind.

A fine, streaky fume was rising from the river. A small crowd had gathered by the road that led nowhere. I stopped near the house with the boarded-up windows. From here I could see the windings of the river covered in mist, the dried-up meadows and rusty lichens of smouldering peat.

People were kneeling around Joseph Car, who was saying something as he stood motionless amidst the faithful. Among them I saw the partisan and Count Pac, and Regina, her head lowered in oblivion, and the Korsaks, gazing at the speaker with adoration. Romus was half lying, half kneeling at the edge of the crowd. The railroad man was standing in the road, an uncertain spectator and observer.

I saw the slender figure of a woman next to Joseph Car. It seemed to me she was looking in my direction, at the other cliff of the valley, the summit of which was red with the last reflection of the already invisible sun.

I felt someone's heavy breathing behind me. I turned: It was Sergeant Glowko, sweaty, covered with thick dust.

"Ignorant lot . . ." he threw out bait.

I did not reply.

He evidently regarded this as disapproval, for he said in a conciliatory manner: "My old woman is kneeling there too. I went home but there wasn't, excuse the expression, a living soul. Couldn't wash or eat."

I kept silent.

"Such, evidently, is human nature."

Suddenly the praying people bowed lower; they almost touched the dry and cold earth with their foreheads. At this moment a gloomy, groaning hymn came to us from over there:

> We're going to God, we keep going to God,
> Through sorrow, despair, and doubt.
> And ever longer my wearisome way,
> And ever heavier my conscience.

Later, they started going down to the river and disappeared into the black ravine. Cries could be heard, and the intensified gurgling of water. Joseph Car also went down to them.

The slender woman set off in the direction of the house. She stopped a moment on the hillock and gazed in our direction. I raised one hand on a sudden impulse, to wave to her. But all at once it all seemed inappropriate.

The woman disappeared into the house that was distinguished from the others by the red sorb tree.

It was as though the railway tracks, drawing energy from somewhere in this unusual heat, had become individual heaters. Count Pac, in threadbare sandals, had already stepped twice on lost screws. Jumping on one leg, he muttered something to himself, and we greedily caught at this muttering made up of unarticulated disapproval.

"We'll boil at work like this," said the partisan. "This is the eightieth screw. I'll never travel by train any more."

"I consider this an equivocal occupation altogether," the count remarked. "Whose head did it enter to build a siding in a hole like this? As it is, no trains will ever come here."

"Count, can't you breathe in another direction? My back is all drenched," the partisan moved away in distaste.

Pac reddened: "How m-m-many times have I s-s-said I'm not a count?" he blew his nose and wiped it, peasant-fashion, with the sleeve of his bright shirt.

"Look, look," said the partisan to me, unexpectedly, "even though he's an aristocrat, he has his looks."

Count Pac pricked up his ears attentively.

"Handsome face," the partisan went on, "well-built, such as women go for. Bolero all in flowers, tight pants and those sandals! Oh, he knows how to do well by himself, he knows what to put on. And to be surprised that at parties everywhere the girls ask: 'Why isn't the count here? Without him a party is always a flop."

"This isn't a bolero, my friend, but a sports shirt of special cut," said Pac, modestly.

"If only he'd use eau de cologne sometimes . . . Sure, he has his own odor, he rides healthily like a cock, but the women hereabouts are modest, it doesn't appeal to all of them. Eighty-sixth."

"Eighty-sixth what?"

"Screw."

"You see, sir, my nature is such that I don't like women of easy virtue," Count Pac reflected, gazing at the drab horizon. "I, if you please, like to fight. I appreciate resistance, I adore conquest."

"There, you see," said the partisan turning to me with a hypocritical sigh, "how fate favors some. Whenever I meet Regina, she always inquires, as if in passing, whether the count is well, or how he likes the township, or why he so rarely drops by at the store?"

"S-s-same thing all over again. I'm an ordinary g-g-guy from a poor family," whispered the embarrassed count. "Does she really ask that?"

"Whatever should I lie for? Well, gents, time to light up. Work don't like haste."

We settled ourselves on a slope overgrown with furze. Count

Pac smoothed the crease of his pants and sat down carefully on his handkerchief: "She always looks at me so strangely," said he, blinking.

"Who does?"

"Why, she does, Miss Regina."

"You'd do better to tell us of some incident in your life. You've turned over more than one dozen women, for sure, eh?"

"Oh, sir, you're so coarse," the count pushed him back with huge, bony paws.

We lay for a time in silence. As every day at this time, a white scarf of smoke in the sky was growing behind the invisible jet. Someone above us coughed uncertainly. Slowly we rose up on our elbows.

Ildefons Korsak was bowing undecidedly from the top of the slope.

"Well now, grandad, what's the news? Shall we finish off a pint?"

Korsak shifted uncertainly from one foot to the other and snuffled into his whiskers: "God forbid. I came to see the railroad man."

"Sit down, then."

Ildefons Korsak sat down modestly at one side.

"What are they writing about in the newspapers, grandad?" asked the partisan.

"Oh well, what they have to write about, same old thing. They sent up some sputniks again."

"Well, well, tell us."

"Naught to tell. They always make such a fuss about anything new. I can remember, mister, when the first airplanes appeared. What didn't they have to say about them, such an event, such a boon for mankind! Well, and what came of them? What do you or I, mister, get out of it? It flies over our heads, mister, once a day, devil knows where or why. Same with the sun. So many years they said it moves around the earth, and that was fine. Then, mister, they decided it's the earth that moves around the sun. Well, so what, mister? What's in it for us?"

"You backward old gentleman," said the partisan, and he began flicking off the ants that were walking over his prosthesis.

"Mister, I don't give a curse what will be," went on Ildefons Korsak, "I'm more interested in what used to be."

"You can read books about history."

"He he," Korsak grinned slily, "I know, but what came even

before them? There's the riddle, mister. But nobody writes about that."

A figure appeared in the distance, in the air vibrating over the tracks. It was coming in our direction.

"Who can that be?" asked the partisan lazily.

"A woman, for sure."

"You, count, have only one thought in your head."

"I swear it, after all, it's obvious she's wearing a d-d-dress."

"Where, where?" Ildefons Korsak was interested.

"Well, over there, on the track."

"It's a bush, mister."

"Grandad, you can't see for the life of you."

"And sometimes I can't hear," sighed Korsak. "But there was a time when I could spot a ruble half a mile off."

"Who wouldn't, when rubles were still golden?"

The railroad man came up. His blue smock was unfastened, he carried his dusty cap in one hand. He dragged his left leg almost imperceptibly: "Always lying around, you loafers, lying around!" he shouted from a distance. "You aren't working on your own account, after all."

"He talks well, even though he's a Marxist," said the partisan.

"Not out doors, on the bare ground, you'll all catch colds."

"We're used to it, and the count is lying on his handkerchief."

"P-p-please sir, h-h-how many times d-d-did I say . . ."

"There isn't even a sign of work," said the railroad man, putting on his cap to acquire official weight.

"It isn't right to talk that way," said the partisan severely. "I tightened eighty-six screws."

"If you were putting up a house for yourself it would be almost finished by this time."

"I don't have a house. I lack the possessive instinct."

"I know you, Krupa. Well, what are you standing around for?" Ildefons Korsak took two uncertain steps.

"Mr. Councilor," he began.

"What councilor, what sort of councilor? You've nothing but prewar times in your head."

"I'm a little confused in the head, for at my age a person doesn't hear aright, nor see aright, Mr. Dobas."

"Not Dobas, not Dobas. My name's Debicki."

"Mr. Debicki, I came about the job."

"What job?"

"Well, when we treated you to food and drink after we saved our lodger, you promised me the job of a trackman."

"Well, just look. You yourself say you don't see aright or hear aright."

"That's only in general matters, mister. At work I can see and hear too. Once, mister, I could spot a ruble half a mile away."

"A ruble half a mile off, you say?"

"Ha ha, he caught him nicely with that ruble," said the partisan.

The railroad man took his cap off again and began peering thoughtfully into it. But our superior's meditations were interrupted by the slow creaking of wheels. A haycart was dragging its way along the road beside the tracks, its driver in his sheepskin cap was walking alongside the sweating horse, Romus right behind him. At the sight of us Romus began spitting nervously.

"We're coming from the forest," he said.

"Well?" said the railroad man.

"We're carrying a person."

He and the driver moved aside from the cart and then we caught sight of the remains of a man lying on the bare boards. He wore a jacket and pants, just like those worn by everybody in these parts. His face was covered by a horse's feed bag. Only his bare, livid feet were projecting from the broad trouser-legs.

"The surveyors found him while they were measuring the forest," said Romus, and he hastily spat several times.

"Who is he?"

"Nobody knows. We're taking him to the county hall."

"Well, gee up, nag," said the peasant and he struck the mare's flanks with his whip. The cart moved off, and I went after it, drawn by some horrible curiosity.

"Maybe Huniady shot him?" asked the railroad man.

Romus began spitting still more rapidly.

"No, it wasn't Huniady. He fell into some old bunkers and got killed. The surveyors were measuring the forest to the clearing, and they found him."

I was walking alongside the cart. A livid hand, with a piece of withered moss stuck between the fingers, was dangling and swinging through the side of the cart. I couldn't muster up the courage to pull the sack off the dead man's head.

"Why are you here, young sir?" muttered the driver. "Ain't necessary."

I didn't listen to him. I was staring with an effort at the blackened sack, in which oats had been scattered. Below it could be seen the outline of a thin Adam's apple.

Suddenly I slipped a hand into the cart, and for a fragment of second, lifted the sack. Wide open, motionless eyes and a face with lips parted stared at me. The only likeness it had was the likeness of death. I let the coarse cloth fall in horror.

"Ain't necessary, young sir," said the driver.

I stopped dead. The cart drove on, its wheels sinking into the powdery sand of the road. Romus caught up with the driver. They walked on, side by side, in silence, without looking at the cart, the lad spitting thickly.

Only now did I recognize the sour stench, so memorable and hateful. I held my breath. The cart was already far away, but I still feared to draw breath.

"Well, didn't you ever see a dead body?" said the partisan furiously.

I went back to them. They were standing in the center of the railroad tracks, staring at the fine cloud of dust on the road.

"Accursed forest," said the railroad man.

"They're going to cut it down and flood us," the partisan declared.

"What's that you're saying?" the railroad man woke up and put his cap on.

"I say that when they dam the Sola, the water will flood us. There'll be a lake in place of the township."

The railroad man looked at him sternly: "Don't repeat rumors."

"They're good rumors. And what are we building this siding for?"

"Trains will be coming here, understand, you blockhead?"

"They haven't come for years and years, and it was good so. Now they're going to build a power station, so the railroad will be necessary."

"Shut up, you shit," the railroad man roared, and threw his cap on the ground. Dragging his left leg, he moved rapidly in the direction of the shed where his office was.

"People are irritable nowadays, dear me, that they are," murmured Ildefons Korsak.

The partisan glanced at him without much liking: "And what are you setting up a Greek chorus for, old man? They'll kick you out too. Do you think you are already in the last stage in your life?"

"But where can I go from here? We're used to living here. Aren't I right?"

The partisan picked up a long screwdriver. He walked out between the tracks with lowered head. I too moved off to work. We worked a while in silence. The dry, monotonous heat stuck to our backs.

The partisan straightened up, wiped the sweat from his neck with his arm and, without looking in my direction, asked: "Well, what did you see?"

"Nothing."

"You must have seen something, as you lifted the sack."

"A corpse like any other corpse. And nothing more."

"Well, and what did you peep in for?"

"I don't know."

He turned and looked at me with hostility: "All right, let's say you don't know. But it would be better if you knew."

Count Pac picked up the railroad man's cap and carried it to the bank where Korsak was sitting: "Just look," said Ildefons, "butterflies flying about. I don't remember seeing anything like this at this time of year as long as I've lived."

"Yes sir, you're right," sighed Pac, "everything is topsy-turvy these days."

"Count, was that a hint?" asked the partisan.

"Goodness, no. You misunderstand me. I had the weather in mind," Pac explained hastily. "I don't know whether you gentlemen have noticed that of late the winter hasn't been winter, nor the summer, summer."

"Ah, everything has changed, changed," said Ildefons Korsak. "People are different, and nature ain't what it used to be. And all because man wants to be wiser than God."

Some strange and distant voices cried out. We started looking around, until finally Korsak was first to look into the sky. "Look there. Wild geese flying back to the north. Just look, mister."

The count dusted off the railroad man's cap, hesitated a moment, struggling against the urge to try it on, but in the end laid it down on a whitish clump of furze. Agitated black ants crawled over it immediately.

"This weather will end badly, I'm telling you," said the partisan.

The railroad man came out of his little shed and also gazed at the sky.

"They're flying to their death, chief," shouted Ildefons Korsak.

The railroad man dropped his gaze to us: "You're waiting for the end of the world, eh?"

"We're not waiting for anything. We're all right," said Count Pac hastily.

The railroad man wanted to say something but restrained himself and went back to his office with a shrug.

The tracks, corroded by rust, were quietly humming. Someone's cow, coming back loose from the meadows, had stopped between the tracks. She looked at us persistently with her dark eyes. I was stifling and felt faint again.

I sat down on a heated tie that smelled of creosote. Yellowish drops of resin were oozing from the knots, the last vestiges of a dead tree's life.

"What did you come here for?" the partisan unexpectedly asked me.

"You speaking to me?"

"Yes, you. Who sent you here?"

"Do I look like one of them?"

"You look as you should. But that's not the point."

"I don't ask you anything."

"I'm on my own ground here."

"Don't bother me. My head aches. I feel tired, very tired."

"But why have you come to us?"

"I don't know. That's the way it worked out."

"Why do you poke your nose in everywhere, why do you ask questions, why are you restless?"

"All I want to do here is work. Nothing else concerns me."

"Then why did you do what you did, you know what, the other evening?"

"I didn't do anything. I'm sick."

"For whom are you looking here?"

I burst out coughing. I covered my mouth with one hand, and later asked: "I . . . I'm looking for someone here?"

"Yes. For whom are you looking here?"

"Let me alone. I don't want anything. I'm very sick."

"Just look at him, he's sick. A man like an animal, weighs a hundred and eighty pounds."

Count Pac tittered nervously.

"Such times have come," said Ildefons Korsak, "that young people fall sick. Apparently healthy and strong, but one puff of air and they're gone."

"Yes, yes, Mr. Korsak," the partisan admitted, sitting down on a long track. "It started like a party. But the party didn't come off. People are getting sour, they're irritable, everyone has a pain."

"A very apt metaphor," said Count Pac. "But what is it you have in mind?"

"Your brain has been numbed by eroticism," said the partisan, annoyed. "I have you in mind, and him too," he pointed at me with his prosthesis, "all of you. Not too long ago, you were paying court, but now you sit licking your wounds."

He picked a thin stalk of cornflower from between the ties and crumbled the faded flower absently. A huge horse fly buzzed penetratingly with its tiny wings, dancing above his head.

Someone emerged from between the township buildings that were plunged in dusty heat. We rose eagerly from the tracks. Count Pac dropped a screwdriver which fell on a pile of hooks used for hammering in the tracks. A tall woman was taking a shortcut through a dead little field.

"Whoever can that be?" asked the partisan uncertainly.

Count Pac tittered, "Don't you know?"

The partisan jumped across a ditch overgrown with dry grass like a cow's ear, and began to climb the slope carelessly. Then he stopped on the edge of the steep incline and waited for Regina.

She came up, looking furtively to one side: "God be with you."

"Not worth bothering God with work like this," said the partisan. "Here on business, Miss Regina?"

She pouted contemptuously: "With the likes of you? What sort of business would I have here? I'm going to the river."

"True, it's Saturday. Can I scrub your back for you?"

"No thanks, I'll manage."

"Please don't feel shy. Why all this fuss?" he stretched out his hand to take from her the bag with towel and large new bathmat, but she evaded him and ran toward the tracks.

Count Pac snickered, hiding his face in a flowery sleeve.

"Why d'you pick and choose like an organist on an organ?" the partisan shouted from above. "After all, everyone knows you need a man."

"Look, a man has turned up. Nice to know," she said sarcastically. She straddled the hot tracks and we looked at her strong calves, hips like loaves of country bread and breasts which would have sufficed for all of us.

"Yet nobody has complained until today, praise God," said the partisan, and he began coming down toward us. "And it wasn't with such little princesses that I had dealings."

"More familiarity than acquaintance."

"We could get to know one another."

"I don't wish to," she raised one hand sleepily in order to straighten a disobedient lock of her abundant hair, flaxen from the sun. She froze in this gesture a moment, allowing us to relish the mature charm of her body. Count Pac began breathing heavily.

"Oh, the slut," sighed the partisan quietly, and he kicked the railroad track which, God knows, was innocent.

Regina lowered her arm, tugged her dress and slowly moved off in the direction of the meadows and river, hidden in a grove.

"May children make a slingshot out of you-know-what if I don't get her," said the partisan stubbornly.

He went out of the edge of the tracks and shielded his mouth with his hand: "Regina! Regina!" he shouted.

She increased her pace without looking round.

"Regina!"

She began running across the meadow, which was dun as scorched sheepskin.

"Regina!"

She rushed into a group of alders. Her progress was indicated only by the spasmodic shaking of branches.

The partisan struck his hip with his prosthesis once and again in order to straighten its position, then began going slowly down to the river, to the place where the woman had disappeared. Count Pac coughed with a nervous titter: "L-l-let's go and take a l-l-look," he said. "She's g-g-going to bathe. She's shameless."

Seeing I didn't stir, he rubbed his hands uncertainly: "G-g-give you m-m-my word, it's w-w-worth seeing."

Very embarrassed, clearly ashamed of his weakness, he set off after the partisan.

The railroad man came out of his shed. He shook his head, gazed after the workers as they moved away, then approached us and picked up his cap: "And you, Korsak, aren't you running after them? Or have you forgotten your glasses, eh?"

"Not me, Mr. Councilor," said Ildefons, abashed. "One year it was as though they removed that by hand. I don't even remember too well. It must have been after the first war, when everything was still reckoned in marks."

The railroad man banged the track with his boot: "Well, thanks be to God, you haven't been breaking your backs at work today," he stated gloomily.

Ildefons Korsak was pursuing the interrupted course of his deliberations: "But once, mister, I too was interested in women. Only I was very delicate, and my sister used to watch me, so where was I to sin under such circumstances, mister? Well and so it somehow flew away."

The railroad man transferred his hostile gaze to me: "I want to talk to you."

"But what about me, mister foreman?"

"Go home, your sister has certainly cooked up something bitter for you."

"But what about the job?"

"Be off with you. We'll all be in hell before we get this siding built."

Ildefons Korsak was left alone between the tracks. He snuffled into his greenish whiskers, gazing at the blades of grass which flourished shamelessly between the ties.

Sun and dust floating in the hot air were visible through cracks in the office walls. The railroad man sat down behind a crooked little table and pulled a page of the calendar, from under which the redness of a holiday looked out. Then he pedantically straightened a junky exercise book which, apart from personnel matters, contained all the official aspects of the undertaking.

"Well, what about it?" he asked.

I gazed at him in astonishment and met a look that was heavy and hostile.

"Who sent you here?"

"Nobody. I came by myself."

The railroad man picked up a pencil, played with it a moment, then drew something on the outside cover of the exercise book.

"You can tell me frankly," he said all at once.

"But I've nothing to tell."

"Well, yes," said the railroad man, and he tapped his pencil on the table top.

Silence that lasted for a while, filled with the voices of crickets roaming somewhere outside the thin wall.

"After all, I can see you're not made for this work. I've an eye for that. I know right away what's required. Maybe they sent you from some control office?"

"No."

"Then maybe it's about this dam on the Sola?"

"I'm sick, mister railroad man."

"Nobody comes here for a cure."

"Am I disturbing anybody?"

The railroad man again sketched something on the exercise book. He glanced out of the corner of his eye to ascertain if his ambiguous manipulations were having any effect.

"Whether or not you disturb anyone, I must know why you

came here. There was very nearly a misfortune. If not for the Korsaks . . ."

"I was poisoned by something I ate."

The railroad man fixed his gaze into my eyes.

"Well yes," he said, "well, yes."

He opened the exercise book and read something attentively for a while: "So you don't want to explain?"

"I've nothing to explain."

"As you think best," said the railroad man, and he stood up from behind the table.

I went out to the tracks. I could feel the railroad man's gaze on my back. I walked in the direction of the township, jumping across from tie to tie. Then I turned around: he was standing motionless in front of his shed, official cap hanging down in his hand, watching me.

In the high grass dried to whiteness on both sides of the railroad embankment lay sparsely scattered hillocks of graves. I knew that in the higher ones, better looked after, with beechwood crosses, there reposed the partisans. But the lower hillocks, like ancient molehills, concealed the bodies of Russian prisoners who'd tried to escape from German transport trains. All these graves straggled in little streams toward the meadows and the Sola, marking the trace of the hopes of men fleeing from captivity.

I came out on the sandy road. At its end, by our house, stood the cart. The mare had plunged her head into the sack of provender and was lazily defending herself against horseflies. The peasant in his sheepskin cap was tampering with something under the cart.

I recognized them. Alongside, in the wretched shade of a chestnut tree, lay Romus. I wanted to turn back, to find another way, but they'd already caught sight of me, and Romus had raised himself on one elbow with an almost imperceptible, lazy movement.

I walked up, holding my breath.

"We're still here," said Romus. "The shaft broke. He's out of luck after death too."

I tried to avoid looking at the interior of the cart. But my eyes, in strange haste, kept running foul of that oval bulge covered with cement sacks.

"He couldn't have killed him," said Romus.

"Who couldn't?" I asked, with a constricted heart.

"Well, him, Huniady. Sure, after so many years no ammunition would be any use, would it?"

"And you don't know him?" I asked.

"Whom?"

"Him." I dared not point.

"No. Probably not," said Romus hesitantly. "That's an accursed forest. But maybe you want to take a look?"

"No."

"Sure, you already looked."

The peasant crept out from under the cart with some loops of wire in his hands.

"See, mister, he'd sooner work in discomfort underneath the cart than take the dead body off. He's that superstitious."

The peasant began to untie his whip from the railings of the fence. I could see the white face of Miss Malvina in a window of our house.

"Mister Glowko! Mister Glowko!" Romus shouted.

The sergeant came out into the road fastening his belt. He was still laboriously munching the last mouthfuls of his dinner. His official equipment clanked with buckles.

"Bah, mister," he said to me, "in former times, when one person died in ten years, people used to be scared, excuse me for saying so, to leave their homes after dark; everyone remembered such an event a long time. How much talk there was later, fright, amazement! But now the time has come when death lies at every turn. Maybe the world has outlived itself. . . . Harap, you ready?"

"We can go," said the peasant. "High time, dusk not far off."

Romus began rising in an unusually slow fashion from the hen-bespoiled grass.

"You stay behind, why not?" said Sergeant Glowko with dislike.

"I'm bored."

The peasant whipped up the mare's dusty flanks:

"Get a move on, nag."

The cart creaked and began moving into the misty lividness of the road. Sergeant Glowko walked alongside, holding the cart stake, and behind him flowed Romus, as unreal as a nightmare.

"Good evening," I heard someone's voice.

I turned around, my throat tight. I bowed clumsily.

It was she. She was holding a large basket made of spruce twigs, filled with paradisiacal apples: "I'm on my way back from Podjelniaki. See what a fine crop there's been this year," and she held out her hands and gave the basket of fruit to me: "Why don't you try one?"

I took an apple, entirely suffused with red, and slowly bit into it, eyeing the girl. She had the face of a schoolgirl, a face familiar to me from somewhere, as if recalled from a long past dream and not in the least suited to a body shamelessly plump with womanhood.

"I just had to get to know you."

Again I bowed clumsily. She was looking at me without embarrassment, with a smile that was neither naïve nor challenging.

"You interest me a lot. I've spied on you several times."

I felt still more stifling.

"That's not a healthy curiosity."

"You don't think so?"

"There isn't anything of interest in me. Is it worthwhile to believe in gossip?"

She was still gazing at me.

"Very well. Since you're so bashful."

"Excuse me."

"Could you help me?" she suddenly asked.

I took the basket from her and we set off along the tracks in the direction of the meadows. I watched her attentively out of the corner of my eye. There was that sort of nonchalant carelessness in her attire that usually has its origin in a taste not of the best. And also she walked at a relaxed pace, yielding as it were to a dancing rhythm. I already knew that this was a collection of traits of a person living in an aggressive and hostile environment.

She sensed that I was watching her. However, she didn't confirm the fact, so as not to scare me away. A huge flock of rooks was circling over the river. From there, up above, it looked as though plant lice were attacking the large and twisted carcass of a caterpillar.

Suddenly she stopped and, continuing that dancing motion with her hips, said: "My name's Justine."

I'd already opened my mouth but she forestalled me: "No need. I know your name."

And she fell silent. A white strand of gossamer rubbed against my cheek and flowed upon her, on her neck that was smoky with sunburn. The very fine, slender thread, like the little silver chain of a medallion, caught on to the moving pulse of her artery. "I'll wait for you every day, miss," I said unexpectedly.

She glanced at me, amazed: "What?"

I blinked, not very sensibly, urgently seeking some justification which would erase the clumsy offer.

"Let's go, it's late already," she said, as though nothing had happened.

She moved ahead with that accentuated step of hers, apparently careless but — I'd have sworn — in fact calculated.

"She controlled that nicely," I said to myself. "Watch out. You can get your fingers burned here."

And suddenly I felt easier, that persistent stuffiness having gone away.

"Did you say something?" she asked, not completing a half turn. I could see the outline of her cheek and a fragment of raised eyebrow.

"Nothing important. It sometimes happens that I talk to myself."

We walked for some time in silence. Finally she stopped, again with an incompleted movement: "I think we'll be friends," she said.

"I don't believe in friendship too much."

"Yes, I know. People say that in such cases it isn't possible to be friends. But we're not flirting, are we?"

And without waiting for my reply she moved forward. We were passing the deserted house. Now, as I was going that way for the hundredth time, it seemed to me that this building was reminiscent of an old manorhouse with its porch bared of lime, running into a garden overgrown with grass as tall as a man. And I suddenly noticed the outline of former garden paths, and sparse trees set in deliberate order, and there even seemed to flicker somewhere the violet skirt of a woman strolling alone.

"I like this house," she said, but the remark seemed banal and out of place to me.

"It's certainly haunted," I said, to conceal my annoyance. She stopped and looked me in the eyes.

"Have I offended you somehow? Excuse me, I always run ahead. It's a habit."

Suddenly she took my arm and again I became stiff with amazement.

"Excuse me, maybe it's uncomfortable?"

"Not in the least," I said, hastily. "I implore you."

She smiled and glanced at me, rocking her bent head in time to her step: "Well, good," she said, finally.

"What's good?"

"Must you know everything?"

Here was their house already, swallowed up in black bushes of lilac or jasmine. She stopped at the start of a clay path. I handed her the basket. She rocked it steadily, striking it with her knee. She was silent. I didn't know how I was supposed to end this walk.

She evidently sensed my uneasiness, for she turned back to me, smiling in her own way, and swaying her head rhythmically, asked: "Maybe you'll take an apple for the journey?"

But she didn't put the basket forward, so I had to go closer. She looked down as I reached for the basket that was rocking in ceaseless movement: "Well, go and choose."

But she did not stop that monotonous movement, so all I could see in front of me was the revolving surface of the basket full of red apples. "I can't decide," I said, in strange expectation.

Then she suddenly stopped the movement of the basket, and leaned over to help me. For an instant I felt the warmth of her breasts on my temples, I saw her little hand with short, apparently bitten finger-nails. She gave me the first apple that came to hand, leaving her fingers in my palm a fraction of a second.

We both straightened up, I all sweating and uncertain, as though I'd committed a punishable crime, she friendly, as though abstracted, smiling. She again began rocking the basket with her persistent rhythm. We were both silent.

But this silence became unbearable, so I absently bit into the apple, though I didn't want to, and glanced at her. I could have sworn that now I saw something like sorrow in her, and again I felt clumsy, as though I'd done something inappropriate.

"So I suppose it's until we meet again," I said, not loudly.

"Mh," she nodded, but did not walk away.

I smiled, in order to confirm the ordinariness of this goodbye. But she didn't reply with a smile, only gazed at me persistently, and it seemed to me she wanted to tell me something.

All at once she turned away and ran down the steep path toward the house. I stayed there, a little disappointed, but also somehow festive. I began going down after her cautiously, and something almost like admiration of myself began creeping into my feelings.

Then I suddenly caught sight of him, as he stepped off the veranda among the lilac or jasmine bushes that were already blackened ready for winter. Then she suddenly appeared on the edge of the path. And I saw her throw her basket to the ground, run to him, cuddle him somehow inappropriately, with that lustful softness of hers, that shamelessness, while he with the gesture of a sated man embraced her, his property, then picked up the basket of apples.

Thus they went into the house hidden by the red sorb tree.

"Well, you see," I said to myself, with relief. But it wasn't relief at all. "Well, you see. How often has life taken your common sense away from you?"

And sudden vindictiveness seized me. I turned back once more in the direction of their house: "You just wait, you'll see me again," I said.

I set off back. I walked along for a certain time until I sensed someone's presence. I looked up. Romus was patiently flowing alongside: "You're talking to yourself." He bared his teeth.

"I have the habit, you see."

"Supposedly people who've lived a long time in isolation talk to themselves."

"That's not true."

I could feel his intrusive stare. I increased my pace involuntarily.

"You like her," he drawled.

I stopped violently: "What is it you want of me?"

"I don't want anything. But you fancy her."

"Be on your way."

I set off in the direction of home. Romus walked behind me with the step of a lunatic, and it was apparent he was with difficulty revolving laborious thoughts in his head.

"But we don't like her. Regina's something else."

I was silent.

"Neither one thing nor the other," Romus again spoke. "But Regina is so much of a woman, it's awful. You can take a look at her for yourself. She goes to bathe in the river. But today it's too late. The count likes to take a look, he has a taste for that."

I was walking faster and faster, and Romus' nasal, drawling voice remained somewhere in the background.

Later, lying on my bed, I was watching the blood-colored glow as it crept slowly across the wall toward the bare pine planks of the ceiling. I heard the Korsaks leave for the prayer meeting; later heard hymn singing flowing here along with the river's evening chill. Then they came back, talking sluggishly. The gate in the fence banged, they went into their apartment. The last drop of red in the demijohn on the window sill went out.

The door creaked. Miss Malvina peered intently into the darkness, trying to discern me in the dusk: "Do you want anything?"

"No, thank you."

"Some buttermilk, maybe?"

"No, thank you very much."

She stood a moment on the threshold, undecided: "Nothing bothering you?"

"No. Everything is fine. I'm going to sleep."

She kept silent a moment, then: "Well, just be careful. Please sleep well. For bad thoughts there's only sleep, nothing more."

She waited for me to answer. "Well then, good night," she said finally.

"Good night."

She listened to my breathing and when I turned over impatiently on the bed she quietly shut the door.

She and her brother muttered anxiously together for a while longer; at last the gilded crack under their door went out.

I tossed angrily on the bed and the jangling of the springs resounded a long time in the heated room.

Someone's cautious steps around the veranda aroused me. In a fraction of a second I was on my feet, mastering the violent beating of my heart. Some sediments of recollections full of terror, nocturnal fears, dreads of conscience enveloped me with clammy stuffiness. I could feel the shivering of my feet on the cold floor. Very slowly I began to distinguish the outlines of furniture, the misty gleam of the mirror, the square of the window brighter than the walls, with the globe of the demijohn, and the shape of the door to the veranda. Only now did I realize where I was and what the time was.

I tiptoed across the dark room, keeping my balance with outstretched hands. Finally I hit upon the door. I stopped on the veranda, holding my breath. Someone was creeping up to the next window.

I could see a dark, crouching figure pressed to the window pane. The nocturnal visitor straightened up a little and stared for a long time into the dark abyss of the window. Finally he tapped.

He stood a moment, vigilantly crouched, waiting for a reply. He tapped again. I could hear the impatient, fearful clank of the window pane loose in its frame.

"Who's there?" called Regina in a sleepy voice.

"It's me, do you hear?"

"What are you making such a noise at night for?"

"Open up, I want to tell you something."

"Tell me tomorrow."

"For God's sake, open up, else it will be the worse for you."

"Go away, you'll waken everyone. What will people say of me?"

"If you don't want to open the door, then come outside to me."

Silence.

"I'm not going to leave you alone. What is it, am I any worse than the others?"

"I don't go with anyone here. Why do you pester me?"

"Regina, open the door, I have something to tell you."

"Tomorrow."

"I'm going crazy, Regina. Why are you fooling with me?"

"It'll pass, go to bed."

"Regina, Regina," the partisan suddenly whined, "I can't go on any longer. I can't do anything, or think straight, I've become a complete fool."

Silence.

"Regina, I've got something buried in the ground here. If you want we can leave tomorrow."

"Quiet, or I'll call people."

"I have relatives abroad. You'll live like a lady."

The partisan puffed and blew angrily, and in this puffing and blowing there were tears: "Will you come out?"

Silence.

"Will you come out?"

He raised a fist: "Oh you God damn bitch . . ."

A terrifying clatter of broken glass resounded. Little pieces tinkled over the stones for a long moment.

The partisan went unsteadily to the veranda and laid his head against its cold frame. He stared into the interior without thinking and evidently caught sight of me, for he approached my door and stopped on the threshold: "Did you hear?" he asked.

I caught the sour smell of vodka: "I woke up this instant."

"Did you ever see such a bitch? I'm too small for her."

He took a few steps forward and caught hold of my shirt: "But do you know that the daughter of a government commissar fell in love with me? She was my orderly — not orderly, what am I saying, she was my slave, my whore. You know that in those days I ruled this county; even the Germans took off their caps to me."

He let go of me and went back to the door. I could see his stooping shoulders against the background of the star-scattered sky. They were twitching spasmodically. He blew his nose time and again, and groped at his face with his fingers. Then, without turning, he muttered to one side, "Well, don't get mad. Let's forget it, it's not worth while."

He banged his prosthesis with all his might against the door frame until all the window panes rattled, then rushed down full tilt, hit the gate with his chest and ran out into the road. There he stopped a moment, ran his prosthesis over his tousled hair and set off in the direction of the railroad.

> *A partisan's faith goes*
> *Along a road 'midst village huts.*
> *A pair of eyes shines in a window,*
> *And lips red as a rose . . .*

His song died away somewhere in the strange, starlit, and exceedingly quiet night. It seemed to me that even here I could hear the rise and fall, the uneven murmur of the Sola flowing untiringly south.

"Has he gone now?" someone whispered uncertainly.

In the rectangle of the door stood Regina, covered only by a thin chemise. I could clearly see her breasts, loosened for the night, swaying lazily.

"Yes."

"God, I had the fright of my life. Can I come into your room for a moment?"

"Please do."

She sat down on my bed, while I stood in the center of the room.

"He broke a window."

"Seems he was a little drunk."

"Only please don't tell anyone."

"Of course not, Miss Regina."

"It's been going on like this for six months. I'm scared to go out of the house."

"He loves you."

Suddenly it became quiet.

"That wasn't a wise thing to say. What can he, a man like that, know about loving?"

"I don't know, miss. It seems to be things aren't easy for him."

"Easy or hard, I'm not for him."

I kept silent. I couldn't see her face hidden in the gloom.

"But your bed's hot!" she exclaimed in a different voice.

"I was asleep already."

"Well yes, what else is there to do in such a place? People go to bed when the hens do. I was at a party in Podjelniaki, but some peasantry came so I left, though one forestry official made eyes at me in a big way."

I was silent.

"Brr, it's cold," she suddenly shivered and clasped herself with her naked arms. "The nights are cold already."

"Yes, after all, it's late autumn."

"Where did you live previously?"

"In many places. I never stayed anywhere long."

She deliberated a while over something, finally she asked: "You're on your own? Don't you have any family?"

"I'm on my own now."

"And you came here of your own free will?"

"Yes."

"I don't believe you." I could sense coquetry in her voice.

I was silent.

"Well yes," she whispered. "Time to sleep. Excuse me for disturbing you."

She sighed. I didn't even notice when she was at the door. Against the background of a sky holed with stars I saw the outline of her strong body under the flowing streams of her chemise.

"Thank you," she whispered.

"Good night."

"Good night."

Her bare feet resounded on the veranda, then the door rattled and everything fell silent.

I shaved carefully for the first time in several days, then set about cleaning up the room. Miss Malvina, overhearing me bustling about, opened the door slightly. I stopped in the center of the room with the broom in one hand and looked at her in an unfriendly way.

"Thank God, everything will be all right now," she said timidly.

"I don't understand you, miss."

"But I know what I'm saying. A person mustn't allow bad thoughts into his heart."

Behind her I could see Ildefons Korsak writing laboriously in a thick exercise book, dipping his steel pen nib into a huge, dusty inkpot.

"When a person looks in the mirror, that means he's well," she added.

"I shan't come to dinner today," I said.

"And I was preparing such tasty pancakes, like back home in the East.

"I'll be back late."

"But where are you going? Wouldn't it be better to pray with us; a prayer never yet harmed anyone."

"I want to see the forest. I thought of this a long time ago."

Regina walked by the veranda, humming in a deep alto voice. Through the crooked window panes I could see her bare shoulders bedewed with water, and her loosened hair. With a forceful gesture she splashed soapsuds out of a bucket, watched for a moment as little tongues of water, mossy with dust, flowed among the roots of the buckthorn. Then she went back to her room.

"That forest is evil. Better not go unless you need to," said Miss Malvina. "When there's no work, it's better to occupy your thoughts with something, there, like Ildek does. He, mister, always spends Sunday from dawn to dusk sitting over his exercise book, and he writes and writes endlessly. But I don't prevent the poor man. Let him write for health's sake. Better this than loaf around among people, or — God forbid — drink vodka, or get up to some foolishness."

I smiled, which clearly provoked Ildefons Korsak, for he rose from his writing and came to the door.

"What do I have to write about, Miss Malvina?" I asked uncertainly. "In order to write, a person must reach some thought or other. But my head's as empty as an old pot."

"But what sort of thought is needed for writing?" interposed Ildefons Korsak. "I've read at least five haystacks of books in my life and didn't find a single thought. In the Old Testament you can find all the general thoughts and the particular one a person needs to somehow get himself to that coffin of four planks."

"All the same, you write."

"I do," Korsak reflected. "Sure I write. But I have no anger against anyone, nor gratitude to anyone, so it isn't of present times that I write, mister. As for me, mister, in my book there will be everything the human eye has forgotten, or even that which it never saw."

"And did you ever read your book to anyone?"

"Did I read it?" Ildefons Korsak was surprised. "Why read it now? People will find it some time and read it. You found that cross of the old-time insurrectionists in the river, didn't you? At one time that was a sheet of iron, and those words they printed on it meant only as much as they wanted them to. But now you have cleaned the rust off the old cross, hung it around your neck and you read the inscriptions every day. Evidently it has some significance for you, although you're not an insurrectionist and you don't recall old-time customs."

"Go on, go on with you, poor man, and don't turn the gentleman's head with your nonsense," Miss Malvina interrupted.

"Well, that's how it is, too," said Ildefons Korsak, returning to the table. He sat down at his exercise book and began to read the latest fragment he'd written. It was difficult for him, so he started again from the beginning, stumbled on an unsuitable word, groaned painfully and peeped cautiously in our direction to make sure we could see his torment. Then he chewed the end of his penholder, gazing in anguish at the window sooty with dust.

I shifted the demijohn with its exuberantly bubbling Japanese mushroom, scraped the remains of the spread that had been served in my honor off the top of the radio cabinet, then straightened the winter landscape on the wall. It glowed with the red light of sunset, reflected many times in the innocent snow and reminded me of something from old times, something dead, something of unfulfilled hopes.

Then I took the unwanted broom out to the veranda. Regina was standing at her door, her face lifted high to the sun. With a feminine sense of the practical she was giving herself a sun-tan and at the same time fixing her hair with hot curlers. She wasn't in the least embarrassed to be only in her petticoat.

"Hot again," she said, without looking at me. "You'll see, something will come of this."

"That's so. A whole month without a drop of rain."

"Excuse me for not being dressed. But I woke late. And soon they're coming to fetch me. In a taxi."

"Fancy that. So you're not going to prayers?"

"Not today. The Lord God may forgive me. They're coming all the way from town."

"Were you ever in the forest, miss?"

"Why on earth go there? Better if it burns down. I haven't any business there."

"Well, I wish you success, miss."

"And I don't advise you to peep in there. The only one of us who goes there is the railroad man. They killed his wife and children during the war. He buried them on the very spot, by the pitch factory. They say that's why he's so abnormal. But in my view, a person must live for the present, not remembering what used to be and not thinking what's going to be. Am I right?"

"Surely, Miss Regina."

"You too should go to your own parts, and bring a woman back with you."

She rattled the curlers, checked their temperature with a licked finger. Bright drops of water still lay on her arms: "You don't say anything?"

"I wouldn't want to bring anyone here."

She turned her face to me and laughed suddenly: "Maybe I'd suit you?"

"I don't know whether that would be an advantageous decision for you, miss."

She was silent a moment, finally said: "You must have been of a better class once."

"Am I worse now?"

"That isn't it. But I feel that things aren't right with you."

The hens had gone in under the bushes, and they began loitering among the roots, hidden in their lairs from the sun. Somewhere not far off bees were buzzing on a high note.

"If I've said anything wrong, forgive me."

"Nothing wrong, Miss Regina."

"Oh, you're completely out of this world," she blew on the curlers and shook her head with the fresh curls. "Why should I waste time here with you? It's quite cold."

And with this she went into her room. I looked at my reflection in the window pane and heaved a sigh on beholding yet again that same thin, uninteresting face. I moved toward the gate.

"Don't go far away. This is an uneasy neighborhood," Miss Malvina called after me.

Romus was lolling in the burdocks. Without any greeting he followed me with a terrifyingly sleepy gaze. Then he collapsed helplessly on his back and slowly made a hole in the grass with his head, seeking a place where the sun could not penetrate.

On the railroad track I unexpectedly met Szafir. He was walking between the tracks and attentively inspecting our recent work. Seeing me, he hesitated, then said:

"Good morning."

"Good morning."

"I happen to have some business to discuss with you."

". . ."

"I've been looking over your personal file."

". . ."

"You ought to come and see me."

"Do I have to?"

"You don't have to. The position is that you've been living here some time, but we still don't know one another."

He was looking at me haggardly. And I didn't know whether his intentions were good or not.

"I feel bad. I want to be by myself."

Szafir dropped his gaze to the earth and kicked a stone which rolled and rebounded between the tracks: "The position is that this is a difficult neighborhood," he said. "Once this used to be our district, see. During the war our units were stationed here. But now the position is that this is a most backward region. Haven't you noticed? There aren't any young people here. They've all run away to the towns; only old people with their superstitions have stayed behind. All kinds of people, a conglomeration from all over the world, all homeless. That's the position here. Are you here for long?"

"I don't know. I myself don't know."

"I too came here not too long ago. Somehow I never had the luck to reach the end of a job anywhere. Such is fate. Will you drop by?"

"I don't know. Maybe later."

"People say all sorts of things about you."

"Is that a threat?"

Szafir suddenly looked up and smiled unexpectedly: "Are you afraid of threats?"

He wanted to say something more, but clearly decided not to, for he turned and walked away with his crooked gait.

Then I stopped near that house hidden in the old bushes. The red sorb tree was moving its yellowing leaves almost imperceptibly. A slender and thin wisp of smoke was suspended over the blackened chimney. I stood there like a criminal, behind a dead lilac bush. I gazed intently into the black windows in which there was tranquility and stillness. I knew that someone might come up at any moment, that I'd have to seek awkward excuses, but I couldn't tear my gaze away from this house.

Somewhere behind me the vesper bell of the monastery resounded, summoning the faithful, of whom there were none in our township. It resounded busily, with a sort of urgency, and its echo, stifled by the distance, wandered through the oak glade on the far side of the river. I coughed once and again, too loudly. No one looked out of a window.

So I went into a dry meadow that smelled of burning. A broad column of heated air was quivering above the peat bog. A lost stork had wandered into this deserted place and, suspecting the fire smouldering, the flame blazing under the turf, it suddenly rose into the air, flapping its ponderous wings.

"See, we meet again."

She said this puffing at a milkweed flower entangled in gossamer. I stopped, dismayed, in the middle of a pace.

"Don't you know where to look for me?" she asked.

"Yet I've found you."

"But you wasted time unnecessarily over there near the house."

She was lying on a blanket, an open book nearby. A transparent cloud of flies was circling around her head. She didn't ask me to sit down, so I stood about ten paces from her, in the center of the burned-out field.

"Well, what?" she asked.

"I'd say 'Nothing,' but that would be impolite, wouldn't it?"

She started swaying her head in that peculiar and irritating way she had.

"I've talked about you with my husband. He told me you'd met by the river."

"Is he your husband?"

"Are you surprised?"

"Why should I be?"

She placed the commonplace flower between the pages of her book and again stared steadily at me.

"Don't you want to ask where we're from and what links us together?"

"I don't ask because everyone keeps asking me questions."

"You know what? You're nice."

"I want to do better."

She turned over on her back and pulled up her knees. She was certainly looking at the sky, but I couldn't see her face which was veiled by streams of fine, clear hair.

"And where are you off to?"

"To the forest."

"But there aren't any mushrooms this year."

"I'm looking for a job as gamekeeper."

"Oh! Witty too."

She again turned her face toward me.

"Do you want to make friends with me?"

"I already said I would."

"But maybe you're a seducer. The terror of the neighborhood. Well said?"

I went in the direction of the Sola's steep bank. Startled frogs jumped from under my feet into the winding current of the river.

"Please wait."

I stopped.

"Please come back."

I returned to my previous place.

"You know what, I bought myself a new hat yesterday. It will change everything for me, for sure. Well said?"

"Well said, for sure."

Again she swayed her head in that haunting, catchy rhythm.

"Aren't things going well?" I asked.

"Well, sure. Before we met yesterday, I fell. My side is all bruises," she clutched her blouse but I hastily looked at the ground. "I wanted to show off to you by coming down the road near the monastery. I tripped over a root."

I was silent.

"Oh, how taciturn you are."

"I have to go."

"Then I'll come with you."

She rose, carelessly gathered the blanket and book, and handed me the bundle dripping with pine needles.

"Please carry that."

We went down to the very edge of the river. She put a bare foot into the water.

"Oh, how cold."

"Are you able to cross to the other side? It's shallow here."

"You must hold me."

I took her dry palm. We waded across the river, stumbling on hidden stones, sinking into the ticklish water plants. She pulled up her skirt, which was already wet in several places.

She suddenly stopped in the middle of the river.

"Do you remember my name?"

"Of course. Justine."

We were holding hands, walled in by rapid water that bore the reflection of black banks. It looked as though we were searching for something lost in the shallow river.

I pulled her by the hand.

"No, no!" she cried in sudden fright.

"What are you scared of? After all, the water will carry you off in a moment."

She glanced at me intently, then moved ahead toward the far bank. I let her hand go. Struggling against the current, she waded by her own efforts to the first alders.

"I'd surely be able to swim across this river in a deep place, too. Well said?" she said, already in her usual tone.

"Well said."

"Are you angry with me?"

"If I'm angry sometimes, then it's only with myself."

She walked toward the oak glade with that curvaceous, rhythmic step of hers. I walked after her, avoiding the large, bristly pine cones. We started to climb the gentle sloping bank on which young oaks grew. Then she stopped and pressed her entire body to a cracked tree trunk.

"I was never here before."

"Nor was I."

"The whole valley and our house can be seen."

"It's recognizable by the sorb."

"Isn't it! You've noticed that too?"

I sought a cigarette. "See how it looks, you fool?" I asked myself quietly.

"Did you say something?"

"Nothing particular. Sometimes I talk to myself."

She began telling me something or other about her childhood or schooldays which didn't concern me in the slightest. I looked, without sympathy, at her not too pretty face, somehow asynchronic, composed of two small halves, all at once alien to me, stripped of the charm which had previously come into being in my imagination but now had been all of a sudden dashed, and I was bored, I was clearly bored, wishing her to go away, to return to the other bank.

She stopped talking and eyed me a moment longer with the gaze that had so often misled me. Then she set off into the depths of the forest.

"Well, all right," I told myself, "it's just as well it happened this way."

She didn't turn around or ask what I was saying. She walked on more and more slowly, until she stopped in an incompleted movement. When I came up level with her, without looking at me she said:

"Please give back the blanket."

I grunted, surprised. She glanced at me angrily.

"Do you hear, please give the blanket back."

I automatically handed her the bundle.

"I'm not going any further with you," she whispered, and unexpectedly she started running downhill toward the river. She ran with arms outspread as though into someone's embraces, and the impetus puffed her skirt and blouse, which slipped out from under her belt. Then she disappeared in the ravine of the river and for a long time I couldn't see her. When I was about to move on, she appeared on the other bank. She was again walking in that way of hers, head bent to one side.

Absurdly, I wanted her to look back. I waited for that a long time, but it didn't happen.

Beyond the oak glade began sparse pine woods, full of high and faded grass. I came across rusty rolls of barbed wire and caved-in hunters' trenches thickly overgrown with wild strawberries, many of which were flowering again. Then the forest imperceptibly descended toward a valley, and here the first spruces appeared, powerful, gnarled, and black.

Soon I found myself in the gloomy spruce forest. I was walking between high, withered ferns, plunging into their dense tangles, stubbornly walking into the depths of the unknown woods.

Here it was dark. The trees moaned alarmingly, though I recalled that back in our valley we hadn't heard the wind for a month. My throat dried up, my painful feet got caught more and more often in intrusive weeds.

I sat down on an old trunk. Red ants were running rapidly about, dragging white larvae, which they hid under a bone turned gray by rain. Somewhere a woodpecker was tapping with monotonous fury. In front of me stood a dead tree with black scars, towering toward the sky, a tree killed by an artillery shell.

I rose and set off again on my way. I had to. This was why I'd got up that day, shaved, licked my hand wetted in the water of the Sola. So as not to dream terrible dreams, so my heart wouldn't suddenly thump with a stifling memory, so as to liberate myself of this burden moulded by the years.

I proceeded like this a very long time. I'd lost track of time and didn't know whether I was walking in a straight line or whether I was circling around one and the same spot. I couldn't see the sky, it was hidden by the precipitous branches of the spruces. A gloom, a damp gloom, was thickening around me, and in this gloom was a sort of ridiculous terror, the terror of solitude or the terror of enslavement.

I realized I would measure this forest from end to end, I would get to know its secrets and if I didn't find anything — then I'd postpone the deadline for some time.

Something flickered among the trees. I stopped, gasping for breath.

"An animal, of course. A doe, or a fallow deer. These forests are famous for fallow deer," I said to myself as calmly as I could.

Then again I moved on into the unending undergrowth of ferns that would never flower. Their dry stalks caught my clothing with a glassy hiss, while I stubbornly trampled down the hostile thicket. Crouching to the ground, almost blindly, I plunged ahead.

Finally I reached a thin clearing and fell upon the coarse moss. For a long time I gasped into the ground with my hot breath, without the strength to raise my head. Then I turned over on my back.

Between the black branches I caught sight of fragments of blue sky, scraps of light ductile as fresh honey. I gazed at these traces of life, gently brushed by the ceaseless movement of the tattered branches, and felt safer.

Later I sat up and looked around. Not far away was a deep gap in the withered ferns. I dragged myself in that direction and became numb like someone struck down by a long-awaited misfortune.

In an area of bare earth I could see a shallow tunnel already silting up, with two red stones, begrimed underneath, moldy with dried-up ash over both its banks. At the bottom of the tunnel lay coals mingled with sand and entire wood knots that hadn't been consumed by the fire. I knew I would find something more. In grass burnt by the spattering of a bonfire I quickly discovered some empty cartridges from which the powder had been shaken out in order to light a fire of damp wood. I turned the empty cartridges with their untouched percussion caps between my fingers, realizing that everything that was to have happened had already happened.

I rose slowly. For a moment I struggled with an enormous fear, then I called out, not loudly:

"Korvin!"

Not even the echo answered.

"Korvin! Korvin!"

The forest was murmuring with its hidden, somber life.

"Korvin! It's me! It's me!"

I drew air into my lungs: "Korvin! I'm looking for you! Korvin!"

Clenching my fists until they hurt, I walked with long, clumsy paces through the forest, stifling my fear and emotion. I kept shouting, "Korvin! Answer! It's me! I've come to you."

Snow is falling. Great flakes are dropping straight down to the ground, because there is no wind. They melt immediately, devoured by black mud in which a stray bit of light from the streetlamp wanders. In front of the store stands a line of silent people. Someone is smoking a cigarette, protecting it from the moisture in his palm. Plumes of snow are growing on men's hats.

At the end of the street I can see a tunnel with beads of faint lamps. In its opening a crowd of snow-covered people is shuffling about. They are moving monotonously around something that lies in the middle of the street. A streetcar comes up and stops in front of the gathering, its bell ringing impatiently.

I still have time, twenty long minutes. So I approach the crowd and stop behind the men's backs. I listen to their stifled explanations: "He jumped out, mister, and slipped, and the driver didn't have time to brake."

"He never jumped out. He was walking along the sidewalk and threw himself under the streetcar."

"Rubbish. After all, that woman over there saw it herself. He was coming back from work. Look how slippery it is. It's easy to have an accident."

"You telling me? I was walking behind him all the time. He looked like he was drunk, or else he was sick."

"Ah, whenever there's an accident they always say afterwards he was drunk."

"Still a young man. This shows the way life is. He left home early in the morning, but he surely never thought he would never return any more."

"If people had lifted the streetcar right away, maybe he'd have survived. But the driver made a fool of himself, he went into reverse and then drove straight on again."

"But it seems to me as though he did it himself, voluntarily."

"Who'd take his own life in times like these? It's just frightening to go out into the street."

"Things work out differently for different people. Who knows what sort of life he led?"

"Horrible time of year. They'll have to dig his grave with a crowbar."

"To him, mister, it's all the same. He doesn't bother his head about it any more."

"As if the war wasn't enough. To die by your own hand. . . ."

I push between the people and stand over the man sprawled over the rails. No blood to be seen; black, squashed mud covers everything. And this suicide looks like a rag trampled in the gutter. Only the white of one eye glitters phosphorescently in the reflection of the electric light.

Several streetcar men are clumping around him in their heavy, felt boots. Only at this moment do I see the deserted streetcar, the one that ran over the man, inside the tunnel. I imperceptibly draw my sleeve up and search a long time for the hands of my wrist watch. Sixteen minutes to go.

"Pick up his package from the ground," says someone behind me.

"That's not allowed. It's not permitted to move anything until the militia come," the streetcar men reply.

"Maybe he was taking something home. Why is it to be wasted?"

"It's all one now," one of the streetcar men shrugs.

Someone pushes my back.

"Haven't you had your fill of looking? Well then, stand aside."

So now I'm standing by the sidewalk knowing it's not worthwhile looking at my watch. But I look just the same and find out that barely a minute and a half have passed.

I go back. After all, I can wait by the door. I dread the moment when they begin lifting him, to place that muddied human scrap on a stretcher. I don't want to see his face, devoured by death.

So I turn back, I go to that plasterless building, its windows not entirely filled with dirty light. From here I look once again in the direction of the tunnel. And I see that it is empty already. Far away, at the other end of the tunnel there creeps a half-empty streetcar. So it had all ended, in the twinkling of an eye, not even a trace remained.

Every few moments the hunched figure of some passer-by disentangles itself from the snowstorm and disappears in the door of the building by which I am standing. These are my judges. They don't see me, they don't even guess that I can be hiding here behind a notched drainpipe, apprehensive, smeared all over, stripped of all the conditions I had stammered out years ago. I glance at my watch: another nine minutes.

I think to myself: people are right. He's past it now. One way or another, but now everything is behind him. Another seven minutes.

It's hard for me to stand a long time by this drain pipe filled with a monotonous gurgling. So I set off with short steps toward the door. I spend a long time kicking snow off my shoes, I fumble the door handle with deliberate helplessness. Finally I'm in this long passage which today has an entirely different meaning. Another four minutes.

"Did you see the accident?" someone asks gently. "A disastrous time. Dark, wet, everyone in a hurry. They pushed him out of the streetcar."

"It seems he threw himself out."

"Oh no. People are just gossiping, as always. Going in?"

"No. I'll wait here for a while."

They all disappear into the big hall, but I shield myself with my back and wait. Two more minutes. Might as well go in.

A lot of people. They know it's going to be sensational. They are feverishly whispering to each other. I can feel many curious paris of eyes on me. I sit down in a corner. Naked light bulbs are strung high under the ceiling. Some damp stains on the walls. This is precisely the hour.

Finally they take their seats at the head table. I can hear nothing of what is being said. I am biding my time. This goes on insanely long, and I can distinguish jokes, and laughter, and anger, and malice, and pathos, and boredom in this current. As usual in a human gathering.

Finally they start talking about me. The creak of chairs can be heard. I know what that means. Everyone is turning in my direction.

And I rise and walk a very long way on my benumbed feet to the table covered with green baize.

I stand facing the gathering. Before me I can see a pyramid of faces, in which I can't distinguish eyes, nor brows or lips. I can hear a separate stifled hum of voices.

"Tell us your curriculum vitae," says the secretary, and he seats himself more comfortably, ready to relish a bit of knowledge which he already knows through and through.

I've written scores of curricula in my life. But today I'm producing a special one, appropriate to this assembly. True, too.

And as I hem and haw laboriously, sounding out each word, I see you before me on that night.

You were sitting at a table that smelled of fresh bread, encircled by the livid glow of a carbide lamp you'd made of empty food cans. You were reading Zeromski's novel *Ashes,* the Bible of your generation, bound in dark blue cloth. It wasn't easy going for you, this book and the previous ones you'd earned for your work, chopping wood, digging the garden, bringing water, from two old folk whose only wealth in those unusual times was a collection of old books.

The wind was howling outside the window, pots quietly grumbled on top of the kitchen stove, while a transparent spider was cautiously lowering itself down an invisible thread attached to the old electric lamp with its big porcelain egg shade. You were reading idly, not understanding much, permeated with a vibrating uncertainty by the fear of solitude. For the hundredth time you recalled that hour when your weapon was taken away from you and they expelled you from the unit. Going back in memory to that moment, you considered it once more, scrupulously, uncovering unexpected and ever more threatening elements. You lived again through that shameful return, when after the emblems and military insiginia were stripped off your uniform, you crept home at night, fearing both the Germans and your own people.

From the next room, through the half-open door, you were listening to your mother crying in her sleep, although she didn't know anything about your disgrace, for you'd lied to her, declaring your unit had been disbanded while you'd obtained an important and secret task in the conspiracy.

Listening to your mother's broken sobs, you moved the book out of the circle of baneful light and gazed at the window pane filled with the reflection of a flame, fine as an arrow's barb and of your head, your hair licked by a blue glare.

And then, from out of the dense wind, the strained growl of a motor approached and rattled the window pane. In one moment you'd extinguished the light and stood in the door of the hallway appalled by the thud of your heart. Then you went out on tiptoe to the front of the house, to the old flagstones with which part of the yard was paved.

You caught sight of the black mass of a truck standing at the crossroad, two bright lantern lights, and you could hear foreign speech mingled with the wind. And without knowing why, you looked in the direction where that house stood, excommunicated and detested, in which lived an alien vagabond, a wanderer without faith or citizenship. Between the trees you could distinguish the feeble reflection of a window, or properly speaking a triangular crack in the obscurity, gleaming like a cat's eye.

You ran there through the gardens behind the house, jumping fences and beds dug in for the winter, avoiding dog kennels full of hostile snarling. Finally you found yourself by the stone wall, partly sunken into the clay hillside, and you leaned toward this window. In the triangular crack you caught sight of part of a room, seen from above, a bare floor awash in soapsuds, the semicircle of a wash basin and the feet of a child being rubbed dry by someone's hands.

You tapped cautiously at the little pane. Someone came to the window and, without drawing the curtain aside, asked: "Who's there?"

"It's me," you replied automatically. And then, realizing how ineffective this introduction was, you whispered feverishly into the sash-joint: "Escape, escape! The Shaulis have come! Escape!"

Then you hid behind the well, waiting to see if he believed you. You could hear a dull thumping from inside the dwelling, and realized he was hastily pulling on his boots, hitting his heels on the floor. Then the door squeaked and the cracks of the hallway filled with a wavering light. At the same time, many footsteps clattered in the street and someone opened the garden gate.

You wanted to cry out, to warn him, but it was already too late. He was standing in the door to the hallway, surrounded by a glow of light from the lamp with which his wife was lighting his way. Once again you recalled his appearance: a tall, lean figure with a helpless, crouched back, black hair, and swarthy face with prominent lips that sometimes smiled without the participation of his eyes.

The Shaulis came into the ray of light. Reflections shivered on their helmets like great cockades. They said something to him and he replied, faltering and staring at the ground.

"Laba naktis," they said to his wife, and waited for her to close the hallway door.

Then they led him past you, prodding him without anger: "Ejk, ejk ponas."

You walked around the well, hiding behind its wet carcass. You followed him with your eyes until the moment when he merged into the night, and even longer: until the roar of the engine resounded, and the truck, whining in low gear, rolled along the steep road.

For a long time you shivered by the well, pressing the mossy planks with your fingers, and you could not collect your thoughts. Then you shifted your gaze to that window huddled close to the earth. And suddenly you went to it, kneeled down on the slippery turf, and pressed your face to that window pane where there was the triangle of light.

A woman was standing with her back to you in the center of the room. You could see her bright, reddish hair enveloped in the light of the naphtha lamp, and her drooping hands. She stood thus a long time, beside the unemptied washbowl, amidst bubbles of soapy water which were bursting one by one.

And you could not tear your gaze away from her, although you were freezing, dressed only in a shirt, although you could not control your chattering and spasmodically shivering teeth.

The child cried out. But the woman didn't move, she remained an enormously long time, in that strange stillness until at last, when your legs became numb with cold, she slowly raised her hands, froze a moment in that attitude, and then, with a lethargic movement, drew her blouse over her head.

Only when you caught sight of her nakedness, shameless and without meaning, you leaped away from the window, struck with horror. You ran home the same way, appalled by thus getting to know a woman's body.

Then you dozed on the kitchen sofa, under a half-open window. You could hear all the neighbors' clocks striking, and you awaited the dawn. And when a cock crowed somewhere, your sensitive ears caught, in the murmur of the wind, the thud of the earth under the feet of many exhausted people.

You hurried out into the garden and burrowed into the wetness of old raspberry bushes. You saw them come into the yard, shining their flashlight, and beating on the door. You were drenched in sweat and the dew that had formed copiously before dawn.

There must have been an automobile in the street, for you could hear from thence the stifled murmur of a crowd of prisoners herded in the back.

They ransacked the house a long time, accompanied by the groaning voice of your mother. Finally some of them came out in front of the house. One pissed on your head, others chatted sleepily, smoking cigarettes. You were so frozen that you couldn't extricate your hand which had become entangled in raspberry stalks.

Then you heard the order to search the garden.

"Nie reikia," said an unseen Shauli.

"Reikia, reikia," urged an officer.

They moved off, trampling down gooseberry bushes. Then you had an attack of terror, the like of which had never been your lot during months of partisan action. You rushed blindly in flight, smashing the raspberry bushes, injuring yourself on tomato props, tripping over fresh lumps of earth. You ran in this state of shock until you fell into a pond covered with goose feathers. Here, choking in thick muddy water, you came to your senses. Drenched in slime you dragged yourself to the bank, your bare feet stiff with cold. You knew very well that the origin of this terror was that day on which they'd led you, disarmed, beyond the halting place. But you couldn't rid yourself of it. It caught you by the throat in sudden waves, like contortions, and you rushed, you had to rush, to the nearest door and to bang desperately on the rain-washed, clean planks.

Nobody opened. You could hear whispering inside, steps creeping behind the wall and tense waiting. But no one lifted the latch.

So you ran to the next house. You beat against the door, the walls, the windows. You groaned, writhing with pain, for the cold had already become pain. You stared imploringly into the window panes, beyond which something loomed obscurely, perhaps someone in there was struggling with his own conscience.

Then you caught sight of that edifice which meant more than anything to your dear ones. You passed the belfry, pursued by dogs, and gained the rectory window. You tore at the shutters, weeping in despair.

"Who's that? Who is calling?" you finally heard a voice, but not of the priest, only of that man who rarely left the house.

"It's me, Paul. Please let me in, please open the door, I'm dying."

The silence lasted a long time. Finally that same voice replied: "It can't be done. The Shaulis are going around the houses. It's not allowed."

You burst into tears, fell on your knees, striking your head on the foundation. Dawn was rising. An awakened rook was gliding over the church, beating its wings against bursts of wind. It was becoming lighter and lighter.

"Go away. Don't endanger other people," said the voice, muffled by the window's double glass.

Humiliated, you rose from the earth. You stood thus a long while on trembling legs, and felt the sudden passing of terror in yourself. And then you were surprised by everything that had happened.

You wiped saliva from your chin, rubbed the mildew-smelling slime from your hands and set off toward your house, quite openly, along the middle of the road.

You didn't hide in the curves of the fences, you didn't look around fearfully, you walked with confidence on your frozen feet, surprised by the calm around you. But after all it was early morning, and the first smoke was rising from some houses. However, you knew that the hidden eyes of people were following you on this journey.

You walked like this a very long way, falling asleep on the way, until you caught sight of the wide-open gate. You entered your home and here you suddenly came to, amidst the overturned furniture, scattered clothing, upset milk.

"Mama," you said, sleepily.

No one replied.

"Mama, I'm back," you repeated.

The neighbors' clock struck six.

"Mama, I'm terribly sleepy."

Silence.

"Mama, answer me."

You went into the other room, which was as disordered as the kitchen. Your mother's mattress had been kicked to the floor. You lay down on it, seeking its hidden warmth.

An alien presence awoke you. You pulled apart your encrusted eyelashes with the utmost difficulty. Neighbors were standing in the doorway. You felt a drop of sweat trickle through your hair and roll ticklingly over your brow, down your cheek, and a drop of warmth fell on your bare collarbone: "Where's my mother?" you asked.

They stirred angrily: "Where d'you think? They took her away. They took her into town."

"But what for?"

Again that hostile stir: "Ask yourself why. You never were any use to anyone, and now you're driving your own family to death."

"God, how hot I am."

"Get up, and go rescue your mother."

You rose from the mattress and staggered, seeking to regain your balance. You saw in front of you the little shrine of the Ostrobramska Church and there were straw flowers, many straw flowers, under the faded picture. Suddenly you crossed yourself.

The neighbors moved away from the door to let you through.

You staggered to the town, which rose in the distance veiled by mist. And when you finally entered its walls, joy seized you, for soon you would see your mother, and all this muddle would be unraveled in a moment.

You pushed your way through the crowded little streets, stubbornly elbowing passers-by, until you reached a large building with an enormous number of bars at the windows. Naked chestnut trees stood around it, and the place was as familiar to you as to other inhabitants of that town.

A sentry was standing at the barrier, dandling a fine machinegun, such as you had dreamed of out there, in the unit. You wanted to greet him with some gesture, you even moved one hand and with this hand raised to the sky you moved in his direction, leaning against the wall, which flowed toward you, then moved away again into the mist.

Then, all at once, you were grabbed under the arms, and you sensed that the hand on the left belonged to a man, and that on the right to a woman.

"I'm going to get my mother," you said, quietly.

"You're sick," you recognized a woman's voice, "please listen to us."

"But my mother is in there."

"Please don't say anything. You'll be able to rest right away. In this house."

"But I'm to blame . . . to blame . . . to blame."

"Very well, but be quiet, they're looking at us."

Then there were stairs, passageways, some hasty running about, and the smell of someone else's apartment. Old-fashioned, mousy, like a faded illustration. And later surely some kind of dream, involving all the people you'd known up to then but who today had undergone sudden strange and cruel events.

"Well, it'll be all right," said the man.

"I apologize very much for the trouble," you stammered out, with difficulty.

"That's what we're here for. It's our duty," said the woman.

You reflected a moment: "I was going to get my mother."

"I know, I know. But this morning they took them further. To the Reich."

You rose suddenly: "I have to go."

The woman — no, she wasn't a woman, but a girl with warm hands, stopped you: "That's pointless. You can't help and you'll die. They won't find her any more."

"You must go into hiding," the man added. "Each life is valuable now."

You saw their concerned faces over you, and that is why you had to say: "I was thrown out of my unit."

The man straightened up: "What unit?"

"Hurricane's."

It grew quiet, you heard the ticking of the watch the man wore. You knew both were gazing at each other in consternation.

"I'll go away," you whispered.

The man's high boots squeaked: "Show this man the way."

The girl took you by the sleeve and led you by another route. You found yourself in a yard full of corded logs, you passed one black gateway, then another, and came out into a street drowned in terrifying light.

"This is Wielka Street. Can you find your own way?" the girl asked.

You nodded.

She turned away swiftly and ran in the direction of the labyrinth of passage gates, and you didn't even manage to remember her face, nor the color of her hair. You gazed at the place she'd touched on your shirt sleeve, still able to feel her warmth.

So you went home, or not really home, but to your settlement, which had given you childhood and youth but now had become hostile and alien. As you could not spend the nights in your own home, expecting the Shaulis at any moment, you chose an empty lot on which someone was to have built a house in 'thirty-nine but didn't have time, and who had gotten lost somewhere in the world.

So you moved into this garden of rank, wild weeds, already touched by the first frosts, and you placed your mattress which you carried from home in a shed intended for cement.

The neighbors knew where you were hiding, but they did not oppose your decision, but neither did they support it with benevolent help. You lay there a dozen days or more, living on turnips you had brought from other people's gardens, and you remembered nothing of those days, except the patter of rain on the tarred felt roof, the murmur of the wind so rich in its intonations.

It seemed to you that all this lasted only a couple of weeks, but it may well have lasted longer, since the glitter of frost crept into the shed, climbing higher and higher on the door planks. Sometimes, waking, you touched with horror your spiky hair, cut by ice. Between the cracks of the boards you could see stars and the blurred outlines of trees, but all this was lined with a feeling of alienation.

And one such night, when snow was falling and had awakened you by its silence, you had a strange encounter. Some man or other was standing in the shed door, motionless, as though pondering. You sat up on your mattress under the heap of rags and cement sacks, but he was rooted motionless, and would have seemed to be a tree trunk were it not for his warm breath, which rolled into the shed like dense steam.

"Winter is here," he said, after a while.

"I'm better now. I'll be leaving this shed soon," you replied.

"Where will you go?"

"To the forest."

"But there is no return to the forest."

"I'll find some other unit."

In the settlement, dogs were howling, predicting a hard winter.

"It isn't easy to be an alien among your own people," he said.

"I meant well. It worked out strangely."

The snow creaked under his boots: "Find some suitable company for yourself."

"But where shall I find it?"

"You aren't the only one of your kind in the world."

You gathered a handful of loose snow from a crack and tasted it. It tasted of the roof, bitter.

"Farewell," said the man.

And he vanished. You didn't even hear the snow squeak, for the dogs again resounded with their somber howling.

Then suddenly you realized you should have asked him about something, that he had left too soon, that you needed him. So you ran out, then stopped in the snow-covered garden without knowing what to do.

And you began seeking his fresh tracks in the snow. You set out on a track that soon proved false. You ran from one field edge to another, from clumps of grass to heaps of twigs, until you suddenly caught sight of that window, this time with a different-shaped crack, not triangular.

Your heart beat more fiercely; you knew you were saved though you did not completely understand the meaning of this salvation. Swamped in the first snowdrifts, you scrambled to the window and glued your eye to the pane which was frosted over by a fine pattern. Your breath veiled the cold glass with mist, but in spite of which you could see in the clear fragments of the pane the woman, reading a sheet of paper folded in the shape of a letter.

You kept waiting for a man with flakes of snow on his stooping shoulders, and with black hair, to appear in the circle of light, for him to speak to her, bathed in the reddish light. But no one entered the house, and it was very quiet, and the woman remained as motionless as a figure in an engraving.

But then she suddenly rose from the stool and, with a slow movement, again drew the blouse over her head. And again, between the cracks of frost hardened to the pane, you saw female nakedness totally revealed, but you did not run away, you absorbed it, overcoming a great grief by this sacrilege, as heavy as human remains.

"Any questions?" cries the secretary after a long silence.

A man rises. I can see the white blotch of his face and the bright gleam of a gold tooth: "You've been telling us of a period when you belonged to an underground gang. Can you inform us what is now happening to its leader?"

I'm prepared for this question. And yet my heart starts beating so loudly again that I'm afraid the audience will hear it. Then I notice a half-filled glass in front of me. I reach for it and slowly drink the water, which tastes like summer rain. "No, I don't know. We parted by chance, and I don't know what he's doing, or even if he's still alive."

"But do you realize it's your duty to tell the truth?"

"Yes."

"So can you tell us what his pseudonym was?"

I reach for the glass again. Empty. I pull out a cigarette, twist it round and round in my fingers and then put it aside. "No. I don't remember his pseudonym."

A very long pause of significant silence.

"I don't remember. We very often changed our pseudonyms for security's sake. I don't remember. I'm afraid I might accidentally give you someone else's."

"But surely your unit must have had some name?"

"No, it didn't. This was a group which had separated itself from a large unit which later was disbanded. Simply a dozen or so very young people. We wanted to fight to the last man."

"What for?"

I pick up the cigarette and am surprised at how crumbled it is. I look at the scraps of tobacco scattered on the red cloth.

"In any case, these are well-known matters which don't need explanation," the secretary interposes. "We know very well the circumstances under which you young people went underground."

"Yes. Though it's strange he can't remember either his leader's pseudonym nor the name of the unit. Yes, it's strange."

And he sits down. Now I notice he's bald. The naked light bulb is reflected on his skull.

"Anyone else want to ask any questions?" says the secretary in a weary voice.

The pyramid of faces is cut across by lines of smoke. Someone comes in and takes a long time to close the door, causing it to keep squeaking. But no one turns in that direction. All the heads are motionless.

He rises again and his gold tooth gleams. I hold my breath.

"I should also like to know whether you fired at our men."

"I was a soldier, after all," I say, and I feel this description to be somehow inappropriate, and a sort of condemnation suddenly arising in the audience. "I was a soldier," I repeat helplessly, "so I fired."

"How many of our men did you kill?"

I reach for the empty glass and replace it on the same spot: "Clashes usually happened at night. I fired at those in front of me, but I didn't know whether I hit or wounded, or killed any of them."

"You don't remember a definite case of murder?"

His white face is insistently rooted in the center of the dark wall. I know he is looking into my eyes, and I know he won't believe me: "Yes, there was such a case. I got the order to carry out a death sentence."

"To shoot a man?"

I shift from one foot to the other, and lean with all my strength on the podium: "Yes," I say, "yes."

"Who was it?"

"I don't know. I only got the address and description of this man."

"What did he look like?"

The secretary gets up: "Is this essential?"

The other man's tooth hastily gleams. "It is for me. These are important matters. Surely I have the right to know everything to the end?"

The secretary sits down and looks at me:

"He lived in an isolated house near a railroad. It's difficult for me to say anything, for it was night. I only remember he was tall, with dark hair, sallow, with protruding lips."

I hear the abrupt noise of a chair pushed back. Only now do I notice that behind me is the clerk's small table, covered with sheets of hastily written notes. Next to him a woman with white hair and eyes hysterically wide is swaying. A copying-ink pencil is quivering in her hand: "That was my husband . . . My husband died like that . . ." she whispers.

I turn to her and now stand with my back to the audience: "I didn't kill him," I said.

"Explain what you mean," cries the secretary, and he rises as though he wants to help me. "This is very important."

I swallow thick saliva that doesn't let itself be swallowed: "I had an order to kill him, but I didn't."

"In other words, you didn't carry out the order?" the secretary prompts.

"I did. I had to."

"How's that?" the secretary gets agitated. "Did you kill him or didn't you?"

Staring at the woman's heavy clumsy boots glistening with

moisture, I seek appropriate words: "I shot him. I shot him so as not to kill him."

The woman bursts into tears. She turns away from us all and weeps into her sleeve. She seeks blindly with her left hand for her handbag which isn't on the table.

"What do you mean about 'firing without killing'? How do you know the results of that shot?" the same voice asks from the audience.

"I know, because I didn't want to kill him."

"Yet you fired?"

"I know for certain that I didn't kill him."

"But why didn't you want to kill him, since you went there to carry out the sentence?"

I am silent. The woman turns around and sits down again at the table, covering her face helplessly with one hand. I make an enormous effort to remember. But I can't. I have seen many such faces fraught with affliction in my life. "At that time I'd already stopped wanting to kill people," I repeated quietly.

"But you went with a bandit's assignment?"

I am again standing with my face to the audience. I know now there is no way back. I'd lived through this hour many times during sleepless nights, but today it oppresses me most heavily. My head aches. My hands feel so heavy that I have to rest them on the podium: "One night our patrol went into a village on an assignment. Some men from the security police caught them. They killed them off, every one of them. At that time the frosts were very severe. The bodies of our men froze stiff in the middle of the village. We had to chop them out of the earth afterwards."

"That's a lie. Our men didn't behave like that!" shouted that man in the audience. "Admit you're lying!"

"I'm not lying."

"Propaganda! Bandit propaganda."

"I saw it myself."

The secretary gets up. He places his pencil on the table for a moment: "These are tragic matters," he says, "and surely it isn't necessary to speak of them here."

"On the contrary," exclaims a man in the audience. "He must give all the details. His unit may exist to this very day."

"Yes, yes, you're right," the secretary agrees. "Everyone understands that when a man makes a decision, he must take all the consequences of that decision, isn't that so?"

He looks at me expectantly.

"I've told you," I say, in agony. "I haven't anything to add. I don't want to remember those days. I don't want to know about them."

Suddenly the tear-stained woman exclaims: "So why do you want to join us? Why are you entering our organization?"

I stare at the red cloth with which the podium is covered. I can see the separate threads of the fabric and wonder how out of so many crooked and clumsy knots such a wide expanse of smooth cloth can be formed? I don't want to betray anyone. I want to be loyal to myself, but I don't want to betray anyone.

"Did you hear my question?" asks the woman.

"I don't want to betray anyone," I whisper.

"Speak up, we can't hear," someone shouts from the audience.

"I can't betray anyone, because later I'll never be able to rid myself of it; I'll wander around until I die with it." I know they can't hear me. But I want to shout, shout, before it's too late.

The secretary rises: "Allow me to answer for him. People with various backgrounds come to us. They're making a choice that is not easy to make, they're denying everything in which they grew up, to which they were attached, which was the cornerstone of their existence. They are pushed by a natural desire to grasp the very bounds of human thought, this element of life which makes for injustice, which elevates the strong and ruthless, and which degrades the weak and honest, which awakens in a man egoism aimed against his fellows, which keeps increasing the general feeling of unhappiness and hopelessness, chaos and despair . . ."

I hear the secretary's voice as though from a great distance. And to me it seems that a heavy and stifling dream is permeating me with nightmares and terror. I lean lower and lower over the red stream of cloth, stubbornly repeating to myself, "I don't want to betray. I don't want treachery."

The forest was becoming thinner. Thick sheets of sunshine were breaking through the bare tree trunks. I knew that after-dinner time was approaching.

I stopped by a shriveled raspberry bush and mechanically picked off some red, living berries. They tasted bitter, unripened. I could feel the violent beat of a pulse in my temples: "Korvin!" I shouted, yet again. But now without that earlier hope.

Birds' wings flapped somewhere in the treetops. I raised my head, looked at the fragments of ashy sky. A dry and stifling heat filtered in from above.

"Korvin," I cried in an undertone, for the last time.

No one answered. My legs hurt, so I set forward heavily to suppress the insistent ache of my bones. I no longer had any strength left. I wrenched my feet off the ground with difficulty, stumbling over the uneven forest undergrowth. I was walking as though along a wild animal's track beaten out in the faded forest grass.

Then I saw before me a shallow, though very steep, cliff with sparse juniper bushes. And this obstacle seemed insurmountable to me. I threw myself heavily to the ground, crushing a warm molehill.

Ahead of me stood a mound overgrown with heath, and down below, in the dell, ran a barely marked trail skirting the junipers. The heath was especially rich and restful for my eyes.

All at once I heard some rustling in the brushwood, as though someone had squirted water on a heated piece of tin. Sideways, without raising my head, I caught sight of a couple walking along the forgotten little pathway.

First I recognized that festive skirt, puffed out with petticoats, and the thick yellow hair. Only later did I notice the unnatural stiffness of the man's left arm. Regina and the partisan were walking along close together, their hips pressed to one another. There was some expectancy and the painful torture of closeness in their movements.

The partisan glanced furtively around. Later he stopped her. He gazed at her with feigned wonder, which freed both of any responsibility: "Shall we sit down here?" he asked.

"Isn't it damp?" she said, indifferently.

"How could it be? Look at the heath."

He went up to the juniper bushes: "Look, here will be fine. There's even some sunshine."

I wanted to go away. But I couldn't get up. I knew I couldn't startle them now, that something very bad would happen were I suddenly to sweep down the cliff to where they were, in the bottom of the ravine. I knew this from their pallid lips, staring eyes, and restless hands.

The partisan took off his jacket and threw it on the bed of heath: "Sit down," he said, with difficulty.

They sat down at a small distance from one another. They looked at the sun. They were sitting with their backs to me, but I knew their faces were tense.

The partisan swallowed: "Perhaps we might smoke?"

She nodded. He took out a pack of cigarettes. They spilled onto the heath. He took a long time gathering them up with his one hand. Finally they both lit up, unaware that the flame of a badly extinguished match was creeping over the silvery moss behind their backs, winding into the red rings of the pine needles.

The partisan stopped smoking first. He had noticed the smouldering moss and was furtively stifling it with his dead hand. They sat a while longer in anticipation.

Then he timidly placed his good hand on the back of her neck.

"Stop it," she said.

"What are you scared of?"

"Someone was shouting in the forest."

"You were hearing things. Who'd come to these lonesome places?"

"I distinctly heard someone calling."

"The forest is big."

He began stroking her neck, which was glossy with sweat. Then he turned her face towards him. Both closed their eyes. Kissing her, he turned her over on her back. Then they abandoned shame.

They kissed voraciously, writhing on his crushed jacket. She sought his head with both hands, gripping his hair. He started to unfasten her blouse, but could not manage with his one hand so finally he ripped it with all his might, and shimmering circles of buttons rolled into the undergrowth.

He extricated her large and heavy breasts from confinement. She pulled him to her. They slithered down on to the narrow path, linked in this embrace, breathless. His left hand lay motionless, as though hidden behind his back. Blades of pine needles stuck between the leather fingers.

Finally he crushed her to the ground and with uncoordinated movements began making the final preparations. She gazed at the sky with enormous, wide open eyes, her mouth open, and the tips of her white teeth showing under her lower lip. He fell upon her with his entire weight, with a sort of desperation, and all at once froze.

Then she began to kiss him hastily, blindly, drawing him to her. I could hear their violent, hoarse breathing, and something like horror caught me by the throat.

Yet again he furiously grabbed her under him, for a brief moment he struggled, and his breathing changed into grunting. Then he became motionless, hiding his head in the angle of her collar-bone. She began stroking his head soothingly, seized a handful of his hair, raised his face, and plunged her lips upon his.

Once more he threw himself desperately upon her. She wanted to receive him, she cried out briefly, staring unseeingly at the sky, but he withdrew from her with a groan and fell face-down to the ground.

They lay thus for a long time, breathing more and more quietly and slowly. Her eyes were closed but there was no calmness in her face. Finally, without raising her eyelids, she reached down to cover her naked thighs. He certainly sensed the gesture, since he met her hand halfway and began kissing it frantically. But they still dared not look at one another.

Then she sat up, hiding herself with the edge of her skirt. He was still lying with his face plunged into the moss. I felt a drop of cold sweat rolling down my back.

Slowly she rose and walked aimlessly down the little path. Her full, shameless breasts swayed lazily in her open blouse. Only after a time did she feel this nakedness, and wrapped herself in a lilac-colored batiste.

"Regina," the partisan said helplessly, without uncovering his face.

She was walking away with a heavy, tired step.

"Regina," he repeated, almost inaudibly.

She disappeared in silence among the trees.

Then he rose and sat up staring blankly at the earth. Later he shook himself, as though he wanted to shake off something horrible, and began thumping his prosthesis crazily on the ground. He hammered at the crushed leather like an animal in its death pangs.

Finally he got up, retrieved his jacket and aimlessly brushed the spruce needles off it. He walked away in the opposite direction.

Only now did I notice that one of my legs had gone numb. Filled with a strange terror, I hopped between the junipers, dragging my alien, unfeeling leg. I instinctively made for the direction where the sun should be sinking toward its setting.

I don't know how long I walked, but finally I stopped at the cliff of oaks, which descended to the river. A large, spikey pine cone jumped from under my feet and rolled down with large bounds.

The water was cold and already dark with the approaching evening. I emerged on the other bank, and suddenly became aware that our township was far to my left, and that while wandering in the forest I had lost my instinct of space.

So I went back along the edge of the alders, avoiding the smouldering peat beds and a burial mound much riddled with molehills. The song of some people praying by the river came to meet me:

Lord, our God, hear our prayers!
Thou art with me, and I with Thee.
Thou gavest me life,
Thou shalt be my end . . .

Then I stopped nearby and watched the gathering. They were kneeling in the meadow, praying with terror in the face of the unknown. Above them was suspended a sky, unnatural and breaking all the known laws of heat.

There I saw the Korsaks, and the count, and Romus. Today even the railroad man was closer to the assembly. But I could not see Regina. Perhaps she was standing hidden behind her husband, who was neither leading the prayers nor receiving them.

So ended my day.

I dragged myself home, sat down on the threshold of the veranda and listened to the pain that ached throughout my body. At times it seemed to me that this Sunday had been a dream, a dream from earlier years, a dream it was impossible to forget.

The gate creaked. Regina walked quickly in, covering her bosom with crossed arms. She passed me with her eyes fixed on the ground.

"Good evening," I said suddenly, and was startled by my own voice.

She stopped. I could see her back with a heather stain over her shoulder blade.

"Good evening," she replied.

I felt a great bitterness, but she was evidently grateful for the greeting, as she said, choking on the words: "Oh dear, it's not worth leaving the house. I went to town and was bored to death there. It would be better to stay home, to do something, to sew or even read. Oh, I'm a fool, that I am."

She stood there a moment longer, then suddenly ran into her room.

The sun had already set. Only the insulators on the telegraph pole were still leaking redness. A great flock of birds was wheeling under the sky.

At that moment I heard Regina's desperate, violent sobbing. I froze into immobility, beset by this unabashed, penetrating weeping.

Our work was simple. We drove enormous spikes, known as "castilles," into the ties, reinforcing the horizontally placed tracks on their iron foundations. We used special hammers as an all-purpose tool, something halfway between a pickaxe and a pile driver. We did not hurry too much: the siding was not large, and the first train was not supposed to arrive from the north until the end of the following month.

Count Pac folded back the collar of his shirt to halfway down, revealing a large expanse of ill-looking chest. He stood facing the sun, and it was apparent that he was greatly relishing its work. When he finally decided he had found a position proper to effective sun-tanning, he brought an old-fashioned birchwood snuffbox out of his pocket and offered us cigarettes of his own manufacture. "I don't want to be indiscreet," he said, "but why is it you chose to come here and nowhere else?"

I kept silence, lighting my cigarette carefully. The count was observing me with his tiny and very bloodshot eyes. "Pardon," he said finally, "but you see, sir, this township is small. Everyone has been living here for years, and they don't much go for newcomers. You know it's so, don't you?"

"But I don't want anything from anyone, and I don't interfere with anyone, Count."

Pac turned away violently: "Ec-ec-excuse me, sir. I am no-no-not a count."

"That's the title they give you."

"It's go-go-gossip, slander," said the count, vexed. "I'm a man of the people, with democratic beliefs."

"But, Count, I see nothing degrading in your social origins. Many aristocrats joined . . ."

"Goddam it," shouted the count, as coarsely as possible. "I s-s-screw the aristocracy. We had three acres and cultivated them laboriously. I have ev-ev-evidence, and papers to prove it. G-g-goddam it."

Here Pac blushed on realizing how many improper phrases he'd used in a moment.

"You don't have to insist on your origins," I said, in a conciliatory manner. "You should rather have adopted the attitude of a Red count. That's more picturesque. And what a beautiful tradition, too."

"You think that would have been better?" asked Pac, confused.

"Of course. One could mention many names that mean something in our contemporary life."

Count Pac blushed still more, and suddenly bared his large, bad teeth: "Unheard of!" he screamed. "Are y-y-you talking about those idiots? They're d-d-degenerates. Th-the-they qualified for the madhouse as long ago as the eighteenth century. And the r-r-rest are nouveaux-riches, upstarts who bought their titles from the Hapsburgs with money obtained from usury, s-s-sixty years ago. There's no genuine aristocracy today!"

"Well, you see, we've finally reached agreement."

Pac cooled down after his sudden outburst: "Pardon, excuse me. I've explained my background to you, and now please stop making remarks."

Someone was approaching us, walking between the tracks. Count Pac seized his hammer with alacrity and spat into his palms with all the skill of an old woodcutter.

"Take it easy," said I, "why all the hurry? It's the partisan."

And in fact the partisan Jasiu Krupa emerged from the gray air that was vibrating with the heat. Without looking at us, he got his hammer out of the ditch and went between the tracks.

"Good morning," said Count Pac, intuitively sensing that his hour had come.

The partisan kept hammering in silence.

"Good morning," cried the count again. "Obviously Sunday was a success. It'll soon be noon."

"Get away from me, otherwise . . ." the partisan muttered, not stopping his work.

"Yesterday the State liquor store made something from you," said Count Pac, and he winked at me mischievously with one little red and blue eye.

The partisan kept silent.

"Or maybe it was the little ladies, the girls from the variétés?" the count quipped.

The partisan straightened up and glared: "Get away, you noble orphan, you, or I'll lay you out with this hammer."

Pac beamed happily: "I saw you, yes I did, setting off yesterday for a little stroll with Miss Regina."

The partisan turned pale and dropped his hammer: "What's this you're gabbling about?" he asked, in a stifled voice.

"How's that? You went across the river into the Solec forest. After mushrooms, for sure, eh?" laughed Count Pac, happy that fate was giving him dominance over his inveterate tormentor. "When will the banns be put up, may we know?"

The partisan bent down, picked up his hammer and gazed at its slippery handle for a long time: "As if I'd marry such a woman as that," he said, dully. "How do I know who else she's been with before? She's a strumpet, a homeless whore. The devil brought her to us."

"He, he, you're only saying that. But you'd gladly turn her over once and again, wouldn't you?" said Count Pac, rapidly blinking his little eyes.

The partisan squeezed his hammer until his fingers turned white, and struck a powerful blow with it: "She's just the thing for you. You ought to marry her yourself," he said, simply in order to have the last word.

The count plastered a sticky curl of dirty yellow hair across his brow: "Why should I marry her?" he asked with relish. "Why burden myself with trouble? As long as my acquaintances have wives, so have I. None of them has complained yet."

He fell silent, dashed by the stare of the partisan as he stood leaning on his hammer.

"I've my own methods," he added, after a moment. "I like a woman to be satisfied."

The partisan stood motionless, crouching to leap: "You misshapen rice pudding," he said, with loathing. "Take a look at yourself in the mirror."

The count was somewhat taken aback: "I'm speaking the truth. Women don't appreciate a man's face, but something else."

The partisan grabbed his hammer by the handle and began approaching the count. Startled by the turn of events, Pac retreated helplessly, shielding himself with both hands: "What's wrong? You've humiliated me, and yet you still bear a grudge. I never pestered Miss Regina. I like her, sure, but after all I know you two are fond of each other. Mr. Krupa, excuse me, but what's wrong?"

"What's wrong is that if you start to jabber crap once more, I'll smash your head, get that?"

"But after all, I never said a bad word about Miss Regina."

"I wish a thunderbolt would strike her down. She thinks she will catch me. I never fell in love with girls like her; if it wasn't for democracy, I'd be the mayor today. I'd be taking music-hall dancers out for a good time. Don't let that whore make up to me, for I'll give her such a thrashing that the bubbles will come out of her ears." The partisan stopped and wiped dried froth from the corners of his mouth. For a moment he gazed furiously at the appalled Pac, who kept retreating. Then he went back to his position and furiously began beating spikes into the tarred ties.

"I don't understand it at all," the count whispered to me. "Did I say anything wrong? Sure, his hangover is giving him a bad time, and that's why he's furious."

Miss Malvina appeared at the top of the slope, leading a red cow on a chain: "God be with you," she said, politely. "There's such fine clover here, let the creature feed up before winter comes."

She sat down daintily amidst the aromatic furze, and the cow descended into the ditch where, at the bottom, a little patch of fresh grass had survived in the remaining moisture. A ribbon of smoke, left by an invisible jet, was growing in the sky.

"Here's midday," she sighed. "And you gentlemen will evidently finish preparing this railroad track soon. But who for? We, thank God, have no need of trains. We've somehow managed without them all our lives, and we'll manage without them in our old age, too. The first time we ever got into a train was when they brought us to this Poland. We traveled a whole week, sir, we traveled and traveled, we had our fill of sights."

"So you haven't heard what we're building it for?" asked the count.

"People say all sorts of things. They gossip until they've talked themselves out. We used to live peaceably too, but once we saw that train, we had to look for a new place in our old age."

"Nobody will ask your opinion this time."

"But where will Ildek and me go? Mister, here we have a nice little house, and a milch cow, and a garden patch. Better to die, mister, and not live to see the day."

"Water will flood the whole place. There won't even be enough dry ground to be buried in," said the partisan abruptly. "Maybe that will be for the best."

"Please don't blaspheme," Miss Malvina murmured. "Back home in the East, near Ejszyszki, long ago, some Jew wanted to set up a factory. But people wouldn't let him, for they were scared of the smoke and feared that their creatures would drop dead at the noise of the engines. So he flew around all the government offices, even to the General himself, yet nothing came of it. For the people wouldn't have it. That's how it goes in this world."

The monastery vesper bell resounded. The cow, finding a scrap of shade, sank to the earth with a groan. Miss Malvina tugged at the chain: "Oh, you creature. She's as lazy as a human being, that she is. And only yesterday, sir, someone was shouting in the forest, crying for help."

"Who could be shouting?" exclaimed the partisan. "What will people think up next?"

"Romus heard it, and so did other people. Something is in the wind here, mister, only what can it be?"

"Maybe Huniady?" I asked, without looking at them.

"Huniady?" the partisan straightened up, and I could feel his gaze on my back. "What would he have to shout for?"

"Who can tell?" said Miss Malvina. "So many years. It wouldn't be surprising if he'd gone out of his mind. They say he comes from our region."

"Do you think everyone was born near Ejszyszki, miss?"

"A man saw him and talked with him. But then he disappeared. They say he left for foreign parts."

"Do you believe in Huniady?" I asked the partisan suddenly, and looked up. I met his watchful, vigilant gaze.

He struck his prosthesis on his hip, to straighten it. "I don't understand what you mean?"

"Could he have survived in those woods until today?"

"Why not? It's the only place where he had a chance to hide. A lot of people knew him. And there was a price on his head."

Miss Malvina shivered superstitiously: "Better not talk about such people. He's a bandit, the like of which the world never saw."

The partisan shifted his steady gaze to her: "Maybe someone did him an injustice? Maybe he had no other way?"

"It's not our business," Miss Malvina sighed. "God alone will judge."

"But it's terrible to live like an animal," said Count Pac, quietly. "He's already expiated his guilt."

"Everything in the mind and the heart falls into forgetfulness," said the partisan, "but conscience lives as long as man lives."

I sat down heavily by the track. I leaned my spine against its heated edge, and breathed in the air filled with the smell of stubble and smoke.

"You're still poorly," Miss Malvina remarked. "You must take care of yourself. The sun is as strange as it is in July. Sickness may come from it. And this year began strangely too. The storks came when there was still snow, then those winds, the likes of which I never saw in all my life. But I remember when I was still a little girl that people said Judgment Day would come the end of our century. Yes, yes, though no one knows the day nor the hour. And Miss Regina didn't go to the store today. She's in bed, mister, under a quilt, and she says she caught a cold in town."

The partisan went back to work slowly. But I could sense he was attentively listening to Miss Malvina's words.

"Such is the life of a single woman. She dresses up fine, she paints her face with rouge, and everyone thinks, 'Oh, she's really enjoying life, and giving the goods to others.' But if people were to hear how she weeps at night, how she sobs in her sleep . . ."

"Miss Regina can't complain, surely; she never lets a party pass," said the partisan, dully. "She isn't doing herself any injustice."

"Mister, I don't think she really wants parties. She flits around so because she's afraid to sit alone at home. She laughs and dances, flirts perhaps sometimes, but doesn't allow any intimacy."

The partisan had turned his back to us and was gazing in the direction where the reddish tracks, running toward each other, finally joined under the ash-colored sky. A thread of gossamer got stuck in his hair and vaguely tickled his bristly cheek. Lost in thought, he drove it away like an intrusive bee.

"Take a rest, gentlemen, take a rest," some unknown voice suddenly cried. "Maybe His Excellency the Count would play to us on the piano, in the shade?"

The railroad man was standing on the slope, looking at us somberly. His black smock, something between a mechanic's apron and a poor summer coat, was crumpled and soaked with dirt. His official cap was reminiscent of a stale compress stuck on his head: "These aren't the times for you gentlemen. Your lot can only be the fate of millionaires. Lie down in the garden, eat something tasty, and watch other people working."

"There now, he knows the human soul." The partisan was amazed. "He speaks right to the point."

"I know you, Krupa. If I were to use force on you, you'd start singing a different tune."

"But there's been an end to force, hasn't there?"

"Lucky for you. If it depended on me, you'd have built not only a siding by this time, but a three-story railroad depot."

"Oh my goodness," Miss Malvina interposed hastily. "You gentlemen talk so nasty. People are nervy these days, oh how nervy they are! Everyone walks around in a bad temper, and looks at other people with the eyes of a wolf. It's all on account of that accursed war. Everyone got exhausted, and no one has any relish for life."

The count tittered nervously.

"And what are you baring your teeth for?" asked the railroad man in an ill-tempered voice. "Do you think you're better than other people because you graduated from universities?"

"God forbid, Mister railroad man. I was educated at home," said Pac, with alacrity. "Just so that I can read and write."

"Then why do you keep all those books in your apartment?"

"I don't know how they got there. Maybe someone threw them away. I had a hard childhood, sir. How could I go to universities?"

"Don't you deny it. I can tell a penpusher right away."

"Yes, that's true," sighed Miss Malvina. "More than one person has had his head turned by books. At home back East, there was one such near Ejszyszki, who read and read books all day long. And once, later, he called out to everybody that the earth moves round the sun. We laughed at him, poor man, but we didn't know he would end up in the madhouse. For when the war came . . ."

"Better watch your cow," the railroad man interrupted aloofly. "That's the fifth pancake she's dropped on the track."

"Oh goodness," Miss Malvina took fright and jumped nimbly to her creature, which was standing between the tracks with her tail uplifted.

The railroad man wanted to say something more, but he merely shrugged resignedly and went off toward his office, dragging one leg.

The partisan gazed after him and spat into his palm: "There goes an old failure of the Revolution."

The railroad man turned violently: "What's that you're saying, Krupa?"

"I said, 'Old failure of the Revolution,' " repeated the partisan, loudly but indistinctly.

The count tittered, gnawing the handle of his hammer. He was afraid to reveal his joy, so he merely jiggled his arms spasmodically and gazed with eyes popping at the railroad man, who began unthinkingly to fasten his smock: "I can't hear you, Krupa."

"Nothing important. I'll tell you some other time."

"I know you, Krupa," said the railway man, helplessly. He hesitated a moment, then set off for his hut, glancing back at us unobtrusively.

Miss Malvina tugged at the disobedient cow and very breathlessly said: "It isn't nice to talk of a person so. He's the way he is, but he's had a hard time."

The partisan went back to work. Count Pac followed suit, after tidying his sticky hair coquettishly.

"You aren't from here," Miss Korsak turned to me. "You don't know anything. But during the war he was with the Communist partisans and killed a German in these woods. When his turn came, he ruled over the entire township. And later, sir, he went up, he left for a big town. He was severe to people, very severe. Maybe because wicked people had killed his family. And he lived in the town, holding a high position, but later on he came back here. They dismissed him, supposedly because he don't have a good enough education. That's how it is."

The tracks resounded pure and clear under the hammer blows. Their rapid voice tightly filled the slumbering valley.

"That's how it is," Miss Malvina repeated. "He's a strange man, that he is. Sometimes on Saturdays he goes away and comes back on Monday. Where he goes and why, nobody knows. Some people say he visits the grave, others spread the rumor that he drinks vodka in solitude. That's how it is."

Listening to the singsong and rather sleepy ramblings of Miss Malvina, my gaze wandered around the valley, which was permeated with gray dust. Then I caught sight of a moderately spry object plunging out from the riverside undergrowth. It was Romus. His movements betrayed a state of powerful indignation. In these manipulations of his he reminded me of a swimmer struggling with a rapid river current.

Miss Malvina fell silent, fascinated by this unusual phenomenon. Her unnatural silence attracted the attention of the partisan and of Count Pac. Both straightened up; it grew quiet in the valley, and all of us watched motionlessly while Romus was struggling with time and space.

"He's yelling something," whispered Miss Malvina.

In fact we could hear a sort of distant groaning and some deranged syllables.

"Obviously he's suffering from paralysis," muttered the partisan, growing impatient.

"Mister, he's still a child," said Miss Korsak.

"The child of a hippopotamus."

Meanwhile Romus had covered a minuscule part of the way and — overestimating his achievement, he felt he was already close to us — began waving his hands like a lunatic, expressing immense indignation.

"Mister, he's shouting," exclaimed Miss Malvina in a tremulous voice.

"I bet he'll make it by evening," the partisan said.

The count threw down his hammer: "Maybe we should go and meet him."

We descended the slope in silence, toward the dense thistles sprinkled with wool fluff. Miss Malvina struggled feverishly with the cow which failed to understand the significance of the moment and put up stubborn resistance.

"Well, and what is it now, if you please, folks?" shouted the railroad man who had emerged from his office, intrigued by our silence.

"Romus, it's Romus running," explained Miss Malvina, nervously.

The railroad man, taken aback by the uncommon spectacle, asked no more.

Romus, in the heat of the day, was of his own free will executing movements which in certain of their elements resembled running.

Finally he reached the first line of thistles and scrambled through them for a long time, arousing clouds of spherical fluff. In the end he came to a stop in front of us, eyes popping, and began to puff violently, holding his sides.

"What is it, you orphan, speak up," the partisan became agitated.

"He's choking, poor thing, he can't breathe."

Romus, gasping hoarsely, doubled up, groped in the dry grass with an outstretched hand, then collapsed heavily on the ground:

"They . . . they . . ."

"What? Who?"

"They've come."

"For Heaven's sake. Who has come, my child?"

"They have. They've come."

"Speak up or I'll give you a kick in the pants," said the partisan in a trembling voice.

Romus flung himself down on his back and folded his arms: "They've come. To put up the dam. From town."

We glanced at one another, understanding everything at once. The partisan was first to leap up. On the way he grabbed his hammer and ran down toward the river with long bounds, his prosthesis pressed to his side. After him went the count, who had previously straightened the dotted kerchief around his neck, and finally Miss Malvina and I, driving the stubborn cow.

We ran in silence, marking our way by the startled tinkling of the chain which dragged in the stony road. I caught sight of the railroad man out of the corner of my eye. Romus dragged himself back through the thistles.

We stopped by the bank of the river as it gurgled monotonously between the alders. We were silent as we stared at the opposite bank, where the gilded oak thicket rose.

There we could see three small huts erected on rocks, a few planks carelessly strewn about, a concrete mixer bespattered with cement, a pile of shovels near an anthill and some tractors driving away on enormous wheels.

The railroad man ran up and stopped beside us, breathing heavily. He covered his mouth with one hand, as though trying to stifle violent uneasiness. Romus came up from the rear.

In this autumnal landscape, the assembled building implements offended by their incongruousness; they upset the order of nature and predicted the unknown. A flock of crows was circling under the clear sky, upset by the arrival of strangers. The thundering of the tractors gradually melted away into the gray dust of the turn of the valley that was closed in by a curly-headed belt of blue forest.

Only now did we perceive men moving around the building site. There were not many. They looked perfectly ordinary. And yet even I, not a local, shared the tension of those gathered on the river bank.

The partisan suddenly shouted "Hey there!" and held up his hammer in his clenched fist. They could not hear. The murmuring of the Sola cut us off.

"Hey there, you oafs!" the partisan called out again.

Someone on the other side stopped and looked toward us. We could see the red outline of his face, but not his features.

"You motherfuckers, d'you hear?" the partisan shouted.

And he threatened them with the hammer.

The man who had stopped gazed at him a moment. Then he went back to work.

So we stood silently, and the whisper of the Sola changed slowly into a murmuring like that of the wind, then into an increasing roar lined with thundering. We listened to this with strange dread, and were afraid to look at one another.

Suddenly Miss Malvina sank to her knees. She raised her face up to the ashy heat and began to pray desperately in a droning, mournful voice: "O God, O God, take us poor people under Your protection, look upon our abjectness. Count our days, which were born with tears and are passing away in pain. Measure our sufferings, weigh the burden we carry. O God, O God, straighten our path and give us a light death when the end comes."

Not until now did I understand the cause of that rumbling noise that rolled toward us from across the stream. The workers had started up machinery hidden behind one of the sheds.

Someone behind me coughed uncertainly. I turned slowly. Sergeant Glowko was straightening his copious accoutrements.

"Look there," the partisan said to him, "they'll drive us out along with the rabbits."

"This ain't my district," replied Sergeant Glowko without conviction. "Maybe they'll go away before winter. Many people have started to build here. In the thirties they wanted to breed horses, later Hitler put up a bunker for himself in the forest, and in the olden days insurrectionists built an ammunition factory, but it caught fire from gunpowder. The earth remains, and the people remain."

"But don't you know, you fool, that they're going to flood all this, that there'll be a lake here?"

"Don't call me a fool, don't, excuse me."

Miss Malvina was still kneeling, moving her chapped lips soundlessly. Finally she sighed and said, "The Lord God will punish them. Terrible divine punishment will come upon those people for their pride, for improving God's handiwork."

She sighed again, and rose. Without looking back, she set off toward the meadows, the cow after her, like a prisoner at hard labor with a clanking chain.

I glanced in that direction, and only now did I catch sight of Joseph Car standing in front of his house with a group of motionless people. Behind him smouldered the redness of the sorb, which was continually in my thoughts.

Toward evening, lying on the old bed which was witness of many confinements and deaths, I surveyed the furniture in my room. I had the sensation that the gloom was shadowy water, and that I was resting at the bottom of a huge lake. The first chill of evening had already entered the house, and the floor boards were creaking under its weight. Behind the wall, which was thin as a partition, proceeded the stifled and sleepy discourse of the Korsaks.

My gaze lighted on the chest of drawers, industriously devoured by woodworms, on which the old radio stood. It always smelled of bog plants and I had never looked into it.

Drawn by idle curiosity, I rose from the bed and went to the aged piece of furniture grinning with bare locks, whose durability had been tested by looters of various armies and eras. I pulled out the top drawer; it was empty, its bottom bestrewn with fragments of herbs. In the second I found some gingerbread, dried to the consistency of cement, with someone's greedy tooth marks on it.

Not until I reached the bottom drawer did I discover a large bundle of old papers. I glanced through the yellowed records of someone's fate in the last war. Here were passes issued by long-forgotten institutions of the Occupation: *Arbeitsamt* documents, doctors' certificates spattered with Latin diagnoses, in which a word ominous as a winter flower was often repeated — tuberculosis. A youthful face looked out at me from an identity card, expressionless, neutral, likeable only for its youth. I read his name, which was certainly false, inspected the rubber stamp, doubtless forged, and tried to recreate in my mind the life story of this man, who had left behind him, like a handful of ash, this faked trace of his existence.

"In the dark like this, mister?" I heard Miss Malvina's voice behind me.

Embarrassed, I slammed the drawer.

"Go ahead, please don't mind me. Those aren't our papers."

"Whose are they?"

"Nobody's. They were left behind by some unknown man. Ildek knocked a plank out of the wall of the house, and found those papers underneath. Someone had hidden them, no one knows when. He never came back for them. Maybe he died, or went away to far-off places."

"Once I too, far from here, hid everything that concerned my childhood and youth."

"That's how it happens. Happy is the man who dies in the house where he was born."

"I was looking through them and wondering what happened to mine. Have they rotted in the earth? Or did someone dig them up?"

"What's there to wonder at — the older a person, the oftener he goes back to his youth. They, mister, want to find warmth as they used to under their father's sheepskin jacket. Please don't sit there by yourself in the dark. Please come with us to prayer. We must pray, pray as much as we can. As you live longer, you'll understand me. Everything passes — fame and glory and talent and riches and joy and pride. But fear remains, the fear old people have, as you too will understand, mister, some day."

"When I begin praying, it will mean I've surrendered. And I don't want to give up yet."

"What's that you say? I don't understand aright."

"Nothing that matters, Miss Malvina. I want to be by myself."

The little old lady sighed: "Maybe someone is praying for you, though you don't even know it. Well, time to go. The people are gathering already."

"So you didn't know that man?" I pointed to the chest.

"But we, mister, are from a different part, from the East. Maybe one day he'll come back. Maybe human hatred, or his own shame and conscience have cut him off from this place. He'll come back, mister, years later, if his life hasn't already ended. Good night to you."

"Good night."

She went out. I heard her and her brother go to the gate, which slammed dully, like a tree falling in the forest. Then the secret echoes of the deserted house beset me. A sort of painful terror slowly mounted. Involuntarily I checked the door, full of somnolent darkness, and the window, which let in a few glimmerings of stars. Once again I pulled out that drawer, trying to catch in myself that undefined sorrow for that which was irrevocably gone.

Someone scratched at the door. I shivered and felt a sudden, violent warmth.

She was standing on the veranda. I could not see her face very well.

"Am I interrupting?"

"Not in the least. Why should you?"

"I was passing, and it seemed to me that a light was on in your room."

"Just so, I'll switch it on right away."

I began feverishly searching the rough wall for the switch. Finally I groped to it, and a small light bulb with dead flies stuck to it glowed under the ceiling.

We both blinked.

"Good evening," I said, cheerfully.

She smiled: "Good evening."

"Please come inside. There's nothing to sit on here."

"How so? The bed? Fine."

She sat down and began swinging her leg. That monotonous, provocative rhythm again: "I was in Podjelniaki. I play with the children in the orphanage there. I have to. Maybe you aren't aware that I'm an orphan too, and was brought up in an orphanage too. Right after the war we even went begging a little. I could sing reasonably well, and was a boneless child. Even today I can still do the split. Don't you believe me?"

"Why shouldn't I? Do you remember your parents?"

"No. I don't even know whether my name is really mine. They found me during some battle or other. Someone was fighting someone else. Maybe partisans and Germans. I myself don't know."

She swayed her head in her peculiar fashion, and it was hard to tell whether she was telling the truth or lying. I squatted at the foot of the bed. The room seemed hideously bare in this feeble light. We were sitting there as if on an empty stage.

"Maybe you're a witch's child, left as a foundling for humans?"

Without interrupting the rhythmical swaying of her head, she said: "Maybe."

And she gazed at me steadily: "I will bewitch you."

"I think that's already happened."

She didn't smile; some belated fly buzzed out of the twilight to begin circling the lamp mournfully.

"Badly said, surely?" I said.

"Well said."

"And what will come of it?"

She reached into her handbag and drew out an apple, looking as though covered with red wax: "Would you like it?"

"Thank you."

"I talked to my husband about you."

"Is that good or bad?"

She shrugged.

"Have you been with him long?"

She bit into the apple and gazed at me with a scrap on her lips.

"I would like to know something about him. He reminds me very much of someone."

"It must be six years. Yes, six years."

"And before that?"

"Before that, I didn't know him."

"Do you know where he comes from?"

"I never asked. He used to be a teacher."

The fly on the ceiling fell silent. We both looked in the same direction.

"At one time people disliked him very much. Perhaps that's why I fell in love with him."

"Has he changed now?"

"Yes. He has lived through a great deal."

"Wasn't he wounded once?"

She glanced at me inquiringly.

"Excuse me. It's not important," I said.

Again she began swinging her legs.

"Assuredly you're an enchantress. Well said?"

"Very well," she smiled knowingly, approving that I had adopted her style. "I bring unhappiness to everyone."

"Including yourself?"

"Myself too," she said rapidly and glanced sideways at the floor, which was riddled with huge cracks.

"Don't you go to the prayer meeting?"

"Are you making fun of them?"

"Not in the least, miss. I don't feel I have the right to."

"I've brought you something."

"I'm very curious."

Out of her handbag she took a yellow chrysanthemum, dipped in dense redness. The flower had already faded. I accepted it in such a way that her fingers had to touch my palm. She snatched her hand away violently: "You have hot hands."

I stretched my hand out: "Yes. That's my peculiarity. Please check."

She hesitated a moment. Finally she cautiously and uncertainly took my hand, then at once let it go.

"Well said?"

"Very well," she said, without looking at me. "I have to go now."

"I'll go with you."

"No, no, that isn't necessary," she said vehemently, then added, "No, thank you. What for? It's peaceful here."

When we went out to the veranda, I barred her way. She pushed me in the chest with enormous force, so that I barely managed to brush her hair with my face, and I staggered against the door frame. All the window panes tinkled with a tiny shiver.

She ran past me quickly and I heard the gate rattle. I went out in front of the house. Some apples she had scattered were still rolling down the path. I picked one up, already covered with the moisture of dew.

"Well, well," I said, surprised at myself.

I opened the gate and looked for Justine. But it was dark. The uneven, frantic song of the people praying arose from the river bank.

"I will kill you," I suddenly heard Romus's breaking voice. He was holding the fence, and he spluttered thickly with his dry lips, expressing great indignation: "Why have you latched on to her?"

"Go to bed, Romus."

"Why have you come here? It all started because of you."

I went into the garden, shivering spasmodically. The night was coming on, cold, underlaid with light frost.

"I will kill you. You'll see."

I threw an apple in the direction of his whining. He sensed the flight of the apple in the already heavy dusk and jumped aside at the last moment. "I saw everything. I know everything."

I went into my room and sat down on the bed, looking at the window which I expected to be shattered by a rock. But all was quiet. A damp coldness was creeping into the room, enveloping my legs with a troublesome, itchy feeling.

I lay down, even though I knew it would be difficult to fall asleep. I summoned up into my memory calm and motionless landscapes brought out of those rare moments that were without fear, until finally faces and fragments of events from the past began to beset me in my shallow sleep. Suddenly, with a hysterical shudder, I awoke, filled with the rapid beating of my heart.

Someone was shouting somewhere, and I had the sensation that it was the war, that a wounded man was shouting.

"Regina, I want to tell you something! Let me in for just a minute, Regina!"

The woman's voice answered him, indistinct and stifled by the wall: "You've no shame, you goat. Get away from my window. You damned pervert."

"Regina, be quiet, for God's sake, people will hear you. I was upset, because I love you, you bitch. It was all on account of loving you. Let me in, you'll see."

"How dare you! How dare you come near women?"

"Regina, Regina," whined the partisan, listening for the door to creak. But Regina no longer answered. He stood there at her window, helplessly rubbing the moisture off his worn, leather arm.

I lay still, tensely waiting for him to go away. But he did not go, and I could hear him sigh from time to time. I couldn't fall asleep. When I finally pressed my eyelids tightly with relief, thinking he had gone off into the night with his despair, his hoarse breathing would suddenly resound and it all started over again.

Two enormous excavating machines stood not far from the sheds. Their long necks were stretched upward, and it seemed as though their toothy jaws were reaching for the yellow leaves of the oak thicket. A pile of cement sacks rose alongside.

Two workmen with rolled-up trouser legs were sitting on the river bank, beside fishing rods stuck in the ground. They stared motionless at their floats which cut out slender furrows in the water's shining mirror. In front of one of the sheds, concealed in the deep, early evening shade, someone was playing a clarinet.

One of the fishermen pulled up his line and extricated the hook from the water. It was bare, and drops of water fell from it, glimmering with the light. Fastening another piece of bait to it, he suddenly shouted across the river: "Hey, fellow, do you have a store here?"

I said nothing.

"Where can we buy vodka, d'you know?"

His companion, without looking at me, said with deliberation, "Leave him alone, can't you see he's a half-wit?"

But the first fisherman pursued his friendly intent: "Little father, how come you've been struck dumb? Ears overgrown with spiderwebs?"

"He's some thick-witted rustic," the other added loudly. "Sure, and the lice have ate up his brains."

"Father!" shouted the first. "Come over here, we'll show you something."

"Come on, come on, don't be scared."

Then, all at once, drawn on by some childish impulse, I made a provocative and indecent gesture, well-known to all street urchins.

The workmen jumped up as briskly as though going to collect their pay. They started feverishly looking for stones in the riverside undergrowth.

"Damn his eyes! Did you see how familiar he is with Boy Scouts' signs?"

"I tell you this isn't the last time they'll show us such signs. I know these country folk."

Stones whizzed over my head, one after another. I began running back across the dried-up meadow, accompanied by their curses.

"Look, look, he's quick on his feet! May your guts burst, daddy!"

"Just you wait, we'll come over and get you. I'll kick you in the ass, you old show-off."

"He's not all that old. Just look how spry he is on his pins!"

"Good thing nobody saw. To have to take that from such a fart . . ."

They went on complaining of their humiliation for a long time, until their voices slowly died away in the riverside twilight. I stopped at the foot of a slope and rested for a while after my burst of running. In front of me, above, was the familiar house and the red, club-shaped sorb tree.

I walked up slowly, gazing at the windows, which were filled with the reflection of the sky. But the house stood quiet, as if disemboweled. A colored blouse was hanging up to dry on the line, stirred by invisible gusts of warm air.

"Good evening."

I stopped abruptly and started looking for a cigarette.

Joseph Car was standing among the bushes of blackened jasmine, and it seemed to me he was waiting for somebody.

"Good evening," I said, slowly, as if wanting to gain time.

"Did you get a look at them?"

"Yes."

"They've been carting up their machinery and equipment since dawn."

"Do you think it's true about our township?"

Only now did I notice the copious drops of sweat on his forehead and the encrusted foam in the corners of his mouth.

"I've seen the plans. They're not informing the inhabitants so as to avoid panic."

I don't know why I thought he hadn't recognized me and was regarding me as a chance passer-by.

"Why don't you come and visit us? My wife likes you very much," he said, unexpectedly.

I was embarrassed and that surely must have been apparent, but Joseph Car was staring through me at the smouldering peat bog and the flat burial mound riddled with molehills.

"I've been ill. I was feeling bad."

He was staring fixedly but probably couldn't see me: "Yes, my wife's an unusual person. Have you fallen in love with her already?"

I almost choked from the smoke. I stared into his eyes with determination but perceived nothing. "Forgive me, I really don't understand," I gabbled, violently knocking the ashes off my cigarette.

"Everyone is in love with her. That's the sort of person she is. Surely you were an orphan, like my wife. You both have something in common: a naïve trust and the shrewdness of homeless people."

"I don't know. All in all, I don't know what to say."

I could have sworn I was talking to a blind man. He sought for a leaf at random and tore one off a bush: "It's a shame about this valley. It remembers many things."

"I'd like to have a talk with you some time," I said.

Now he saw me. The crumpled leaf dropped from his hand: "Please leave this place. As fast as you can."

The rapid voice of the monastery bell resounded from the township and continued toward the river, which was already covered by the oak thicket's intense shade.

"Before you get too attached. Before you find your place."

"But why?"

"Go away. You won't find what you're looking for here. The water will flood everything, the town will be covered for ever and only the legend of a town at the bottom of the lake will remain."

"But how do you know what I'm looking for?"

He smiled with his lips but nothing else. Only now did I notice that what I'd taken as a high trimming of hair was grayness. I held my breath and waited for his reply.

"How do I know? Everyone is searching. But most often for that which is already far behind us."

The bell stopped tolling. Its echo moved deeper into the forest and finally disappeared.

"Please leave. You simply must go."

"I haven't any place to go back to."

"This isn't the place you're looking for. There will be no peace here."

I trod on my cigarette stub: "Can you read the future?"

"Does it surprise you? I know how to read many things."

I saw a kind of incomprehensible tension on his face. Again he was gazing through me at the valley as it became filled with dusk.

"I must talk to you. About things very important to me. Enormously important."

"I want that too," he said, quietly. "Please come some day when it seems essential to you."

The clarinet was playing in back of me. It reminded me of something I couldn't define. But I was certain I had heard its nasal voice in a similar landscape and under similar circumstances.

"But please consider whether it's really worthwhile," exclaimed Joseph Car. "Whether it has meaning."

"I'll come. I'll most certainly come."

And I went away without saying goodbye. I don't know whether he stayed to watch me or whether he went into his house. Again the dense flock of birds was patiently circling over the valley.

And here was the deserted little manor house, hidden in an orchard which was turning wild. I stopped not thinking by the fence without railings. I gazed at the trees frozen in stillness, and among them suddenly caught sight of a cherry tree covered with white flowers. It stood as though snow-covered among the apple trees that were dying before winter.

On the way back toward the railroad lines I kept looking

round, and sought out this white little tree imprisoned among the black, forked trunks.

In the next room the buzzing of voices was compounded with terrible scrapings of chairs. I guessed the Korsaks were celebrating some occasion or other. I could tell by the pieces of unwanted furniture shoved in disorder into my room. Mr. Ildefons's blackened exercise books lay on the broken radio, also his flaked penholder and the large inkpot shimmering violet with encrusted ink. I had an enormous urge to pick up these notebooks filled with someone else's intimate thoughts, but a kind of embarrassment or shame at myself prevented me from taking the step.

So I sat on the bed and stared at the window, which was filled with the aluminum sky.

"I'll settle what I have to settle, then I'll go back to where I came from," I said to myself.

In abrupt moments of silence in the next room the distant voice of the clarinet disentangled itself from the twilight, bearing fragments of old tunes remembered from goodness knows where.

Suddenly the door creaked. Miss Malvina, in an aureole of red light, was looking toward me: "In the dark like this?"

"I'm resting."

"But please be so kind as to join us. We're sitting and having a bite to eat, and there's fruit liqueur with herbs."

"My head aches."

"A drink is good for worry," the nasal voice of the railroad man exclaimed, behind her. "I used to know all sorts of sayings at one time, but now I've forgotten 'em."

"Pray step in and don't scorn us."

"Come on, come on," shouted the partisan. "It's at night that the worst absurdities come into a person's head."

"Mr. Jasiu is so tactless," said Miss Malvina with distaste. "What was, is past. Why recall it in vain? Please, please, we're waiting."

I went into their kitchen and blinked at the light of the naked bulb.

They were all sitting at the table, which was already stained with vodka and sauce from the pickles: Mr. Ildefons, the railroad man, the partisan, Count Pac and Sergeant Glowko. Their cheeks were flushed and they leaned their elbows heavily on the table top.

> On a kolkhoz the life is just great,
> One does the reaping while eight others sleep.

But when the sun scorches
He too runs away . . .

Mr. Ildefons suddenly burst into song.

"Be quiet, you scatterbrain," cried Miss Malvina. "When he's wound up he always sings the same thing. Don't you know any other songs?"

"I never heard that song before. What language is it in?" asked the railroad man gloomily, and as his elbow had slipped off the corner of the table, he kept his seat only with the utmost effort.

"Well, let's drink to success," Miss Korsak eagerly raised a glass of greenish liquid. "He's a poor man, sir, he's feeble. The doctors took his insides out."

"But can I know what he was singing?" the railroad man insisted.

"One glass is enough for him. Then he gets all muddled, poor man."

"But I could hear it was about kolkhozes."

"Sir, he served in the Red cavalry under Budionny, and only now in his old age he sometimes gets confused."

The railroad man pondered, touching his lips with his glass. Then he lurched, grabbing for his balance lost for some unknown reason, and said: "Well, here's to us."

"If you please, here's a roast rabbit."

"Where did you get it?" asked the railroad man suspiciously.

"Mr. Jasiu brought it, and I roasted it."

The railroad man looked attentively at the partisan, who was gathering crumbs from the table with his prosthesis and slowly tipping them into his mouth.

"You have a gun, Krupa."

"Good God, who said I did? I handed it in when I had to. And the rabbit? It was running down by the river, slipped up, hit its head on a mushroom, and the damage was done."

The railroad man pondered laboriously a long time, then said: "I know you, Krupa."

Bare feet pattered in the hallway. We all looked in that direction. Two little boys were standing on the threshold, both begrimed about the hair, with a little girl, in something that was neither a long dress nor a night shirt: "Daddy, come home! Mama says so!" shouted the oldest.

Sergeant Glowko was suffused with a sudden blush: "Coming, coming. Tell your mother I'm coming."

The children ran out into the yard and, to vary the monotony, slammed the gate with all their might.

"How come you're so timid?" asked the partisan. "Aren't you allowed to sit with your friends for a while?"

"All very well for you," said the sergeant, embarrassed. "My old woman gets mad at times, oh so mad, pardon the expression, and she hits me too."

"Got to be brief with women," the partisan banged his leather fist on the table.

Sergeant Glowko blinked and, to avoid the touchy subject, asked earnestly: "And where's Miss Regina? She wasn't in the store again today."

Miss Korsak clapped an open palm to her forehead: "Right. Where is she, poor girl? Sitting by herself, for sure. Please go get her, someone."

"I'll go, I'll go," Count Pac offered, and he moved briskly toward the door. The partisan watched him with a hostile look.

Glowko bit into a pickle, and shook his head: "Ugh, he's interested in women, that one is."

"He's young, sir, and fickle."

"Who says he's young?" asked the partisan somberly. "He only pretends to flirt, to avoid suspicion."

"No, no," the sergeant protested. "Last year, when that schoolgirls' camp came this way, he followed them ten miles. And his eyes, pardon the expression, were like the eyes of that rabbit. He has his own strength, you can't say he don't."

The railroad man swayed on his stool: "Well, here's to us."

At this moment Count Pac forcibly dragged Regina into the room, bad-tempered, sleepy. She gathered her unfastened blouse together over her breasts.

"Please, please come in!" cried Mr. Ildefons, and he blinked fearfully.

"And what makes you so bold, for God's sake?" Miss Korsak groaned. She stared at her brother for a long time with an appalled expression.

"They don't let a person sleep. Good God, how much vodka they've drunk."

"Please take a seat, here," Mr. Ildefons ventured yet again.

Regina sat down between him and the count. She did not look toward the partisan, who was afraid to raise his head from the table top.

"What was I going to say? A bit of roast rabbit? You men, pour the vodka."

"Vodka at night? I'll never get to sleep afterwards."

"Miss Regina, Miss Regina, you're so sleepy, so nice and warm, may I kiss your hand?" The count made eyes at her.

"Well, here's to us," said the railroad man, somberly.

We all drank up. Regina choked as custom requires of respectable females. The count threw himself upon her, to kiss the elbows of his fair neighbor: "What beautiful hands, the hands of a pianist."

Suddenly the partisan banged the table top with his prosthesis. For a moment there was silence, while he stared dully at a plate of snacks.

"Daddy, come home, else mama says she won't let you in," cried the children from the threshold.

Sergeant Glowko groaned helplessly and began looking round for his gear, which had disappeared somewhere during the banquet.

"Sit down," said Count Pac. "Are you afraid of your wife?"

"All very well for you to talk," he complained in a damp voice. "And here I sit, on this here stool, as though it was hot coals . . ."

All the same, he settled himself more comfortably, for the children disappeared as rapidly as they had come. He sighed heavily, and reached for his newly filled glass.

"Now, let's drink so all of us can stay here," said Miss Malvina, ceremoniously.

It grew quiet. The railroad man raised his reddened eyes to her: "Stay where?"

"Here, on our land," said Miss Malvina, uncertainly. "So they don't drive a person out into the world in his old age."

The railroad man turned his glass in his hands, moving his lips soundlessly: "A person can live any place."

Miss Korsak sat down by him eagerly: "You're in a high position and everyone in the Party knows you. You only have to say a word in the right place."

"But don't you know it's a question of more far-reaching matters?"

"Yes, we know, mister, though we're only simple people. But they could set up their dam, mister, beyond the Solec forest, where there's nothing but empty fields; no people live there."

"We can't teach them anything. They have better heads there than ours."

"But what if we don't let ourselves be resettled?" asked the partisan, provocatively.

"I know you, Krupa."

"I know you, too. This is your last stop. You've tried your luck everywhere, and yet you came back to us."

"I went where I was told to go."

"We, mister, aren't against anyone. This government too is all right for us. No matter where we go in our old age, as things are, we've left our own land behind once before."

"If we all act together, they certainly won't evict us," added Count Pac.

The partisan stretched out his leather hand toward the railroad man: "You know very well this is our promised land. And there's nothing in the world to go looking for."

The railroad man pushed the table violently: "So all of you are buying me up with this drinking, like some pre-war mayor?" he said, rising from his stool with difficulty.

"Oh goodness, who would dare?" cried Miss Malvina. "We're doing it out of the goodness of our hearts, so the State don't lose, and we too don't come to any harm."

"Don't come to me with such talk. I've been kicked around enough in my life. But I won't let you do it. You want to make a pig out of me for the sake of a glass of raw liquor?"

"Have you already forgotten what it used to be like, in the old days?" asked the partisan, quietly.

The railroad man slowly turned to him: "And who's supposed to remember? I remember, I remember everything, and will remember forever. But you won't work me over. I'll go to my grave the man I am."

The count giggled nervously, squeezing Regina's elbow.

"Yes, I've eaten and drunk at your expense," said the railroad man, irrelevantly. "When I close my eyes, the lot of you can fly up and drag what is yours from under my carcass."

"Do you bear a grudge against us?" asked the partisan, and he too stood up from the table. "Have I done you any wrong?"

The railroad man raised his fist and wanted to say something but merely opened his palm, stared helplessly at his tobacco-stained fingers, and made a gesture of resignation with one hand, as though he wanted to dispel thick layers of livid smoke: "Where's my cap?"

The partisan sat down on the bench again: "Under the table."

The railroad man made yet another gesture and, without reaching for his cap, set out toward the door. There he collided with the children as they rushed breathlessly into the room: "Daddy, come on, mama is waiting in front of the house."

"Coming, coming," muttered Glowko. But when the children had left, he added bitterly, "It's all right for you."

Count Pac tittered, and half embraced Regina.

"It's turned nasty, somehow," said Miss Malvina, mortified.

We were silent. Suddenly Korsak swayed and banged his head on the table.

"Sssh. Let him lie. He'll rest, poor man," his sister said, hastily.

I suddenly noticed that the partisan was watching with somber attention the carryings-on of the count, who was just pouring herb liquor into Regina's glass: "Well, Miss Regina, your health."

The partisan banged his empty glass on the worn table top. We all looked his way, except the count, who was giving Regina to drink from her glass like an infant, with the utmost care: "See, it's good."

He moved his long face, with its sparse yellow hair, closer to hers and whispered in her ear. She laughed drily, turning away from her suitor.

Again the partisan banged his glass and glared stubbornly into the opposite corner.

"What was I going to say?" said Miss Malvina. "Oh, yes, he's a stern man, very stern, but after all he was born here, he got married here, he buried his family here."

Sergeant Glowko sighed and looked painfully at the door: "It's all the same to me. Only there must be order."

Count Pac tittered for the third time.

"And why do you snigger like that, idiot?" asked Miss Malvina crossly, as she stood up to clear the table.

Undeterred, Count Pac again whispered into Regina's ear. She was listening to him with that typical gesture of tense attention and caution. The partisan banged his glass on the table. Suddenly Ildefons Korsak sobbed in his sleep.

Miss Malvina stroked his shaggy, sea-green hair: "Hush, poor man, he's dreamed something terrible."

The count pulled Regina and her stool closer to him. He hastily licked his dry lips with the tip of his tongue, trying to control his wandering hands: "The vodka's bitter, isn't it, Miss Regina?"

"I can take it, I'm not complaining."

"I was thinking of something else."

"Your thoughts don't interest me."

"A stone, a cold rock, not a woman," said the count, peering into her décolletage.

"Don't be a bore, all right?"

"Pardon, I have serious intentions toward you."

"You're tipsy."

"To give myself courage, miss. You smell of herbs, it's your hair, isn't it?"

The partisan's stool scraped as he turned toward the window, where our dim reflections were present in the panes.

Again Count Pac began whispering hastily, seeking out Regina's hand under the table with his sweaty one. There was a rumbling in Sergeant Glowko's stomach. He shook his head mournfully.

"You're beautiful, miss, you act on me not only spiritually but physically too," breathed the count, in a conspiratorial manner. "Physical association is of primary importance. You really suit me, upon my word you do."

"Count," the partisan exclaimed suddenly in a hollow voice.

The count lowered his whispering and drew even closer to Regina.

"Count," said the partisan, louder.

"Count yourself," Pac turned on him furiously.

The partisan stood up slowly and approached Pac, poking his prosthesis under the latter's nose: "Sniff this."

"Sniff it yourself."

"It smells of the herbs which will cure you right away."

"Miss Regina can choose anyone she likes."

"What did you say?"

"What you heard."

The partisan tried to hurl the count to the floor with a skilful grasp, but Pac held fast to Regina's arm and stayed on his stool. The partisan staggered with a little fragment of the count's shirt collar in his hand. The glasses flew about, bounding on the floor.

"For Heaven's sake, help! Mr. Glowko!" shrieked Miss Korsak.

The partisan had grabbed the count's shirt and was trying to tear him from Regina: "Let go of her, d'you hear, or I'll belt you!"

Suddenly Regina freed herself with one twist from Pac's sweaty hands: "Be off, you pigs!" she screamed hysterically. "You're boors, you need whores! What do you animals know of love? Oh God, cursed be the day I came here."

And all at once she rushed blindly for the door, overturning stools along the way. She hit the frame with all the force of her shoulders and hips, so that the electric bulb under the ceiling began swaying rapidly. Then she rushed into the hallway, reeled there for a moment like a moth, and finally found the exit.

Later we heard the furious slam of her door. Ildefons Korsak mumbled something with his lips plunged into a puddle on the table and raised his head, blinking: "Eh? I didn't catch. Did anything happen?"

The partisan put the count's ripped-off collar on an empty plate, then wiped his prosthesis on his pants. Pac was still gazing, wide-mouthed, at the open door.

"Back home in the East, unthinkable," said Miss Malvina, musingly. "There's present-day intellectuals for you."

I rose and went cautiously to the door. A sudden chill had seized me, and I went out in front of the house with its burden on my back. The sky was again filled with stars. The red end of a cigarette was glowing not far from the gate.

I went out into the street.

"Good evening," said someone's voice.

"Good evening."

"Having a good time, I see."

"Szafir?"

"Yes, it's me."

"Why don't you come in?"

"Nobody asked me."

Somewhere far away a dog was howling. The little glow let up for a moment, cutting out the drawn features of Szafir's face from the darkness.

"You're a strange man," he said. "You see nothing but your own hump. It's quite impossible to make contact with you. Don't you see that everyone is living differently, that they've forgotten what they used to have?"

"Am I so exceptional?"

"Well, sure. Look around, everyone worries, or is happy, or they work, or rest, ordinarily, without eccentricity."

"I'm not better yet."

"I know what sort of sickness that is. I too fell sick in my time. I was a secretary in a big factory. A strike broke out. You know, a strike against the People's authority. I went out to the workmen. The fact that they wouldn't listen is nothing. I knew them all, but now I couldn't recognize them. They threw stones and spat at me. I knew they were in the right, but I was in the right too. Then they pulled me off the platform, without ceremony, and put me into a wheelbarrow. But they didn't wheel me out. The older workmen wouldn't let them. Maybe because I'd gone out to meet them. I hadn't hidden along with the rest of the management. I got sick then."

"My sickness is different."

"So be it. But a man can't live that way. Do you think anybody here understands you?"

"Surely everyone has been sick with something or other."

"People are normal, you can believe me. It's you who have something out of order."

"I don't know. No doubt you're right."

"But I need you."

"What for?"

"Something bad is going on here. I can smell it."

"And I'm supposed to help?"

"What else?"

"But I'm not normal."

"Pah, that's only a manner of speaking. Wait, where are you going?"

"My head aches."

"Wait a minute."

He wanted to come after me, but it was dark, and he lost me in the gloom. I tripped over a rail: it was terribly cold. Until then I had only known the hot smell of heated iron.

I knew I was going to that dark house. I wanted to be there for a while. I sank into mole hills with warm interiors. Then I saw the outline of the deserted homestead and the crossed poles of the wrecked fence. I scrambled across and went in among the trees. The tall grass was wet, foreboding a hot day. It seemed to me I could hear a cricket chirping.

And all of a sudden, for no reason, my heart began to thump. Pushing aside overhanging branches laden with moisture, I penetrated ever more rapidly into the depths of the wild garden. Then I stopped on the stone slabs in front of the house and began attentively to gaze into the darkness.

"I'm completely frozen. Where have you been loitering so long?"

"How do you know I've been loitering, miss?"

"I already told you I'm an enchantress."

She came out of the darkness and gave me her hand. I retained hold of her cool fingers.

"Your hand is hot."

"I've already told you that's my peculiarity."

We set off down the overgrown path. The white cherry tree came to meet us, like a ghost.

"Please talk. Why are you silent?"

"I'm just wondering what to say."

"Look, a flowering tree."

"I picked it out in the daytime. We'll meet here, all right?"

"Aren't you afraid of the commonplace?"

"Yes. But one sees the commonplace only afterwards."

"I don't know anything about you, but I'm very curious."

"And is that the enchantress speaking?"

"Oh, what sort of enchantress am I? I'm unlucky. Today I broke a vase, a souvenir. Hopeless, well said?"

"Well said."

"Oh, here's the fence. Now maybe we can stand still a while."

I didn't know whether she was serious or joking. She was drawing something with the tip of one toe on the grass of the little alley.

"This new hat didn't help me at all," she exclaimed.

But I kept silent in sudden rage. This auto-ironical tone of hers angered and confused me.

"Well, it's getting cold," she said, a trifle too loudly, as was her habit.

"If you don't object, I'll put my arms around you."

"I don't object."

I put my arms around her. I could feel the girlish frailty of her shoulders under my hands. She did not yield to my gesture and we stood rather awkwardly.

I gazed into her face and caught the faint glimmering of her eyes: "Warmer."

"Well, of course," she said, again too loudly, canceling out in this way whatever intimacy I had created.

"You little fool," I whispered.

"Did you say something?"

"No, nothing important."

Then suddenly a drop of dew fell on to her cheek from a branch. I hesitated. And then, awkwardly, I raised a trembling hand and started to wipe the moisture off her face. She gazed into my eyes, but in that gloom I could not see what she was thinking.

With abrupt determination I leaned down and kissed her cool lips. Then I drew her to me and kissed her longer, wanting to bring her mouth alive with my own lips. This lasted a long time, before she began to respond, before she revealed her little teeth, which tasted of apples.

I rocked her in my arms and felt her pulse on me. Then we drew breath violently, as though after a long dive.

"Oh dear, my head is swimming," she said, unnaturally loudly.

"Let's walk. We mustn't stand still. It's cold."

We drew near to the house, which was transparent with holes in the roof.

"Shall we go in? It'll be warmer inside."

She didn't answer. So I broke a rotten plank and crept in: "Please come," I put out my hand.

"But maybe there are rats?"

"It's an empty house. Nobody has lived here for fifteen years," I said, leading her through the large hallway.

We entered a big room. The sky could be seen through cracks between the planks that boarded up the window. I felt something soft underfoot.

"There's straw here. Shall we sit down?"

Again she didn't answer. I drew her to me. We were now sitting on old straw smelling of cellars.

"It's romantic here, isn't it? Well said?" she asked loudly.

"You little fool," I whispered.

And I put my arms around her again. We kissed for a long time, and I rocked her in my embrace more and more, until at last we were touching the straw with our sides, and we stayed like this, half lying, half sitting.

But when I touched her breasts, when I held their warm roundness, suddenly in my memory I saw the forest, the steep slope, the path covered with pine-cones, and the face of the partisan, desperate, drenched in sweat.

Abruptly I pressed her down to the rustling straw, but at that moment she pushed me with both hands with unexpected strength. I swayed and sat up with a clatter among the scattered bricks of a demolished stove.

And she began crying. Violently, spasmodically, with such frenzy that I became really scared.

I rose on my knees and thus, kneeling, began to approach her, in order somehow to stop this strange, frightened weeping.

But then she jumped up from the straw and avoiding the scattered logs and planks, ran with unusual agility out into the garden.

When I got out in front of the house, she had already gone. I ran in the direction she must have taken. Finally I caught sight of her as she walked along, stumbling, black and strangely tall against the background of vague whiteness arising from the river.

I barred her way. She stopped, wiping her face with both hands. We were silent.

"I wanted to ask you something," I said, quietly.

She kept silent, sobbing.

"I wanted to ask you something," I repeated, helplessly.

She moved away, passing by me in a wide half-circle. I turned after her and said: "Does he have a scar on his right side?"

Silent, she walked away into the night.

"Does your husband have a bullet scar?"

It was dark and quiet. I could hear the distant murmur of the Sola, concealed in the undergrowth. It was like the stifled quarreling of a group of people. And then, as once before, a distant rifle shot resounded in the depths of the forest.

The cart, its bottom strewn with pea pods, drove up to the house. The same carter who had driven the man found in the Solec forest now took a blackened bag of feed from under his seat and slung it over the horse's head.

Miss Malvina came out to the porch, attracted by this unexpected arrival: "Mr. Harap wants us?" she inquired.

"Mh," the carter muttered.

Miss Korsak thought a moment: "Going to town?"

"Mh."

Miss Malvina glanced up at the sky, in which a snowy trail was growing. The invisible jet aircraft was moving north, as every day.

"Are you taking someone with you?"

"Mh."

"You're not talkative, Mr. Harap."

"Mh."

Mr. Ildefons came to the door, somehow haggard, clutching his trousers over his sunken stomach.

"Harap has come," said Miss Malvina. "He's driving into town."

"It didn't come off too well yesterday, it didn't," whispered Ildefons Korsak, and he snuffled in his greenish whiskers. "People don't know how to have a good time nowadays. That's the way the world is now."

All at once the door to Regina's room opened. She stood there tying a silk kerchief under her chin, ready for the journey. Behind her was Romus, dragging two plain fiber suitcases and a large bundle tied with rope.

"Good God, what's this?" cried Miss Malvina, pressing both hands to her bosom. "Angels and ministers of grace defend us! I don't understand."

"Goodbye miss, goodbye sir, it isn't me that's bad, please don't keep anger in your hearts," said Regina in a stifled voice.

"Romus, throw my luggage on the pea pods in the back of the cart."

I emerged from the shade of the dead acacia and stopped halfway to the cart. Romus passed me with a grimace of superior knowingness. He carefully buried the suitcases in the layer of vegetation in the cart, which creaked like wires.

"Good God, have we offended by a hard word? Was it bad living with us?"

"Everything was fine, thank you for your goodness, and for everything, but my time has come to leave," said Regina in a broken voice.

"So suddenly, so unexpectedly? Good God, had I known, I could have at least roasted a chicken for you."

"Thank you very much. I don't need anything."

"But where are you off to, little Regina? What will a woman do on her own? People are like wolves nowadays, they bite the weak before you know it."

Regina passed me, her gaze fixed on the ground. She stopped by the cart, absently undoing the knot on her bundle.

"There are people everywhere," she said with her head bowed low. "I'll go to town. And what happens then will be in God's hands. Maybe I'll go abroad, to my brother."

"Why right away to foreign countries? It's a terrible thing to travel so far."

Regina turned violently: "And what do I have here? What sort of life do I lead here?"

Miss Malvina was silent a moment and then said sympathetically, "I know, I know, my child. What can you find among simple people like us?"

"When I go to America I won't forget you. I'll be sending you packages," said Regina, with an uncertain smile.

She began climbing onto the cart, her sunburnt, ruddy calves gleaming. Then she sat down on the horse blanket and looked once more at the strange house, stuck together of parts that didn't match, and at us standing in the hot sunlight. Harap tugged the reins and gee-upped — but Regina suddenly stopped him. She jumped off the cart and ran toward us.

It seemed to me she had forgotten something and I even wanted to glance toward the carelessly open door, but Regina slowed and stopped unexpectedly in front of me: "I wanted to say goodbye to you," she said, shyly, and she suddenly looked into my eyes: "It's as though you weren't around. You never spoke, you never wanted anything, you held no grudge against anyone."

I remained silent, not knowing what to say.

"But I got to like you."

I felt the presence of someone behind me, insistent and hostile, but after all I couldn't turn around: "And I like you very much, Miss Regina."

"We'd have made a good couple. I'd certainly have married you."

"You are very nice, Miss Regina."

"You say that out of politeness. But it's the truth."

"I'm not joking either."

She smiled youthfully and said, with cautious facetiousness: "You should have said the word. Too bad."

"Too bad. That's what girls have always said to me. But it was already too late."

"May you at least end up a success."

Confused, I felt warm all over: "I don't understand."

"I know what I'm talking about."

Someone was breathing heavily behind me.

Unexpectedly she came up, took my face in her hands and kissed me on the mouth: "Goodbye," she said. "Goodbye." She wanted to say something else, but only swayed as if trying to regain her balance, and impulsively she set off toward the cart.

"Regina!" someone behind me shouted.

It was the partisan. He was standing at my back, nervously wiping his prosthesis with his good hand. Regina sat down resolutely beside Harap and began absurdly to cover her feet tight in the pea pods, as if during the frosts of February.

"Aren't you going to say goodbye to me?" asked the partisan hoarsely.

She said nothing and did not look in our direction. Once more she nervously tied the colored corners of her kerchief under her chin.

"Regina, watch it, for your own good, stay here!"

She tugged at her rug: "Why don't we start?"

"Mh," Harap muttered, and he clapped the horse's flank with his whip.

The cart turned sharply and moved off north, in the direction of the narrow outlet of our valley, drowned in woods as blue as smoke. Regina did not look back a single time.

The partisan rushed after the departing cart. He pressed his prosthesis to his side, jumping over the many stones left by the floods. He ran thus for a long time, but nobody knew whether he wasn't able to catch up with the cart or whether he didn't want to. Finally he halted on the hilltop, gazing after the departing people, whom we could no longer see.

Romus was lying by the fence, in the shade. He was spitting rapidly, which meant a state of excitement. A yellow butterfly started flying along the road, but nobody noticed it.

"Well, there now," sighed Miss Malvina. "Everyone else can go off into the world, but we're doomed to stay here and live."

Ildefons Korsak set off at a crooked trot to the sheds. It was evident he had been waiting a long while for this moment.

Miss Malvina glanced once again at the sky, at the sun vibrating with the heat: "There will be some misfortune, that there will. Who ever saw such things at this time of year? The judgment of Our Lord is close at hand," she sighed, and went into the house.

The partisan was coming back along the ashy road. He walked heavily, raising clouds of floury dust. He stopped beside me and, gazing once more in the direction Regina had taken, said: "There, the slut. Did you see?"

I said nothing. He banged his prosthesis against his good hand and set off toward the railroad.

Not long after Regina's departure, I was witness of an unusual event. Before noon, along the road by which Regina had departed, we noticed a huge cloud of dust, from which emerged a strange object, reminiscent of a low billiard table. This thing swayed dangerously in all directions and gleamed terribly with nickel fittings.

We threw down our hammers and even Romus rose sleepily from the hot, dry grass. We all stared, wondering, at the unknown phenomenon.

Not until after a long pause did Romus say: "A taxi. A taxi's coming from town."

The partisan turned pale all of a sudden. Cautiously, as though creeping, he moved to meet the newly arrived car. We also went out to the road. We stopped behind the partisan.

A flat, green automobile, big as a railroad car, turned and stopped by us. First, a short and stocky dark man got out, who immediately intrigued us by the gold buttons on his check jacket. After him there emerged another man, tall and very grizzled, with a set, angry face.

The dark man with the gold buttons raised the hood of the car and unscrewed the cap of the cooler. Jumping back nimbly from the stream of boiling water, and after wiping off his hands, he said: "Some roads you got here. Congratulations."

"We didn't build them," said Romus, in a bored voice.

The partisan gazed eagerly through the dusty windows of the automobile. But the interior was empty. A bundled-up raincoat, a little brush, crumpled maps, lay under the back window.

The short dark man eyed Romus: "You must be the local intellectual?"

Romus, taken aback, shifted from one foot to the other.

"A philosopher, ha?" pursued the dark man. "The local Spinoza."

Romus focused his attention on himself, supposing that something wasn't in order. But he failed to find a ready answer, for his questioner all at once lost interest and began expounding something to his silent companion in English.

Then he turned to the partisan, who certainly looked the most reasonable: "Is it far from here to the Solec forest, my good man?"

The partisan pointed to the opposite bank of the river with his prosthesis: "The forest begins there."

The dark man undid two gold buttons over his round belly and explained: "This man is a journalist from the West."

We bowed politely, the grizzled newcomer also bowed his head civilly.

"Your locality interests him," the dark man went on. "He knows it's going to be flooded, and that's why he wants to write an article about you all for the foreign press."

He stopped, looking at us expectantly. Count Pac straightened his collar, which was untidily opened at the neck:

"We're very pleased to meet you."

"Do any of you gentlemen know the Solec forest well?"

We looked at one another doubtfully.

"We need a guide."

The grizzled newcomer said something briefly in English.

"He says," the dark man explained, "that he'll pay well for your services."

"Romus could, he knows the forest, he's from here," said Count Pac.

The visitors looked at Romus, who was persistently digging with one foot in a hot rut left by a tire of the automobile. Obviously he was struggling inwardly, oscillating between pride and greed: "Why not? I can take you," he said finally, with unnatural moderation.

"Then let's go right away. No time to waste," the dark man decided and he began locking the car doors carefully.

"Unnecessary caution," said Count Pac. "Nobody here is interested in cars. It can stand in the middle of the road for a week."

The dark man raised his plump hand, the keys gleaming: "Oh-ho, I've my own opinion as to that. Our nation is inquisitive and very patient. They can demolish a car right down to the last screw. Let's go."

They set off toward the river. First the interpreter with his gold buttons, then the Western journalist, and last Romus, navigating lethargically and spitting copiously to one side. They were about to go down to the meadow when the dark man stopped abruptly, remembering something: "Oh, yes. Did any of you gentlemen ever hear of Huniady?"

Thistle fluff floated over our heads. The clarinet resounded from the river.

"Huniady. That's a pseudonym," added the dark man, "Once he commanded a big unit here, he ruled the entire county. Now he's supposed to be hiding in these woods."

The partisan hesitated. However, he moved carelessly toward them. I went after him.

"People make up various stories, you know how it is," he said evasively.

All of us began walking toward the river.

"We have certain information that he's still alive today."

The partisan looked at them cautiously out of a corner of his eye: "We never heard anything of the sort. Who'd survive so many years in solitude?"

"Is someone around here playing the clarinet?"

"Workmen. From that building site."

"So nothing's been heard of Huniady recently?"

"We're not from here, you see. The old inhabitants may know something," said Count Pac. "We aren't interested in such things."

The dark man said something to the grizzled man, but got no answer.

"That means nobody has met him in recent years?"

"Whoever met him didn't live to say so," said Pac.

The dark man with gold buttons suddenly stopped: "You said you'd never heard of Huniady?"

The count looked in confusion at the partisan: "People say all sorts of things. Who'd believe in such legends?"

Soon we stopped at the bank of the Sola: "What's that smoke?" asked the interpreter.

"The peat is on fire. Due to the drought."

"But how can we get to the other side?"

"There's a bridge at Podjelniaki," said Romus.

"Far?"

"Three miles."

The dark man looked round helplessly: "That's a long way. Is the river deep?"

"Not very. It's dried up. We cross at the ford."

The dark man wanted to interpret, but the journalist made a gesture indicating he understood the significance of the conversation. In silence he crouched, and began untying his shoelaces.

They took their shoes off, turned up their trouser legs and walked into the water. The grizzled man held his camera up, no one knew why, as though afraid of wetting it. Romus led them across the Sola like St. Christopher.

The workmen on the far side watched this crossing suspiciously. There were already more sheds, some sort of machinery was put down under tarpaulins, and the field path had become a broad road.

Romus and the newcomers reached the other bank. They slowly climbed the slope of the green oak thicket until at last they disappeared from our sight.

"Maybe we should go after them and see what they are really looking for?" asked Count Pac.

The partisan pulled on a cigarette: "I'm not interested."

"But you're a local, after all. You must know what concerns you."

Krupa let out a fine cloud of smoke: "Count, please take off like a hunted boar, O.K.?"

"I'm n-n-not a c-c-count, d'you hear?" Pac glared at him furiously. "I'm w-w-warning you. I know s-s-something about you t-t-too."

The partisan took several steps toward the count: "And what can you know about me?"

Several workmen had gathered on the other bank. Shading their eyes with their hands, they were gazing at us with insistent attention: "Hey, you," one of them shouted, "come over here to us."

Seeing our reluctance, he repeated: "Well, come on, come on."

Count Pac couldn't help himself: "But what for?"

"We'll show you something!"

"Show it to your whores!"

There was a sudden stir among the workmen. Cut off by the river and therefore helpless, they began hurling the most inventive curses in our direction. We walked away without haste, showing provocative contempt in our lazy movements.

"Joe, bring the rifle! Hurry up!" one of them cried, so that we would hear.

The partisan exhibited to them an expansive hole in his work pants.

"Well, here boys, splash yourselves!"

Behind us we heard a threatening moan and the violent stamping of feet by the insulted workmen. But we were already far away, we were in no danger.

We didn't go back to work, but it was too early to break up. So we went into the Korsaks' garden, where the afternoon heat was filled with the scent of dried-up corn gourds. We knew they would soon be back and therefore felt a sort of ill-defined and ambiguous uneasiness.

The partisan pulled a forgotten carrot out of the dry earth, wiped it carefully on his clothes, and began gnawing it with his widely-set teeth. The count watched him, unconsciously imitating his bites with his own livid lips.

Mr. Ildefons appeared in the door of the house, pen in hand. He smiled at us knowingly and said, "It isn't allowed, mister, to write with the words we use every day. They're ordinary words, and there's no strength in them. And how ugly they are, crooked as a tumble-down fence and crooked in the ear. Written words have to be beautiful, mister, the most unusual expressions and so arranged that it looks like poetry. I know that, mister."

"Well, and when will you finish your writing?" asked the partisan, continuing to gnaw the carrot.

"When will I finish? God alone knows. But I will surely finish it some day. There has never been such a book, mister."

At this point he raised his pen to his eyes, examined it as it glowed with dried ink like an amethyst and then, smiling mysteriously, went back to his labors.

"Why are they so long?" said Pac.

The partisan turned over to the other side and stared at the road. Sleepy hens were bathing in the hot sand. Someone was coming from the other end of the road with a heavy tread. Short, almost dwarfish, he was dressed in greasy peasant garments. On seeing us as we loitered in the garden, he stopped at the fence and looked curiously in our direction.

Finally he called out, in an unnaturally high voice:

"Greetings in the name of the Lord."

Neither the partisan nor the count replied to this salutation. So I rose on one elbow and said, "Greetings."

Only now did I recognize the passer-by as the youngest of the monks, who most often went to the township for errands at the store.

"Store closed?"

"Yes. As of today," I said.

"Will it be for long, sir?"

"I don't know. Probably. The manageress has left."

The partisan turned over and closed his eyes, as if tired out by the heat.

"Left?" the monk echoed. "That's bad."

He was standing hidden by the railings. I could see only his inquisitive, rapidly blinking eyes.

"Is it true they're going to evacuate us from here?"

We kept silent.

"You gentlemen must be of that sect, for sure?" said the monk.

The partisan sat up violently: "Go away, go away, cleric, and don't annoy people."

Taken aback, the monk walked several yards away from the fence and bowed to us, almost to the ground. He waited a moment as though waiting for a reply, then set off in the direction of the monastery, which lay on the hillside like a white limestone rock.

Then we heard the rumble of the engine, and the chickens scattered, cackling, toward the fence. The green automobile stopped at our gate. Both newcomers dismounted, as did Romus, scratching his calves which had been pricked by undergrowth.

They came up to us and sat down heavily on the rocks in front of the house.

"Don't you have a restaurant here?" asked the dark man with the gold buttons. "Of course I don't mean an elegant place of superior category. A tavern would do."

"There isn't any," said the count.

"Or a store?"

"The store is closed."

"Well, what a country I'm in!" said the dark man, and whispered something to his grizzled companion, who was staring intently at our house.

"But may we rest a while?"

"Why not, please do," said the partisan, shrugging.

The Western journalist rose and went up to the house. He scrutinized the door, windows, faded planks, as though he meant to buy the tumble-down old place.

"Did you find Huniady?" asked the partisan, blowing off some black ants that were running over his prosthesis.

"Maybe we did, too," said the owner of the gold buttons.

"Did he say anything interesting?"

"Of course. He said he has many acquaintances in the area."
The partisan suddenly choked with that snort of his, and glanced at the newcomer.

"I remember you from someplace," said the dark man.

"Me?" the partisan was surprised and wiped his mouth with his good hand.

"Yes, you. I remember your face very well."

"You're mistaken, my friend," the partisan laughed, uncertainly. "Sometimes it seems so to a person. Faces can be alike."

"Didn't you live in Rozan before the war?"

"No. I didn't."

"Odd. I must have met you at some time."

"It's a sort of obsession," I suddenly put in. "Many people suffer from it. I too have the impression I know this foreigner's features from some place."

The grizzled journalist turned and looked at us. The dark man said something to him, rapidly. The foreigner came up and eyed me for a while. His face was neutral and surely not memorable. Yet I must have seen it somewhere, though younger, brighter, and cleaner.

Then he walked away, took out his camera and pointed it at the house.

The partisan instantly jumped up and leaped at him: "Not allowed! *Verboten!*" he shouted, raising his prosthesis as though about to strike.

"You crazy?" hissed the dark man. "Not allowed to photograph that broken-down old place?"

"Not allowed," the partisan repeated. "We don't want him to."

"My dear man, he's a foreign journalist, after all. He'll take pictures of you all, too. They'll be printed in the world's greatest newspapers."

"We don't need our pictures taken."

"You don't want the whole world to know about you?"

"What's his name?"

"Who?"

"Well, him," said the partisan, pointing to the journalist.

"An English name. You couldn't have heard of him in this hole."

"It's late," said the partisan, "and the roads here are rotten."

"We can pay well."

The partisan went back to his place and sat down heavily: "Go somewhere else. Are there so few interesting places in this country, then?"

"I remember you from somewhere, I'm sure I do."

"From a dream. Sometimes a person will dream for no reason."

The dark man said something to the journalist, and fastened up all the gold buttons on his jacket.

"What's he jabbering about?" the partisan asked the count.

"How should I know? I don't know any English," said the count, hastily.

"Aha, yet you know they're talking English."

The newcomers walked to the gate. The dark man shook his head: "You aren't very hospitable."

"We don't like strangers."

"Maybe we're prophets. Maybe we've brought news for you all."

"We know everything. We don't expect any news."

The dark man turned and they walked into the road without saying goodbye. The interpreter stayed by the car, but the journalist set off up the hill and walked a long time until he stopped by a clump of buckthorn.

From there he gazed at our valley, at the sandy roads, the peat bog overgrown with weeds and the bare oak glade from which the Solec forest began.

Then he all at once knelt down, as though he had caught sight of something sublime. We rose in surprise and walked onto the road without a word. The foreigner was kneeling on the sloping hillside, and it might have seemed that he was praying to our valley.

Later he came down toward us and plunged into the green box of the automobile without a word.

"At one time the Saints Cyril and Methodius came like this," said the dark man. "Look." And he showed us a strange knife, with the sign of the Cross on its handle.

Romus laughed hoarsely: "They found that in the river. I saw them."

"Don't you believe me?" asked the dark man. "Too bad."

"You regard us as children," said the count.

"Is that bad?"

The dark man got into the car: "Goodbye."

They were about to drive off when the partisan abruptly struggled in the direction of the car's open window: "Will you give me a ride to town?"

"Why not?" replied the interpreter. "Get in."

"I'll be back," the partisan whispered to us.

The automobile moved in the direction in which the Sola flowed, and where now the reddening sun hung in the west.

"He's gone after her," said Count Pac and walked away in the opposite direction.

I wanted to open the door into the hallway, but felt someone's presence behind me. I turned. Romus was shifting from one foot to the other as though burned by the heated stone slabs of the porch.

"What have you got to say, Romus?" I asked.

"Please go away from here. That's good advice."

"Trying to scare me?"

"Maybe, maybe not. It will be better for you if you leave."

"Do you think I have some private business here?"

"I don't know whether you have or not. But I think it's worth your while to listen to me."

"Did someone send you to me?"

"I came of my own free will. But they don't like you here. Here everyone has his own business, and it's better if there are no strangers."

Once again, from somewhere behind the hill the great flock of birds flew out, to bid farewell to the day in the valley.

"You know, Romus, maybe this time you're right."

He waited expectantly for what else I would tell him: "I'll leave. I promise you I'll be gone the day after tomorrow."

He was standing motionless, but I could not see his face as it was hidden in deep shadow.

"Don't you believe me?"

"It's better if I do, mister."

I went into my room, which was filled with a reddish glow. I knew that a struggle with enervating insomnia awaited me again. So, seeking all symptoms of tiredness in myself, I undressed cautiously and lay down on the bed. The rapid sounds of the monastery bell came through the window. Then followed a terrifying silence, such as everyone remembers from holiday nights in childhood.

I don't know how long I lay like this. Surely a very long time, for when the awaited knocking came at the window, my legs were already frozen with the pre-dawn chill.

I lit the lamp and opened my door. On the threshold was the partisan, blinking in the feeble light.

"I've come back," he said.

"Please come in and sit down."

But he remained on the threshold. "I came half the way on foot," he said.

"I'm leaving the day after tomorrow."

He paid no attention to my words.

"Do you know what I went for?" he said.

"I can guess."

"Ah, there are times when something comes over a man . . ."

I caught sight of reddening icicles of caked blood on his swollen upper lip.

"Did you get hurt?"

"In town I met some men from the building site." He was silent for a moment. "You know, she loved me. A man finds that out best in bed. D'you believe me?"

"Please sit down, here's a chair."

"They beat me up in town. But I didn't find her."

Again he fell silent for a long moment.

"Maybe just as well, eh?"

I didn't reply.

"Maybe just as well," he repeated, then he turned away and disappeared into the night, which was filled with thin, terribly cold mist.

I was wondering whether to go in and close all that which had been waiting for a solution for years. That which always returned at unexpected times like a stifling recollection. That which weighed me down every day because it was unfinished.

On the far side of the river, incomprehensible traffic swarmed, aimed against this valley. I could see new machinery and new loads of building materials. Single, muffled calls resounded from over there.

I looked at the house and the tall sorb tree, whose fruit would be strangely sweet after the first light, nocturnal frosts. I hesitated, waiting for that impulse which would lead me to the veranda overgrown with the withered vine.

So I entered the path between the dead jasmine bushes. The house was silent, covered by a dry heat full of the odor of the smouldering peat bog. I wiped my forehead and looked at my fingers bedewed with warm sweat.

The clarinet of the unknown player resounded, and at that moment I entered the dark hallway with its smell of herbs. Gropingly I sought for the right door. I found the cold lock that had been forged by a blacksmith. I knocked.

"Come in," said someone in a stifled voice.

I started looking for the doorknob, scratching my nails on the jagged planks.

"It's open. Please come in," I heard the same voice.

The knob's rough mechanism clanked and I saw just such a room as I'd expected. A table covered with a cotton-backed cloth, a small shelf of books, fragments of souvenir-fetishes on the walls.

Joseph Car, wearing only a shirt, rose from the couch. She was lying beside him, in the brownish shadow.

"Surely I'm intruding," I said in confusion.

"Please, please come in," said Joseph Car, fastening his shirt at the throat.

She also rose from the couch, straightening her rumpled blouse. Without looking at me, she lazily began to fasten her hair by the window, outside which the day was hot beyond the stalks of the vine thicket.

"I'm leaving in a few days."

"Ah," muttered Joseph Car, but he didn't ask for how long I was leaving, or why.

The room contained the furniture usual in those parts, but it was arranged very differently, bearing witness that its owners were newcomers. I could remember such rooms from the war years.

"I've come to talk," I said.

"Yes, yes, I remember. We mentioned this."

She turned around and looked at me. Her foot, stretched forward, was executing barely perceptible rhythmical movements.

"Well, just now," said Joseph Car, "you wanted to go to Podjelniaki, Justine."

She went to the bench, took her basket woven from spruce roots and stopped in front of me, as though waiting for something. He approached and embraced her intimately. They both looked at me, and it was as though they wanted me to remember this for ever.

"Well, go, go, my child," he said at last.

She suddenly cuddled up to him and kissed him shamelessly on the mouth. I felt a warm drop of sweat trickle down my nose.

"It's hot," I said. "It hasn't been as hot as this before."

They were holding hands, and I felt particularly stupid. Then she slowly let his hand go, finger by finger, in a manner that struck me as exceptionally unseemly.

"Maybe there isn't going to be any winter at all, what do you think?" she asked, a fraction too loudly.

I said nothing.

"Don't you believe in the end of the world?"

I wanted to reply and, what's more, to reply with a hurting, sarcastic reproach, but nothing came to my mind.

"Well said?" she asked.

"I don't know. Probably."

She rocked on one foot, gazing somewhere to the side, then abruptly ran out of the room. Again I noticed that the clarinet was still piping across the river.

"Please sit down," he said, pointing to a stool.

I sat down, and he began walking about, taking short steps, by the couch. I could see the glowing window in front of me, like the opening of an oven.

"Well, what is it?" he asked, stopping in front of me.

I felt he did not like my visit, that he'd disliked me from the very beginning, from our first talk on the river bank. And that he was covering up his dislike with polite reserve. So I didn't know how to begin, or from what angle to breach this unfriendly wall.

"I want to ask you something," I said. After these words I felt suddenly discouraged, as a result of the cautious concentration in his black eyes, half hidden by his eyelids. I noticed dried shreds of foam in the corners of his mouth.

"It's tremendously important to me," I added.

He stirred: "I'm listening."

"Szafir — you know him, don't you? — considers me abnormal." And I fell silent, unable to find the right words.

He stood there, stooping, vigilant, with caution in his hunched shoulders: "Yes, I'm listening," he said, quietly.

"Everyone has some incidents in his destiny, which weigh on his later existence like rocks. You see, I've gone round in a great circle in my life, and on returning, certain matters have become important to me. Perhaps even more than they were when they started. For now, apart from their anecdotal value, I'm seeking some greater significance in them, some meaning which determines the order of our being. Did I express myself clearly?"

"Well," he hesitated, "not too. But I'm listening."

"That is of enormous importance to me. In my life I've had many opportunities to make choices. I remained in torment. Because I want to find a meaning in this. You'll agree that it's been our lot to live through a great deal. Our experiences could be spread out between several generations. No doubt that's why we feel the need for some summing up, some conclusion, I don't know, I really don't, some sort of order that would justify it all."

"This means that you're coming to me like those people from the township."

I caught sight of her outside the window, slowly walking along the path that climbed the russet hill. At the top she paused and gazed for a long time in the direction of the river. Then she sat down, taking the basket between her slender, gold-colored knees.

"No, I don't need a faith from outside. I want to find peace in myself."

He straightened up and moved off again. He walked to and fro across the room, until he finally stopped at the window and caught sight of Justine sitting there. He turned around rapidly, caught my glance, from which he realized that I too could see her.

He smiled with his blistered lips: "You've answered yourself," he remarked, quietly.

"I'm counting on an answer from you."

He stopped, separated from me by the table: "I'm no doctor," he shrugged.

I swallowed some thick saliva: "Why did you choose this place? The same valley with a river running through it, the same railroad line going by, with an oak thicket on the other bank."

He was gazing at the tablecloth with its pattern of cool colors: "There are very many areas such as this. It was in valleys like this that the first towns in our country were formed. You can learn about this in school."

"That isn't so. This valley is exceptional in its peat beds, in the river full of souvenirs, in the forest which has seen many generations of armed men. I remember just such a valley from my childhood and youth and so do you. Do you know that whenever I want to picture to myself the life of people in settlements, whenever I want to describe a landscape in a striking way, I always see this valley, recalled in the most minute detail?"

"Surely you don't think I'm subject to childish sentimentality? I came to this place by chance. Things somehow worked out between me and these people from the township."

She continued sitting on the hilltop, as before. It almost seemed that she was listening attentively to our conversation from a distance.

"Do you recognize me?" I asked, quietly.

He was not looking at me: "I don't know what you're concerned about. You came here recently, you're living at the Korsaks. That's as much as I know about you."

"Don't you remember anything from years ago? Please consider, I beg you."

He took out a handkerchief and wiped his sweaty face for a long time: "It's hard for me to say. Maybe we once met by accident. I was a teacher, I've seen many faces, and forgotten many too."

"You couldn't forget me. Any more than I could you."

He pressed the arm of his chair until the joints of his fingers turned white: "You're tiring me. Please let's drop this meaningless talk."

I got up from the stool and went over to him: "I remember you. I remember you very well. Please look at me."

He raised his eyes. Our looks met. I saw a muscle in his cheek begin to twitch.

"I would like to forget you. But I remember you all the time."

We've been walking a very long time already. The snow is deep and thick, so it is difficult to march. I glance often and anxiously at the sky. A snow storm is threatening. The moon has been in a halo since early evening. We need snow; it will cover our tracks.

February. The air, stiff with frost, could be sliced with a knife. The stars are timidly sparkling from under covering of frozen mist. The howling of wolves accompanies us all the time. Sometimes far away, sometimes so close and unexpected that we shudder, glancing furtively at one another. "Quiet," a lad with a pink face and scant elflocks of hair stuck like a wig to his white brow spits superstitiously, then crosses himself many times. "Falcon" tries to walk between us, as though our presence would save him from the devil.

We're walking at an uneven, though rhythmical, pace. Hoar frost has settled on our eyelashes and brows, and gets into our eyes. The bullets in Quiet's mess kit rattle like the bones of a sinner.

From time to time, someone fires a shot in the woods that surround us on all sides. We stop to listen fearfully, while I say in an off-hand tone, "A tree cracking in the frost."

They sigh with relief and we move on again, along the little-used road that is full of unexpected, troubled shadows.

"Who'd be roaming around this wilderness in such a frost?" Quiet calms himself and us.

"But what if they have arms?" asked Falcon quietly.

"Come on, Falcon," say I. "After all, it's a farm with no owner. Who can have arms there? Unless the forester hid some sawed-off shotgun. More noise than damage."

We're talking with difficulty, for the biting air is as stifling as the steam on the top shelf of a steam bath. It is difficult to stammer out a word to the end.

"I need a stove," says Quiet. "A big stove with oak logs. To thaw out my bones."

White fluff slithered down from a branch. We stop instinctively.

"Hear that?" asks Falcon.

"Wolves," I calm them.

"No. I can hear sledges. Their runners are creaking in a frozen rut."

"No, no. In this silence a man hears whatever his fancy prompts."

"Much further?" asks Quiet.

I look at the compass strapped to my wrist. Its aquamarine pointer trembles uncertainly, pointing north. Then I open the map case. I need no flashlight. Everything can be seen on the ordinance map.

"If I haven't mistaken the way it's another two miles."

"Not far," Falcon rejoices.

"Not far."

We walk on. Around us, the forest is suffused by moonlight.

"Nice," I say to myself. And I think it would be worth remembering this sight. As though it might at some time be useful to me.

"What's that you're saying?" Falcon asks, uneasily.

"Nothing."

I keep myself under control all the time. As though acting in front of a hidden but ever-present audience. I am remembering the landscapes, states of personal feelings, discoveries contained in unexpected wartime situations. I drive them into my memory like lectures I shall have to deliver at some time in someone's presence. Maybe they taught me this at school, at home, or in books, of which I have read several tons.

Falcon stops sharply.

"What's up?" I ask.

"Sssh. Don't you hear? Sledges. Horses neighing."

We prick up our ears in the silence which is lined with the murmuring of sleeping earth.

"Oh, come on," say I. "Fear has eyes as big as a rabbit's."

"Why should I be scared?" Falcon moans. "I've been through three round-ups. I was in a hayrick when they poked it with bayonets."

"I used to like lobbing grenades, one time," says Quiet. "Now and then we'd grab a hog into the sleigh and be off. But now it matters less and less. They're prowling on every road."

"Do you know how many degrees below zero it was today?" I ask.

"I know," Quiet mutters. "Let's go, let's get it over."

The snow squeaks terrifyingly, even though we are trying to walk as quietly as possible. At times one of us trips, and his weapon clangs heavily. The forest is beginning to thin out lazily to the sides. In front there is more and more hazy whiteness lined with a yellow tint.

"I swear someone is riding. Don't you hear people's voices?" asks Falcon.

"You're all nerves," say I. "You should have stayed behind."

"Let's wait a while here in the forest," Falcon urges. "There's a huge clearing ahead. They'll knock us off like so many pheasants."

"Three in the morning. It's a long way back. Let's go on," I decide.

We walk in stubborn silence. Somewhere to the right, in a black strip of forest encircling the great clearing like a bow, the wolves are baying.

"Those wolves are howling for bad luck," Quiet whispers, entangled in frosty steam as though in a veil. "This winter will finish us off, confound it."

Falcon was forging his way ahead. He runs like an old elk, impatiently pulling his neck out of his snow-covered collar. Suddenly he turns back and rushes towards us, cutting through frozen lumps of snow with his boots.

"I told you so, damn you," he hisses. "There are people riding."

"Where?"

"Over there. Toward us."

We stop, breathing fast and heavily. We stare at the opposite end of the forest edge, where our road disappears. It is true, something is indistinctly looming there, against the dark blue background.

"Ssssh," Falcon says again.

First of all, we catch the infrequent and slow talking of men, reminiscent of a river struggling with the roots of submerged tree trunks. Then the squeak of sledge runners studded with iron, and the neighing of horses can be heard.

"Follow me!" I order.

I set off running to the left, to the wall of the forest. I don't have to speak, or tell them to make sure their tracks coincide with mine. They know it well, they do it out of habit. But the snow is deep, at first I sink up to my knees, then to my groin, then to my waist.

I struggle as though struggling with the current of a mountain river. The frozen undergrowth snaps heavily, tearing my clothes. I can hear my sheepskin jacket losing hold like an old feedbag.

But already we're in the forest, in the first clumps of juniper hidden under piles of snow. I throw myself down by the nearest tree trunk and start licking its chilled bark, which is filled with the smell of resin. The others fall beside me. I draw off my mittens. At once my palms stick to my frozen weapon.

"We'll be lucky if they don't see our tracks," I whisper.

Quiet groans. He starts blowing on the catch of his automatic, so as not to freeze his fingers.

All at once we stiffen. A long line of sledges is driving into the middle of the wide clearing. They are driving slowly, in close order. They are approaching the spot where we turned off, leaving deep tracks like those of wild boars.

I draw the bolt of my automatic. Quiet and Falcon do the same. We stare at this strange procession. The first sledges have passed the point that was critical for us; now the rest are driving past it.

"They didn't notice," says Falcon, with relief.

"Don't hollo until . . ." I warn him.

An icicle flopped heavily into the snow immediately in front of us.

"Good God," Quiet suddenly moans. "Do you see what it is they're carrying?"

We're crawling almost to the very edge of the forest.

"Chairs or something. Whole cartfuls," Falcon whispers.

Quiet gets up on his knees: "Chairs, you idiot?" he stammers, "they're men."

"What men?" asks Falcon, in a strained voice.

"Frozen to death."

The head of the column is now driving into the forest from which we just came. One of the drivers whistles piercingly on his fingers; someone from the last sledge replies in the same way.

Involuntarily I take my cap off: "It's the lads of Kmicic they're carrying," I say. "They caught them the day before yesterday, and now they're driving them through the forest to scare people."

The sledges, bristling with protruding arms and feet on which the light of the moon gleams reflects on the ice crust, plunge into the forest.

They too take off their caps. Quiet begins to cross himself fervently, in the Ruthenian manner. He bows low to the frozen partisans in a sort of animal frenzy, like a dying rhinoceros which bangs its snout on the indifferent earth.

We remain thus a long time, although the procession has already penetrated some time ago into the forest.

"They'll put an end to us too," says Quiet, in an undertone. I know things aren't well with them.

"Get up!" I order.

They rise from kneeling and we reluctantly return to the road, then proceed into a lane of wolves' howling.

Before four o'clock, we emerge to a branching of the road that leads to the farm. Falcon crouches over the trampled snow.

"Tire marks," he says. "Trucks drove this way not long ago."

"Coming for milk, surely."

He says nothing, but I know he isn't convinced. We walk more and more cautiously between naked alder bushes toward a clump of trees, amidst which the hidden farm lies sleeping. We tread as lightly as birds. Were it possible, we would glide high above the snowy path.

From invisible buildings, a dog barks. Of course they stop immediately: "It's baying at the moon," I say. "What are you stopping for?"

"Where's your moon?" Falcon points to the sky.

True enough. Clouds edged with light have already covered half the firmament.

We move on. Branches catch at our sheepskin jackets. A heavy weariness burdens our shoulders. I drop off to sleep for fractions of seconds and then fragments of my childhood appear, incidents at home filled with warmth and tranquility.

Falcon stops. And says nothing.

"What now?" I ask.

"I see a little light," he says, anxiously.

"Where?"

"Over there, under that tree."

We stand motionless for a moment.

"Yes, there it is," says Quiet.

"I don't see anything."

"You have to wait for him to draw, then the cigarette end glows."

They're right. For an instant a red point glows, deep in the blackness of the trees. I reflect briefly: "Got to go on. We must check. Maybe we're seeing things. Maybe it's a night watchman."

They are silent, and in their silence there is dislike bordering on hatred.

"Tire tracks and a sentry smoking a cigarette. What more do you want?" Falcon asks in a whisper.

I turn around and walk toward the outbuildings. I know they won't leave me. Again the blood-red little cloud gleams under the tree. Then, all at once, I catch the sound of what seems to be the stifled weeping of many people.

I begin crawling in the direction of that little glow. The alders shield me, but then it isn't possible to crawl any longer, the red cloud appears a few paces from me. I can even distinguish the dull stamping of feet shod in Russian-style felt top boots, and hear the clank of a tommy gun against metal buttons.

I turn back and look for my patrol. However, there's nothing around except snow and naked alder branches. It's getting darker and darker.

I have to risk it.

"Falcon, Quiet!" I breathe, covering my mouth with one hand.

No one answers, only that weeping, that human moaning coming from God knows where, begins to take on the shape of a protracted song:

"Quiet, answer!"

Again the blood-red circle glows in the dark. It seems to me that in it I can discern the features of a human face.

"Falcon, come here!"

But no one answers. So I rise from the snow and try to catch at some meaningful thought. Only now do I begin to realise that this weeping, this lamentation, is only a song being chanted by men somewhere in the farm sheds. Now I can even recognize separate words, which form themselves into the verse of a popular Russian front-line song:

> *The famous front-line family met the lad,*
> *Comrades and friends everywhere.*
> *But he couldn't forget the familiar street.*
> *Where are you, sweet girl, where's the family hearth?*

I hoist the machine pistol over my shoulder and set off back, without attempting to conceal myself. I notice my cap is still stuck in my belt, after I'd wedged it there in the clearing. And the bones of my skull ache with the frost. I touch my hair and am surprised to find it as frozen as a brush soaked in water. I put my frozen cap on. Frost drips out of every seam.

Suddenly I hear the crowing of a cock behind me. Cocks usually crow just before five. And such urgency denotes a change in the weather. But a fragment of the story of St. Peter and the three cock crows comes pointlessly to mind. I try to recall it and to arrange it in proper sequence. I wonder why such a thought should have crept into my mind on this night, of all nights.

First one shadow, then another, rises from the underbrush. I don't even bother to unsling my gun. I know who it is that is timidly coming up. "The cock is crowing," I say. "Doesn't that remind you two of anything?"

"Of home," says Quiet, uncertainly.

And he sighs. We walk more and more rapidly, more and more briskly, as though coming back from the fields.

"Troops are stationed there," Falcon exclaims. "That's for sure."

"What if there aren't any?" I ask.

We're marching at a good pace. It's surprising that we have that much strength left at dawn.

"I keep thinking of Kmicic's men," says Quiet, abruptly.

Not long now until dawn. But it is growing darker and darker, as though real night is only now coming. Trees are no longer cracking in the forest. Clearly the frost has lessened.

Suddenly something touches my cheek with a delicate coldness. I glance at my sleeve. The first star of a snowflake shines in the blackness of my jacket.

We walk a very long time, half asleep, half awake. The snow storm grows heavier. We feel out with our feet the ruts in the road, now covered with fresh snow. Finally, alongside the bare larch tree, a shout stops us: "Halt, who goes there?"

"Oldster," I reply.

"Watchword?"

"Shield. Reply?"

"Sword."

Rabbit helps us lift the juniper bush off the square of frozen moss. We open the lid and go down into the bunker. Rabbit seals us in this hole with the juniper and a lid of spruce chips.

Then he asks, with an ambiguous smile: "Bladders empty?"

"Why?"

"The Swallow is spending the night with us. In case of need we go up top."

Our cave is dug in a hillside. We scattered the excavated earth in the forest. It is reminiscent of a country cellar. We boarded up the walls and ceiling with spruce poles and covered it with pine. In the middle, a fire is blazing in a little iron stove. It can only be lit at night. Patches of red light flicker across the sleeping people, revealing for a moment someone's mouth open as if to shout, a clenched fist, a discarded boot glistening with the moisture that drips incessantly from the tangled ceiling.

I see Korvin's reddish burnous and Swallow's short sheepskin jacket by the stove. "Swallow" is what we call Musia, our orderly girl. They're sleeping together, cuddled up to one another as always. One of the girl's bare feet, bitten by the blood-red light, is sticking out from under a Russian sheepskin jacket.

"Take a good look. You'll have enough," whispered Quiet. "There, that's our bitch."

And he slumps down on a layer of leaves alongside Falcon.

I kneel by the stove and open the little door which is pink as a translucent body. I throw in a knot of wood oozing resin. A handful of sparks scatters on the ground, while the stove sets up a cheerful, brisk roaring.

All of a sudden the short jacket swells up, the bare foot disappears and unexpectedly I see her face, swollen with sleep. She throws Korvin's hand from her shoulder, gazes attentively at my hands, then at the empty sacks we've thrown down by the ladder.

"You're back?"

"As you see."

She nods sympathetically.

"Well, that's all right then. Come here by us. You'll get warm at the stove."

She moves over, making room for me between herself and the blazing "jug," which is sizzling like melted tallow. I lie down beside her, we cover ourselves with the sheepskins as though they were the roof of a tent. The snowstorm streams monotonously across the vaulting of the bunker.

"We couldn't do anything. Troops were there," I say.

After a moment Musia says: "Korvin told me about you this evening, you know?"

I hold my breath. Her hand creeps in, finds my shoulder and pats me on my stiff joint.

"He recalled German times. I'd heard of such an incident, but I didn't know it was you who. . . ."

I press her hand with my cheek to my shoulder: "It's true. Things went wrong."

"Are you still fretting?"

"It wasn't glorious. Do you know what it meant? I have been out of things for almost a year. They avoided me as though I had the plague. Only recently did Korvin take me on."

The commandant tossed in his sleep and groaned. She covered him tightly in his burnous with her free hand. Snow, devoured by the flames, crackled in the chimney pipe.

Again I feel the warm moistness of her breath: "Oh, Oldster, Oldster," she sighs.

"My pseudonym is all I have left from better days."

She strokes my forehead with her warm hand, and I suddenly fall upon her with my whole body and nestle my face to her breasts, which are imprisoned in the material of her uniform. Musia embraces me, entwines her hands around my shoulders: "Go to sleep, Oldster," she whispers.

"Very well, chief."

That response of hers is maternal in nature. So I feel like a criminal. I stiffen, motionless, stifling the ambiguous impulses in me. Not until she falls asleep do I cautiously touch her neck with my lips. Musia is breathing calmly, her warm breath regularly fills the sheepskin canopy. So I start more boldly to kiss her chin, her parted lips, the coarse down on her upper lip. She is defenseless, cut off by sleep. I watchfully steal embraces, full of painful shame, until I at last fall asleep in her warmth that smells of autumn leaves.

Then sleepy chattering disentangles itself from nocturnal apparitions, and in it I recognize the voices of Quiet and Falcon. I open my eyes slowly. Against the background of the spruce twig ceiling I see a sallow face with protruding lips, encircled by the sickle of a black beard. So I scramble out from under the sheepskins and report: "Captain, sir, sergeant Oldster . . ."

"Quiet, lie down," says Korvin.

With this growth of beard he looks older than I do. His appearance somehow influences his surroundings. He treats me leniently; I treat him with respect. Musia, by the green wall, is sewing on a button.

"Do you have anything for breakfast?" asks Korvin.

Rabbit places a hunk of bread sprinkled with meal and a few heads of onion on the box. He begins cutting the bread into pieces.

"There are as many of us as there were Apostles," he says. "Thirteen."

"I wonder who'll be that last one," says Korvin.

I am carefully pulling on my boots: "With Musia, we're fourteen."

Korvin glances at me from under his brows.

"Of course we're fourteen, that's a good number," Musia cries.

Quiet is rolling a cigarette, then he looks for a little coal in the ashes: "What's all this talk about anyway, there were twelve Apostles."

"No, little father," Rabbit stops cutting the bread. "There were thirteen Apostles, as many as us. Commandant, your portion."

"Give Musia hers first," Korvin orders.

When my turn comes, I refuse: "I don't want any, I'm not hungry."

Again I see Korvin's eyes, which seem ironical: "Come on, Oldster, what's the fuss? Take your bread."

"No, I don't want it."

"He's embarrassed," Musia explains, in a conciliatory tone. "Take it and don't talk. I've seen more than one patrol come back empty-handed."

Korvin smiles with his lips only: "See, even Swallow stands up for you. Eat it, don't make such a fuss."

I keep a stubborn silence, so Rabbit goes back to the box and puts my share aside.

They munch the bread, baked of flour ground in a handmill. Musia chews a quarter of an onion, chokes and starts to cry.

"Eyes stinging?" asks Quiet, kindly.

"Oh, what a life I have with you all," she puts her bread to one side and pulls a thread between her teeth. Then she inspects her trench coat with one arm extended: "Hardly did I get here than your lice crawled all over me."

She pulls off her jersey and scratches round her bra while we, not in the least aware of the unseemliness of the situation, gaze at her with hungry eyes.

"Come, Musia," Korvin scolds her. "Have some self-respect."

"What's that? Aren't I a soldier like all of you?"

Rabbit collects bread crumbs and slides them into his mouth: "Captain, the bread is all gone, sir."

"And yesterday we saw Kmicic's lads," Quiet exclaims. "They were carting them away like so many frozen boards."

Korvin lies down on his back next to me: "Light the stove."

"Afternoon is coming, sir," says Quiet.

"In a snowstorm like this nobody will notice the smoke."

He takes the map case out from under his head. He starts moving a finger over the German staff map: "I know. Swallow brought a report from the inspectorate. An informer gave them away. They caught an entire platoon by day while they were asleep."

Musia puts on the coat, slowly fastens all the buttons. Her black hair is full of golden larch needles.

Staring at her insistently, we scratch ourselves, mostly in private places. A glow has again burst out in the stove, and the warmth brings on itching. A monotonous grating noise fills the damp cave.

"What day is it?" asks Falcon.

"Christmas Eve, had you forgotten?" asks Musia. "We must think of getting a tree."

"Some carrion would go down well," Rabbit sighs.

Musia puts on her muddy boots: "There's a sentimental one for you."

My share of the bread and the portion of onion are lying on the box as before. Drops of moisture fall heavily on the drenched floor. And overhead the blizzard rumbles on.

Korvin turns around and looks at me: "At dusk you're to take a patrol out."

"Very good, sir."

"But I warn you, it won't be an easy job."

"I understand."

"Not yet you don't. You must get rid of that reptile who betrayed Kmicic's men."

Musia leans over Korvin: "What are you two talking about?"

"Don't interrupt, Musia. This has to be done properly. I've been writing out the death sentence all morning."

He eyes me inquiringly. I don't really know what this is all about.

"If you don't want to execute him yourself, you can draw lots. I'm not going to force anyone."

Although he is younger than I am, I can see winding threads of gray in his beard.

"Do you still remember Gudaje?"

He shuts his eyes for a moment: "Do I remember him? That doesn't matter. Then I forced myself. Maybe I should be grateful to you?"

Falcon is mumbling in a corner. He thinks he's musical. The stove-pipe end grows redder. The dew drops that fall on it hiss long and painfully.

"All right, Korvin, I'll do it myself."

"I said you can all draw lots."

"I know what I have to do. I'll fix it."

Musia takes Korvin's dark mop of hair between her hands: "I'll go with them."

"What for?"

"I know the way. We'll get there faster."

Korvin yields to her caress, but I can sense tension of some kind in him: "He'll find his way. I learned my trade from him."

"Let me go, Korvin. We'll bring back something for Christmas Eve," Musia begs.

"Would you go with Rabbit, too?"

"Are you jealous, maybe? But what rights do you have over me?"

"Well, all right, Musia. Go, if you want."

Falcon gets up and starts walking about our cave packed with vegetation soaking in moisture: "It certainly is howling up there. How many Christmas Eves have there been like this?"

"Have to cut down a little tree," says Quiet.

"Don't you have enough Christmas trees here?" Falcon mutters, and he starts humming.

Korvin turns over on his stomach, supports the swarthy face of one of the Three Kings in his hands: "If only we can hang on till Spring, lads," he exclaims. "They're going to bring us a radio transmitter in March. We'll be a special unit. This won't last much longer, I can tell you."

Thus the sleepy day rolls by, filled with lazy recollections and sloth. At times we suddenly fall silent, and then it seems to us that scraps of a carol reach us from somewhere on the edge of the wilderness, that the wind is pressing the smell of frost and the odor of poppy seeds ground in an earthenware pot through the cracks of the cave lid.

"What's the time?" I ask Korvin.

"You've time, it's only twenty after three."

"I'd like to go right away."

He looks at me attentively: "It's still light."

"I'd like to get it over with."

"I told you already, you can draw lots."

"No, no. I'm taking it on myself."

"You've changed, Oldster."

"Everything costs me more."

He looks away, as though embarrassed by my frankness: "You can leave any time," he says. "They'll be going home in the spring," he indicates Quiet who is gnawing a straw. "I know that. It's easier to keep in hiding around the hut in summer."

"What about you?"

"Me? You know my affairs. I still have to meet my brother. I'll hang him as I planned; then I'll be free."

"You're still thinking about that?"

"Yes. He won't let me sleep."

"How do you know he's alive?"

"He assuredly got out whole. And now his time has come."

"He's your brother, all the same."

Korvin hides his face in his mussed-up sheepskin jacket: "Do you know what I went through on account of him? Wherever I showed myself, from morning to night, I could feel people's eyes on my back: Bolshevik, Bolshevik, Bolshevik. Once I came home in the evening and he was sitting at the table. In front of him were those papers of his, illegal stuff or something. I went up and spat at him. He stood up and hit me in the face for the first time. Then he punched me for a long time like a stranger, he made the blood run out of my ears, nose, mouth. In the night he woke up and listened, to see whether I was still breathing. 'I'm your father,' he said, 'and either I'll make a man of you, or I'll kill you.'"

I get up and put on my jacket. Falcon and Quiet also get ready for the journey. Over the jacket I pull on a cloak that is still damp, steaming on one side from the heat of the stove. Musia is standing by the ladder, ready: "Captain, I report departure of the patrol, one plus three."

Korvin gets up off the ground. I can see white drops of saliva on his black beard. He is tired from his unexpected report. He is breathing heavily: "The reptile lives in a house that used to belong to a German. Near Turgielany. In any case, Musia will show you the way."

From his map case he pulls out a page torn from an exercise book, folded in four: "Here's the death sentence. Take care not to lose it."

The wind has scattered snow into the stove. A handful of sparks mixed with leaves falls to the ground. The little red flames go out one after another. The stove murmurs like a samovar. Only the clink of glasses is missing.

"What are you waiting for?" Korvin asks.

"My respects, Korvin," I say, and suddenly embrace him.

He frees himself from my grasp: "What are you fooling around for?"

"I don't know, Korvin. Maybe because it's Christmas Eve."

"Get going. Come back soon."

Rabbit is already climbing the ladder to open the flap: "We'll wait," he says. "Not a single one of the Apostles must be missing."

"Musia, well, Musia," says Korvin quietly.

Swallow salutes carelessly. Korvin waits for her to come up and then kisses her shamelessly before our eyes. But the girl is already silently climbing the tarry steps of the ladder.

Up above, a sharp and biting wind is blowing. It gathers up the fresh snow and carries it around the wilderness in broad sweeps. Musia pushes her bear-like paw under my arm.

"Walk in my tracks," I say.

"I prefer this way. It's warmer."

"Which of the Apostles are you?"

"Which do you think?"

"Chief, I think you're Mary Magdalene."

"You talk nicely, but why 'chief'?"

"I'm right, surely."

"You're stupid, Oldster."

We walk in silence for a time. I can feel the barren taste of snow on my lips.

"Do you believe in what people call miracles?" she asks.

"Such things don't happen in war time."

"You know, I just can't imagine what it will be like after the war. I never even think about it."

"Do you love him?"

"Whom?"

"Korvin."

"Oh, you're a fool, Oldster. I like him, as I like you. Have to live somehow."

I try to free myself from her hand, which is lost in her huge mitten.

"Did I say anything bad, Oldster? Love can't be born in such filth, under bullets. Do you know lice are already crawling all over me? I sleep with him on the understanding, get me, that it's easier for him. I've put everything off until later. I know what it's going to be like. I've thought it all out."

"I understand, chief."

"Don't talk like that, all right?"

"It also seems to me that this will come to an end some time. And we'll start a new life, such as we've never seen. We've got to hold out. I think everything will turn out well, don't you?"

"Surely."

Wolves are calling. We are walking along beside an unfrozen stream. Abruptly a bird of some kind tears itself from the water and hastily flies away into the trees, flapping its wings. We pause, startled by the presence of a living thing.

"A duck," says Quiet.

"Where would a duck come from at this time of year?"

"They do occur."

"Odd."

Falcon moves ahead: "This is an odd evening altogether. Even animals speak with human voices at midnight."

The snow squeaks monotonously under foot. I can feel the chill of the folded paper, bearing the death sentence, in my pocket. Quiet is rattling his canteen as though he wanted to dispel evil thoughts.

"Korvin usually went on this sort of patrol himself," Musia remarks.

"Does he like it?"

"Of course not. I once saw him throw up."

"You know his background?"

"He doesn't talk about himself. But I know something is devouring him."

Quiet stops abruptly. He listens, sticking his ears out of his frost-covered sheepskin jacket.

"Now what?" I ask.

"Sledges."

"You're imagining things."

"You said that the other time."

"Peasants stealing wood."

"Peasants' horses have bells. But these are moving as quietly as ghosts."

"Can you hear anything, chief?"

"No, nothing."

"Let's go on, then."

We set off. The wilderness becomes thinner. More and more white clearings, with bushes bent under deep snow. The distant howling of wolves accompanies us all the way.

Now Falcon stops and turns his head back toward us. He raises a hand. We hold our breath. Somewhere among the trees, we don't know whether far or near, there resounds the noise of sledge runners, like the tearing of thin cloth. It seems to us that we can hear the muffled talking of the drivers and the measured thump of hoofs with sharp nails breaking icy snow.

"They're carrying Kmicic's lads," says Falcon, in a whisper.

I keep silent. And I don't know whether that weird funeral procession is driving through the wilderness or whether it is the secret life of the forest that constitutes these stammering rustlings in which we are seeking a meaning we shall always carry in our memories.

Then everything grows quiet. We move on.

"Remember your first day with the partisans, chief?" I ask, no longer feeling the warm curve of her hand under my arm.

But Musia, behind me, is struggling with the deep drifts, and doesn't reply. In the stifled rustling of the wilderness I seek the echo of those accursed sledges. I think of that which has already taken on the shape of a fairy tale deeply ingrained in the memory, like a millstone.

You were sitting on a low couch covered with oilcloth. A young nurse, who could scent conspiracy as though it were perfume, was tying up your leg with a bandage soaked in plaster. You were telling the miserable story of your leg for the tenth time at least. That when all of you were carrying a railroad track, the German overseer shouted, displeased with something, so that as a result you all let go fearfully of the steel bar, which fell to the ground, then rebounded from the ties and hit your foot slightly, though even that was enough to break two bones.

What mortified you most was the fragmented way in which you narrated the cause of the accident. You were ashamed to say you'd been frightened by the German's sudden shout, so you lied that he issued a sudden order to drop the weight, and you were a fraction of a second too late in letting go of the big pincers by means of which tracks are lifted.

The nurses nodded their heads understandingly, while the TB patients beyond the glass door, hoarse and coughing, had come to whine for a medical certificate that would protect them from the *Arbeitsamt*.

Your leg hurt very much, it was swollen and discolored from an internal hemorrhage. The nurse tossed it about like a rolling pin, while you hissed and bit your lips.

"Well, it's nothing much," said the sister. "It'll grow back together in three weeks."

Like all young nurses, she had the face of an angel, but it was an angel from the highest sphere of heaven, lofty, above everything. You knew very well that the hearts of these angels only beat when they are attending heroic wounds brought out of the forests. So you watched mournfully, holding back your groans, as the angel wound a terribly cold bandage round your unlucky leg, which itched with throbbing like a sackful of bees.

"Maybe we should make you a walking cast?" she asked.

You groaned with cautious approval. So you obtained an iron saddle bow under your heel and later you waited in a chair for a long time while the plaster hardened.

The nurse was already poking about in little glass cupboards as though she'd forgotten her patient. The TB patients, mostly malingerers, were rattling around in the next room. A raised German voice thundered from a wall daubed with oil paint, and it was altogether a humiliating, enormous gibbering.

You wanted the little minx to humble herself, so you tried blackmail and groaned alarmingly. She turned round and gave you an indifferent glance: "Please don't fuss. People endure far greater suffering nowadays."

You were ashamed, though greater and increasingly vague anger permeated you. And she said: "I can give you a small glass of alcohol. Your leg will hurt less. Do you want some?"

"Yes," you groaned.

She handed you a medicine beaker filled with a scalding liquid. You swallowed it down, struggling a long time with your breathing passages in which the devilish concoction stuck. She watched your struggles.

"Shall I lend you a cane?"

"No. Thank you," you replied, and you felt a still greater influx of rage.

So you got up from the chair and, stretching out your arms like a bird with broken wings, began hopping to the door. You repelled her merciful hands, cool in their studied samaritanism.

The TB patients fell silent, startled by the unexpected sight. Their hoarse and terrifying coughs, dragged up from their viscera, only started again when you tottered out into the sunlit street, filled with a Sunday and holiday crowd.

Hopping on one leg, clutching the fences, you reached the park and sat down heavily on a bench. Beyond the iron fence and rusty acanthus leaves you could see the street with its broad sidewalks, the town's most fashionable promenade. A crowd of strollers was moving down both sides, touching hats to one another ceremoniously, as is usual on early Sunday evenings.

But ever-increasing fury seized you. So you struck vindictively at your leg, large as a snow man, on the bench, and waited for the already warm plaster finally to burst.

Then, among the crowd flowing from the right, you caught sight of the ruddy face of a German officer. He gleamed energetically with eyeglasses, he stretched and strutted, laughed like a stallion: hahaha. Attached to his arms were two German *Schwestern*, bright in black capes. They were gazing at him, engrossed, while he expanded in the crowd, snuffing haughtily and gurgling joyfully like a turkey cock.

Your rage, inflamed by the alcohol, attained its highest point. Now you saw your degradation with the most terrible clarity, a man with that plaster cast on one leg and the abjectness of these passers-by, pushed by an arrogant German. From the way his full and gleaming lips were moving, you could guess the insulting words with which this officer was humiliating your fellow countrymen, and was showing off to his lazaretto hens.

So you experienced a violent and terribly painful humiliation and realized that the bold Occupant must be punished immediately. Without thinking, you jumped up from the bench and tottered into the street. Amidst fiery spots of anger you sought the braggart, who had just passed. So you hurled yourself in pursuit. You limped quite a while, elbowing aside the passers-by before you finally caught up with him and barred his way.

The sight of you confounded him greatly, for he stopped and reached into his pocket, certainly with the intention of finding some coins. But it seemed to you he was reaching for his holster, so you hopped up on one leg and hit him in the face with all your might.

The nurses screamed, one very shrilly, the other moderately. His crystal eyeglasses fell to the sidewalk and rolled under the feet of passers-by. And you caught sight, all around you, of faces congealed in horror, you felt violent terror and without thinking hurled yourself into the dense crowd, then into the park gate.

You ran down a shady path, breathing heavily. The terror gradually quieted down within you, especially as you couldn't hear any sounds of pursuit behind you. At last, quite calm, you slowed down your pace, or properly speaking, your hop, and began to wonder why nobody was chasing you.

You reflected this way and that, considering the matter in extreme detail, until you were all of a sudden seized by the worst possible and unusually painful thought. For you realized your deed had gone unnoticed, had been made light of and perhaps already forgotten. For you realized that the braggart officer, the arrogant Occupant, had not suffered any damage to his honor nor to his physical exterior.

So in a momentary decision you resolved to set the matter right and to seal it. With all the strength of your other leg, you hobbled down an alley parallel to the street, in the direction in which the German should be walking away.

Indeed you soon saw him again. He was already erect and lordly, though a trifle out of countenance, maybe also because he was trying to impress the *Schwestern* with special zeal, while they kept nodding. Fixing his loose eyeglasses on his nose, he was no doubt telling his lady friends that he'd been startled, that he hadn't expected a cripple, that it was Sunday, who'd have thought it? As he did so, he waved his plump hands, as if to demonstrate what he could have done to such an intruder, how he could have humbled him.

So you rushed through an iron gate into the street, and caught up with him again, hearing his victorious and male laughter. Until you barred his way again and saw his horror: popping eyes and bared teeth, as at the sight of a ghost.

You hit him in the face three times with vigor and force, until he started helplessly to protect his face with both hands. The nurses screamed hysterically and seized you under the arms before you noticed.

Howling like old she-wolves, they dragged you down the road towards a gendarme, who was striding without haste in your direction.

Some days later you were brought before the military court of an infantry division. Your fellow-prisoners said goodbye to you with the sign of the Cross, regretting your youth, your unfulfilled years.

For striking an officer off duty, and in accordance with the regulations of the German army, you were sentenced to three weeks in jail.

Through the bars of the improvised stockade you could see the supply depot and enormous numbers of boxcars crammed with people caught in raids, who were being carted away to the death camps.

Late in the fall you emerged to freedom and smashed the plaster on your leg against the first street lamp. For a long time you scratched the stiff, white calf and then set off helplessly in the direction of the suburb from which the road led to your settlement. You still could not understand why your deed had been treated so lightly and without due respect. Even now, when passers-by disappeared hastily into gateways at the sight of German boots, you could proceed on your journey undisturbed, armed with the prison discharge papers, covered with solemn rubber stamps and signatures.

The unachieved deed took on more and more the form of a grotesque anecdote the further it receded in time; it weighed exceedingly on your memory. You wanted to clothe it with a total and serious offense. The audience, consisting of your relatives, friends, and acquaintances, was well disposed toward you.

Early in the winter you set out for Hurricane's unit. You met them in a small farm house, full of old furniture and books. A string of sausage and rusty flitches of bacon were hanging from the ceiling. At the table, in a circle of naphtha lamp-light veiled by an aquamarine little shade, twin sisters were softly singing old songs about Polish manor-houses. The farmer, bronzed by the winds, a goodnatured member of the lesser gentry, was bustling about offering food and drink.

By midnight everyone in turn had come. First, or perhaps not the very first, was a young forest Apollo, elegant in a German airman's fur jacket, with a pilot's cap carelessly unfastened under his chin. He was called "Bold," and was leader of your convoy. Then several peasants arrived, equipped with enough provisions for several months' stay in jail. Then someone from the town came, bringing a fifteen-year-old boy, apparently the only son of a professor's family. The lad sat down at the table and began laboriously writing down pseudonyms that might be considered.

But the elder of the twin sisters, watching him with increasing affection, suddenly stopped singing "A little white manor house stays in my memory" and pinched his cheek: "There, you dumpling," she said, "I could kiss you to death."

Thereupon everyone seized spontaneously on that pseudonym: "Dumpling! Dumpling! Let's call him Dumpling."

The lad pushed the girl's hand away, protesting with tears in his eyes. It wasn't for this that he'd battled six months with his parents, not for this that he had gone without food, not for this that he had begged for permission, to lose everything with this horrible pseudonym. He had dreamed of something loftier, more somber. But now — Dumpling!

"Take your ear-flaps off, Dumpling," said Bold. "You'll catch cold."

But the boy snatched off not only his ear-flaps, but also his gloves, handkerchief, scarf, and took some note-pads out of his pocket, hurling them all into a corner: "You'll see what Dumpling can do! You'll get to know Dumpling!" he shouted, red with fury.

This touched everyone. The farmer sniggered silently, so that his belt wobbled on his belly like a narrow horse collar.

Then Bold rose from the table and spent a long time fastening his equipment. The sisters couldn't take their eyes off him. The red glow of the stove poured in from the kitchen. Crooked shadows shuffled aimlessly about on the whitewashed walls. Anticipating the moment of separation, the sisters struck a more mournful note.

"Don't go by way of Turgielany," said the farmer, "a German unit is stationed there."

"Many of them?" asked Bold.

"Around five."

Your leader made a contemptuous gesture. Then he eyed you all attentively: "There's still a pistol left with five bullets," he said, solemnly.

"For me, they promised me in town," Dumpling leaped up.

Bold pointed a finger at you: "You, you," he said, when you hesitated, "I hear you're valiant. You slapped a German officer's face. So it's yours.

And he handed you a rust-eaten pistol, naked, without a holster.

Then there was a wide plain of mud, whitened slightly by frost. You all set off toward the stars of the Big Dipper, which was suspended over the horizon. Dogs barked in the darkened hamlets, you could even hear a harmonica cackling somewhere in the distance. There was a smell of smoke and Shrovetide.

Dumpling toddled along hurriedly to keep up with your pace. Finally he caught up with you on a causeway bristling with willow roots, and grabbed you by the sleeve: "Do you have the pistol?" he asked.

"Uh-huh," you muttered.

"Do you want us to be friends?"

You laughed, but he squeezed your elbow: "I'm going to stick by you."

Then you both walked a long time, side by side: "You know, I'm never going to agree to people calling me that. I must have a true pseudonym."

"Well, think up something better."

"I must earn it. You'll see."

A livid glare was swaying over the horizon. Then a pair of blue headlights emerged. You pressed your bodies to the icy mud as a truck rolled along the road close by. This first taking cover from the enemy made you true soldiers.

"Once we've got guns, a truck like that won't pass by unpunished," said Dumpling quietly, and he shivered as though from the cold. "You'll see."

All of you walked on for a long time until at last, out of the depths of heavy sleepiness, alien singing emerged, cut as though with a knife. Bold stopped and you too. He shone his flashlight at the map. He cleared his throat uncertainly: "Turgielany. The Germans aren't sleeping. They're celebrating, that's for sure."

We kept silent.

"To go around would add another six miles."

"We can scoot through the village. Nobody will notice us," said Dumpling.

The lads were silent.

"That's so. I've already bruised my foot," said the man from town who had brought the boy.

"Well, all right, let's try," Bold decided, and he cocked his rifle.

All of you moved off on tiptoe and penetrated between the first buildings.

"Got the revolver?" Dumpling whispered.

"Yes."

"I'll be close to you, remember."

You cocked it. The handle rapidly grew wet in your convulsively clenched palm. You could hear your own heart beat.

"*Halt! Wer da?*" a sudden shout froze you.

Then everything proceeded chaotically. A round of shots flashed, which you did not hear, shocked by an unknown feeling. You jumped violently to one side, smashing the poles of a fence, you ran across someone's premises filled with escaping dogs, you rushed between sparse trees lit up by another round of shots fired to greet you. So you fell to the frosty earth and watched drunken Germans walking between the trees, calling out pitifully. Someone fired in your direction, it was Bold for sure, and in a sort of hypnotic state you leaped unarmed several yards ahead, against the Germans.

It looked as though you had already got mixed up with the enemy. Your heart was thumping so strongly that you thought it would strike against the stony earth through your thin ribs, resounding like a railroad cistern.

Then, all at once, with the remains of your consciousness or, properly speaking, with the last scrap of your self-esteem, you remembered the revolver. You pulled the holster in front of you in your clenched palm and intently sought a suitable target. Several yards away, a little to the front and to one side, you saw a figure pressed against a tree trunk. You aimed at this fading shape and pulled the trigger twice. The first thing you remembered was the fact that your shots were not heard. The second was that the figure of your enemy detached itself from the trunk and sank very slowly onto the frost, like a coat falling off a hanger.

Later you heard Bold's terrifying cry: "Follow me! That way!"

And you ran to the right, pursued by rays of luminous bullets that streaked low across the ground like crazy glowworms. You rushed through a frozen meadow, full of puddles laced with ice which splashed as though they were window panes.

In the morning, when you were all asleep in your quarters, First Lieutenant Hurricane, the commandant, arrived. He took off his field jacket, sat down by the window and looked at you as you lay in a row in the straw. You all got up like civilians, clumsily, yawning, and he smiled, measuring you up and down, as future soldiers.

"All in order, Bold?"

"Yes, sir."

"All have arrived?"

"All, Lieutenant."

You were all standing in front of him, in your town raincoats, struggling against persistent sleepiness.

"One of us isn't here," said that man from town, timidly.

"Who?" asked Bold.

"Dumpling."

"How's that? Why not?"

"Well, he's not here."

"Maybe he's sleeping somewhere else?"

"He wasn't with us when we came here to the quarters."

A sudden silence fell.

"Who was last to see him?"

All kept silent. Then you exclaimed: "I was. In Turgielany."

"And then?"

Hurricane rose and came up to us.

"Then we didn't see him again," said one of the boys.

"He's the professor's son, isn't he?" asked Hurricane.

"Yes, sir. He was with him," and Bold pointed at you.

"You didn't see him again after Turgielany?"

"No, sir," you replied, quietly.

Hurricane was silent a moment: "We'll wait till evening. Maybe he got lost during the shooting."

But Dumpling still hadn't come back by midnight, when you fell into a shallow and fearful sleep, permeated with dull coldness. All night long, round and round, you dreamed of that frantic first skirmish. In ceaseless repetition you saw those two little flames emerging from the muzzle of your revolver, and the rag, which had been a man a moment before, sinking to the ground.

Then at dawn you woke up chilled to the marrow, although everyone around you was lying undressed, with their covers tossed off. You got up, strapped on someone else's belt, under which you tucked a revolver with three bullets.

Later, you entered the next room, where a company of old veterans was sleeping. Creeping over the men as they slept, you searched all their haversacks, taking from them three rugged, coarsely made hand grenades.

You went out in front of the hut. Hens were pecking at horse manure. Thin smoke seeped from the chimneys and crept lazily between the houses, becoming shallow clouds in the gardens. A sentry looked at you doubtfully: "Where are you going?" he asked, as you set off along the road back.

You didn't reply.

"Stop! Stop! Where are you going?"

And he eased the catch of his rifle. But you didn't look back. You were walking with your head bowed, as though searching for something in the fine snow.

"Stop, or I'll fire!" the sentry shouted, helplessly.

But then he fell silent and gazed blankly after you. You were trudging along steadily, and you knew very well that nothing would stop you from doing what you had planned. You passed some hamlets, crooked crosses by the wayside, and little cemeteries covered with frost, the basic element of country landscapes.

Finally you entered Turgielany. People stopped, straightened up over unfinished labor, watching you in fear and amazement. By your step and the revolver stuck under your belt, they guessed your nationality. But you marched down the center of the street like the leader of a patrol coming back to safe quarters.

So the peasants glanced at one another significantly and smiled indulgently, surprised by their own mistake. Now they were certain you were a policeman, staying at the German post.

But a moment later they turned toward you again, troubled by strange doubts. It seemed to you that the village had suddenly fallen silent, and that you were walking alone in a mute hedge of human eyes.

You penetrated between those well-remembered trees, and found that particular tree from your dream without any difficulty. Under it, a stain of blood smouldered with frozen redness in the thin snow. A thick rosary of drops ran toward the guardhouse, barricaded by log walls between which were placed sand sacks that had turned into stone.

You set off along the track of blood, expecting with painful tension that the line of red drops would suddenly stop, giving you hope. But the line thickened, became ever more monstrous. It looked as though someone had been swinging a bucket of blood, more and more impatiently.

Then you saw the entry into the German fort and a sentry with snow on his helmet, gazing longingly at a new sauna nearby. Succulent clouds of smoke and steam were pouring from its empty attic. Inside could be heard the shouts of Germans and the crack of birch twigs, with which the bathers were flogging themselves.

You stopped in front of that steam bath and listened eagerly to these cries of frolicking, pleasure, the victorious awareness of existence. You stared intently at the blank triangle of attic under the straw roof, and you knew very well there was no ceiling inside.

The sentry took off his helmet and woolen skullcap. He scratched impatiently at his tousled head. You clearly saw that he couldn't wait for his turn.

And when the yelling of the men, crazy with drunkenness, mounted to one great shout of liberation, you reached into your pocket and pulled out the grenades. Carefully, like a scrupulous salesman, you tied them with string as if they were so many beets in a bundle, and with your teeth you pulled the safety pin out of the one that had dark-green glaze covering.

And then the sentry caught sight of you and in a flash realized what you were aiming to do. He shouted out hysterically, as though he wanted to warn you of some misfortune, threw his helmet and skullcap on the ground and began struggling with the frozen catch of his rifle. But before he could raise the weapon to his eye, you carried through your calm, measured attack and hurled the grenades into the open triangle of the attic. Then you and the sentry both waited a long while, staring with all your might at the tarry walls of the bath house.

Finally the roof split into two, emitting skyrockets of sparks and fleshy steam. Then the heated stones of the bath exploded and the door fell out into the snow and a naked man clutching his red belly tottered over it. Next another leaped out, and collapsed immediately in the snow, vomiting blood. After them crept a third, clutching a ripped artery with one hand. Only now did you notice they were shouting, but it was not exactly shouting. The naked men howled as they set off at a run, but the white snow held them to the ground like glue, and they rolled unrestrainedly in the cold snow, and glaring blood stains corroded the surface voraciously.

"Did you ever hear, Oldster," says Swallow, "of a miracle happening during a war? During a war only baffling and confusing earthy things happen. And what happened to him?"

"Who?"

"Well, that boy."

"I was telling you. Afterwards a legend grew up around him. I heard later that he wasn't a boy at all, but a girl in disguise. And that his father, the professor, went round the villages until the end of the Occupation, looking for his child."

"What do you think, Oldster — will anything be left of us?"

"Someone will surely survive and will write down lies, which means the truth as he'd like to find it in the memories of his youth."

"What will you do after the war?"

"I don't know. But I don't want to live just any old way."

"Nor I. After all, we've already seen everything it's possible to see in this world. Just have to make a choice."

It is getting darker. The snow becomes grayer. The barking of dogs can be heard. Quiet groans at every step. He always does, for he believes that this groaning breathing eases effort.

"There won't be any stars tonight," says Falcon.

Quiet sniffs the frosty air: "It smells of Christmas Eve celebrations, of food and sprats. It's time already. Soon they'll be sitting down to table."

"How many days do they celebrate where you come from?" asks Falcon.

Quiet reflects, listening to the creak of snow underfoot: "Depends who you are. Poor farmers four, at most five days. But the rich go on celebrating up to two weeks. They stop only after Twelfth Night."

"All we have left of it is the fasting."

"I'd take that kind of fasting: hot potatoes, steamed lentil soup with gray salt and bread kvass. Do you know how good that is?"

Falcon doesn't, but he sighs with approval. The wilderness is behind us now. We are accompanied only by sparse thickets and an azure row of alders. Somewhere in the darkness the distant light of a crooked window blinks from time to time.

"It's as though we were carol singers!" Musia exclaims.

"Some carol singers!" I say, and feel in my pocket for the paper Korvin gave me.

"It's deserted. No one on the road."

"Who'd go out of doors on this evening? Almost a sin."

"If you wish for something today, it will come to pass in the coming year."

"I'm wishing," I say.

Again she pushes her hand under my arm. I can see the thick puffs of her breath in front of me.

"And what did you wish?"

"Don't be inquisitive, chief."

"You don't have to embarrass me, Oldster."

"Is it far?"

"Is what far?"

"Well, you know."

"We have to get to the railroad. Then about a mile along the tracks . . . I'd like to be the most beautiful girl, the richest, the most likeable. For everyone to love me. But that won't ever come true, Oldster."

"You're still very young, chief."

"I'm simply a woman."

"I know that, chief."

"How can you know, you puppy?"

She stops abruptly. I stop too, holding her hand, which she didn't have time to remove from under my arm. We stand like this, cut off by the thick walls of our sheepskins. I can feel warmth filled with desire mounting inside me. Behind the dense steam that pours from our mouths I can see her blinking in a teasing manner, her eyelashes covered with hoar frost.

"You're a virgin, I know that, a woman perceives anything like that right away."

She leans her sheepskin jacket, heavy with her breasts, against my cloak: "Well, what did you wish, you puppy?"

"That I'd like to be the wisest and best of men, and that all women would love me."

She gazes at me a long time, then covers her eyes with her white lashes: "I'd like to meet you, some time after the war."

"And I'd like to meet you, too."

"That's only your manner of speaking, Oldster."

We press each other clumsily, lost in our stiff, frozen clothing: "Really, it's true. I meant it," I whisper.

She remains silent. And all of a sudden it seems to me that something dark, like a ladybug, is creeping down her frost-parched cheek: "Swallow, what's happening?" I ask quietly, taken aback by this turn of events.

"Nothing. This is a stupid evening."

"Musia, I honestly . . . "

"All right. Don't say any more."

She extricates her hand from mine and secretly wipes her cheek with one sleeve, as though to wipe away a snowflake: "I myself don't know what came over me," she smiles, screening her face with one hand. "It's all silly. Why are we standing here?"

We want to move on, but Falcon stops us. He and Quiet are listening, their coat collars open.

"What now?" I ask.

"We can hear the sledges. They're carting Kmicic's lads."

Crouching, we stare a long time into the darkness. Quiet cocks his automatic rifle. Something not unlike a groan muffled by distance emerges from the heavy silence.

"They're singing a carol somewhere," says Musia. "There's a village not far away."

And she wants to move on. But I stop her with the muzzle of my automatic rifle: "No, wait. That's surely telephone wires resounding, to mark a change in the weather."

Musia looks round and says: "You're right. We've reached the railroad."

We walk down from the road: we take a shortcut, drowning in snow, and push on toward the railroad cutting.

"But I tell you I distinctly heard sledges! This is the third day they're carting them. Even on a night like this," exclaims Falcon.

"They know we can hear them," Quiet shudders unexpectedly.

The two black lines of track run into the darkness. We walk through their monotonous, dull ringing as though through a chasm full of crickets.

I go ahead of them: "Attention. Prepare for action."

I can hear them cock their automatic rifles. I know they're blowing on their rifle butts, covering the catches with their warm sleeves to thaw them.

We are walking faster and faster, because I am involuntarily increasing my pace. Sometimes a heel clangs on a rail that is taut with frost. Slowly a bluish flame, burning as feebly as a rotten stump, grows lighter in front of us.

I turn around. Swallow is pattering along quickly on her little feet in the rear of the patrol. She slips on the iced-up ties.

"Here?" I ask.

"Yes. The door opens from the field," she says rapidly.

Finally we see this house in front of us. Large, brick, solidly built by the Germans for the sentries who guard the railroad. Overturned rolls of barbed wire stick up out of the snow, there is a cement bunker to the left of the well.

"Go up to the windows," I give the order to Quiet and Falcon.

I wait for them to disappear round the corners of the house. Then I go up to the dark door, climbing the two stone steps that are sprinkled with sand. The conduits are humming as though under pressure from the tidings people send one another on this night.

I try the door handle. Locked. So I strike my hand on the solid oak planks, but my mitten muffles the sound. Behind me I can hear the rapid breathing of Swallow.

I strike with my rifle butt. Inside, the door to the hallway rattles. It seems to me that the slight warmth of the house, smelling of heated tiles, is enveloping me.

"Who is it?" asks a hoarse, male voice.

"Us. Friends," I reply, as calmly as possible.

"Who's 'us'?"

"Friends. Carol singers."

Inside there is silence.

"Please open the door, please don't be afraid."

"Isn't it too early for carol singers?"

I change my tone: "Open, or we'll break down the door."

The man inside reflects a long time.

"We want to talk to you. Open the door."

I hear a thin voice, surely that of a child.

The man opens the door.

"Hands up!"

Slowly he raises his hands, which are surrounded by curly steam as though in a bath house. I push him with the barrel, and he retreats, and thus we enter a large room in which there is not much furniture. A little tree without any chains, angels, balls or candles, sprinkled only with lumps of wadding, stands on a worn chair. I see a dark-haired little girl by this tree, reaching up on tiptoe and holding a skein of wadding. She looks at us with interest, in which there lurks the pleasure of an unexpected Christmas Eve adventure.

Now I look at the man. Between the sleeves of his country jersey I see a swarthy face, a mop of black hair, protruding lips, which look swollen. Involuntarily I lower my automatic and press it against my cape, as though to cover my heart, which has begun to thump violently.

After a long moment of silence, the man asks: "Can I lower my hands?"

I am mouthing thick saliva, and cannot manage to answer.

So he lowers his hands. I search in his eyes for a sign that he remembers, for the spark that would remove all doubts. But hunched as formerly, he is gazing at me with taut attention, with blank fear, and only now do I realize that I haven't shaved, am wearing odd clothes, have grown older since that time.

"Is there anyone else in the house?" I ask, in a deliberately low voice, and I gaze at him with fear in my eyes. He is afraid of my soot-camouflaged automatic, and I am afraid he will recognize me.

"No, I'm alone," and he glances toward the tree where the little girl is standing with wadding in her hands.

I long to ask about that woman I know, whom I have in mind forever, who unwittingly revealed the first nakedness of woman to me. But I prevent myself in time; I still hope not to be recognized.

Ice is flowing like knotty roots from the window panes to the sills. Wadding, adorned with straw flowers, lies between the double windows. A stove is roaring, somewhere out of sight. The Christmas tree smells of church. I don't know what I must do, so I wait until a drop of melted snow trickles down my cheek and moistens my parched lips.

"Well, what happened, Oldster?" asks Swallow.

I take several steps into the center of the room, concealing the man from Musia.

"Oh God," I suddenly hear her voice.

I turn. She is standing in front of the stranger and staring at him with wide open eyes: "Oh God. Can it be?" she repeats.

The man smiles almost imperceptibly, with his lips only. Then he smooths his hair down, as though afraid that the untidiness of his appearance will surprise this girl, wrapped up in her snow-covered sheepskin jacket.

I knock the ice off my boots: "Take the child out," I say.

Musia is still staring at the man: "No. I'm staying here."

"D'you hear? Take the child out."

"No. Let me stay."

Rage seizes me. I go across and push her by force into the hall-way. Then I go back. He's standing in the same place, rubbing his elbow, which evidently went numb when he had his hands up.

I open the door to the next room, which is in darkness: "Go along," I say to the child.

The little girl holding the wadding goes out obediently, but doesn't shut the door entirely. I want to slam it, but she wedges herself in the crack and resists. I struggle clumsily for a moment.

"I'm afraid of the dark," she says.

"Shut the door for a moment," the man cries. "This gentleman is leaving right away."

"Let there be a little crack, a little tiny crack."

"Shut it only for a moment. Then I'll call and you can open it."

"But I'm afraid."

I can see the child's clenched, white fingers on the edge of the door, and feel an increasing throbbing in my temples.

"Shut it this minute, d'you hear me, you shit ass!" the man shouts.

Her fingers open slowly and disappear, then the door closes quietly, without creaking.

A window pane quivers. It's Falcon or Quiet tapping impatiently. We both look at that window, rich as tapestry, then our eyes abruptly meet.

I see his entire forehead is covered with copious sweat. His swarthy, lean cheeks are trembling with sudden twitching. It seems to me his shoulders are undergoing some kind of strange and uncoordinated vibration.

"Can I open the door now?" we suddenly hear the uncertain voice of the little girl. She is standing in the half-open door, still clutching the wadding.

"Close it, you bitch!" he yells in a hoarse voice.

The little girl disappears. I begin groping with shaky fingers in the pocket where the death sentence is. I run my fingers over the cold and slippery interior, but can't find the paper I touched so often on the way here.

Something bad is happening to the man. He has turned his face toward me, he opens his mouth as if to catch his breath, and from this uncoordinated movement of his lips I recall a phrase from somewhere: "It's hard to be an alien among your own people."

His hands begin to twitch as though he were patting his loins, his eyes go out of line and he gives the impression he is staring at something on my chest. So I instinctively reach there and find the automatic, steaming from cold.

Then he suddenly falls over on his back, striking his head with full force on the floor. I run over to him and see the whites of his eyes turned up, and can hear an odd gurgle emerging from his mouth, on which I notice a drop of blood.

The window panes resound from the banging of Falcon and Quiet.

"You must kill him. You must kill him," I stammer to myself. "That's the order you got."

I hear the door creak behind me. So in desperation I raise the automatic and search for the catch with one finger. I find the catch regulating the fire, and without thinking shift it from "burst" to "single" shot.

Then I shift the foresight to the right side of his chest and pull the trigger. Almost at the same moment as the noise of the shot I leap out to the hallway. Here I collide with Musia, who grabs me desperately with both hands. I tear myself away and roll down the steps into deep snow. I pick myself up, drenched in burning snow up to my elbows and run wildly toward the railroad tracks.

Later I take huge strides along the track, and the frosty wind strikes me, taking my breath away. Behind me the limping footsteps of my patrol keep drumming.

We thus flee in silence for a long time, as though chased by numerous pursuers, until we finally emerge on the road which leads to the wilderness.

"Wait for me, by God, I can't go any faster, I'll croak," Quiet cries, behind us.

"He's right, no one is chasing us, after all," says Falcon.

We slow down a little, listening to our own choking breaths.

"You've lost your cap," cries Musia.

I feel my head.

"It doesn't matter."

"Maybe we'll go back?" Falcon suggests.

"No need. What for? I have another in the dugout," and I increase my pace.

We're running again, and it seems to me I can hear a far-off carol.

"Why did you cry out 'Oh God!'?" I ask in a broken voice.

For a long time Musia can't catch her breath: "Don't you understand anything?" she answers with a question.

Now I'm sorry I spoke. I increase my pace still more.

"Did you have a good look at him?" Musia asks again.

I am running, slipping in sleigh ruts. I press my head down into my wet collar. I don't want to hear Musia.

"Stop, wait for me, you devils!" Quiet calls, from the rear.

And when I slow down, he catches up with me and asks: "Why didn't you fire a burst?"

"It jammed," I say, hastily. "It jammed after the second shot."

"But you only fired once."

"He got it. I saw it myself." And again sudden rage seizes me: "What's it to you, you shit? I had to carry out the sentence, and I carried it out."

Quiet falls silent, shocked by my violence.

Again I increase my pace, I am almost running, and they limp after me without murmuring. I am seized by a terrible coldness as well as by sweat. So I stick my hands in my pockets and then, immediately, in the very first instant, I find the paper, no longer necessary.

"We're not bringing anything back from patrol this time either," groans Quiet behind me.

"Oldster, Oldster," whispers Musia, "where are you rushing to at this rate?"

I know she wants to catch up to me and fasten to my arm.

"Oldster, after all, nothing happened. We killed a reptile," she tries to deceive both herself and me.

I crumple the paper in my pocket into a little ball and later drop it, unnoticed, in the snow. I know it will drown in this fluff, the rain will wash away everything written on it before the grass breaks through and the trees turn green. I know that this white, soaked leaf will be carried away by some bird to make a nest of it.

"But it's hot!" exclaimed Joseph Car after a long silence. "An unusual year. Do you know the Apocalypse?"

He took a handkerchief out of his pocket and wiped his brow carefully, watching me out of the corner of his eye.

"I read it during the war. I don't remember anything of it today. Do you believe in prophecy?"

Sleepy flies hit against the naked light bulb that has a little enamel saucer over it.

"Do I believe?" he repeated my question. "I believe in everything that is beyond the literalness of our life."

The clarinet resounded again beyond the river. The unknown musician monotonously continued that same roughly composed tune.

"And that's why you came to me," he remarked. "They all seek the same thing from me."

In his face I read unforgotten reactions, fleeting grimaces, well-known wrinkles. However he was gazing at the floor, and a dense shadow concealed his face.

"I'm neither a quack doctor nor the founder of a religious sect. I haven't laid down any liturgical or moral rules. My religion is hope, which can be found in all beliefs, or even outside of an institutional dogma. You see, I've lived through a great deal; in the end I reached understanding. I came to understand that the lack of fulfillment which accompanies us all the time can and must be appeased in our lives."

He picked up a small ash-wood ruler and began playing with it. I noticed the horseshoe-shaped marks of someone's teeth on the mottled wood and thought that a dog must have surely been biting it like a bone.

"You'll probably say I haven't brought up anything new. I agree, and I could disavow my program, or rather my lack of program, even more strictly. You should know that in my time I was a specialist in atheistic literature. I possess wide knowledge in this field and above all a frightening self-knowledge. Yet I decided on this procedure, and it is a yardstick of my liberation, my freedom amidst people."

He tapped the ruler on his sweaty palm and all at once looked into my eyes: "Why did you lay violent hands on yourself?"

I rose from the stool and went over to the window: "Let's not gossip. I've come to you with something else in mind."

"Do you want to join us? It's the simplest thing imaginable. We pray every day by the Sola, but without prayers, in words supplied by the moment and the mood. The only permanent formula is our song, which has grown from day to day, composed by no one knows who. Please come this evening. Your presence will be a christening and a priestly consecration all in one. It is very simple. And in this there's no trickery that a sceptical mind might want to track down. You'll be a co-creator and servant of this new faith, a religion of the most democratic kind."

Outside the window, through the tangle of vine, I could see the path and the hill, but she was no longer sitting there. All that remained was a faded flower, which the hot wind was rolling across the dry ground.

"Before eternity catches up with me I'd like to come to terms with the things of this world," I said.

He rose from the couch: "I appreciate your irony. I too have calculated my risks."

I turned my back to the window.

"Are you looking for Justine? She's gone to Podjelniaki."

I kept silent.

"You are looking for Justine, aren't you?" he repeated.

"After all, you know why I've come here," I said, quietly.

"Indeed, a most dramatic tale. If true."

"Absolutely. You know it very well."

He smiled with his lips alone: "You're fond of Justine, aren't you?"

I licked salty sweat from my parched lips.

"Please don't deny it. I know everything. She's told me of your meetings."

"I don't understand."

"She's a depraved girl. Or rather, a fatal woman, eh? A woman-child. Well said?"

I wanted to grab him by his dry throat, marked by the outlines of veins. He caught sight of my hatred and smiled with his pro-truding lips, on which tiny drops of clotted saliva showed.

"A grown man, whose life has been eroded by superior notions, and an enigmatic girl."

Suddenly I regretted my sincerity and the effort put into this unsatisfactory meeting. He tapped the ruler more rapidly against his palm, which glistened with sweat: "I'm talking about you. No-body else. Secrets fascinate you. You're a secret devourer of tasty bits, an ugly scoundrel."

I took several paces toward him. He shielded himself with the ruler, held in both hands on a level with his chest.

"You know what I'm getting at," I said, with difficulty.

He smiled crookedly. I noticed that his left cheek had started twitching rapidly. His eyes widened, the yellowish whites gleam-ing.

"You want me to tell you that I'm the man whom you've been encountering continually all your life?"

"Yes, that's what I want."

"Very well, then. I'll show you the mark of your bullet," he put one hand into the opening of his shirt over his chest. "I'll tell you how I lay wounded on the floor, listening to the child crying. How passers-by mistook my calls for the shouts of a reveler at the holi-day table, how those men who were carting the frozen bodies of the partisans of Kmicic drove past my house. How I traveled to the county hall amidst frozen corpses, licking snow from their hands, for I was suffering from a fever that was haunted by spec-ters and ghosts. I'll remind you of all our meetings, when I saw in your eyes that you were being bated to death as I was, when I had a presentiment that fate would join us together and you would search for me to the end of your life, just as I search for my own purification."

"You used to be different."

"I was and always am with the weaker."

I listened to myself, surprised not to feel any relief. It seemed to me as though we had exhausted all the oxygen in this dusk-filled room and were in danger of suffocation.

"What more do you want of me?" he asked, with difficulty.

"I don't know. Nothing now, I suppose. Although I had pic-tured this moment quite differently."

Outside the window, the voice of the clarinet wandered on,

mingled with the murmuring of the river. The long ribbon of sunlight had already crept from the hallway door and begun climbing the blackened fir planks of the door.

"I've been searching for you and him for years. First in my memory, then in people's tales and the columns of newspapers. Every name seemed to be yours. Then I began looking for you in little townships like ours, which we've all left forever. What I've lived through up to now is like a handful of stones brought up from the riverbed. Now I shall forever be fitting them into ever new configurations and search for the meaning behind all this."

Someone's feet pattered for a moment somewhere behind the wall. We both looked out of the window. A shimmering heat that smelled of burning oozed through the twirls of the vine. Then we waited for the door to open and for her to appear on the threshold. This waiting lasted a very long time. His forehead, under his black, curly mop of hair, became covered with dense sweat. Since nothing happened, I approached him and put out my hand. "Thank you," I said and then at once words failed me. But he didn't give me his hand. "Thank you," I repeated.

"What are you thanking me for?"

"I very badly wanted to meet you."

He put his hand onto his cheek, which was twitching convulsively.

"Look," he said, hoarsely, "I could lie to you and leave the matter as it stands. But after all, you don't need easy consolation, do you?"

I was silent, trying to part my unyielding lips. My heart began beating rapidly and irregularly.

"I'm not the man you're looking for. Because I can see your fear and your helplessness, I could easily assure you that I've taken part in your life. But I think it would be better if you really found what it is you need. So go on your way; maybe you're already close."

"You're lying!" I shouted.

He suddenly clenched his teeth, as though holding back great pain: "In every man you'll see those you did an injustice to. Every face will seem familiar to you, in every face you'll find the traces of the suffering you caused. You know what drives you from one place to another. Do I have to tell you?"

I grabbed his chest abruptly by the shirt, but he hurled himself back with unbelievable strength and stood for a moment swaying, his teeth strangely bared. He struck convulsively at his creased trousers with the hand that held the ruler, as though wanting to beat dust off them. Then he stammered something and hurled his whole body with a sort of angular movement at the door leading into the next room. The door shook a moment, then returned to its frame.

I sat down on the stool and looked at the window, waiting for her to come back. From there I could see the slope of the meadow, the insurrectionists' grave-mound and the blue, thin smoke over the smouldering peat bog.

From the next room, in which he had hidden himself, I could hear something like a jabbering conversation and stifled banging, as though someone was lazily threshing pea stalks and pods.

I waited like this a very long time. I should have left, but something made me sit it out and bring the matter to an end. So I started examining the frugal contents of the room, searching for some traces that would confirm my suppositions.

"Maybe he's right?" I asked myself in an undertone. "Maybe it's not important whether they're among the living, or went away long ago."

So I began once again reflecting on the past and his present-day behavior. I felt frustrated and cheated. My rage against him grew all the greater.

The sun's reflection had already crept to the wall above the door. Only now did I catch sight in the window of the vibrating skein of the red sun. But still he didn't come back. When at last I thought he'd long left the house and there wasn't any point in waiting any longer, the door suddenly creaked.

I looked up with a start. He came in unsteadily, as though after a long sickness and gazed at me in astonishment: "Oh, it's you. Good evening."

"Good evening," I said, taken aback.

He sat down on the couch with a groan and put aside the ruler, blackened in several places. "Terribly hot today," he said in a tired voice.

It seemed to me that a sudden redness was glimmering in his mouth. I thought to myself that it was probably the reflection of the setting sun on his face.

"Have you walked by the river?" he asked.

He gazed at me with the tired look of a man who has come back from a long journey.

"Yes, I've been down to the Sola."

"More and more people and machines."

The sound of the clarinet penetrated the room, it started to reverberate softly on some glass utensil or other.

"I feel bad," he said, with a sigh. "Drop by sometimes. Justine and I will be very happy. She likes you."

I rose all at once. He gazed absently at my clenched fists and yawned. Then in sudden alarm, I saw his mouth was full of congealed blood.

I don't know why, but I thought it better not to ask any questions. He fell on his back on the couch and stared at me dully from between half-closed eyelids: "You mentioned leaving," he said, quietly.

"Did I? I don't recall."

"Maybe it just seemed so to me."

A mosquito emerged from a dark corner and resounded intrusively over my head.

"Please come to us by the river. We pray there every day."

I wiped my face with my shirt-sleeve. The mosquito was buzzing right into my ear.

"Too bad you're leaving," he said in a whisper. Then he added, "But maybe it's for the better."

I wanted to seize him by the arms, lift him and shout into his face that I would never leave, that I would stay, that I would entangle myself still more in the affairs of this valley. But he yawned again, not embarrassed by my presence, and again I saw his wide open mouth full of blood.

I left without saying goodbye.

Everything was dried up, deprived of water. Only by the monastery some sparse rectangles of winter wheat were glowing. And it seemed that a light chill was drawing from there, from this shrill greenery, which shyly permeated my damp shoulders.

The demijohn was standing in my window, wrapped in yellowed gauze. In the brown fluid in this demijohn floated the Japanese mushroom, a cure for all sicknesses. The eyes of old women and bewhiskered men watched me attentively from their faded portraits in my room. My room smelled of immortelles, from which palms had been made, a souvenir of olden days.

I knew this room of mine through and through. I'd pondered over its details many times. I also knew that somebody's papers, the account of someone else's life, were lying in the chest of drawers.

So I pulled out the drawer, notched by plunderers, full of the smell of woodworms and once more looked through these documents and the bland, commonplace features of the man in the photo.

I felt certain I'd seen that face not long ago, aged and altered by another way of life. It looked at me, at the local people, at our house, with the same dogged mouth.

"He's right," I said, ashamed of myself. "I look for meanings everywhere. Every face I see grows over with the thicket of memory. I shall never extricate myself from it. He's right."

My shadow was very long. It moved across the face of the mole-hills like the enormous hand of a clock. I almost felt I could feel its weight.

I went into the garden, which was bare of leaves. A ruddy light lay on the white cherry tree. I stopped at the edge of a flower bed overgrown with wormwood. I looked around cautiously. She wasn't here.

So I entered the porch overgrown with foliage, between wooden columns cracked wretchedly down their entire length. I removed the familiar plank that closed off the entrance.

Inside, I caught sight of several panels of thick light dividing the large room into oblong sections. The light entered here through cracks in the windows boarded up with planks. I remembered this sight.

The blackened straw, on which I'd lain with her, rustled under my feet.

"Justine," I called, in an undertone.

Nobody replied. I went into the first section, framed with light.

"Justine," I repeated.

Then I entered the second section formed by the beams of the setting sun.

"Justine, I've come."

I cut through the next sections and found myself on the threshold of another room. Here lay the demolished tiles of a stove; it was as gloomy as an aquarium.

"Answer me," I said.

Distant singing started up somewhere outside the thick walls of the house.

"She's not here," I said, astonished.

In my left hand I was holding a bit of spider web, which I had torn off on the way here. I raised my palm to my eyes. A large spider marked with a white cross hastily let itself down on a long thread, but I'd forgotten whether this was a good or bad omen.

A little later I found myself in the orchard, looking at the crooked roofs of the quiet township. The loud pealing of the vesper bell reached out to me from that direction. The monks were reminding us of the night which was soon to arrive from beyond the Solec forest.

I walked in the direction of the river. Already from the distance, from the top of the slight hill where the sun-scorched meadows began, I could see a group of people praying on the bank of the Sola. Joseph Car was kneeling among them.

> *We're going to God, we keep going to God,*
> *Through sorrow, despair, and doubt.*
> *And ever longer my wearisome way,*
> *And ever heavier my conscience."*

They were all there. The Korsaks and the partisan, Romus, and Count Pac. For the first time the railroad man was down on one knee among the people; he no longer avoided them but had become a part of the collective. The undecided sergeant, Glowko, was standing amidst the worn ruts of the unfinished road and gazing with neither reproach nor with approval at his wife who, with the children, was praying most fervently. Only Regina, the passionate and independent Regina, was not there. She had gone off into the world to seek a better destiny.

Workmen had gathered on the other bank of the river. They were watching the people praying and comments, which were brief but juicy in their hostility. The clarinet yet again returned with monotonous persistence to that dull and laboriously overworked tune. I thought I could see the outline of the seated figure of the player in the brownish shadow of a plank shed.

One of the workmen threw a stone into the river by our bank. A splash of water, gleaming like a rainbow, fell on the congregation. They ignored this aggressive act, merely raising voices full of hostile sublimity.

"Hey, Baptists! Who're you praying to?" the workmen shouted.

"They're praying to that black man!" shouted someone from the hut.

"He's their Christ."

Another stone flew across the river and fell down near Pac. Bits of moss, spiky chestnuts and wood cuttings scattered. One of the projectiles hit Romus in the back. The boy staggered, fell on his hands, and then began to rise slowly from the ground. All at once he froze in this sleepy movement, with his face raised to the sky: "Look, all of you!"

Everybody turned their heads in that direction.

"Look! There, over the forest!"

And unthinkingly they rose from the meadow, staring at the ragged line of horizon along the northwestern edge of the sky. The workmen also turned their backs to the river and moved their gaze in the same direction.

An enormous white cloud, glowing along its edges and paved from beneath with leaden shadows, was flowing out from behind the distant line of trees, as though from the very center of the Solec wilderness. It swelled in a strange circular manner until it took on the shape of a bearded head with its mouth open to shriek. And it looked as though heavy shoulders, the torso, and whole body of a giant, coming in the direction of our valley, would soon emerge from beyond the horizon.

Miss Malvina suddenly cried out and fell on her knees. Now everyone in turn knelt down in intense silence. The clarinet stopped halfway through an unfinished phrase and at the same moment the bell ceased after the third part of the prayer for the dead.

Then the unnaturally high voice of Miss Malvina, penetrating as the cry of a crane, resounded:

> Lord, our God, hear our prayers!
> Thou art with me, and I with Thee.
> Thou gavest me life,
> Thou shalt be my end . . .

Everyone was singing, filling the valley at this strange early evening hour with overwhelming supplication.

But the cloud began to decay, rolling into a lividly outlined dense ball, then slowly plunging back into the motionless wilderness. The sky was again empty, ashen, glimmering with heat.

I walked diagonally across the meadow. The grass, like singed hair, rustled underfoot. I could hear a completely different rippling of the river, impatient and sharpened. I plunged into a naked clump of alder; half dried up, the Sola was darting in a narrow current between felt-colored rocks. Black roots, like the legs of huge spiders, immersed themselves cautiously among bearded water plants.

All at once I stopped. I still had time to withdraw, I still had the opportunity to call off my decision.

But she said, without looking round, "The air is terribly sultry, well said?"

I could see her crouched shoulders. She was sitting on the river bank, staring at the narrow stream, a tortuous branch of the Sola.

"A cloud has appeared. Maybe there'll be rain at last."

I sat down next to her. She didn't look at me. Her chin was supported on the knees of her drawn-up legs. The back of her neck, under the braided knot of her hair, was bestrewn with minute drops of sweat.

"Could the river dry up entirely?"

"I don't know. Probably not the Sola."

"I've been sitting here for an hour. It looks to me as though there's less and less water flowing."

"I was looking for you in the empty house."

"You were looking for me?"

"Yes."

She kept silent, motionless in that pose, as though huddled up against the cold.

"You wore out my husband. He stayed in bed all afternoon."

"We talked."

"What about?"

"Past things."

"Do you know one another?"

She twisted her head, looking at me from under her lashes. Only now did I notice the traces of freckles on her temples that were covered with the fine skin of a sick child.

"What do you think?"

"I don't think anything," she shrugged. "It seems possible."

"Did he never mention that we'd met already at some time in our lives?"

"No. He doesn't talk to me about such things. He puts me off with jokes. He can do that."

Banks of sand lay on the shore, brought by a flood. I picked up a handful of the hot grains: "Everyone is waiting for me to leave here."

She too poured dry sand into her palm edged by her sleeve: "I keep wondering why you did it."

"Did what?"

She kept gazing: "You know what. I asked before."

"I was sick, that's all. Poisoned, or something."

"Please don't be ashamed. After all, such a time can come upon anyone."

"Enchantresses too?"

She smiled sadly. The warm sand flowed rapidly from her palm: "What sort of enchantress am I? I just said it for the sake of saying something."

"But I'd prefer you to be an enchantress."

"What if it turns out that I'm not?"

"Then I'll never again come to meet with you."

She started to rock her head rhythmically. She gazed at me from sleepily half-closed eyelids: "All right. I'll try to enchant you."

A cockchafer flew past. A May bug. We could hear its humming, which sounded strange in these alders stripped of life.

"You see," she said all of a sudden, "I don't know my parents. I remember hearing something about this at the orphanage. It was suspected that I was a German child. You know, a foundling. Maybe that was during the German retreat, but that's clearly impossible, I'm certainly older than that by several years. So maybe partisans broke up a German convoy somewhere, in which German families were coming back from Russia."

I eyed her dark hair threaded with rusty strands as though singed, her very round face oval like an infant's and an old-fashioned dimple in the chin.

"No, that's impossible. You don't look like a German girl."

She was swaying her head rhythmically and looking at me in a manner which might have been called challenging. But I knew it was merely an unconscious mannerism, a sort of gape.

"How can you tell? They even advised me to apply to the Red Cross."

"Please don't do that. Please stay with us."

"I'll stay. Of course I'll stay."

Now she was staring at the very fine trickle of sand which kept flowing from her palm into a small clump of straw flowers growing flimsily in the black earth.

"I know already that I'm going to be in trouble on account of you," she said all of a sudden.

"What are you saying?"

"I'm right."

And she glanced at me with a smile I didn't yet know.

I took her hand. Her palm was cut across by a deep scar, like a special line which life had granted her.

"What's that?" I asked.

"I don't know. I've always had it."

I kissed her open palm. She slowly withdrew her hand. Suddenly I embraced her.

"Well, and what now?"

"Well, nothing," she smiled, abashed.

"How's it going with the enchantments?"

"Not too well."

We were talking for the sake of talking. Both of us were in a state of tension. The arm I'd put round her was trembling, and I knew very well that she was aware of that. I turned her face to me, and kissed her.

"No," she whispered, leaning back.

"Why not?"

"No."

And she rapidly plucked a tiny flower stalk.

"Here, it's for you."

I wanted to say it was commonplace, I wanted somehow to put an end to this ludicrous situation, but all I did was to take the flower and place it behind me on the still hot sand. The clarinet could be heard again and I had the impression that its sound smelled of the chill of wet river-plants.

I embraced her unexpectedly. She struggled desperately but then was weighed down by nothing but passivity. I kissed her a long time before her lips came to life and began responding. Then we leaned apart, to draw breath.

"I have to go now," she said, but made not the slightest move to get up.

"There's still time. The sun has only just set."

"I ought to go back."

Again we kissed interminably, until we lost balance and fell on our backs, feeling the warmth hidden in the sand.

"You can see the stars," she stammered into my ears at last.

I glanced up instinctively and saw a single drop gleaming with an aquamarine light: "You little fool," I whispered to myself.

"What?"

"Nothing at all."

She was heavy and passive. She was shielding herself with arms as thin at the wrist as a sunflower stalk. I pulled away both her hands in turn, while she gazed intently at the sky. Finally I spread her out on the sand and then my memory unexpectedly brought back to me the partisan's despairing face, the red spruce needles stuck to his damp forehead, his mouth spasmodically gasping for breath.

I threw myself up her wildly, but she languidly curled and turned her face to the ground. With feverish hands I turned her toward the sky again, clumsily overcoming one resistance after another, until finally, when I was already on the frontier of liberation, that which had to happen, happened. It happened without her participation.

Then we listened to our bated breathing. I had the impression we had been heard throughout the valley. I glanced at her face.

She was lying with eyes closed, covered with the dew of sweat. She was almost ugly.

Then I felt a kind of pressure in my throat. It seemed to me I had a long way to go to get home and would never get there.

"Are you happy?" I whispered, to stifle my uneasiness.

She kept silent. And it almost seemed as though she was asleep. A black ant was walking across her hair dipped in the sand. I flicked it away, then shook off particles of sand gleaming with red light. I could see right in front of me her chapped lips, the whitened tip of her nose and her brows, from which the black had rubbed off. She was lying motionless, with her skirt raised indecorously. I covered her girlish thighs with a stealthy movement. Once again the outer world returned in the gurgle of the river, the stifled murmur of the forest, the intrusive voice of the clarinet, magnified by the evening stillness.

A branch cracked somewhere behind me. I looked that way but saw nothing except the deserted, motionless undergrowth.

Then she rose from the ground and sat up, shielding herself from me with her shoulders. She fastened her blouse, straightened her hair, arranged the folds of her skirt, but would not let me see her face.

So I embraced her uncertainly and began kissing the back of her neck with its hair dry as straw. She straightened up, raised her head, exposing her taut neck to my lips. I therefore drew her to me, while she began nestling against my hands.

Then she turned her face up and gazed at me for a long time. I couldn't guess her purpose.

"What have you got there?"

I looked inquiringly at her.

"On your chest, under your shirt."

I undid the buttons. She reached in and held up to her eyes the black iron cross.

"What is it?" she whispered.

"An 1863 insurrectionist's cross. I found it in the Sola."

"Something's written on it."

"Yes. 'Gospodi spasi ludi twoja.' "

"Why do you wear it?"

"I myself don't know. I found it and wear it."

"I'd like to have one too."

"Come, let's look for one in the water."

We went into the strangely warm water. The water plants seized our feet in their shifting tangle. An ever deepening gloom was creeping from the roots of the riverside trees.

"It's getting dark."

"Yes."

"Surely we won't find anything."

We waded a long time, gazing into water overflowing with night. I heard a movement of some kind on the bank. I took a quick look and caught sight of branches stirring and a motionless human figure. She also straightened up in the middle of the river.

"It's the trunk of an old willow," she said softly. "I remember it well."

"We won't find anything today. We must search some other time."

"All right," she whispered. "In the daytime."

On the bank she struggled with her shoes, which wouldn't go on her wet feet.

"I'm worried," I said.

She was silent, carefully tapping the stubborn shoe.

"I'm worried," I repeated quietly. "You know about what."

She reached gropingly for my hand and all at once kissed it with her cold lips.

I turned her around so that her face was illuminated by the anemic moon. Her features were subdued, softened by weariness. She tried to sway her head in that peculiar way of hers, but then immediately froze into her previous position. I shuddered, sensing the moist warmth of her arms.

"Come, let's sit a while longer," I said quietly.

"We must go. It's cold. You're shivering."

"Let's wait."

"No, no," she said hastily and set off in the direction of the meadow.

Then we heard a stifled clattering, like that of an animal in flight. The branches of the alder thicket crackled along the river. These sudden noises soon blended into the monotonous chattering of the Sola.

"Someone was here," I said.

"It only seemed so, I'm sure."

I listened for a while to the meager life of the night. On the other side of the river a light glimmered in the workers' huts, some man there called out imploringly.

"Someone saw us," I whispered.

"What of it?"

We walked across the meadow toward the rust-colored glow of the peat bog, behind which stood the mound of the grave heap. I took her hand, and with my fingers sought that line engrained inside her palm.

"I'm afraid I've lost all my powers of enchantment," she declared. "Well said?"

"I don't know."

"Tomorrow I'll go to Podjelniaki. There's a castle hill there that used to be Prussian. There are supposed to be dungeons. A solitary place, you know? I have to find the appropriate herbs and, generally, get back into shape. Well said?"

"Anyway, it happened," I said to myself, still surprised.

"What?"

"Nothing. I'm one of those people who worry all the time."

We stopped under the hill on which their house stood. From the windows enormously lengthened rectangles of light cut by the crosses of the frames reached out toward us.

"Here we are," she whispered. "Please stop here."

"I'll accompany you to the garden."

"No, no," she said, hastily. "I can find my way."

She pressed my hand very lightly and swaying as though in a dance repeated from memory, began to walk away in the direction of her house.

"Justine!" I suddenly called in an undertone.

She stopped but without turning back, gazing at the bright windows. I caught up with her: "Aren't we going to say goodbye?"

I wanted to kiss her, but she bent her head and I barely rubbed my cheek on her hair. She started running uphill in a narrow corridor of light.

"Justine!" I called.

She disappeared among the lilac bushes, then the door rattled. I climbed the hill and sat down, with the windows of their house at a small distance from me. I could look inside through broad cracks: a wall with a piece of Polish tapestry on it, and the couch, on which Joseph Car was lying.

Later I saw Justine's back. She was walking slowly up to the couch, and I saw her hair evenly braided, the sleeves of her blouse rolled up and a black shawl thrown over her shoulders. In the few seconds since our separation, she had transformed herself into a dainty woman coming back from a boring walk.

She sat down on the edge of the bedding and said something to him. He gazed intently into her face, then all at once turned away to the wall. Then she began stroking his head. They remained like this for a while, and it looked from where I was as though they had gone to sleep in this position. The shadow of the lampshade swayed on the whitish wall.

Then he buried his head in her skirt, which must have still smelled of the river. She stroked his elflocks faster and faster. His shoulders were clearly trembling; finally, she reached with her free hand and the light went out.

I was sitting motionless, collecting my thoughts. I was sorry. I had the pointless wish to throw a stone at the window, on which the moon's thin horns were reflected.

"You made a fool of yourself," I told myself. "You made a fool of yourself like never before."

I rose heavily and set off toward the railroad. It seemed to me as though someone was following me. I stopped and listened to the night. It was silent. A broad patch of mist was white above the river.

"Just as well. Now I can leave," I whispered.

I caught sight of the solid outline of the empty house in front of me and the trees of the orchard lurking in the gloom.

"Where shall I go to? Where?"

Suddenly I heard the sound of someone's footsteps. Someone was approaching out of the night. A black, crooked shadow stopped a few paces in front of me.

"Talking to yourself?" asked the passerby.

"It's a habit."

"Ever been in jail?"

"No. But I'm often alone."

I tried to identify the familiar voice. The passer-by groaned strangely and for a moment I lost sight of him. Then I heard him clapping his pockets. He was looking for matches. In the feeble circle of reddish light I recognized the face of the railroad man.

"You take walks at night? That's a city habit?" he said, coming closer.

I caught the smell of vodka. He leaned against me, as if afraid I would melt away into the darkness.

"I like the night too," he said. "It's safer at night."

"I'm going back home. Shall I go with you?"

"Aha," he laughed hoarsely. "You think I'm drunk? You don't have to, kitten, I'll get to where I want to go."

His cigarette glowed up for an instant. I saw that he was seeking my eyes with his: "I drink a little," he said, quietly. "It's true I like to drink a bit before night comes. But that makes sense. See, kitten, I've had my fill of death in my time and I feel as though my own wouldn't scare me. Until all of a sudden I wake up one winter night and I look, and ice grips my throat. And the way I felt that time has stayed with me ever since. It dies down sometimes in daytime, it's afraid of the light, the carrion, but when night comes, it sucks and bites my innards."

In silence I stared at the little fiery tip, which glowed with each word.

"But once I was a man like a lion. I could carry a 360-pound weight on my back. Sometimes I wanted to leap up and strike at the sky with my chest and see it break in two. You see, kitten, a rat coils up, squeaks and kicks the bucket, but an ox dies painfully, it digs out a whole well under itself."

"Are you scared of Huniady?" I asked abruptly.

The cigarette went out. The railroad man staggered: "Who said I'm scared?"

"People do," I lied.

He was silent a moment, trying to spit out the cigarette. "I know him, and he knows me. There was a time when I chased him all over the county, and even further. Who was afraid of who, kitten?"

"Did you ever see him?"

Again the moist odor of alcohol enveloped me.

"Several times he made arrangements to meet me, but he never came."

"Do you know what he looks like?"

"Nothing particular. Like anybody. They said he was bearded, swarthy, tall. And mind you, kitten, that after all the amnesties, when the outlaw bands quieted down, he left a message for me with some people. That, mind you, he'd come to me, he'd have to come at night. And that I was to wait for him always. It was I, kitten, who brought a platoon of sappers from the county town and mined those German bunkers in the Solec forest, as I knew for sure he was lurking there. And I'm waiting, kitten, I'm waiting for him all the time. And I've been listening for twelve years to hear a mine go off. Because he can only come to me by way of Heaven."

"Shall I take you home? It's late."

"I've no need of a house at night."

"Why don't you go away from here?"

"You see, during the referendum — ha, how long ago that was! — he caught me in a village and tried to burn me up in a hut. My flesh was already singed; then I vowed to myself that if I got out of that stove, then I'd not die anywhere but on our own land."

A single distant shot resounded from across the river, somewhere in the depths of the forest. We both fell silent, straining our ears. Once again all was quiet.

"Did you hear that?" I whispered.

The railroad man breathed out heavily: "An old tree falling," he said, hoarsely.

"Someone was firing."

"What's that nonsense?" he seized me by my shirt front.

"But I heard it distinctly."

"What are you sniffing about here for, what are you looking for? You heard me: a tree fell."

I was silent.

All at once he let me go and said wearily: "Well, be on your way. It's late."

"Let me help you."

"Be on your way, I said," he raised his voice.

I set off in the direction of the railroad tracks, but he stood there listening to my footsteps, to make sure I was doing what he wanted. Then he turned and walked away into the darkness. But he did not withdraw very far, for I could hear his footsteps and the rustle of branches in the orchard. Then the porch steps creaked, and a plank groaned as it was wrenched out. The railroad man had gone to spend the night in the deserted house.

I set off for the tracks almost at a run. I rushed on in this manner, gasping for the cool air. But at one moment it seemed to me that the sound of someone else's hurried footsteps was mingling with the sound of my own. I slowed down and finally halted between the tracks that were gleaming in the greenish moonlight.

"Romus," I said in an undertone.

No one replied.

"Romus," I repeated, "speak up."

In the ditches running along the track crickets were singing like wires in winter before a thaw.

"Romus, I know you're following me."

I felt with my foot for a piece of granite in the gravel. I bent down and picked it up: "What do you want from me?"

With sudden rage I threw the stone into the darkness. I heard it fall and roll for a long time, invisible, down the dried-up slope. I threw several more fragments of rock into various parts of the gloom. But there was a stubborn silence all around. Not until later did a cockchafer fly out of the heart of the night, abruptly hit something, and then instantly fell silent.

Miss Malvina rose with a solemn expression. She was wearing

a black dress with a yellowed lace jabot. She gazed at her glass, which was filled with some liquor of her own making, and said:

"This is a sad anniversary for us, but there's no help for it. Other people have such splendid festivities, but ours, shameful to say, is poor, oh dear me it is. It must be seventeen years already, mister, since they put us into boxcars and brought us to this here Poland."

Ildefons Korsak sighed wearily and touched his glass to his whiskers, that were reminiscent of water plants. Without looking in his direction, Miss Malvina rapidly slapped his hand.

"Fie, how forward he is. Let me have my say to the end. Well, and so we came and we found this valley, just the very same as ours near Ejszyszki. For which, God be thanked. But such earth, rich as butter, mister, sweet-smelling, light as a feather, isn't to be found anywhere. Because at home in the East, the forests were different, and the fields more even, and the rivers calm. All our people have stayed there, they died off in various wars, or were killed by wicked men, or from tainted air. They lie there, mister, buried in their own soil and they praise the Lord God. But as for us, poor wretches that we are, it's terrible to think of death. A person can live any place, but he must die on his own soil."

The railroad man whose hand had already grown stiff during this prolonged toast, scowled and muttered impolitely:

"Well, here's to us."

Without waiting for the others, he ceremoniously filled a measuring glass. The slow sounds of earnestly functioning Adam's apples resounded. The railroad man snuffled into the sleeve of his official smock.

"I know what you're drinking to, miss. But it's different times today. There's no better or worse land, all land is good."

"Oh, Mr. Dobas, I meant no harm. We always drink on the anniversary; we remember. We're without politics, we're plain folks, we like any government."

"My name's Debicki," said the railroad man somberly.

The guests started looking round the table for their favorite snacks. But today's setting had some sort of deeper significance, it was painfully demonstrating against the approaching fate. There were no mushrooms marinated in all kinds of sauces, no ripe pork sausage which usually melted in the mouth like a spider web, no potato cake fried in butter, no tomatoes drowned in cream, no pancakes, no Lithuanian-style meat dumplings strained of bouillon, nor any other dishes for which the house of the Korsaks was celebrated. So they resignedly reached for the slices of pickle and carelessly sliced cheese already overgrown with a slippery patina.

"Your people let us down good," said the partisan, munching the sour pulp of a pickle.

"Did anyone here say something?" the railroad man was surprised.

"I'm speaking to you, you friend of the working people. You let us down nicely with that democracy of yours."

The railroad man moved away a plate of cheese and placed his cracked palms heavily on the table: "What sort of grudge do you have against me, kitten? Do I bathe in luxury like a pre-war voivode? Do I ride around in a limousine, or buy a seaside villa, or loll in the silken sheets of an actress?"

"That's just it," said the partisan. "That's why I hold a grudge against you. Because if you went after money like a voivode, if you took potshots at mirrors in bar rooms with your mistresses, if you built yourself palaces, then at least I could hope to make something out of you for myself. Is it normal for a minister to go around as bare-assed as me? No, grandpa, a system like this has no future."

"You be careful talking about the system. I remember very well that you served under Huniady."

"But I surrendered when the time came, didn't I?"

"You left him alone in nothing but his underpants in winter. You surrendered because I had my grip on all of you."

The partisan turned white. He began thumping his prosthesis on the table top: "I didn't leave him alone. He still had a platoon of soldiers."

"I know your wolfish solidarity. Why do you hide the fact that you used to be with Huniady?"

The partisan rose suddenly: "I never betrayed anybody, you Security cop, hear me? I left him at that time because London gave the order. Anybody who wanted to could go back home."

"Didn't Huniady look for you afterwards?"

"He's looking for you to this day. Why don't you stay home, nights?"

Miss Malvina seized the partisan by his jacket and drew him back to his seat: "My dears, why go into politics? No good ever came to anybody from politics. Ildek, poor child, you'd better sing a song."

Ildefons Korsak, who had woken up from a deep meditation, reached instinctively for his full glass.

"Oh not that, you're poorly, better sing a song for the gentlemen."

"Why not, I can sing, but only in Russian."

"Good gracious me, don't you know any other songs?"

"No."

"You served in all sorts of armies, you've seen the world, but you can only sing in Russian?"

"All songs are beautiful, but Russki songs are the most beautiful of all," said Mr. Ildefons stubbornly.

"Why waste time singing?" cried Miss Korsak, brightly, seeing that her brother was on the verge of performing. "We'd better drink up."

"Well, here's to us," exclaimed the railroad man in an alarmingly modulated voice.

The talk stopped for a moment and then the bang of the gate was heard. Someone ran rapidly across the yard. Sergeant Glowko, who had not even had time to swallow his vodka, seized his cap from the window sill and concealed himself with remarkable skill behind the cupboard. A little boy and girl rushed into the room. They stopped by the threshold, dazzled by the lamplight.

"Is daddy here? Mama ordered him to come home right away," said the little boy, knowledgeably observing the already somewhat messy table.

Nobody could find an answer, so all gazed helplessly into each other's eyes. Finally, seeing the urgency of the situation, Miss Malvina declared in a sweet voice: "Your father hasn't been here. He's still on duty, for sure, poor creature," and she choked dreadfully, either from the liquor of her own production, or from the evasive reply.

The children remained undecided a moment, treated by the revelers with hypocritical smiles, and then disappeared into the dark hallway and only the rapid patter of their bare feet could be heard.

"Merci," said Sergeant Glowko mournfully, as he slithered out from behind the cupboard. "My God, how shameful. To hide in corners from my own children . . . Oh, that accursed wood alcohol."

He sat down again at the table, resigned, and reached for his full glass.

"Here's to us," said the railroad man, stressing each syllable. Cautiously he poured the liquid into his throat, with traditional elegance, so that his Adam's apple wouldn't work vulgarly and, having lifted his head high, he closed his eyes for an instant. Opening them slowly, he lowered his head and shook himself, puffing sulphurously: "Thank you for the refreshment," he said and bowed deeply to those present. In passing he picked up his official cap from the floor. "I enjoy three, maybe four glassfuls."

And he began aiming for the door. Finally he regained his balance, determined the proper direction and moved sharply toward the way out.

"He can't take much," said the partisan in a passionless tone.

Some tin sheets rattled in the hallway. Miss Malvina smiled knowingly: "He's gone to the privy."

"Never mind, he'll get to where he must," said Count Pac. "He'll straighten out before night like a lancer."

Ildefons Korsak, who had been attentively watching pickle juice dripping off the table all the time, suddenly burst out singing, in Russian, in a chesty voice:

> The boat is going at full steam,
> We'll feed commissars to the fish.

"Sssh," Miss Malvina hissed, "did you fall headlong into a ditch, or what? Oh Blessed Mother, he's ill again, for sure. He's got insides like a perch. Barely does he take a little glassful than a sort of bedevilment comes over him."

"He sings well. Let him sing," the partisan commanded.

"No! God forbid!" shrieked Miss Malvina. "Oh, you're accursed, you fought for all the emperors, you made a revolution, who taught you, you booby, such meaningless words?"

Ildefons Korsak snorted through his greenish whiskers and fixed his sister with a stern eye:

"Be off! Don't you dare, or I'll trample you to death with my horse!"

Miss Malvina promptly stuck a large piece of pickle into his mouth and very neatly seized his head, pressing it to her bosom with one elbow. Korsak struggled a while like a pike nailed with a spear.

Miss Malvina turned her face toward us, taut with effort but also benevolently smiling: "What a thing to think up!" she said, turning her brother's cry into a joke. "Wherever is he going to get a horse in a town like this? And Mr. Paul sits there all the while, he don't eat or drink nothing."

"But he isn't missing anything," said the partisan.

Sergeant Glowko raised his glass with a sigh. I timidly followed his example.

"You were getting ready to leave, mysterious passer-by?" said the partisan, looking at me over his glass.

"Yes, I'm leaving soon."

"We won't stop you. And please remember who helped you come back from a long voyage."

"Oh, why remember what's past," Miss Malvina interposed.

"I'm not reproaching anybody."

"A strange business," the sergeant nodded his head. "Not an old man yet, healthy as a bull, but the devil tempted him."

"Oh goodness, the times are upsetting these days."

"It's not the times, miss," said Sergeant Glowko, sternly. "Them folks in the towns, excuse me saying so, do naught but read books and sit in the movies. That way they get water on the brain. Did you people ever see an ordinary man take his own life?"

The partisan and the count glanced at one another furtively, not knowing whether to accept the honorary title of "ordinary man." But luckily Miss Malvina again intervened: "And what's going on in the world, my dears? What do they write in the papers?"

We were silent, uncertain, until the partisan finally muttered: "The count's the only one who reads. Let him tell us."

"I warn you, I'm n-n-not a c-c-count," Pac reddened. "S-s-sometimes I r-r-read when I g-get hold of one b-b-by chance."

"Don't be embarrassed," Sergeant Glowko put in, "it's permissible to read newspapers, if I may say so."

"The same as always. They've sent up another sputnik."

"Who has?" asked Glowko.

The count blinked: "The R-r-russians."

"Aha," said the sergeant, approvingly.

"At home in the East, sir, there used to be a certain man, Holob the blacksmith. Oh how talented he was, how learned, people came to him from thirty miles around. He could have built himself a hayshed of gold, but he just kept on saying 'No.' All he did was to stare at the moon through great big eyeglasses; in the daytime he'd grind away without a moment's rest. He was making a machine as big as a stable."

"Well, what happened?" the sergeant put in.

"Well, one night he disappeared."

"He'd flown to the moon, for sure?" asked the partisan sarcastically.

Malvina Korsak glanced at him solemnly: "Maybe he did, if it's in human power."

"Ach, ignorance," said Glowko, uncertainly.

"But what do we know of what has been and will be? It doesn't often happen that a strange man appears among us, lives for a while, then disappears without trace. I remember at home near Ejszyszki . . ."

"Give over, miss, before night comes," objected the sergeant. "We'd better drink up."

"What's our Regina doing now?" sighed Miss Korsak. "Maybe she's gone far away, to foreign lands, maybe she's become a great lady already."

"Let's drink up," said the partisan.

"She was a good woman, and so pretty. Everything about her in its right place, as it should be. Not like them you see today. They walk along, mister, and nobody knows if it's a he or a she."

"Let's drink up," the partisan repeated stormily.

"Evidently that's the way it was meant to be. Maybe we'll hear of her some day, if God grants."

"Let's drink up," said the partisan yet again, but he drank nothing, only gazed at his cloudy glass of rocking vodka.

I furtively swallowed my dram and felt good. I thought I was dozing in my family home by the hot stove, listening through a shallow slumber, through the narrow channels of reality, to the evening chattering.

"Here come the children!" the count suddenly cried.

Sergeant Glowko, with amazing agility, again jumped behind the cupboard with his unfinished glass. There he struggled with his breathing and it was evident that he would soon start to cough.

"Daddy here?" asked the little boy.

"Go home to bed, my child," said Miss Malvina, sweetly. "Poor little creature, you shouldn't be wandering about at night. Here's a present, a little cucumber pickled this year."

"We've already had supper," said the little boy.

"Go home, what's good will be lost, but your daddy will be found."

The children ran out. Sergeant Glowko came back to the table like a bear with a sore head. He put his glass down.

"Since you're from the East, miss, you surely think that anything is allowed."

"I said that because you have to know how to behave with children. A child has its own common sense."

"But somehow it wasn't nice."

Oh you little apple, where are you off to?
The OGPU will catch you, you'll never come back.

Ildefons Korsak suddenly began singing.

"Be off, away with you, accursed one," Miss Malvina jumped at him. "May the wolves catch you, he's woken up and is off again."

"Miss, do you know what he writes in those exercise books of his?" asked the partisan.

"Well, he writes to be read, such fine things."

"Have you read them?"

"Why should I read them? It's a game."

"Back home one time, I was still working as a bricklayer," said Glowko, "there was such a case. A guy in thin pants arrives: mister engineer, mister foreman, comrade workman, this and that, he wrote something down on paper, and later it turned out he was writing out a book. How ashamed we was, pardon me, I can remember it to this day. Later they wrote in the papers that he'd gone crazy. That's how it goes."

Once again Miss Malvina fixed an arm lock on the head of her enfeebled brother.

"Help maybe?" the count offered. His eyes were already veiled in a strange mist.

He moved forward on his stool and embraced Miss Korsak.

"Oh goodness, what's this?" squeaked his victim. "I'm on in years, y'know."

"Hush, hush," whispered the count, shutting his eyes. "A woman's young as long as she wants to be."

"Good God, help me all of you, now this one's drunk. And someone is looking in the window."

We looked at the pane. Outside was night. The glass reflected the vague outline of our own figures.

"No one's looking," the count whispered. "I'll take the other hand too, it'll be more comfortable."

"He's stuck to me like a leech," said Miss Malvina, already calmed down from her terror. "Aren't there enough girls for you in the neighborhood?"

"Miss, you'll still outdo more than one young lady."

"Goodness gracious, the things you say," declared Miss Korsak, and she unexpectedly tittered.

The partisan banged the table with his prosthesis: "Enough of this tomfoolery."

The worried sergeant straightened his unfastened side arms: "Right, maybe we'd better drink up, excuse me."

"You're so bumptious. After all, I'm a spinster," Miss Malvina pleaded.

"And I'm a bachelor, and not a bad one at that."

Here Count Pac put his bony face, gleaming with yellowness, to Miss Malvina's cheek. She squeaked in a strange, festive voice.

The partisan banged his prosthesis on the table top so that all the glasses jumped: "You're a swine, count."

Pac let Miss Korsak go and turned in the direction of his opponent. He gazed at him with glassy eyes, and it looked as though he was seeing him for the first time ever.

"What did you say?"

"You're a sex maniac, you beast."

Count Pac rose from his stool.

"And you're a Jew."

A sudden silence fell.

"Who is?" asked the partisan in a stifled voice.

"Well, you are. You're a Jew."

The partisan tried to laugh easily: "See that, all of you? He's gone crazy."

"You're a Jew," the count repeated.

The partisan ran his tongue over his parched lips: "People, I don't understand anything."

"You're a Jew," the count said again.

The partisan looked around at all of us, seeking help. He pressed his prosthesis to his hip with all his strength: "My name is Jasiu Krupa."

The count took a step toward him: "You're a Jew."

"People, how can I be a Jew if my name is Jasiu Krupa? Surely you don't believe this idiot?"

But we kept silent, startled by this unexpected turn of events. Sergeant Glowko, sensing that we would place certain hopes in him, ineffectually fastened a nickel button on his uniform.

"Can a Jew be called Jasiu Krupa?" asked the partisan, desperately.

"I know, and you well know about this," said the count, staring at him with colorless eyes. "There are people who know you from before the war. Remember that guy who came with the foreign journalist? Remember how he stared at you?"

The partisan blinked, then raised his good arm, wiped his eyes and gazed for a while at the surface of his palm. Then he bent his artificial arm at the elbow and began going up to count Pac, kicking stools out of the way.

"God, he'll kill him!" Miss Malvina shrieked.

Sergeant Glowko tried to jump to his feet, but entangled himself in his own eagerness and fell down under the table.

They interlocked in the middle of the room. For a moment they struggled, each trying to push the other away. With an effort Count Pac bared his large yellow teeth and it looked as though he were holding a corn cob in his mouth. All of a sudden they lost their balance and were carried into a corner of the room, up to the red-tiled stove. The partisan bumped his head on an angle of the metal pipe. Dried-up fragments of clay, with which the chimney pipe was packed, scattered over the floor. Miss Malvina was standing with her mouth wide open and didn't notice that pickle juice was dripping onto her bare feet.

They bounced back from the stove and again rolled into the middle of the room. The count, clinging to the partisan's collar, tried to kick him with his knee. Then with an abrupt movement the partisan struck the leg on which the count was putting his whole weight. They crashed into the wall, the lamp began rocking violently, illuminating them as they struggled by the wall.

Gradually the partisan gained the upper hand. He thrust his heavy prosthesis under the count's chin and using it like a wagon stake squeezed his opponent's throat with it. Count Pac's eyes protruded, he was staring sideways, a little upwards, into the partisan's livid face: "You're a Jew," he rattled.

The partisan groaned and, sobbing intently, began to mash the count's dry throat with enormous force. At this moment we noticed that blood was pouring from the count's nose, that he was choking in it, that he was close to suffocation.

At the sight of blood something burst in me. I myself don't know when it was that I threw myself at them. Mastering my disgust, and maybe that is why I felt nothing, I separated them and then started to drive them apart like snapping dogs. Clenching my teeth to stifle my nausea, I struck out with my fists against soft, passive resistance.

Abruptly someone seized my hand and clung to it with all his weight.

"Stop it! Stop it!" shrieked Miss Malvina.

I went back to the table and stared at them in amazement, while they got up from the ground with the utmost difficulty and could not stand by themselves. The partisan's face was burst open as though he'd been hit with a flail, while the count couldn't move his left hand, which had evidently been wrenched from its wrist.

"Always the same when a third person interferes," whispered Miss Malvina.

"Excuse me," I said, "excuse me. I wanted to separate them."

Finally both were standing on their feet. They slowly came

back to consciousness. The count blew a huge blood clot out of his nose and stared at it in terror. Now, Sergeant Glowko also found his way out from between the table legs. He appeared amidst us, stern, his slightly soiled cap on his head.

"Good evening."

We turned to the door. Joseph Car, in a black coat, was standing on the threshold.

"What's going on here?" he asked, in a weary voice.

Miss Malvina picked up one of the stools and sat down modestly: "Nothing. They quarreled a little. Everyone knows young men . . ."

We were all breathing heavily in the same rhythm. I noticed that Ildefons Korsak was asleep, with his head stuck in a cupboard drawer.

"We're celebrating an anniversary. Perhaps the last in this place," Miss Malvina added.

"You oughtn't to do it like this," said Joseph Car, calmly. "Isn't there enough anger among people?"

The partisan unfastened his puffed-up lips with difficulty: "He said I'm a Jew. Do you believe I'm a Jew?"

Joseph Car smiled with his lips only: "Our land has always been hospitable. Anyone who wanted to could become an inhabitant. And in this lies her beauty, that the unhappy people of all countries created her nation."

"But do you believe I'm a Jew?" the partisan repeated, stubbornly.

"No."

The partisan jerked himself off the wall with his back and came out staggering into the center of the room. Here he stopped and stared a while at the floor. Then he raised his good hand and wiped his eyes, looking at the back of his hand. All at once he staggered and rushed obliquely toward the door, where he seized Joseph Car by the shoulders and stopped. Then he ran his hand down Car's body, bent as though looking for something in the black coat, finally groped for the prophet's hand and lifted it to his lips.

"That's not necessary," Joseph Car snorted. "What's this?"

Sergeant Glowko involuntarily took off his official cap. He twisted it rapidly in his stiff fingers which never bent.

Joseph Car discreetly wiped his hand on his coat tail. I realized that he was one of those people who are afraid of infection.

"They told me you'd left," he said, looking at me.

"No, I haven't left."

"I was looking for you."

"Here I am."

"Oh, it isn't important."

Ildefons Korsak was tasting something with his lips in a dream.

"A strange night," said Joseph Car, quietly. "And a strange day will follow it."

We kept silent, listening to the roaring in our aching heads.

"Go to bed, all of you," said Joseph Car. "It's late. Leave your anger outside the door. Good night."

He turned and walked out.

We remained for some time in the same places where he'd left us. The partisan mechanically rubbed his prosthesis on his wide pants turned up at the ankles. Count Pac was still staring at that appalling blood clot, while Sergeant Glowko was struggling with some unpleasant idea which pinched him.

"Merci," he said at last and went out, but we knew he'd stopped on the stone porch and was listening into the night. The count set off after him and finally the partisan staggered uncertainly to the hallway.

"I'm going through the gardens," I heard the sergeant say. "Excuse me, but I don't want to meet the children."

Then he scrambled through the fence, evidently tearing out a rail.

"What are you doing here? What are you waiting for?" he asked someone hidden in the night.

Miss Malvina shook her head helplessly. She began with uncoordinated movements to extricate her brother from the drawer.

I went across into my room. I had the impression that something in it had changed. The mirror was dead, the narrow triangle of moonlight was not lying, as usual, on the wall, the window barely appeared as a dim shape in the blackness of the wall.

A partisan's faith goes
Along a path 'midst village huts.
A pair of eyes shines at a window,
And lips red as a rose . . .

It was the partisan singing. Slowly his voice died away in the night. I went out to the front of the house. There wasn't anyone about now. I suddenly felt a chill on my fingers. I raised them to my lips. They were still moist with vodka. For a moment I held them in front of me, level with my eyes, before I realized that the wind had risen and was rushing in impatient gusts into the garden.

"Why a strange night?" I asked myself and went out into the road. Unthinkingly I set off toward the railroad tracks, which were veiled by a high-pitched ringing sound. But it wasn't grasshoppers. It was the drooping wires of the new telephone line resounding.

I kept stumbling as I walked, and a spacious murmuring, like the voice of a distant sea, came to meet me. I passed the empty house, in which an unfastened iron bar was clanking metallically.

"Someone is following me," I thought.

In front was the rectangle of their window patiently stained by the elflocks of a clump of black lilac.

"He was right," I said quietly. "I see too much, hear too much."

That window of theirs somehow pained me. For a moment I struggled against the desire to go up and knock at the cold pane as I had formerly done on so many occasions with all kinds of intentions. Illuminated windows of human dwellings will be an obsession of mine to the end of my life.

I didn't tap. I continued toward the river. On the opposite bank, further to the left, an electric bulb was swinging over the building site. Now I knew that it was the forest which was murmuring, or properly speaking the depths of the forest, and that this enormous voice was coming toward us from there.

All at once I stopped. I listened a very long time.

"No. It's the night chattering," I comforted myself.

Then I found our place. The Sola was rolling patiently and in silence through a channel filled with water plants and moss. It was quiet in this growing murmur of the awakening forest.

Gropingly I found the sand bank. I plunged my fingers into its warm interior as into a dog's coat. Then all of a sudden I felt the need to find that commonplace flower which had screened our game.

I crawled on my knees, groping at the bitterly cold and sticky earth. Then I suddenly caught sight of three motionless figures behind a net of branches, like the trunks of trees smashed by a storm.

I rose to my feet clumsily, regaining my balance with difficulty. The alcohol ticked in me with a hot throbbing.

"Who's there?" I asked loudly.

It seemed to me that one of the tree-trunks bulged suddenly like a bat taking to flight.

"Who's following me?"

At this moment I caught sight of a broad burst of flame and with the noise of the shot in my ears I fell into the river.

Struggling with water plants which seized me by the legs, I pressed desperately toward the opposite bank. I'd been fired at by a sawed-off shotgun. Hence the fire and the drawn-out detonation, hence too the wideness of the aim.

Grabbing at roots, I dragged myself up the steep slope. Here I crouched in the undergrowth, gasping for breath.

The Sola was gurgling and its arrhythmical bubbling indicated that the current was encountering an obstacle which hadn't been there before. I seemed to hear a stifled exchange of opinions. I pricked up my ears in the dark; someone was crossing the river, someone was certainly wading through the water.

I began going up the sloping side of the oak glade. The forest had already so often given me shelter in my life. I clutched the dry, slender clumps of grass. Then I stopped at the top.

Below me the night was chattering with hostility. A large pine cone rolled downhill, clattering in the ferns like a rabbit. They were coming after me. They were standing still now and listening, as I was, to the cone rolling toward the river.

I started running straight ahead, stretching out my hands like tentacles. I rebounded from a tree, plunging ever deeper into the growing roar of the forest.

I don't know how long this flight lasted, as I was half asleep, in a state of drunken stupor, which suddenly overcame me with weariness.

Abruptly two outstretched, hard arms brought me to a halt. I hit my forehead on something that clanged, and I fell to my knees. Under them I could feel the elastic springiness of flower stalks, probably late dahlias. So I put out my hands and found a square post in front of me. I began groping upward until I came to the cross arm. I was kneeling in front of a cross.

And then, unexpectedly, for the first time in years, I instinctively crossed myself.

I found some matches in my pocket. The first went out, but in the fragment of a second for which the light lasted, I saw a tin label. The next match, shielded from the wind in my hands, revealed the inscription: "Adela Debicki." I also caught sight, subconsciously, of another name under that of "Debicki," smeared clumsily with oil paint. I wanted to light a third match to read the entire epitaph, but remembered the old army superstition.

So I sat down on the grave and turned my face in the direction from which I'd come. It was completely dark. I could scarcely make out the shape of my own outstretched hands.

"I'll take a rest here," I thought. "Later I'll go back and go cautiously around the grave mound."

Then again a red light flared up and I could see many pine trunks and the shadows of bushes. The noise of the explosion quickly died down in the forest rocked by the wind.

I felt a burning in my throat and started running blindly, crazily, into the depths of the forest. I was scared, scared as rarely before, of this ferocity of my pursuers and of this isolation.

Some kind of moisture sprinkled my brow: "I'm wounded," I whispered, putting one hand to my face.

But then, unexpectedly, some cold drops fell on to the back of my hand. I slowed my pace and lifted my face to the sky. Heavy rain covered my temples with coolness.

This monotonous pouring rain lessened the terror of the forest. I stopped running. Now I was walking at an easy pace, knocking into trees. I listened, my shoulders benumbed, to what was happening behind me.

"Where are you running away to?" I asked myself quietly. "And what are you running away for?"

I continued vigorously for some time, but then I sat down on a large mossy rock reminding me of a sleeping bear.

"After all, you yourself were seeking this."

"After all, nothing has changed."

"After all, what does it matter?"

I sat thus for a long time, suddenly devoid of terror. I waited for their footsteps to resound and for myself to light the third match.

But nobody came. The night was filled with the monotony of autumn rain. I leaned my hands on the rock and felt the chill of metal. I began feeling the rock on which I sat. I cut one hand on some jagged iron rods.

I was seated on a piece of a German cement bunker, chipped by an explosion. Before I became aware of the nearness of mines, I clambered on to the pile that was overgrown with young birches.

Here I stopped, full of uncertainty. Terror returned and made itself felt with an overpowering shudder.

I was standing amidst a hill made of cement ruins. The heavy rain lashed my face and exposed hands painfully. Something had to be done.

Holding my breath, I cautiously put out one foot. It did not encounter the resistance of any wires. So I pressed it down hard and reached with my other foot.

Then unexpectedly the ground gave way under me and I fell into a black pit, my left foot getting stuck with a terrible sensation of heat.

When I came to, I lit a match. Around me were dried-out little branches of a Christmas tree stuck behind twigs of young spruce, with rotten straw on the floor, and above me the black opening in the roof that crowned a steep ladder, slippery from soldiers' boots.

The match went out and, although it was entirely dark I closed my eyes so as to shut myself off from all this. Above me the wind resounded, rushing across, rattling the ceiling, remnants of spruce needles scattering over my rain-drenched head. And I waited in terrible fear for the redness of the little stove to glow suddenly and for the hands of Musia, the girl called the Swallow, smeared with the slime of a corpse, to reach out to me.

The rain, which was still falling, washed out my tracks and those of my pursuers. But I guessed the direction in which I'd come, I recognized the lump of cement that had given me rest in the night. My left foot felt like a heated iron.

I limped a long part of the way without knowing whether I had gotten out of the mine fields. Finally I stopped to survey the area of the forest I'd crossed. I was standing among ferns reaching chest-high, which blackened by the rain were reminiscent of funereal plumes.

Behind me was the forest, trees glistening with moisture and plunged in a cloud of vapor, and I could no longer see the German cement nest in which, frozen to the marrow, I had raved through the whole autumn night. I thought to myself that either the mines, devoured by rust, had fallen apart, or that there weren't any at all, that this area of deserted forest had been mined by the railroad man in his imagination, harassed by memories during nights of drunkenness.

I was really hopping on one leg, with my left leg sometimes acting as a support, like a cane. Finally I broke off a stubborn hazel switch, which was soaked and therefore slippery, elastic. I came back like a pilgrim bearing bad news.

I again stopped by the grave of the railroad man's family. I inspected the cross, from which the rains had washed away the lime. I looked for traces of a bullet on it. But the bad atmosphere had furrowed many cracks and scratches on it and I found no ragged hole caused by a bullet.

Finally I halted on the edge of the hill and through the naked young oaks I could see before me our entire valley and the opposite cliff, on which stood the water-soaked white monastery amidst the winter wheat that had been cleansed by the downpour. And it seemed to me I had gone far astray, so unrecognizable was this neighborhood in the bad autumn weather. It reminded me of someone who has fallen to the ground and is dozing in despair at the bottom of a great, opaque lake.

I moved downhill, preceded by merry, dancing pine cones which jumped high among the oaks. On the far side to the right I saw dense, motionless clouds of steam and guessed that the peat bog, smouldering for several months, was dying out, veiling the insurrectionists' grave with a thick and substantial wall of fumes.

Then I stopped at the Sola, surprised. During the night the river had reverted to its former splendor and had even exceeded it, filling its bed with a rushing, foaming torrent.

It was about three miles to the bridge at Podjelniaki. My burning foot drew attention to itself with a hurried, painful pulsing, so willy-nilly I probed the water with my stick. Apparently it wouldn't reach above my chest. I plunged into the river, grasping the roots of riverside bushes.

I was gazing helplessly at the reddish water, opaque with loam, when I heard someone shouting. I looked to my right. Two workmen were beckoning to me with violent gestures.

So I scrambled out of the water and hobbled toward them.

"You crazy, fella?" the taller of them asked.

"I have to get home," I said.

"Don't you see how much water there is?"

"Get aboard," said the other, and he pointed to a raft, hurriedly put together from thick planks.

Then we floated across the Sola, they using boat hooks and eyeing me with unfavorable attention: "Been poaching?" asked the taller of the two.

"Of course not. I got lost in the forest."

"We often hear a single shot in there."

"But you can see I don't have a gun."

"Local people say some famous bandit is hiding here."

"Don't believe people's gossip," said the taller man, distrustfully, "I've heard such tales in plenty of places."

"This is a queer neighborhood, by God," the shorter insisted.

Preoccupied with their work, they were no longer looking at me, and I sat there amidst the tarred beams like a castaway.

"He's the one who was so cocky that time," said the shorter man in an undertone.

"Oh, let him be. See how his foot's swollen up like a log."

"He's a Baptist, for sure."

"I never saw him praying with them."

The short man turned to me, leaning his chest against the bar of the boat hook: "Have you-all founded a sect or something?"

"No, it isn't a sect," I replied.

"Then what is it?"

"Properly speaking, they pray in a secular way," I said. Then I added, "They're unfortunate people."

"Unfortunate?" the short man imitated me. "And where are those people born with a silver spoon in their mouths? Ah, there's still a lot of superstition about."

He was going to say something more but we'd already reached the other bank. I floundered around between the alders, along whose branches huge and strangely clear drops of rain were trickling.

"Thanks," I said.

They didn't answer. The raft was whirling, caught by the current. They hastily thrust their boat hooks into the river bed, tensing their muscles under their soaked shirts.

"We could have given him a push," the short man regretted.

The taller muttered something and soon they had disappeared into the riverside undergrowth.

I stumbled across the soggy meadow, which was soaked and squeaking underfoot. I began climbing the hill, to the left slope of which huddled the house with the red club-shaped sorb.

I don't know why, but I sensed I would meet Joseph Car here. Thus I wasn't surprised to see him on the path winding between the lilac bushes. He was wearing the same black overcoat.

"What happened?" he asked.

"I twisted my foot."

"You weren't home all night. Everyone has been looking for you since dawn."

"Who has?"

Joseph Car's gaze stopped on my face: "Who? Everybody. The partisan, Pac, Romus, even Korsak. They set off around the neighborhood, each in a different direction."

"I was shot at during the night."

"Shot?" he repeated.

"Yes, that's why I ran away. They shot twice in my direction."

Joseph Car's protuberant lips smiled: "You were drinking vodka yesterday."

I wiped water off my face. The rain hadn't stopped.

"I found a bunker, a dug-out, Huniady's winter quarters."

He transferred his gaze to the clouds of steam emerging from the peat bed.

"So what?" he asked.

"Nothing. I know Huniady is living here."

"You're sick," he said, quietly. "You see everything in unnatural proportions and in weird associations. You suspect people of having complexes which they don't have. Please look at them, living their own lives, now better, now worse, they love or dislike one another, they work or idle, are sad or cheerful. But they're normal. They're healthy. It's you who is sick."

He didn't look me in the eye, and that indicated anger. The rain pattered on his coat.

"They call you Christ."

"Who're 'they'?" he raised his eyes.

"The people from the other side of the river."

"They call me Christ," he repeated. "Why me? Maybe we're all Christs and have come down to earth for redemption."

"Whom are we to redeem?"

"I don't know. Maybe something that is outside us, or maybe ourselves, our own life, our acts."

"I don't know anything about that."

"That doesn't have to be learned, it comes of itself."

Trickles of water running impatiently downhill carried dead ants on their crests.

"I'm near the end already," I said. "I'm unraveling and untangling everything."

He looked at me dully and out of a clear sky said: "Justine got soaked. She's at home, reading. You like her, don't you?"

Abrupt rage seized me: "You've asked me that many times."

"I asked you?" he was surprised. "Well, maybe. You see: that's all I have. A person I myself molded. You remember the Golem legend?"

"No."

"It doesn't matter. Pouring with rain, isn't it? Something's happening, something bad. Please go back. That will be best."

And he walked away, down the little alley soaked with water, toward the house.

I wanted to shout something at him, to stop him, to make him accessible, but couldn't find the right word. I began hopping toward the railroad track, stopping frequently to rest. It really was late autumn, the rain smelled of approaching winter.

The monastery bell resounded, forcing a way through the downpour: I looked toward that white building standing heavily across the hill-side. I could see all the monks standing on a wall, except the dwarfish one, who was undoubtedly ringing the bell. They were gazing at the township, at the Sola as it rose hour by hour, and at the other bank where unknown, hasty movements had arisen, a feverish bustling about.

I stopped amidst the tracks. Long lines of rain drops were hanging from the telephone wires. The posts were droning alarmingly. My head started to ache. I gazed unthinkingly around the railroad cutting at the scattered graves of Soviet prisoners whom the Germans had thrown out of the boxcars when they had starved to death. The hands of pious people had raised little memorials to them, but these were now barely visible, marked by the most sacred of signs, the sign of a birch cross.

Someone was running along the track from the siding. His broad smock flapped in the wind like an anarchists' banner. I recognized the railroad man. He was dragging his leg through the wet gravel.

"Welcome, welcome, your gracious highness!" he shouted while still in the distance. "Won't you deign to work?"

"I've twisted my ankle."

"It's always the same with you, if it isn't your head, it's your ankle. Everybody's run off like so many black beetles — and who'll finish the siding? The first train will be here in two weeks, and what am I to tell the engineer? That the intelligentsia fell sick?"

"I can't stand on my leg."

"Pah, this government of ours has made bulls of you. All the lot of you want to do is lie on a couch and think exalted thoughts. But who is to shit and then wipe your ass? If I'd known whom I was shedding my blood for, I'd have done better to lie on a peasant's stove and fart."

I said nothing, for I was terribly cold and could restrain my violent attacks of shivering only with difficulty.

"Let your goddam Anders come on his white horse. Let the lot of you guzzle that criminal freedom of yours. Already I can see how one would rip the pants off another, how one would get the other by the throat, so as to get as much for himself as he can, to fill his own belly and thank God that it's other people who're starving. Now even an engineer's job doesn't suit you, because anybody can get it. You want to be the one and only, the tops; equality gives you a pain in the ass. I can't watch it any longer, it sickens me, I'll take my things and be off, anywhere, by God."

And he hurled his official cap at the rusty tracks.

"You pray along with the rest of them," I said, without anger.

"I do?" he asked, taken aback.

"Yes, every day."

He furtively picked up his cap and began wiping gravel off its soiled peak.

"Well, isn't it allowed?" he asked, aggressively.

"Anyone can pray if he wants to," I shrugged.

He dragged his stiff leg over the stones. He intently examined his already cleaned cap: "The Party forbids us to believe in the Church," he said after a moment. "But this isn't religion, is it?"

"You know best."

"Sure I know. A man alone gets bored sometimes. So he sticks to other people so as to kill stupid thoughts," he twisted his cap uncertainly in his cracked hands. "What sort of a religion is that . . . ?"

I kept silence.

"If you'd lived through as much as I," he sighed finally and made a gesture of dismissal.

He turned and set off lamely in the direction of the siding. He waved his arms as though driving away an intrusive fly. The rain thickened and drummed on the ground like hail.

In my room I fell onto the bed, covering myself with a blanket that smelled of damp. It was quiet. On the opposite wall was the very same picture that greeted me every morning: snow, sleigh ruts, naked birches, and an amaranthine sun setting. Somewhere nearby, as though in the next room, the wind was howling. I listened to its voice as if it were a narcotic, for I would have given anything to fall asleep. But I soon realized that these sounds were a monotonous wailing, a mournful human complaint. Every now and then the weeping ceased; some despairing person must have listened attentively, waiting for me to react. But I lay motionless, my teeth chattering quietly. So the complaint burst out again, even more alarming than before, and thus a stubborn battle proceeded for a token of sympathy, for the most frugal measure of pity.

Finally dramatically accentuated footsteps resounded, the door opened with a painful squeak, and I saw Miss Malvina. She hadn't had time to change her clothes since the previous day's party, and her black dress was crumpled, with roughly torn seams under the armpits. Her usually benevolent and serene face was now contorted by a grimace of desolation, of utmost resentment. Her refined nose, frequently admired by Count Pac, had altered its size and changed color. Gray tears were flowing shamelessly down her cheeks.

She stopped near the door and waited. She waited stubbornly for me to reveal amazement, fright, or at least attention. But I lay motionless, staring at her indifferently. All that could be heard was the sound of my teeth, reminiscent of the rattling of a window pane.

At last she couldn't restrain herself: "It's the end of the world," she moaned, covering her face with worn hands. More tears flowed from between her fingers: "Mister Paul, it's the end of the world."

"Please take it easy. Please take a seat, miss."

She snatched her hands away from her face: "There's no taking it easy. We must go down on our knees and pray to God to protect us," she said forcefully. "The seas will leave their shores, the earth will burst open to the very bottom, eternal darkness will come upon us. That's what awaits us."

"I wasn't home all night. Did something happen?" I said, with difficulty.

Miss Malvina squeaked thinly, another wave of tears flooded her desperately contorted and yet comical face. She sobbed away for a while and then, in a breaking and very quiet voice, explained: "It's Ildek . . . Ildek . . . For the first time in my life he hit me. . . . Now he's lying there and saying the most terrible things."

Something made a terrifyingly raucous noise in the next room: "I'll kill you, you bitch."

With a prompt gesture Miss Malvina opened the door wider: "There, please listen to that. See what that accursed pagan says? I'm an old woman, but nobody ever dared raise their hand against me. But now look, in my old age. I puffed and breathed into him, I carried the poor creature in my arms. And this is how he repays me, the brazen devil. Oh, that the sacred earth no longer bore him!"

"I'll feed your innards to a serpent!" screeched Ildefons Korsak in the other room, and clearly he was feeling ill, for all of a sudden the bed springs clanked.

"Keep talking!" Miss Malvina screamed. "Go on, don't be shy, let a stranger hear what you can do, you rare bird, you!"

Ildefons Korsak groaned protractedly:

"God damn the whole lot of you . . ."

"Oh, oh!" shrieked Miss Malvina. "He's blaspheming! He's blaspheming!"

The bed squeaked, and Ildefons Korsak appeared staggering to the door. He had on the same holiday shirt without collar, a gold stud at his throat. His gray hair, filled with the greenishness of senility, stuck up like a crown of thorns over his temples. Miss Malvina instinctively shielded herself with an elbow.

He stretched out his hands to us. Only now did I see that he was holding his exercise books: "Here they are," he said, vindictively.

And he began tearing the crumpled exercise books with fierce intensity. Later, when he'd ripped them into small bits, as he was standing on them barefoot as though on a snow heap, he stretched out his hands in such a way as to indicate he didn't give a damn.

"There you are," he said. "A present from me to you."

Then he grabbed his pants over his belly, as they had been slipping alarmingly during his activities, turned suddenly, and rushed out of the house.

"He's feeble, sir, his innards are nothing but drains, that's all," exclaimed Miss Malvina in a voice that wasn't her own.

I gazed at that heap of bits of paper. The wind rushed by the house and suddenly struck the rain-soaked window with its fist.

"Did you read that?" I asked.

Miss Korsak began straightening the jabot on her sunken bosom: "Yes, I did," she admitted, quietly. "Just like in a book, mister, silly and laughable. He describes some creatures with three heads, animals, dragons as high as the sky, trees that a thousand men couldn't saw down, poisonous flowers, flies inset with precious stones. And he describes all of us local people, and everyone either a king or a valiant prince. Even you were in it, thrown down from some planet or other, all in a suit of armor which suddenly changes into a penitential shirt. I don't remember all of it, for it was night, my eyes aren't what they used to be, and he writes badly. So I had to skip some pages. And I looked up and there he was, standing in front of me, pale as that wall, scowling, it was awful. I took fright, but he said: 'Laugh. Why don't you laugh? Don't be shy. Why the secret? You can read it by day, when other people are around. It will be jollier for all of you.' I know you have to treat tipsy people with care and tact, so I say: 'Oh, Ildek, Ildek, you certainly know how to string words together, that you do. But why write down such frivolous things — wouldn't it be better to compose a nice prayer or a sacred song, so everyone would have some use from it?' He comes up to me and asks: 'Don't I praise the Lord God in my writings?' I see he's bad-tempered, he blinks his eyes. I say ever so slowly: 'What praise can there be of the Lord God in such a monstrosity? There's more sin and human pride than piety.' So he seizes a handful of my hair: 'You witch, isn't your whole life a sin and don't you offend the Lord God by your scurrilous stupidity?' And makes as if to bang my head on the table. . . ." Here Miss Malvina started sobbing softly: "Just look, mister," she lifted a lock of her hair, "a bruise the size of a watermelon. Just like my hands, all bruises."

The floor planks groaned.

Ildefons Korsak stopped soundlessly, like a ghost, on the threshold. He leaned against the doorpost and fixed an insistent gaze on Miss Malvina.

"You complaining to people, little sister?"

"I'm talking about your ingratitude, brother Ildek."

"But you don't know it all, sister. You gave up your life for Ildek, and he spent half his time in whorehouses."

"You're raving!" Miss Malvina cried, painfully.

"Whenever they took me away to the army, I was always the first to line up at whorehouses."

"Silence! Stop it, you accursed monster!"

"I lay with all the women. With German women, with Russkies, and with Jewesses."

Miss Malvina seized him by the neck of his shirt: "Little brother, you're raving, you're weak, your brains are all mixed up from the vodka! Little brother Ildefons, we shall bear our innocence with us to the grave. That is our wealth, our property, our reward for our whole lives!"

She gripped the material of his shirt so tightly that the veins in his throat stood out like thick ropes. He opened his mouth wide, all black within, and yielding to her struggling, he shouted: "Mongol women, entirely yellow Mongol women, I've had even them!"

She desperately shoved her fist into his empty mouth, until he hit his head on the blackened doorpost. Like a hanged man he kicked the pile of torn papers with his bare feet, gabbling doggedly in his swollen larynx.

"Little brother, Ildefons, wake up," Miss Malvina groaned. "Day is here, the bad night has passed."

Then, all of a sudden, wheels drummed on the cobble stones, someone cried out sharply, then the hind hoofs of a horse being wheeled in clattered rapidly. Finally the cart stopped, the creak of its axles in the sand died away, and the murmur of the rain came back.

Miss Malvina freed her brother, both turned their heads

toward the window. I also glanced in that direction. We listened intently to the rain. Next Miss Malvina, as though in a trance, ran across to the window, barely touching the floor with the tips of her toes. She looked obliquely toward the road leading to town. She butted the windowpane, mossy with dampness, with her forehead, her breath clouding the window until I couldn't even see the gray, soaking wall of rain.

"Nobody there. Nobody came," she whispered. "Illusions. Oh goodness, how cold it is."

And she clutched her own shoulders, covering herself up against the chill of the autumn morning.

"The cart has driven in from town," said Ildefons Korsak uncertainly, holding on to his pants over his sunken belly.

"Who'd come here at this time of the year?" sighed Miss Malvina.

I unexpectedly jumped out of bed on my good leg. Both gazed at me in amazement. But like a turkey with a broken leg, I limped to the hallway, thundering in the empty room.

The cart stood at the gate. Harap, the local carter, was putting the black feed bag over the horse's head. Someone was sitting in the cart, covered by a shepherd's sack.

"And yet someone's come," Ildefons Korsak whispered piously behind my back.

"From some government office, no doubt. Maybe it's the income-tax collector." Miss Malvina crossed herself, taking refuge as fast as she could in the interior of the house.

"It's a woman," I said.

"Where? What are you talking about?" Korsak took fright. "What woman? It's an official, may lightning strike him, they're going to take us away, mister, that they are. I dreamed such terrible dreams."

"Where shall we go to, poor people like us, in such weather?" Miss Malvina sobbed from the kitchen.

Harap threw the reins over the horse's back, dripping with rain, and went round to the back of the cart. He stood on the step and raised the rug. Nickel fittings gleamed in the feeble light. Slowly and attentively he brought two suitcases out from among the pea pods and came up to the gate. He opened it with his foot.

Not until then did the new arrival throw the sack from her head. We saw a woman in an oilcloth coat, her head tied in a big rustic kerchief. She got out of the cart carefully, using the wheel hub like the step of a carriage and entered our yard.

Here she stopped by the hay shed. Rain driven by the wind

lashed her bare, red calves, and she gazed at our house and at us as we stood on the porch. Then she bowed low and hurried toward the door which had long since been locked.

"Regina!" cried Miss Korsak.

She thrust us aside, ran toward the approaching woman and seized the small bag from her hands: "Regina's come back!"

Harap had already gone into the house, while the women kissed desperately, weeping, in the center of the yard. Then I caught sight of the partisan, soaked as a sparrow, behind the black railings of the fence. He stood as though being crucified, leaning back as though he intended to smash the rotten tree stump. Slowly and lethargically, Romus came up from the railroad. Later he stopped beside the partisan and began spitting irritably.

The two women shut the door behind them.

"Look, mister," exclaimed Ildefons Korsak. "We thought she was in America, but here you are, she's come back just like she went."

"She's brought back the same suitcases," said Romus lazily, from the fence.

Harap came out of the house. He surveyed us in silence, then beat the rain out of his cloth cap on his boot leg. He went to his horse, took off the feed bag and, having arranged the bridle with its beet-colored pompom, climbed onto the cart and drove away, without saying a word, along the road filled with clay streams.

"And we've been looking for you all along," said Romus, slowly. "We've been in Zajelniaki, in Podjelniaki, and in Powstancza Gorka, and we looked into the vaults of old castle, too."

"And why didn't you look for me in the Solec forest, Romus?" I asked, raising my swollen foot, which brought me relief.

Romus began spluttering even faster than before. I limped toward the gate, opened it, and went out into the road. Romus turned and gazed at me, as though he'd never seen me before. The partisan rocked, gripping the fence railings with his hands. He gazed at the window at which he'd so often knocked by night.

"Well now, Romus, cat got your tongue?" I asked.

"I said what I have to say long ago," he said, angrily, and evaded my eyes.

I saw someone leaning out of a transom in the house next door, summoning one of us with eager gestures. I pointed to myself with one finger. The protruding hand wagged approvingly.

I limped in that direction, up to my ankles in the thin mud. Finally I stopped beside the hedge, empty as a worn-out brush.

Szafir opened the window wider: "Who's come?"

"That girl from the cooperative store. Regina."

"Has she been away?"

"Yes, she had left."

"Why is there such a gathering?"

"Because she had left for good."

"And she came back?"

"She came back."

Szafir pulled his ragged jacket over his chest. It served the purpose of a comfortable robe.

"I'm not leaving the house today," he said. "You know, my lungs are like a spiderweb. Just a little dampness, and they play like forty-eight bassoons."

"For some people even a day like this is nice."

He gazed at me attentively: "Are you suggesting something?"

"God forbid. I just said that."

He wrapped himself up still more tightly in the jacket: "What was I going to say? Oh yes, I've some business with you. We must call a meeting of the people. And soon, too."

"I'm sick. I already told you."

"The situation is of such a kind, get me, that there's no time to be sick. I'm going to get up too, tomorrow. Paying taxes isn't everything."

"But I'm only here temporarily."

"Don't matter. In fact, that's good. We have to call a meeting. There's only a few of our own people here. Each person is needed."

I wanted to say something, but Szafir had already seized the handle and as he shut the window, he repeated hastily: "No matter what happens, this is our business. We shall have to do it by ourselves. I'm counting on you, a good comrade will be very useful to us. Remember what kind of situation this is."

He slammed the window and for a long time he stood shaking over a flowerpot with myrtle; it looked as though he was laughing at me, but he was only coughing.

I went back home. Already nobody was there. Only the partisan was loitering by the fence. He did not glance at me, soaked to the skin, smeared with the green slime of the railings.

So I went indoors and sat down on my bed. I stared absent-mindedly at the little heap of white paper shreds, marked with the large, clumsy writing of Ildefons Korsak.

Miss Malvina reappeared, still wearing a pained expression. She sat down on the edge of the chair and fastened her eyes, dilated with suffering, on the glass jar containing the Japanese mushroom. Thus she waited for my curiosity.

I shuddered from cold: "Well?"

"He's going to move out. As soon as he gets work, he'll move out."

"Where to?"

"God only knows. There's only a few houses here. The railroad man promised him a job as trackman."

"Who are you talking about, miss?"

She looked at me, offended and with reproach: "I'm talking about Ildek. Our little chicken. What will he do without me? Wicked people will peck him to pieces."

Dragging my fiery leg behind me, I limped to the chest. I pulled out a drawer, from which burst the strong odor of wood devoured by worms: "Do you remember, miss, that there's someone's papers here."

"Some people left them behind," she said, absently.

"Something has to be done about them. Maybe we should send them some place? To the Red Cross?"

Miss Malvina rubbed her eyes: "What for? Where will they find anybody today? They were nailed up in the wall, evidently someone hid them and didn't want people to find them."

"But what if their owner is looking for them?"

Once again I surveyed with rapt attention that face which had always seemed familiar. My gaze followed the rusty flourishes of the signature on his identity papers, seeking to discover the stiff outline of a man's fate.

"So many years have passed," sighed Miss Malvina. "Now water is going to flood it all. Maybe some day some learned men will dig underneath the water and find what we have left behind. Maybe then all this will be more valuable than it is these days. Only God can know."

I went back to my bed, struggling with violent tremors: "What about her?" I asked.

Miss Korsak transferred her gaze to me: "Are you talking about Regina? She's come back unhappy and somehow not like she used to be. She don't laugh or swing her skirt or look a person straight in the eye. 'I've made up my mind,' she says, 'and I'm going to get married.' Because it was the railroad man, Dobas, who found out her address and sent Harap for her."

"He wants to get married?"

"Why not, he's a man, isn't he?"

"He never mentioned this."

"That's how it is, mister. What do we know about other people? They say he wants to start his life afresh. He'll marry and move away before water floods the valley. Maybe that's a good thing. Why live in the past for years at a stretch? Nature wounds, but Nature heals too."

"Is Regina going to marry him?"

"She has to," said Miss Korsak quietly. "Goodness, how the rain goes on and on pouring."

We glanced at the window, which was trembling under the wind pressure.

"The Sola has overflowed its banks," she whispered. "God alone knows if we'll live to see the New Year."

"This rain is necessary after such a drought."

Miss Malvina wiped her eyes: "You're a strange man, mister. Maybe it's better for the likes of you to live your life without knowing where you lived or what people you were with."

"Miss Malvina, I've got terrible shivers."

"Just lie down and cover yourself with the blanket. Get some sleep. A man asleep doesn't sin."

With a sigh she tucked a damp blanket around me: "People say the whole world is uneasy. Everywhere there are misfortunes, earthquakes, floods, disasters the likes of which the world never saw. It seems they even say in the newspapers that in some country, I forget where, a great crowd of people gathered on a high mountain to wait for the end."

The wooden ceiling hung heavily over me, its blackened planks full of interwoven lines, among which I could see faces drawn with suffering and arms raised fitfully to Heaven.

Then the night came early. I extricated myself from a stifling doze like from a heavy feather quilt. I wanted to turn on the light, but the bulb scarcely turned pink and its spiral filament pulsated with a feeble glow until it finally expired. I went to the window: little flames of light flickered in only a few houses.

I opened the door that led to the veranda, which was covered by a red metal sheet. Here the rain was drumming with all its might on the low roof, which was also the ceiling. It almost seemed as though spring was coming with its fitful downpours. But the cold climbed up my legs with a painful itching, while the inside of the window panes was covered by a thick layer of sweat.

"I'll just see if she's waiting," I told myself.

Somewhere in the night that was thick with rain there came a drumming like that of a passing train. The windows clattered, the table shuddered. I found my raincoat in a corner and went out of the house.

Numerous little streams of water were chattering all around as they flowed rapidly toward the road now filled with a cold muck. I lifted up my face to catch heavy drops of rain in my mouth. I drank the bitter water, with its taste of stones, and sobriety gradually returned.

I set off lamely toward the river, which was roaring like a sky-high mill. Scarcely had I passed the tracks than I caught sight in front of me of something like a sheaf of straw driven by the wind: "Who is it?" I asked, "who are you?"

"It's me," the small figure replied, "Father Gabriel."

He illuminated himself with a lantern and I saw his oilcloth coat reaching to the ground, his spikey hood and inside it the infantile, wrinkled face of the monk.

"The Archangel Gabriel, surely," I said.

He laughed eagerly: "If anything happens, we'll invite you to our place, we're high up, the water won't reach that far."

All of a sudden it grew startlingly bright and a thunderbolt plowed with a ponderous rumble into the Solec forest.

"A strange year. People say it's the last," I said when it was quiet again.

"People have been waiting like this for centuries," said the monk. "Every generation has had its own day of judgment marked out."

"Back where I come from, the Jews used to gather in their synagogues and pray all night on the last day of the year by their calendar. The day was called Judgment Day. I can remember to this day that weeping, that despair, that imploring God for an extension of time."

"Please come to see us some day. I'll show you their fine liturgical vessels and old books. A few things survived the war."

"Did they live here?"

"One day the Germans took them away to Podjelniaki and there, under the castle hill, they shot them all without exception. It happened in late fall, maybe precisely on Judgment Day."

"I haven't come across any traces."

"They had an age-old cemetery, but it was plowed up and forbidden during the occupation, and now nobody can even distinguish the site."

"And nothing remained of their life?"

"Did anything remain?" the monk repeated. "Surely only this forest, the river, the hills they used to see."

Another greenish flash of lightning glowed, and we waited for the thunderbolt to find itself a resting place.

"Please come and see us," said the monk.

"Everyone talks to me like that."

"What? I didn't understand."

"Nothing important. Good night."

"Please take care. The river is mounting. By morning it'll reach the railroad."

"Good night."

The Sola was roaring in the darkness. I limped with arms outstretched against the echoes of earth trampled down by cattle. In this way I penetrated among the naked trees of the garden, which were being torn by the wind. I looked for the white cherry tree, but it was no longer there. The autumn rain had ripped the flowers off.

I stepped up to the leaf-filled porch and moved the well-known plank aside. I stopped inside the house, which resembled the nave of a church. The wind was roaring monotonously outside. Above, underneath the roof, something was clanking like the ministrant's clapper on Good Friday.

"Justine," I said, not loudly.

Nobody replied.

"Well, that's all right," I muttered, with relief.

The rain dashed a new wave against the shingle roof, and I felt a sudden disappointment. I took a few paces into the depths of the great room filled with the stench of rot.

"Justine."

Suddenly the cracks in the boarded-up windows blazed with light. I caught sight of her standing in front of me, within arm's reach.

When the thunder died down, I asked: "Aren't you scared?"

"But it was me who caused the storm. Didn't you know?"

Reluctance came over me. I wondered what to say and gazed into the darkness, where the windows were. I was waiting for the next lightning flash.

Finally I found her hand. She was standing motionless, hands crossed on her breast.

"No," she whispered, when I tried to draw her after me to the pile of damp straw.

I sat down: "Completely meaningless."

She stood there in the darkness and was silent: "You're shivering," she said at last.

"I twisted my ankle last night."

Rapid footsteps squeaked; she sat down beside me. I could feel the delicate warmth of her breath: "The river's already flowing by our house," she said, quietly. "It looks terrifying. It's carrying away whole trees with their roots, the fragments of some buildings or other. I even saw a dead cow. Surely we'll have to escape."

"What about them? The men from the building site?"

"They've left. Only machinery and empty huts are left."

"You're cold. I'll put my coat round you."

"No, no," she said, "I'm not cold at all."

I wrapped her in the tail of my raincoat. She didn't stop me, nor did she surrender to my care. She was sitting rigidly, and I could feel her skin, rough with the cold, under my fingers. Raindrops the size of acorns were bombarding the bits of paper that lay around on the floor.

"I have the impression I'm cheating you," I said.

"You cheating me?"

"That's how it seems to me."

"It isn't that simple."

A sudden attack of tremors seized me. I clenched my teeth to prevent their chattering.

"Please tell me what you really think," I said after a time.

"After all, I'm an enchantress. Well said?"

"Oh, you little fool," I muttered, suddenly pulling her to me.

I began kissing her clenched lips, clumsily and without desire. We fell on our backs and through my desperate caresses, I caught sight of the first outline of that steep hill, of the pathway red with pine needles, of the partisan struggling like a fish out of water. I overcame her sleepy passivity, plunged into her warm, lifeless body.

Then I listened, ashamed, to my own heavy breathing. I noticed that the straw was slippery with moisture, my hands were wet, our clothing was soaked with rain. In the little hollow above her collarbone was a warm globe. Moisture from my breath had collected there.

"Are . . . are you happy?" I asked stubbornly.

She didn't reply. So I sat up and tidied her clothing and my own. The wind was slithering across the room, something kept banging nearby, like a door behind a traveler arriving.

"You don't understand anything," she said quietly, sitting beside me.

I took out my cigarettes. She sought my hand of her own accord and took one. Then we both lit up, shielding the cigarettes from the damp that penetrated here through all the cracks in the house. As we inhaled, the red cigarette ends glowing, we looked at one another furtively.

"You're shivering," she said.

"I spent the night in the forest."

She suddenly put her free arm round me. The raincoat slipped off her shoulders, but she was lost in her own thoughts and didn't notice. I snuggled up to her, shaken by more and more frequent chills. She threw away her cigarette, which sizzled a long time, dying in an agony of pink light in the middle of the floor. She embraced me with her other arm and rocked me in that movement she'd learned from me.

"Please tell me whether he doesn't unexpectedly disappear sometimes for a while, as though wanting to conceal the state he's in, his psychic tension, or whatever you call it. . . ."

She rocked me more strongly: "I'm beginning to suspect that you only meet me on account of my husband."

"The information is very important to me."

"Everyone has his own secrets. I don't know. Sometimes he disappears, even in the middle of the night, then comes back as though he's been at hard labor. It's his peculiarity. I've never thought about it."

I was shuddering without ceasing, crouched under the wet raincoat, my head pressed between her warm thighs. She combed through my hair tuft by tuft, as though taking dried spruce needles out of it.

"It's late," I chattered through my teeth.

Her hands fell motionless on my temples: "Let's have another cigarette, shall we?" she whispered.

She coughed at the damp, biting smoke. The river was roaring like a great forest in a storm. I nibbled the hem of my shirt to prevent myself from shivering. A wet bush, bent in the wind, scraped rhythmically against the wall.

She pressed her fingers strongly into my arms and I dared not remind her of the necessity to separate. Walled in by the darkness, she had lost all the features I remembered, I couldn't recognize her by touch, or breathing, or by the smile which, at certain moments, I could guess at.

"Maybe you've changed into a specter already. Well said?" I asked.

"Maybe," and she suddenly drew on her cigarette, and I saw the little teeth in her parted lips and the black shadow of the old-fashioned dimple in her chin.

"Everything's in order," I said. "Enchantresses don't have such an ordinary dimple."

I wanted to straighten myself on the straw, but she again pressed my arm.

"Would you go away with me?" I asked through trembling lips.

She took a long time putting out her cigarette on the floor and then embraced me as before: "You have a fever," she touched my brow with her lips.

"We must go. You'll catch the flu from me."

"I'm immune. I've told you so many times."

"I'm getting something on my lips."

She touched them with her lips. "A girlish affliction. Fever," she whispered to my mouth. "Aren't you ashamed? A great big fellow like you with a girl's soul."

I stirred to free myself from her embrace, but she entwined her hands round my elbow.

"Maybe I'm blackmailing you into these meetings?" I asked. "I myself don't know what to think."

"Nobody will ever force me to do anything."

"I like that very much. I like independent women."

"So I've noticed."

"I have an awful headache."

"Do you want to go already?"

She relaxed her grasp. The throbbing of my pulse was driving into my temples. An abrupt chill seized me, I shivered violently, striking her crouched back with my forehead.

"We must go," she said, softly. "You must drink some tea and raspberry juice before you go to sleep."

"Are you angry with me?"

She rose from the straw, and for a while I didn't know what was happening to her. Then I caught sight of her outline against the background of a window cut across by the stripes of cracks. I had the impression she was swaying her head rhythmically in that dancing and nonchalant move of hers.

"All my hair-do has gone for nothing," she said in her normal low voice that bordered on hoarseness. "I worked half the day and now look, nothing but tatters. I have bad luck, well said?"

It seemed to me that there was some sort of reproach in what she was saying. I rose from the floor and struggled with the raincoat which was as crumpled as a sheet. I wanted to answer, but by that time there wasn't anybody there.

"Justine," I whispered.

I thought she was waiting on the porch. A sudden gust caught me and pinned me against the wet wooden column. The darkness was roaring somberly.

"Justine!" I shouted.

A candle was standing on the radio cabinet in my room. Much time had clearly passed since the moment it was placed there. Curls of congealed wax were suspended over the commode top.

I went up to the window and gazed at my own swaying reflection in the pane. I knew this lean face, overgrown with mediocrity, very well. It always taught me moderation and to be satisfied with what life handed me. Outside, the wind rushed ferociously along the muddy alleys.

Then I heard a monotonous wailing, as though someone were chokingly narrating an unhappy accident. I approached the door and looked through a crack outlined by light. In the middle of the other room, which was a kitchen and dining-room combined, both the Korsaks were kneeling, turned toward the window, which looked out on the east. They were mumbling some disordered prayers, put together clumsily, and in a hurry often bowing low down to the very ground, bows learned from the unhappy people among whom they had passed their entire lives. The candle light fawned upon their stooping shoulders and their silver heads like snowballs. The house was creaking like a ship, weighed down under the burden of this powerful roaring that came from the river.

"Aren't you asleep yet?"

I jumped back from the door, caught in the act of peeping. Regina, wrapped in a woolen shawl, was standing in the veranda door.

"They're praying," I said.

"I could hear them in my room. They've been weeping two hours already. Enough to scare a person. It's obvious that they're from the East. Don't you have any electricity in your room either?"

"No. Someone left me a candle."

"Do you also come from their regions?"

"Yes."

"And aren't you drawn to go there some time, to see what it looks like now?"

"I went a few years ago."

"Well, what happened?"

"I ran along all the old, familiar paths with a swelling heart. Everything seemed strangely small, crowded, poor, entirely different from what I'd carried in my memory."

She sat down on the edge of my bed and pulled her shawl more closely around her.

"One ought not to go back," I said. "A landscape without people means nothing. Now I'm sorry I went there. I should have been satisfied with my memories."

"Are your relatives still living? Your mother, father, family?"

Only now did I notice that I was still wearing my raincoat, from which black drops were trickling to the cherrywood floor. I wanted to take it off, but a malicious chill again ran through me and hurt deep down in the depths of my chest.

"I'd rather not talk of that. My life has gone in such a way that I can neither remake nor correct it. I meant the best, and maybe it was precisely on account of that excessive attention that everything went wrong."

"Please shut the door. I can't bear hearing them," Regina said quietly.

I did as she asked, then sat down on the chair plaited from blackened straw. A warmish stench of rubber oozed from my raincoat.

"So you came back, miss?"

She nodded.

"I stayed at a girl friend's. My very best friend since childhood. How often we used to promise one another we'd never part, that nothing would ever separate us! She got married a few years back, they've a child. She, this Kazia, was good to me like she always was, she loves like she always did, but she was embarrassed, and I felt unhappy for no reason. Along came Harap and waited half the day in front of the house, and we were sobbing away like two crybabies, suddenly I packed everything and when nobody was looking — stole softly downstairs into the street. She, Kazia, didn't run after me, but I could see her at the window, as she stood there to the very end, until we drove out of that street. That's how it was."

She smiled timidly. The candle flame was trying to break away from the captivity of the wick. Ragged shadows like large bats were running across the walls. She gazed at me for a long time and I, embarrassed by her gaze, no longer hid my condition, my teeth chattering shamelessly.

"You've been with a woman," she said.

I wanted to protest, but merely hid my face deeper in my wet collar.

"You've been with a bad woman," she repeated.

"Miss Regina, what are you saying?" I muttered, without conviction.

"I know it, don't try and defend yourself. You have her smell on you."

Pointlessly I beat the tails of the raincoat, avoiding her eyes: "I'm sick. I've twisted my ankle, I've got the shivers."

"You've caught cold, for sure."

"I am running a temperature. My head aches. I'm in a bad state, Miss Regina."

The tips of her teeth gleamed glaringly in her mouth. In this grimace she was ugly and cruel. "You'll survive," she whispered. "You'll get better, for sure. A man only dies when he doesn't want to."

"You know what, miss — I loathe my own appearance, my own body, my own thoughts."

"It'll pass. Everything passes. Otherwise our hearts would have broken long ago and the earth would be going round empty as a snowball."

"Miss Regina, I know myself very well. I see with horror that day by day I'm fading, balding, slowly becoming as invisible as air."

She was staring at the floor, outlining some zigzags with her foot. Then she looked up, her face as always smiling, adorned with shy coquetry: "What sort of talk is this? What kind of chatter? A man and a woman ought not to talk to each other this way. Remember what I mentioned to you before I left?"

The wind rushed through, rubbing against the wall until the shutters rattled. We glanced at the window panes shuddering slackly in the poorly made frames.

"Give me something to make me sleep," she suddenly said in a low voice.

"What?" I woke up from the feverish roaring that was growing in my body.

"I can't get to sleep. I toss from side to side, but sleep won't come."

"I don't have any sleeping pills."

She looked at me sideways: "Haven't you?"

I lifted my gaze to the window pane, which reflected us with an aureole above our heads, like saints.

"There must be some left over," she said, confidingly.

"From what?" I didn't remove my gaze from the window.

"You didn't take them all that time, did you?"

The cold crept up my spine and abruptly began to tickle the

nape of my neck. I shuddered and glanced at her. She was smiling ambiguously, listening to the wind moan as it struggled with the roof.

"What do you want them for?" I asked.

"Insomnia is torturing me, and stupid thoughts tick in my head like a clock."

I rose from the chair and fastened the raincoat: "I don't have any."

"You're lying."

I went to the wall and laid my forehead on its cold, harsh surface. "No," I said. "Please don't ask me that."

I heard her rise and quietly approach me.

"You're sorry for me," she said. "Is it that the goodness of your heart won't let you, or is it your conscience? Or maybe you're scared?"

"Is this why you came here?"

"Human life is the most sacred thing on earth, isn't it? But just look, aren't there enough of us? I feel there's too many. Nobody would notice whether Regina was here or whether she wasn't. The time will come when they'll dismiss us from life as they dismiss people from work nowadays."

I opened the door to the veranda unexpectedly: "Who's there?" I asked.

"It's me," the partisan said. "I'm looking for Miss Regina."

"Please come in."

"No. I'd bring in the mud. Better like this."

He was standing motionless in the rectangle of the rough-hewn door frame. Regina leaned out from behind me: "What is it?"

He shifted helplessly from one foot to the other: "They're putting out various rumors about me here."

"I haven't heard any and don't want to."

"They've thought up such nonsense, such untruths, that I hope it'll stick in their gullets like a red-hot iron till the end of their days."

"He's plastered," whispered Regina, and ran out into the rain, neatly avoiding us.

"Wait, I've got something important to tell you," he rushed after her.

Somewhere through the murmuring a door banged loudly and soon afterwards the partisan's insistent thumping resounded. "Regina, you don't have to let me in, but listen. Everything will be all right. I know that next time it'll go as it ought to. Are you listening?"

He smacked for a while in the muddy clay with his boots: "Regina, I looked for you in town. I knew you'd come back."

Then he remained silent a long time, and I could not make out what he was doing at her door. When I wanted to go away, I suddenly saw his eyes before me in the feeble rays of light.

"What are you sticking your nose in for, you prick with the foreskin exposed," he grated his teeth. "You're the one who started it all."

I retreated instinctively, but he didn't follow me. He disappeared in the rain that had been beating the black, steaming earth for so many hours. It was hard for me to tell whether he'd gone home or was still standing at her door, oppressed by painful grief.

Without taking off my raincoat, I fell on the bed. The dry heat of an oven permeated me. I wallowed in it, seeking a cooler layer of air with my mouth. Misshapen specters protruded in a throng from the opaque depths of the mirror, while others crowded at the window, baring their wolfish fangs, and I fled from them by the sweat of my brow, already close to a liberating reality, yet still plunged in the shadows of a bad dream.

Suddenly I caught sight of Szafir's dishevelled head at the window. He was squirming in all directions and one might have thought he was mocking someone unseen, but he was merely looking for me in the dark room.

So I staggered out of bed and limped to the window. He wasn't dressed, in the opening of his fur jerkin I could see his chest, his ribs patterned like herring-bone. His drenched, bristling hair stuck up in various directions like so many dirty icicles. His mouth was wide open, evidently he was shouting something I couldn't hear.

So I ran out into the street, where it was already day, a dark autumn day covered with heavy rain. My leg hurt and the first puddle in which I wet my foot embraced the shred of throbbing pain like a cold compress.

Szafir was breathing spasmodically, his ribs working like bellows of an organ: "Come to them," he gasped out. "They're there."

"What happened?" I asked, huddling into the raincoat that had stiffened violently and was soaked.

"They've gone crazy. Hurry."

He pulled my sleeve and we ran side by side like a pair of foundered horses. He shouted incoherent phrases through his

wheezing: "They want to get across by the Podjelniaki bridge
. . . They will throw the machines and the shocks into the river.
Religious ecstasy . . . That's the situation."

We crossed the railroad tracks, and beyond a fence of dwarf
pines running along the tracks we caught sight of a large gathering of people praying in the rain. In the middle stood Joseph Car
in his black raincoat, collar up.

He was uttering or intoning an anthem, for his hands were in
constant motion, fluttering over the heads of the faithful like black
branches.

As we ran up closer, the singing stopped and they started to get
up slowly from the slimy earth. Among them I recognized the carter Harap, Sergeant Glowko, his wife and children, both the Korsaks, Romus, the partisan, Pac, the railroad man, and weeping
Regina. They stared in silence and it looked as though they were
expecting us, that they were waiting for just such a turn of affairs.

Now I perceived, behind them, the enormously swollen river
Sola, gray as an elephant, flowing or rather rushing rapidly
toward the south. In the whirlpools of its current it was carrying
piled-up trees, stumps washed out of the earth, hay ricks, while
closer to the shore huge clots of red foam were seething like lumps
of sugar. Such a terrifying roar was coming from it that I thought
rocks as big as our houses were rolling along the river bottom.

We stopped several paces from them and Szafir bent, in order
to pant out the remains of his great fatigue. They looked at him as
if he were a dog scuffling on one spot in an attempt to overcome
the helplessness of its paralyzed rump.

"People," he croaked finally, in a strange voice, "people, go
home. You're not allowed to touch anything from the other
bank."

"Look, he's brought that devil who's already taken a peep into
hell! Remember, the dogs howl when they see him!" cried
Glowko's wife.

I saw the eyes of all these people whom I knew well. They were
gazing at us as at strangers. Hostilely, vindictively.

The sergeant moved a little way from the crowd, gazing helplessly at us and at the soaking wet group: "What ignorance," he
said at last, uncertainly, squinting with one bloodshot eye. "Listen
what the man is saying, excuse me."

And emboldened by the sudden silence he shifted his belt, then
began elaborately to extricate his black rubber truncheon from its
short scabbard. Then he raised it above his head but without

much conviction. With the handle he straightened the peak of his cap, from which water was dripping.

"Well, what are you waiting for? You heard what the man said. There's no cause to cherish religions here. The People's authority, excuse me for saying so, won't overlook it. Better break it up, I say."

He waved his truncheon round and round and fixed his dilated eyes on a little woman who was pushing toward him through the lines of people.

"Zofia!" he cried in despair, recognizing his wife. "I'm on duty."

"I'll give you 'duty,' I'll give you 'People's authority,' you drunk," snarled the diminutive Mrs. Glowko. "You've drunk up a shipload of raw spirits from that authority of yours."

Sergeant Glowko lowered his official truncheon and began retreating in our direction. But she had already caught up with him, had seized his rubber weapon and walloped him straight from the shoulder for the first time.

"Zofia, who're you raising your hand against? Zofia, are you with the reaction against the working masses?" cried Sergeant Glowko and fled briskly toward the railroad. His wife, clutching his coat tails, took great strides after him, laying about him with the black truncheon.

The children started howling noisily, and their cries, like iron grating on glass, cut painfully into our ears. The river was now carrying a broken ladder on which was huddled a rabbit looking like a drenched molehill. A huge gust of wind dashed round the valley corner and struck us with a hundredfold downpour of rain. All of a sudden the oaks on the other side bowed down humbly to the river and the Sola called out more powerfully in a bass voice.

"Everybody's upset," I said through the roar of the wind. "But it isn't worth doing anything silly. After all, so far no one has said that we'll have to leave our valley."

"What's he saying?" voices cried out of the crowd. "What nonsense is that devil saying?"

Joseph Car made several steps in my direction. The other people also moved. They surrounded us in a close, tense circle. I gazed at his face, blackened still more by the rain, at his protruding lips, and his eyes dilated with suffering. His right cheek was twitching convulsively, though he was trying to stop it by clenching his teeth as hard as he could.

"Break it up," croaked Szafir. "Too much is a bad thing. Do I have to explain everything from Adam and Eve? After so many years you still haven't got things straight."

Joseph Car stretched out one trembling hand like a drunkard reaching for a glass of vodka and seized me by the lapel. A little row of small drops of sweat or rain was hanging above his eyebrows. He opened his mouth and I could see it was hard for him to speak, that he was having difficulty in moving his stiffened jaws. He groped at my coat until I felt my flesh creep.

"You," he said in a throaty voice unlike his own, "you've always brought unhappiness to everyone. You must be driven away from human habitations like a mad dog."

"I recognize you," I whispered. "Now I'm certain I recognize you. The same sin links us, the same memory."

Suddenly the whites of his eyes showed: "Let go of my hand," he gibbered, "O Christ, let go of me at once."

And he tried to snatch away his hand, which he himself had entangled in my coat.

"I know why you chose this," I said, quietly. "You always were alien, baited, solitary, relentlessly pursued by the crowd, by the cruel rabble. But now that you're standing in front of them, you're leading them, they belong to you and you won't give up your precedence for anything."

He writhed, bowed down to the ground, gazed from under his brows into my eyes, without the strength to free his stiffening hand.

"It would be better if the river took you. Wherever you set foot unhappiness has sprung up like a thistle. You've been running away all your life, but there's a thorny forest behind you through which there's no return," he shouted, sputtering indistinctly and only I understood his words.

I wanted to throw that bony hand off my coat, and I must have pushed him, for he staggered and, baring his teeth as though in a jeering grin, began to straighten his knees, extended himself strangely above his own height, then raised his arms as though they were wings and all of a sudden fell over on his back. He began jerking his legs and his outstretched arms, his head banged on the ground until it almost rumbled. Foam mingled with the redness of blood that came from his mouth.

We all froze with alarm over him and it seemed as though the whole valley had grown silent. With superhuman force he was battering at the turf, tearing it into little bits, and minute fragments of the black earth tossed around him like so many cockchafers.

"He's dancing!" Miss Malvina shrieked in a terrifying voice. "The Spirit has entered into him! People, he's dancing the sacred dance."

And she fell on her knees, and all the others followed suit.

"We're going to God, we keep going to God, Through sorrow, despair and doubt . . . ," she intoned all at once that one and only song of theirs, the monotonous complaint, the mournful hymn.

And he danced before them, his head ploughing the ground, black redness in his mouth; it looked as though he'd been gorging on cherries.

Then I hurled myself toward him, and they let me, believing I wanted to pay reverence to him. But when I pressed my knees down on his stiff arms like the blades of a mill wheel, when I thrust the iron buckle of my belt between his bared teeth, Miss Malvina grabbed me hysterically by my coat and started pulling with enormous power. But I clung to the sick man, overwhelmed him with my entire weight and could feel him weakening under me, quietening down.

"Don't touch him!" Miss Korsak howled. "It's forbidden! He's a saint!"

"He's sick. Sick, that's all," I said into his hair.

"Let go! Be off, you serpent! The Lord God wants this!"

"He's suffocated the saint," said Harap suddenly, when I grew still, covering Joseph Car with all my body.

Romus emerged from the crowd with the slow movements of a drowsy swimmer and stopped right by my head. I could see in front of me his gaping tennis shoes, gleaming with moisture. He spat a number of times spasmodically.

"It's on account of him," he said drawlingly. "He's guilty."

And he unexpectedly kicked my temple. His tennis shoes suddenly turned black, I raised a hand to my eyes, which I couldn't feel, and then Joseph Car again jerked from under me and, liberated, started to dance.

"He's come to!" Miss Malvina cried.

She unexpectedly grabbed me by the collar, I fell on my back, they rushed toward me, kicked me, hit me, ripped my clothing. In fractions of seconds I could see the darkened sky overhead, evil and convulsively grimacing faces. Later I came to my senses for a while, as they mistreated someone else alongside. I caught a brief glimpse of frighteningly white skin cut thickly across with ribs.

I wanted to get up on my hands, but a leg in a muddy boot

plowed into my abdomen. I fell over again and saw the face of the partisan over me, and his quivering mouth.

"To the river!" someone howled. "Drown them like cats!

They grabbed me under my arms. They dragged me through the battered grass which smelled of gall and drying blood. I gnawed the black earth with pain.

"Look, he's got a cross on his chest!" I heard someone shout.

They ripped my shirt down the front, and cold wet hands groped clumsily for the insurrectionist souvenir. They raised me to my knees, and when I fell again, someone gripped my collar and squeezed me with a dog's lead.

"See, even the likes of him believes in God."

For an instant I caught sight of a bare little tree with rusty flower beds under it. I wanted to tell them something, but convulsions seized me again. I vomited earth sticky with bile.

"Let him pray before he dies."

Someone's fist hit me in the teeth. I felt the salty taste of metal, the taste of the rusty cross. My upper lip started to swell rapidly, and grow stiff.

They wrenched my head backwards by my hair.

"D'you hear? Pray to God the Father."

They grew quiet. They were waiting.

"O Father," I whispered.

"Louder!" Someone thrust his knee into my chest.

"Father," I said obediently.

I could no longer hear the roar of the river. My head was filled with a stifled and mild ringing noise. I felt warm, sleepy: "O Father whom I remember from only one passion, who was lying on a bed stripped of covering, O Father, who bled for many hours until blood lay in puddles on the floor, who saw me with eyes filming over, me surprised by this first secret of life which I recognized in the hour of your death. O Father whom I never knew, whose features I learned from the single photograph that survived, whom I sought out in order to love, in family legends, in the talk of neighbors, O Father whom I have always longed for, whom I was proud of, whom I invented in order to stop being an orphan, O Father who has always been a secret part of my existence, O Father whom I now recall so painfully in years of maturity and I don't know why I want to remember you and bring you back to mind this day, this moment, O Father, remembered for ever in sleep and waking, O Father from the boundary of life and death, O Father with the red altar cloth of a consumptive hemorrhage in your teeth. I salute you, wherever you are, whether in some part of nature or in nonexistence. I salute you, O Father, like a son and I want you to know, Father, that I remember and honor your holy days, that I respect your customs and lessons as I invented them, that seeing old age at hand, a great silent shadow, I yearn for you, unknown Father. . . ."

A muddy hand suddenly thrust the rusting cross into my mouth.

"He's blaspheming!" they shouted.

"Blaspheming at a time like this!"

"Into the river with him! Let him perish without a tomb!"

Again they were dragging me across the slippery turf. I could see, as through a tulle curtain, the remains of a decayed fence and a lifeless garden gone wild.

"But he's heavy, the sonofabitch."

"It's his sins that make him so heavy. Else he wouldn't have gone wandering around like a dog without a master."

"Maybe he killed people in the war?"

"Who knows what he did after the war too."

Suddenly I caught sight of Regina's face. She was walking along, tearful, her lips bitten, staring at me tensely. I wanted to greet her somehow, to smile, but all I could do was to spit out the insurrectionist cross which slithered like a warm wafer on my soaking chest.

"Wait, all of you! Stop!" she shrieked.

I fell to the ground. The clouds were rolling low; if I'd had the strength I could have reached up with my feverish hand and plunged it into their cool, moist bellies.

"Let's throw him into the empty house," I heard Regina's voice.

"Into the river!" they insistently shouted.

"Let God decide," she screamed in a high-pitched voice. "If the water rises and sweeps away the empty house, that'll be a sign that it's God's will."

The clouds, like a great padded parachute, were slowly descending toward the earth until they enveloped me in a feathery pulp and I realized with amazement that they were warm, and were becoming hot, and covered my body with a growing weight, as though someone were pouring warm river sand over me.

I tried to tear myself away from something, but couldn't get away. I strained all my muscles, my heart was thudding desperately, I was choking with effort. This went on for a very long time until finally, after I don't know how many efforts, something split around me and I burst out all clammy into a cold night without a vestige of light. Then I could feel my hands, my itching palms, my legs moving against the cold moisture of dew with a fragile warmth, I could feel my throat swollen with pain and my tongue stuck to the roof of my mouth.

I wanted to rise, but my muscles refused to obey. I was lying on my back, suddenly recalling where I was.

Someone coughed and spat. He struggled with glutinous saliva which stuck to his lips like chewing gum.

"Szafir?" I asked.

"Yes."

"Have we been lying here long?"

"I don't know. An hour, maybe, or a whole day."

"Where are they?"

"I don't know."

I turned on my side and started groping. He heard my scuffling in the wet straw.

"Where are you going?" he asked.

"I want a drink."

I tumbled into the hallway where there was no floor. I caught sight of some fine streaks of cracks, in which a scrap of brightness appeared. I reached for the familiar plank. It was firmly nailed down. Some invisible drops cut my palms like mosquitoes. I wedged my shoulder against the plank, which was smeared with rot. It didn't even budge. So I fell on it with my chest, pressed down with my head, until the dull pain of bones flowed from my brow. There was an enormous roar all around; and almost seemed that we were lying on the bed of a great river.

I turned back to Szafir, who was listening to the creaking of his own lungs.

"Did you get out?"

"No. They've nailed up the door."

"Every once in a while someone was walking around the walls."

"Got to rest. Then we'll both try."

"I'm suffocating in this saliva."

"I remember that the roof leaks here."

We started listening, seeking the patter of single drops in the dense roaring. At last I found a ragged sheet of newspaper and prowled round in the dark with my mouth open, hoping to catch a cool, succulent drop. In the end I discovered it and collected a whole thimbleful under my tongue. Before the drops could warm up in my mouth, I brought this little bit of rain water to Szafir and spat it on to his lips. He masticated a long time, then coughed and said, more distinctly: "Help me turn over on my belly."

We drank the sparse drops of rain in turn, reaching with our heads. Then we fell back to the icy floor, exhausted.

"What d'you think, will the river get this far?" I asked.

"It's happened, it's risen as far as the monastery. We'll find out tonight. Do you believe in God's judgment?"

"Sssh. Someone's coming."

Szafir was silent a while, breathing rapidly: "It's the Sola coming," he said. "It's already close."

"Know what? I'm praying."

He stopped wheezing for an instant. I sensed that he had turned his eyes toward me.

"Every day, evenings, since childhood. I've changed my faiths, views, and hopes, but prayer has remained. It hasn't any words, but is made up of verses from all kinds of prayers which I remember, into which I fit casual supplications and thanksgivings. Often it's an undefined thought, sometimes fear or despair, other times it's longing, forebodings of madness which spend the night within me. This custom between waking and sleep is like kneeling at a solitary, nameless grave."

"But who do you pray to?"

"I don't know."

"Why are you telling me this?"

"I hide it like a mysterious sickness, a shameful ailment, which will appear only after our death. Nobody knows about this."

Szafir was silent, cut off by the darkness. Again there was a noise in the thicket of the homestead, reminiscent of a door knocker.

"Sleeping?" I asked.

"No. I think I ought to conserve my strength. I swallowed my own blood; it'll stay inside me, won't it?"

"Sssh. Listen."

Out of the huge, gray and monotonous roaring a new sound dripped from time to time, as though accompanying the filling of a gigantic bottle.

Szafir moaned hoarsely: "The river has entered the garden. It's flowing among the trees," he said, indistinctly.

I listened to these voices outside, and the pain slowly left me.

"Sometimes, before falling asleep, I have a feeling as if I were running sensitive fingers over the concave edge of grainy material. Then I feel a strange, almost painful despair and see myself from outside as through the eyes of a doctor. I perceive in myself shreds of thoughts, desires, reflexes which are the beginning of chaos and disorganization, they are elements of madness, of earthly existence on the far side of a boundary unknown to us. Once I used to be afraid of that."

"I remember from home a bronze stand with music sheets, a sweaty violin in my hands and the smell of rosin. My father hit me whenever I played a wrong note. My spine became twisted from this hard labor of playing, I walked a little to the side, as if into the wind. In those days I loved the window with its curtain puffed out by a breeze, a window I wasn't allowed to look at," he said, whistling his consonants.

"Szafir," I said suddenly, "Szafir. All this is the result of our getting a handful of playing cards and then to the end we shuffle and rearrange them, seeking order and meaning. Such is our life."

"It's terrible stuffy in here," he sighed. "Couldn't a window be opened? Oh, yes . . . I'm not losing my strength, only I let fall a few drops, the others I lapped up, for I've got to economize, haven't I?"

"I just can't forget. Tell me, Szafir, is it the same way with everybody? For I don't really know people, I don't know anything about them, I see them only by daylight, I comment on what they do according to an order that was inborn in me, but I don't know what they're really like, I don't know what they do at night, in hiding, alone with themselves."

"You snapped up too many of those cards when they were being dealt."

"God, how the rain is battering. It's a cloudburst, for sure. The heat must be draining out of you. Szafir, I'll be back, I'm going out into this day full of autumnal chill to check if I forgot anything, as in a hotel room."

White clouds, freshly washed, are flying low above the trees. Further away is the sky, enormously pure, gleaming with the neatness of spring. This wind which is chasing them, but which we on the ground don't feel, is carrying the chill of the distant Arctic. Experienced people say that at this time the annual movement of the eternal ice is taking place in the North.

We are sitting on the edge of the forest. In front of us is a clearing in a thicket chopped down by the Germans, and railroad tracks are humming vernally. In the distance, almost on the horizon is the debris of the gray buildings of Gudaje railroad station.

Behind us is a night spent in a hurried march. A night with light frost, smelling palpably of ozone. Even now I can hear the glassy crackling of ice in puddles, I can still see in my painful eyes starry bits of the frozen mud which twisted our ankles.

Some bushes have already started to turn green, others stand in little bluish clouds of buds not yet unfurled. The boys are munching last year's blackened cabbage, reminiscent of four-leaf clover. But I can already catch the unbearable smell of bird cherry, a sick smell, a ghostly smell.

"Korvin," I say, "light the fire."

He gets up uncertainly, with his mop of black hair covering his forehead.

"The guard only just passed. We've two hours ahead of us. We've time to cook something," I add.

So he sets intently about the actions he's been trained to perform. In a hole from which a tree was uprooted he finds two suitable stones and digs out a tunnel between them. Quiet brings brushwood and pitchwood dripping resin.

Korvin squats on his thin legs, lost in the bluish cloth of some pants from a German supply unit. He gets out his matches. The sulfur croaks time and again. We watch his ambitious efforts with understanding. But the striking edge is moist, the matches merely squeak on the damp pitch and immediately go out. The brushwood fills with a slack smoke that creeps lazily amidst the liverwort.

"Well, come here, Korvin," say I.

He comes over sulking, mad at everyone. I like him as I'd like a kid from a lower class at school. I still don't know how to free myself of school habits, though I very much want to. And now too, terribly ashamed of myself, I can't turn down an opportunity to show off: "See this," and I show him a rifle bullet.

He nods, still offended, but now tense with greedy, childish curiosity.

"Look."

I push the bullet into the rifle muzzle and smash it. The bullet falls into the weeds and in my hand there remains the cartridge, filled to the brim with little lumps of black powder which might serve elves for stools.

"Sprinkle the kindling with this."

He walks away, carrying the explosive in both hands with respect. A big, meaty flame quickly bursts out, the wood begins to burn, snorting promisingly. Falcon brings a messkit filled with water from a ditch, smelling of snow and rooftops. All at once lively talk bursts out in the quiet of the forest. Someone has groats, another Lithuanian bacon four fingers thick, still another crumbles bread for the forthcoming soup.

"What a sky," Korvin is pleased. "I never saw such a spring before."

But a sudden fear pierces me. He sits down alongside me, leans his elbows on a dead ant hill and gazes at the clouds flying east like great wild geese, at the tops of trees rocking in a quiet, joyful murmuring, and at the old greenery freed of snow, which is now dying under the pressure of fresh weeds.

Furtively I spit on a branch of spruce bright with fresh needles and in this scrap of phlegm I look for red threads. I don't find any. I lie down with a sigh on a pile of last year's leaves. The stifling fear leaves me for a moment.

"You know, Korvin, my father died of consumption," I said, quietly.

He gazes at me with those black eyes of his, filled with kindheartedness: "It's not a hereditary disease, I've heard."

"You think that's true?"

"Sure. You'd look different, a consumptive rarely lives past twenty. And you're healthy, by God, sir."

"Korvin, you know, when we stop for the night, I wake at four or five in the morning, I'm suffocating, I get up and don't know what to do with myself for fear. D'you know what that means?"

"It's the conditions we're living in. I too often wake and can't get to sleep again."

I close my eyes and see the black reflections of clouds on my eyelids: "Korvin, one time I spat blood. Black, repulsive blood."

He keeps silent for a long time. The trees are rustling more vigorously; a cool, tattered breeze has flown between us.

"You caught a cold; it happens often. It doesn't mean anything."

I open my eyes and see his gaze, attentive and surely lying. The spruces circle persistently under the terrifyingly blue sky. I have the feeling that this movement will seize my cold head, bedewed with sweat: "I shan't last long, Korvin."

"That's what everyone says, then they live right up to their death."

I smile, and he widens his protruding, plum-colored lips after me.

The earth smells of mushrooms and mildew. I'm so weak that I can't raise my head. This weakness permeates my legs like a leaden weight, and my hands grip a hazel branch covered with tiny leaves, infant leaves.

"Korvin, I have to make haste. I have little time left."

He brings me a messkit of barley soup covered with dried-up foam: "For you, sir."

"I don't want anything. I'm not hungry."

He stands, leaning over me. I see that the utensil is burning his hands: "Eat it, Korvin. Eat to my good health."

He remains waiting, expecting me to change my mind. Then he sits and starts to gulp down the hot soup.

"Sergeant, sir, we were to report to the rendezvous yesterday," he says suddenly.

"I remember, Korvin. We'll get there tomorrow."

"The commandant is going to be furious."

"This evening we'll attack that little station over there."

He glances toward the clear horizon, then at me: "Our units keep away from the railroad," he says, quietly.

"It'll be the first time."

"Apparently there's been an agreement that we never touch the railroads."

"Do you know, Korvin, that in six months I'll have my own unit?"

He gazes at me a while longer, then goes back to his food. I hear only the scraping of spoons emptying mess kits, the squad is finishing their frugal meal. Slowly the talk, interrupted by breakfast, starts up again; someone begins to hum a country song, heavy with sorrow and hopelessness.

"There's a softness in us, Korvin. Get me? You know what I mean?"

"I know, sergeant."

"It must be smashed. Soon only acts will count."

"It'll be hard to recall these times after the war."

"We'll go out of this cleaner if we go out untouched by filth or vulgarity, like young trees."

"But what if we stay here?" he fearfully pointed to the forest and undergrowth awakening to life.

"We'll leave behind a legend, a memory, a power which the living will use."

"I ran away from home, sergeant, sir."

"So did I, Korvin. They held me by the collar, explained it was better to study, that educated people will also be necessary at some future time. But was that true? Can a man be satisfied with half?"

"I believe that once this war is over everything will be different."

He also is gazing at the sky. Black ants with glistening abdomens are running hastily about the empty messkit.

"We'll arrange things differently, won't we, sergeant?"

I smile, glance at his olive-colored face standing out against the redness of the dead ant hill: "I see you have a program, Korvin."

"No, I don't. But I feel sure that people will be better."

I suddenly cough, putting one hand over my mouth. I remove my palm with the fingers permeated with the pinkness of frostbite and gaze with an effort at the warm hollow, full of drops of saliva which look pink to me, ominously pink.

I hear the martial clash of heels. I look up. Falcon is standing in front of me: "Sergeant, sir, I report that some man is walking along the other side of the tracks."

We crawl to the first trees on the edge of the apiary. A hunched man, with a sack on his back, is trudging along on the far side of the forest. He's carrying potatoes; hauling his poor acquisition he shuffles toward the clearly outlined railroad station on the horizon.

"Don't stop him, let him go," I say.

And I stay on the spot, unexpectedly, since the sight reminds me of something. I watch his heavy step, that of an overdriven horse, the familiar back filled with the rotundity of exhaustion, and the black-covered head.

"He's coming back from trading, a speculator," Korvin whispers.

"There's a man like that lives in our settlement. Nobody knows him and he never greets anybody. He struggles with life as helplessly as a crippled animal. All he can do is help people in the fields. They give him a few potatoes, but more cuffs and insults."

The telephone wires are ringing loudly. A hawk floats high over the forest landscape.

"He walks like an ant, like one of many ants. Let him go on his way."

And I wipe my mouth furtively.

"We see so few people," says Korvin, "that they all seem to look familiar."

I keep still, not having the strength to rise from the damp coldness of the ground. I chew the bitter flower of an anemone and feel its very young taste.

"He's like my brother, the man I hate most of all."

"Korvin, did you know I never had brothers or sisters? That I don't even know the feeling of fraternal hatred?"

"Better not bear the responsibility for shared blood, sergeant."

I glance at him. I catch sight of his profile, distorted by bitterness and his eye, half-closed, angry.

"He betrayed us. The OGPU had taken my father to be shot in 1920, and then he betrayed us."

He abruptly opens his mouth wide: "Look, sir. He knocked out three teeth."

"What for?"

"I don't know. He fought me until he got tired. Maybe he was fighting for his own crooked life, because people ran away from him, but most certainly because I hated him."

"Korvin, do you have any relatives?"

"No," he is silent a moment. "You know, sir, sometimes I thought of going to the Germans and not telling anyone."

He meets my gaze and abruptly lowers his eyes. With a trembling hand he begins to search for something in the waterlogged, thick moss: "I went into the forest."

"Where did you get your pseudonym?"

He pecks the grain of a pine cone out with his fingers and raises it to his parched lips: "Our family comes from Hungary. We're supposed to descend from King Mathias Corvinus. That's the tradition."

All of a sudden I notice beside me a maple tree, still bare and sleeping. A tin gutter pipe has been forced into its trunk, down which transparent sap is dripping into a bottle. I reach out lazily and take the icy glass into my hand: "Who put this here, what do you think, Korvin?"

"Local people, for sure. The Germans don't know about that."

"Well, let's drink up. To your health, Korvin."

"Why mine, sergeant?"

"To your start, Korvin. So that everything goes as we hope."

"How?"

"In general. According to what we said."

I put the bottle to my mouth. The sweetish fluid falls into my throat like an angular piece of ice. My chest hurts, as though ripped by a powerful weight. I cough spasmodically and again wipe my mouth. Then for a long time I look at the trace of juice, which is turning pink: "It went down the wrong way, Korvin, here, drink up."

He wipes the neck of the bottle furtively. I notice it, my throat still tight. He is afraid of catching my sickness.

"Your health, sergeant, sir," he raises the bottle with hypocritical vigor.

You were walking along a road through a ravine with sheer sides and sand that slid down everlastingly. Your mother had just bidden you farewell. She stayed on the threshold, watching you as you turned right and walked away with the heavy tread of an old peasant, in the direction of the town that was drowned in gray snowstorms. She pressed her hands, revealing terrible pink marks, to her sagging breasts, and in her eyes there was trust, the unthinking and irritating certainty that you'd return victorious.

In one hand you were carrying a dark, old-fashioned briefcase, totally ragged, as the thread had long since rotted. Its leather, green with mould, smelled of the leaves with which the floor of the attic was strewn. Your home was a strange house. A pilgrim house, a crossroads house, a house of open doors and windows. All sorts of people came to it, lived in it as long as they needed, then went away into the unknown. For some the road led upwards, for others, downwards. And if they came back, it was always by another track, for in these tiny rooms, divided up according to need like bread, you never saw the same, familiar faces again.

The attic of your house was a large rubbish pile. Everything that poverty could leave behind was collected in its steep interior. Rummaging there, you found unusual objects, often incomprehensible, such as skis hacked out, sharpened, and warped on both sides. There too you discovered wooden boxes with photographic equipment dating from before the first world war, some chemicals of no use to you, stinking fluids, and papers exposed decades ago. It was from here that you brought the briefcase, which was supposed to add dignity and importance to you on this difficult day.

And yet you'd been warned by well-meaning people, and also by unfriendly people, who taught you that it wasn't right to try and cross the boundaries laid down by fate. You hadn't listened to them, and now you were walking along the stony road, while your school friends and contemporaries were walking along the edge of the ravine; they had long ago come to terms with the order of things and were amazed and infuriated by your decision.

So they tipped round stones with their bare feet, and the stones ran rapidly down the sides of the ravine and blocked your way. You jumped over these missiles, taking care that none injured your feet, while they, working themselves up to hatred, shouted: "Hey you, what you got in that briefcase?"

"He's got an awl and a horseshoe!"

"An intellectual — a goat's belly-button!"

"Maybe you'll come back mayor!"

"A mayor who beats eggs for the dogs!"

There were more and more stones. They bombarded you from all sides; one hit your ankle, but you trudged along the deserted road and didn't reply to the taunts of your companions, your friends, with whom you'd started the summer in March with the first swim in the Wisincza river and with whom you'd greeted the winter in November with shared boots to work and play, but whom today you'd betrayed and unexpectedly cheated.

You'd never have let these insults and painful taunts go unpunished, but now you felt something not unlike guilt, so you walked on in silence, yet with stubborn resistance.

Then, when the deep ravine opened out and the town, rising heavily into the sky, appeared, they stopped, for here an invisible field edge cut across, beyond which they never went.

They watched you, shouting without much faith in the efficacy of their taunts; their calling became mournful, increasingly reminiscent of the yapping of puppies. The smell of the settlement, the hot odor of gillyflowers spread around the houses you left behind with them.

Then you decided to rest. You sat down on the bank of the Wisincza, a celebrated river, the adventure of your youth, and washed your bloody feet, so as to be able to put on your nicely soled boots, lovingly tempered with polish, a valuable property, boots which are the distillation of honor.

The river was flowing briskly and disappearing in bright reflections in the dark abdomen of the town. But they were still standing there, high up, halfway to the sky almost, full of the futile hope that you'd go back to them, that you'd give up the insane risk.

However, you plunged into the hot and aggressive city. Your greenish shirt, washed until it was white, and trousers sewn in some old-fashioned style, seemed wretched to you here, unconvincing.

Shielding yourself with the briefcase like an armorial cartouche, you walked persistently to the steep cliff of the town. You passed synagogues located in cellars, orthodox churches scrupulously locked and silent, you even marked a mosque blackened with age. Between these buildings, which your forefathers had erected, you went down a winding street to the right place.

Here an ice-cream man was standing in white muffs. Water was dripping from his box, while he was turning a lotto game in a crooked circle, inviting schoolchildren to have a try, the winner to receive a portion of ice cream that tasted like bland saccharine.

You went into a hall big as a forest, where several hundreds of your contemporaries from all over town and even from the environs were rampaging. They kept up their spirits by comparing their own attire and exterior with those of possible rivals. They were exceedingly noisy, showing off their manners, nonchalance, and certainty of success. In this swarm, this shameless market, you suddenly felt your own nothingness. And you became cowardly. For the first time you discovered the taste of tears.

Then someone came up and touched your head disparagingly.

"What are you crying for, kid? Who harmed you?"

You were spoken to like this, you, the terror of your settlement, an independent person who already knew how to earn a living.

Later the examination subjects were handed out and you, your eyes filled with tears, abjectly and fearfully chose the topic that was most sentimental and stupid: "What tales could a school desk tell?" On the large answer sheets you melted away in humiliation and shamelessly wove into the composition your own topics, dressed up in mawkishness poverty itself, and emotional blackmail.

And yet your life had never seemed to you an object of pity, you were always certain you were living properly, in the full range of delight and pain, flights and descents; it had never entered your head, nor the heads of your schoolmates that you were an ill-used, poor little boy.

So, shocked by your own fears, you dropped tears on those innocent sheets of paper, with timid shyness you saw tears blot the moving words, and you glanced painfully at the professor, a young, stooped man with a swarthy face and black eyes, who was walking among the desks with a smile that took in only his lips.

When all of you went out for recess, you already believed in your total unhappiness because you were an orphan. You became ill-looking, frail, timid. You moved aside for the others with an apologetic smile, you didn't get in anybody's way, you even tried not to breathe, to avoid fouling the air, with its wholesome scents of late spring already merging into summer.

Doing all these things, which had their origin in toadyism, you found your way to a spot where nobody else wanted to come. You established yourself on the far side of a shallow pool with a feeble fountain, which adorned the school yard.

Here you stood with a stupid grin on your face; your little hands, which had trapped more than one frog, tweaking the seams of your pants. Meanwhile your rivals let loose their animal spirits over the entire area. Some even began skipping stones on the pool.

Suddenly a stone, thrown with exceptional skill, bounced some six times across the water thick with plankton and struck you a little below the right eye, almost on your lower eyelid.

You cried out and grabbed the wounded place, your eye immediately swelled up so that you could see nothing with it but the school roof.

You were led down a hallway, glass covers clattered; then your eye and forehead were tied up in an endless bandage. When everything around grew quiet, you saw that the teacher was standing in the white room, that stooping and swarthy man, and he was eyeing you attentively. Beside him one of your rivals, a strongly built boy, was shifting from one foot to the other. More than once he had had to repeat the same grade. You also noticed that he was already wearing the high-school uniform, though without the badge, and was depending — or rather his parents were — on passing the exam. He was glancing furtively at you, with a shade of fear and a great deal of dislike.

"Was it he who threw the stone at you?" said the teacher.

"Uh-huh," you moaned.

"He must be removed from the list of candidates."

You kept silent, gropingly touching the bandage that covered a burning pain.

"He'll lose a year," the teacher added.

You continued to keep silent, not knowing what to say.

"If you accept his apologies, I could forgive him. It depends on you."

The would-be high-school boy opened his mouth and gazed at you tensely.

"Well, do you forgive him?" the teacher asked.

"I forgive him," you said and without any shame burst into tears with your one eye.

"Well . . . beg his pardon," said the teacher.

The big boy took one step toward you and croaked in a bass voice: "Well, I apologize."

"Go to your class," the teacher instructed him, and to you he said, "Stay here."

Then he eyed you carefully while you industriously smeared tears on your left cheek, which did not prevent you from noticing that the teacher's cheek began trembling with a strange tick in time with your sobbing.

"Where are you from?"

"From a settlement."

"Do you know this is a difficult high school for the likes of you?"

"Uh-huh."

"You do have the entrance fee?"

"I don't know."

"Children of state workers have piority in admission."

In utter humiliation you blubbered through snotty lips. You were already capable of any baseness.

"Is this your essay on the school desk?" he took your sheet of paper, stained with tears, from among many others.

"Yes, sir."

"I don't know, you cry-baby, how much longer I'll be professor here," he muttered quietly to himself, holding his cheek with one hand.

"I want very much to study," you whined.

"Well, all right, we'll see," he turned away his face as though he disliked me. "I'm not promising anything. Be off now."

You walked to the door and there you glanced back at him once again. You fixed in your memory those stooping shoulders, the black head and the protruding lips. All at once you were struck with the feeling that you would meet this man again in your life, that something intangible linked both of you for ever. And then for the first time you felt anger and impatience, you regretted your sluggishness. When you took hold of the chill brass door knob, the result of the exam and the further course of your studies were already a matter of indifference to you.

Outside the door was the hall, badly lit by one narrow and high window. You caught sight of several pupils standing motionless by the wall. You instinctively stopped. Then the lout in the high-school uniform emerged from amidst them. He came over to you with a sort of crooked smile, his arms were hanging down lazily and he twitched his thick fingers as though counting money. He didn't stop in front of you but, as though in passing or avoiding you, he struck you unexpectedly in the face with his open palm, so that a sharp echo flew down the hallway echoing against the oil-painted walls.

You froze in horror and almost religious fervor. But they were already walking toward the staircase, talking and laughing casually. You stood there, not understanding what had happened, and felt your cheek cautiously, but found nothing but the burning skin. Then you began looking around helplessly, finally gaping at the window, outside which the schoolboys were jeering at Jews through the railings of the iron fence.

"He hit me in the face," you said to yourself. "He hit me in the face," you repeated.

And now you really wanted to cry. You contorted your mouth comically and blinked your good eye as hard as possible, but the tears didn't come.

Your throat was parched; you sat down in the classroom on the last bench. You were given an exercise in mathematics and drew some geometrical figures or other on the squared paper, repeating in great amazement the same words over and over: "He hit me in the face."

The bell sounded, marking the end of studies for the day. You were one of the first ones out, but on the way you managed to measure yourself against one of the bigger boys. He was only a few inches taller.

You didn't go far down the deserted street that was shaded by chestnut trees. You sat down on the sidewalk and took a pen case out of your briefcase. You carefully inspected the well-used piece of wood, you banged it on the flag stones of the sidewalk to check its stamina. It was still strong. Ash wood doesn't age prematurely.

First the teacher came out. Your unfriendly gaze accompanied him until he disappeared behind the Orthodox church.

Later, the bully and a group of his schoolmates appeared in the door. You rose slowly, stuck the briefcase into your belt and, with the pen case in both hands like a casket filled with jewelry, set off toward him.

He was so fully immersed in his talk that he didn't catch sight of you till the last moment. He stopped with a crooked smile and instinctively handed his briefcase to his friends.

"What d'you want, you clown?" he asked in surprise.

You went up to him, casually rattling the holders in the pen case.

"You, hick, drop that box," his colleagues warned you.

He was shielding himself with both hands, so you thumped him on the gleaming nickel wrist watch. The pen case burst open and flew to the ground, while your victim writhed in pain, putting his smashed watch to his mouth like a wound. Then with your elbow you struck his unguarded cheek and his nose flattened over the watch. Blood spurted, he tried to jump aside behind the others, but you stuck out one foot. He banged his head on the sidewalk so hard that the streetlamp almost resounded. Then you felt a strange chill in your hair and on the back of your neck and you fell upon him with bared teeth.

His friends rushed to help him, but by now you no longer understood what was happening. You were whirling in a dense crowd of bodies, and you kept thinking the same thing — that he'd hit you in the face. Something ripped with a screech, somebody yelped, you suddenly soiled your hand in something warm and wet.

All of a sudden you saw the sky open up in front of you. Then you regretted your weakness, you realized you'd been beaten and humiliated, that you were lying and dreaming of the sky in your stupor. You wanted to moan, you got up on your elbows. At this moment you heard a thundering noise moving away, like a squadron of lancers galloping by in a charge. You saw one of them desperately climbing a slope hairy with grass and come helplessly down again into the street. You caught sight of another rushing back toward the school with the ripped back of his jacket waving like a banner. Your rival, clutching his stomach with both hands, was rushing toward the corner of the street as though he had heard the call of nature. He disappeared and all was quiet.

You got up. Your blouse was hanging on by only one sleeve so you tore it off and threw it into the gutter. Your briefcase had gone. Your pens were still rolling down the sidewalk.

Then your rival peeped cautiously around the corner. You were so exhausted that you hadn't the strength to pursue him. You stamped your ragged boots and he, without waiting, instantly vanished, and all that could be heard was his rapid flight.

The ice-cream man was rotating the lotto wheel. The pollen of a lime flower was floating through the air. A locomotive, lost in the great town, whistled somewhere. And you, with neither your pen case nor your briefcase, the attribute of success, went home from this first examination of yours, with the heavy tread of an old peasant.

"It's getting dark, sergeant," says Korvin, timidly.

So it is. The clouds have already worked through their shift for the day and have departed to somewhere beyond the horizon, red with the after-dusk glow; the sky is perfectly clear, adorned with the first star.

"Tomorrow it will be windy," I say, gathering whortleberries squashed by frost. They taste sweet and make the mouth water.

"The fellows saw a stork in the marshes."

"You're right, it's time," I say to myself.

I rise with difficulty. I'm weak, as though all my blood had left me. I'm afraid of this night, and especially of the stifling time before dawn. With all my power I breathe the air permeated with ozone. I know it's healthy, but my head begins to spin. I lean against the maple tree oozing sap.

"Platoon! Fall in!"

They run toward me with their weapons clattering. They shove and squabble among themselves as they stand in line. They froze during the afternoon and now try to warm up, beating their hands.

I push myself from the tree with my back and go up to them. They're well clothed, all in German uniforms, with solid weapons. That's to my credit. They know this.

"Fellows," I say, quietly. "The commandant has given an order on the strength of which we'll become a company within a few days."

They're listening greedily and I see a frieze of motionless faces before me: "It looks as though after some time we'll grow into an independent brigade. Then we'll work on our own account. You men will be the cadre of this unit."

"If only we could have horses," someone exclaims, uncertainly.

"All Thunderbolt's squadron have horses," another adds.

"I even have my saber buried in the garden at home," Lightning Flash whispers.

Korvin is standing beside me. I feel his eyes on me, he believes in me, he wants with all his might for me to give an appropriate answer.

"There will be horses, fellows. We'll choose the very best. We'll drive the Germans across the whole area, from the lakes to the old frontier."

I light my torch and glance at my newly acquired air-force watch. It's coming up to seven.

"Now we're waiting for the first transport. When it stops at the depot, we'll move off in groups as planned. Remember your job, each one of you. After twenty minutes withdraw in sections to the Smolensk highway. We'll meet there. Now have a smoke."

Hands shielding little flames glow red. Someone puts his heavy messkit down on the ground. Talk begins, laughter, bold mutterings covering anxiety.

"Korvin," I say.

"Here, sergeant," he clicks his heels fervently.

"Korvin," I repeat, "you recall what we were talking about?"

"Yes, sergeant."

"You and your platoon will go next to last. You'll empty the boxcars with people. You'll shoot all the SS men at once on the spot."

Somewhere in the distance a locomotive groans. Sudden movement follows. Men hastily unsling their weapons.

"You hear, Korvin?"

He is silent, but after a moment says: "Very good, sir."

"Repeat the order."

He noisily swallows saliva: "Shoot the SS."

"Any questions?"

He nervously clicks the safety catch of his automatic: "No, sir."

I wipe the dew off my machine pistol. The fellows stamp their feet, treading out unfinished cigarette ends, known as "bankrupts." I see that one man has turned his back on his colleagues and is hastily crossing himself time and again, as though he wanted to accumulate a reserve of blessing.

"There was no order to shoot the prisoners," I hear Korvin's whisper.

"If you want me to, I'll appoint someone else."

He is silent.

"Well, Korvin?"

"No need, sergeant."

At this moment our sentry runs up, all out of breath, trampling down the undergrowth: "Sergeant, it's coming, I saw the sparks."

Everyone falls silent. I hear the dying murmur of the forest. From somewhere far away the heavy clucking of a steam engine working up a slope penetrates to us. It seems as if the engine hadn't the strength, for the heavy puffing dies away every now and then as though checked by a vigilant hand, but soon we hear the pistons working again, closer and closer, ever clearer. I raise my hand.

"Men, follow me on the double!"

We set off in silence in predetermined order along the straight forest edge. We pass dark stacks of snow fencing, waiting for next winter. We run, stumbling in the fragile spring mud, and the bitter air cuts our chests. I'm trying to breathe as little as possible, I am instinctively scared of my own throat which is already as dry as a threshing floor, I'm scared of the tight bands of my ribs, I'm scared of the regular whistling sound which plays within me as in an empty willow tree.

Already the blind, blue lights of the locomotive can be seen. A black cloud of smoke is creeping into the clear, sparkling sky. We can hear the first German shouts.

Then the banging of shots bursts out, they blend into a single transparent substance, they become the air, the hollow atmosphere of this incident, which we shall remember to our dying days.

I rush into the railroad station. A sooty light bulb under a green shade is swaying desperately in all directions. Out of the corner of my eyes I see crouched figures of people lying on a floor that is covered with spring mud. I strike the door of the telegraph office. The glass flies, but I don't hear it tinkling at all. By the desk with the telegraph stands a German railroad worker in a red cap, who raises his hands above his head with fearful slowness. By the walls, Polish railroad workers, confused, raise their hands to the level of their chests, then drop them again, not knowing how to behave in this unexpected situation.

I strip my automatic and hastily begin smashing the telephone equipment with the heel of its butt, I smash the telegraph apparatus and the signal-box switchboard with its changing colored lights. Through a hole torn in the livid paint covering the big window I can see a part of the platform: struggling black figures flicker in the opening, but I can't make out which are my men and which are the others. A woman with her head bared extricates herself with the utmost, mortal effort from amidst clouds of steam, as though out of an abyss. Her mouth is open as wide as possible, but I can't hear her screams. She runs slowly toward me, as if in a dream. For an instant I have the impression she can see me and is making in my direction in search of rescue. Before she disappears, I catch sight of a childish dimple in her chin, filled with saliva.

The windowpane above my head bursts radiantly. Soaked in reddish light, wedges of glass fall onto the shattered switchboard, as soundlessly as if dropped into the thick water of a bog. I see blood on my hands, trickling slowly through my fingers, and withdraw to the center of the telegraph office. The railroad workers are lying on the floor. So I grab an iron box with ticket-office takings and run into the waiting room. I glance at my watch, which has a living, trembling drop of blood on its face. Barely fourteen minutes have elasped.

Falcon staggers in from the platform. On his back he's carrying a bundle of rifles, like a carpenter. I shout to him, but he doesn't hear my voice, nor can I hear my own. So I bar his way and shove the cash box into his hand. He accepts it without understanding and, loaded down by its excessive weight, hobbles toward the exit and into the street.

Through the smashed windows of the waiting room I see steam spreading above the platform and the long red flares of machinegun bursts. Someone is stubbornly ramming his head against the window frame, then moves away into the darkness of the evening. A naked hand emerges every few moments from between the buffers, as if pointing the right way to somebody.

"Gray's" platoon, which was to secure the rear of the railroad station, is now running along the train. I glance once again at my watch. The eighteenth minute of the attack. I urge the second hand on with my eyes. For an instant I think the watch has stopped, but it hasn't; the tiny hair of the hand is going around its section of the watch face with barely perceptible shudders.

I run toward the exit door, where someone is pressing into the corner of a bench, shielding himself with a black, pock-marked sack. In this brief instant, I catch sight of a child's behind, that of a little girl who has covered her head in the iron holder of a spittoon near the leg of the bench, and I see the face of the man with a black sack: round dark eyes and white teeth between livid, fleshy lips. It looks as though he's greeting me with a smile, but it's only a grimace of terror, of tension waiting for quiet. And I know that this grimace makes him a stranger, erases features I've remembered in the form of bitterness and depression.

Already I'm in the street with its angular cobbles. I see a droshky horse which has broken down the railings and is circling round and round, foaming, on a hill encircled by a clasping thicket. Only now does the deafness surrounding my head begin to be penetrated by thinning-out shots and the detonations of explosive charges.

I plunge into the young forest and push blindly toward the south. Now I can hear the firing, retiring into the distance, linked with bursts from automatics. I can also hear the regular, tranquil hissing of the locomotive, a dumb animal amidst men at loggerheads.

Once across the railroad track, I go into the clearing well known to me from the hours of waiting and again enter the forest, thin, quiet, murmuring with the barely perceptible breath of night. Someone is coming after me, someone is panting, gasping air strained through his teeth. I turn my head. Behind me all is deserted, black trees are effaced in the darkness. Now I realize that it's my own breathing I heard. I stop, lean over and for a long time spit the spiky exhaustion out of myself.

Here's the Smolensk highway. A group of men is lurking in a ditch.

"Stop, who goes there?"

"Oldster," I gasp, almost in a whisper.

"Password?"

"Shield. Reply?"

"Sword."

I stumble down into the ditch among shivering men. I press my heart to the stony bank and wait for its rhythm to slow down and grow calm.

"Sergeant, we certainly grabbed arms and ammunition. Four boxcars full of troops."

"A supply train, sergeant. Boxes up to the ceiling in the freight cars. We didn't have time to break them open. Maybe it was butter?"

"If we'd had carts, we could even have gotten away with the axles."

There is some confusion, one man clicks his rifle.

"They're ours. Falcon's back with the miners."

"Did you lay the mine?" I ask.

He can't answer. He nods his head as though he were bowing to me like a peasant, down to the ground.

We go out on the highway and wait.

"It won't go off," says someone. "All they can lay is women."

"But where's Korvin?" I ask. "Korvin!"

"He's here, sergeant," a voice cries. "There he is, under that tree, vomiting."

All at once a mountain of fire rises above the station and the heavy thunder of the explosion strikes us. Someone had staggered and sat down in a puddle, cursing desperately.

"Well, lads. It went off like a elephant's fart."

They start laughing again but in a way entirely different from before. Someone lights a cigarette, another munches a stolen crust of bread, someone else undoes his pants, the buckle of his belt clinking.

I go up to the boy hunched by the tree. I put a hand on his shoulders, which are bent like a bow: "Korvin. Well, Korvin, how did it go?"

He presses himself closer to the tree and doesn't answer. So I pat him clumsily and go back to the road.

"Did everybody come back?"

"Four didn't."

"Sssh, someone's coming."

"Yes, they're coming."

Everyone falls silent, and nobody even asks for the password. Two men are dragging something as long as a mattress. They put it down in the middle of the road.

"We threw our rifles away," I recognize the voice of Quiet. "Couldn't be helped."

"Who's that?" asks Falcon.

"It's Lightning Flash. He must have got hit in the ass, for his pants are full of blood."

I go up to them. The platoon is silent.

"Is he still alive?"

"Who can tell? He groaned a while back."

"Orderly! Dress his wound. And make stretchers."

Later we're walking through the night under the stars of the Big Dipper. We skirt villages which greet us with the barking of dogs. I can hear cautious whispering behind me. Tired feet tramp regularly over the shallow mud.

Suddenly there is a horrifying shriek: "O Christ, dear Christ! I can't stand it!"

I stop, so do they. We're all shivering with the penetrating cold.

"That him?" I ask.

"Yes. That was Lightning Flash."

"Carry him carefully, lads."

We move on. I check my compass and watch.

"That's as much help to him as incense to a dead man," someone mutters.

We proceed, persistently silent. Near me, on the other side of the highway, someone is dragging his feet. I hesitate a while, then ask: "That you, Korvin?"

"Yes, sergeant."

"Feeling better?"

"Yes," he whispers reluctantly and I have the impression he's turned his head away.

I know very well that I must say something to him. I straighten my automatic and only now do I realize that mine is clean, while their weapons are frost-covered, because they'd been heated.

"Korvin, you know I was scared at the beginning."

He is silent, but I'm certain he glances toward me.

"When I joined the unit, I couldn't control my fear during the first weeks."

"Sergeant, I know how it really was, sir. The lads told me."

"Don't you believe them. I was really scared. Not until I got a command, understand, when I was appointed leader, did I stop being really scared. There's some psychological quirk here."

He is walking along in silence, head bowed.

"You'll get a platoon in my company, Korvin."

All of a sudden I shuddered with the cold. A shallow mist is suspended over the fields. This coldness comes from it.

"Did you hear me, Korvin?"

"Yes, sir."

"For Christ's sake, lads, finish me off," Lightning Flash suddenly howls. "May the ground cover this sonofabitch, let him die by someone else's fence!"

We instinctively quicken our pace.

"How he howls, like a wolf, it turns you up to hear him," someone behind mutters.

"We'll hear our fill of it."

Again we're entering forest, high, wild. Somewhere in the depths some unknown bird cries out with a voice as startling as a crane's. No branches stir. Calm before dawn.

The track here is barely perceptible. Brushes of dry heath in the ruts. Clean sand shows white, like snow drifts. We're close.

"May the swine devour your brain, you accursed hangman," the wounded partisan Lightning Flash yells. "May you die like me! Lads, have mercy, I can't stand it!"

And he weeps aloud to the whole forest, and the wilderness does not stifle his wild lamentations; on the contrary, it intensifies and multiplies with echoes. We walk in the steep nave of the sobbing of the dying man.

In the hamlet where the unit is quartered, they carry him into the hut where the field hospital is located. The lads go off to the barn to sleep until evening. But I stay by the porch of this little hospital. In the kitchen window I see an old woman dressing. She kisses a scapula hanging on a brown string and intones the Morning Office in a voice hoarse with sleep: "Lips, begin to praise the Holy Virgin . . ."

The neighing of horses comes from the stable. They stamp their hoofs, shod for winter, on the thick planks that make up the floor. Little flames of kindling appear in all houses of the village. The sentry on duty in front of the commandant's house yawns desperately; he's having a hard time, he groans and can't stop his early morning yawns.

"Oh God, brothers, friends, do something," Lighting Flash shrieks in the dark interior. "I curse you, you bandit! I curse you for all eternity!"

Then he howls on one note, unceasingly, without a break. I feel a chill in my hair, the nape of my neck is cold, the skin creeps. Suddenly I grab the little column of the porch with both hands, drag my heavy body up one step and then another, and I know I must go inside there, absolutely, that I have to get this bestial howling to stop.

In the door I collide with Quiet. The lad looks at me with his narrow little eyes, in which is both understanding and cunning. On his chest I see a German iron cross, a trophy which he didn't forget on this accursed night.

"No need, sergeant. Go to bed, that's the healthiest thing to do," he pushes me in front of him, then carefully closes the door.

I remain alone in the center of the little yard, by a well as moss-covered as an old rock. Quiet turns back at the barn door and shakes his head to stop me from going to my partisan Lightning Flash.

The lads of the sentry company come along the street. They're bringing the weapons we captured. Whole armfuls, like firewood. They salute me with admiration and respect. But there, behind me, the racket starts up again. A stool falls over on the floor, the orderly's footsteps patter and the strange, unearthly howling of the wounded man.

I cover my ears in my coat collar. I go into the stable. In the dirty light of dawn I see two rows of rounded horses' withers. I go over to mine. He is chewing clean hay, pricking up his ears, he shakes my hand off when I lay it on his back.

A tousled figure in a black sheepskin climbs down from the loft. I look at his strong, bony legs, which haven't seen either soap or water in a long time. There's something heartening about those legs.

"Ah, it's the sergeant," he says in peasant style, without any military fuss.

"I came to see my roan."

"He's no complaints, sergeant. He fools around all day, getting fat. Why don't you take him for a ride once in a while."

"You see, Karshun, my ankles aren't strong, and the horse would come in useful."

"How's that?" says the outraged groom. "All the platoon commanders ride horseback, but you, sergeant, go on foot like any raw recruit."

"I'll get into the saddle when each one of my lads has a horse. Get me, Karshun?"

"Get you, yes I get you, sergeant, but nobody gets anything out of you going shank's mare. But I look after the saddle and clean the saber with ash."

"Go to bed, Karshun. I've lost one man, and have another badly wounded."

He is silent on the ladder strewn with straw.

"It's God's will," he said finally. "You today, me tomorrow. Everything is ordained in Heaven. Good night, sergeant."

I cough heavily, something within me creaks, and I wipe my mouth. Then I raise my hand into the blurred smudge of early light. There's a black streak of blood. But I don't know whether it's the one of this moment, or that from Gudaje. I wipe my hand in the horse's coat and he slaps my head with his thick tail.

Then I go to my own quarters, to the hut of an old, solitary widow and fall in my uniform into a high bed that smells of straw and apples. I can hear Lightning Flash howling all the time. I myself can't tell; maybe its wind roaring in the chimney?

Someone is tugging me by the arm. Hastily I dream struggle and plunge into distant memories, but his persistence intensifies and drags me out of the dream into a bright and sunny day. I open my eyelids and see, against the background of the golden ceiling woven of circles of pinewood, the official face of Bold, our military policeman and commander of the gendarmery section.

"Come on, Oldster, Oldster, Oldster," he is monotonously repeating.

I sit up on the bed.

"Hell, I overslept."

"No, it's only midday. The commandant wants you."

I want to set off at a run, but he holds me back: "Take your belt and revolver."

"Don't bother me, I only use them in action."

He won't look me in the eye. He straightens his green armband.

"Take your belt, I say. That's the order."

I do as he wants, tighten my Sam Browne belt and straighten my cap.

"Come," says he.

We go out of the house. The bright sunlight hits my eyes. I blink and see, in front of the commandant's porch, the entire unit drawn up in platoons. First Lieutenant Hurricane, our commanding officer, is standing on the first step. All are silent, frozen into immobility.

I halt at the right wing of my platoon while Bold goes up to the commandant. Some sort of weeping, thin and feeble, bursts out of the neighboring house. Everyone looks that way.

"Is he still alive?" I ask one of my men.

He nods almost imperceptibly.

"Atten-SHUN!" Hurricane orders.

We click our heels according to regulations. Meanwhile he takes a piece of paper folded in four out of the pocket of his trench coat. I can see his fair, almost white hair under his cap and a similarly blond mustache, carefully trimmed. He reads monotonously, unaffectedly: "For continuous infringement of military discipline and failure to comply with the orders of his superior officers, Sergeant Oldster is from this day forward degraded, stripped of decorations and the right to re-enter the ranks of our army, and his platoon is dissolved and demobilized. Signed . . . Attention! Hurricane, first lieutenant, commanding officer XV brigade."

He puts the piece of paper away, but I still can't understand the meaning of his order. I stare with an effort at his face, frowning, whitened with that faded hair and wait for him to laugh slightly, in moderation, as is his custom.

But he is avoiding my eyes, gazing sideways at the ground under our feet and says: "I warned you more than once, Oldster. This had to happen."

Anger is growing within me. I forget the proper stance and stretch out one hand, as if to ask for something: "Sir," I stammer, "Sir . . ."

"No fuss, Oldster."

I try to swallow saliva into my parched throat: "They say our units aren't allowed to attack the German railroad. Is that why, sir?"

"It's because you're a swashbuckler. Bold, proceed."

Bold sticks his chest out like a martinet: "Very good, sir."

Then he walks deliberately toward me. He halts one pace away. He stamps his heels tightly together as at drill and without looking me in the eyes reaches out one hand, unfastens my revolver belt, which he had ordered me to wear, rips off the epaulettes with the insignia of a sergeant. For a moment he reflects, eyeing my clothes like a tailor would, finally seizes the eagle badge on my cap and tugs at it with all his might, but the good material doesn't give way. I dig in with my feet while he struggles with this badge as though it were a thistle burr that won't let itself be removed from a garment. In the end, using all his strength, he rips the badge off and almost staggers, suddenly losing resistance. I stand like an animal subjected to the treatment of a veterinarian.

"Company . . . dismissed!" Hurricane roars the order.

I'm a civilian already. It doesn't apply to me. I blink my eyes unthinkingly, alone in the middle of the big yard.

For several hours the military police in couples take my disarmed men off in various directions. I shall be last to go. Hurricane wants to be sure. He's afraid that if I set off first, I'd wait for my lads later, somewhere along the road.

Again, as yesterday, sterile clouds are moving low over the ground, pulling little lakes of shadows after them. I sit with Korvin on an earthen bench in front of the cottage. We say nothing. There's nothing to talk about. I cover my face with one hand, pretending to think, when one of the villagers crosses the road. The hoofs of well-fed horses clatter in the stable, among them one without a master.

Then a young military policeman with a mousey mustache approaches, his boots creaking: "Come along," he says, as if talking to peasants.

We walk in file like a flock of poultry. The gendarme first, then Korvin, myself at the end. I don't look back but I know the unit is watching our departure. We lived through something or other together. Later they'll sometimes recall us, before falling asleep.

We proceed thus along a field path for a long way, surely some three miles. Finally the military policeman stops and says, sternly, "You're free now."

He turns back without a word of goodbye. We stand there and gaze after him as though after a relative. Not until he disappears among the hawthorn bushes do we set off ahead, heavily.

The winter wheat is already high, a rabbit could hide in it. I reflect that a lot of birch trees grow on our land. No, that's not what I'm thinking about at all. I keep going back to that time in front of the porch and I hear the common voice of Hurricane, I begin to recall each word, to recreate the tiniest nuance in his intonation.

"Korvin, your foot-clout is coming out of your boot," I say.

He doesn't even check it, but walks silently ahead, staring at the sandy path.

I want to say something, I feel the need of relaxing this situation, the dimensions of which I still don't know. And I am ashamed of myself; I embarrass this lad who all at once seems to me worthy of respect.

Again we walk a long time without speaking a word.

"Korvin, you know you're only two years younger than I," I try to smile, even though he doesn't see it anyway.

His silence strikes me as insulting. So I decide not to say anything more.

"I see none of our boys," he suddenly exclaims.

"Uh-huh. They've gone home, for sure," I say, soothingly. "I'm not going to let this go unpunished. I know the way to the district command."

A V formation of wild birds is floating above the clouds. What next? What next? My feet sink into the sand. It's hot. Got to unfasten my uniform.

Korvin unexpectedly stops and gazes at the forest: "You know . . ." he says, "you know, I'm going back."

"Where to?"

I can feel the light throbbing of my heart against my ribs.

"To them."

"They won't have you."

"They must. They can do as they like with me, but they've got to take me back."

"You heard the order, Korvin."

"I must, on my brother's account. I've got to redeem myself."

"Don't be a child, Korvin."

But he won't listen to my arguments. He starts running back, faster and faster, as though afraid I would pursue him. I'm standing helpless in the middle of the road, I open my mouth but can't manage a shout.

Left alone, I gaze at the sky and the road; that's a good direction, I'll make it to town.

The sun is roasting. So I take off my uniform jacket, and notice on my chest the identity disc I had made out of the bottom of a tin can. I recognize my angular letters, made with a wire forming the inscription: "Oldster, December 12, 1942." The date of my entering Hurricane's unit. I throw the disc into a field. It glitters with silver like a mirror and falls into the winter corn. A ploughman will find it some day.

Only now do I realize I am carrying a German uniform under my arm, and the first patrol I meet will shoot me on the spot. I have to get hold of a civilian jacket. Sweat trickles down my nose. I'm scared, for the first time I'm really scared, scared as only a civilian can be.

I go into the shade of some poplars shattered by thunderbolts or cannon shells. The road ascends gently, and when I arrive at the circular hilltop I see below me the molehills of dugouts amidst charred logs and ragged chimneys.

Cautiously I enter this village which doesn't exist. It's quiet, I don't hear any cattle or see any hens. A dead conflagration site. Here's a fence spared from the debris, and on a willow stump overgrown with fine rings of young buds, a rusty homespun rag is fluttering in the wind. I pick it up and find a shepherd's old russet coat, left behind on this fence. I pull it on. It's too short, the ragged sleeves too short also. I hang the German jacket, acquired with so much difficulty, on the willow.

I walk on down a road filled with ash. A big-bellied sack is lying by a well with a broken, black shadoof. I lift the sack, which isn't heavy, it rustles and rye straw leaks out of it. So I throw this provender over my shoulders, soaked with moisture and arousing confidence as the insignia of pilgrimage.

A lark is resounding somewhere. The clouds gallop unceasingly into the eastern sky. I'll get home by evening, easily.

All of a sudden I hear the clatter of planks behind me, as though someone were slamming the lid of a coffin. I look back in surprise, though without fear. I see something incomprehensible. People are pouring out of the dugouts, armed with pitchforks, flails, axes. Their earth-colored faces are angry and frantic. They start running toward me in single file, silent, without a sound, like dogs maddened by rabies.

Suddenly my legs turn limp with terror.

"Help!" I shout piercingly. "Help!"

And I rush off in flight, for a very long time down the middle of the road, gasping terribly through my clenched larynx. Later, I don't know when, I look back furtively. There are deserted ruts pressed between two walls of a pine thicket and a small birch covered all bright green at the turn. I fall on the moss and spit out saliva thick as resin. In it I see a blackish twist of clotted blood. I start spitting faster and faster, more and more desperately, with my lips dry. The patched sack lies beside me, I throw it over my shoulders and move on. Alone against them all.

"I've heard my fill in life of other people's tales," said Szafir. "They'd come to me as to a father confessor in moments when there wasn't help anywhere else. They always complain that someone had done them an injury, they complain about others, their enemies, their neighbors, friends, relatives. And as I look into their honest, tearful eyes, so overwhelmingly human, I know very well that they too were injuring others, just as badly. Then sometimes a bolting machine I once saw in a grist mill would come into my mind. There, similarly, millions of grains of corn were revolving at great speed, tearing the skin off by their own weight and power."

"Someone is walking in front of the porch," I said, softly. Szafir stopped. We listened intently to the night closely surrounding us.

"Surely the rain's stopping. D'you hear?"

"Maybe they've come back?"

"They're thinking of tomorrow. They're afraid. They're afraid that when I get out of here I'll telephone to the county town. But I never will."

"But what if we don't get out of here?"

"If we don't, I'll tell you something that can be told only when we can't see one another. You know, I too could whine and bemoan my fate, shake my fist at the sky, and threaten. But I'm ashamed to, and I'm ashamed of myself because I got my share, my measure of sublimity and of humiliation, and that's supposed to suffice. I must manage with it according to how things are, not bothering anyone else with my own hunger, thirst, cravings. You know, when I was serving in the army, the ones I hated most were those who begged for extras."

"You're talking religion. Strange, coming from your mouth."

"I forgot religion a long time ago. Traces of it remain in me, like a remembered provincial custom, domestic habit, or the teaching of fathers. The meaning of it is surely that we exist, we possess a real physical frame and the awareness that with that as our only endowment, we have to flounder to our goal. I've no right to claim more, my dear nocturnal companion. Anyway, who from? From my near ones, who are as sovereign as I am, or from God, whom I never met?"

"But what if that isn't enough for a person?"

"Do you know what I remember from across all these years, both good and bad ones? One little incident in my childhood. Once I set out to go to town, to the picture show, which was my great passion. I had fifteen pennies on me, stolen or earned, I don't recall now. I walked three hours across the fields, the meadows by the river until I finally arrived, tired and covered with dust like a traveler, at my destination. And then it turned out that tickets cost twenty pennies. Probably you recall your own childhood and you'll understand that never afterwards in my life did I long for anything the way I then desired to see that picture, the name of which I can't remember today. I walked away from the ticket counter for at least an hour, shattered, overwhelmed with despair, close to suicide. Then a big officer cadet stopped me, tall, handsome, the personification of charm and success. He asked me, one of thousands of similar adolescents, the reason for my unhappiness. And when I told him, he took ten pennies out of his only zloty and gave them to me. I've remembered this incident for a long time. Not because I'm sentimental, and not because I saw some symbol in this insignificant event. What made me think was that those ten pennies became the basis of my conduct in life. Later, in the highly colored periods of my life story and in its gray, bitter periods, I regarded it as essential to help other people on every occasion, though my acts met with increasing mockery or sneering. This coarse, primitive necessity which was the beginning of everything may, my dear and refined comrade, make you laugh a little, like an entertaining thing of the past, an unfashionable prejudice, a primitive superstition. But I'm afraid that we, in our ceaseless march onward, in the penetrating digging up of the future, we'll discover this simple content by digging, and then it will seem beautiful and unusual to us.

"Listen, if I wander like a pilgrim from place to place, if I can't find peace anywhere, it's not because I want some kind of reward, not because I'm looking for something that can't be found. I wake up every day and fall asleep with fear, horror, a terrible feeling of helplessness. I could choose resignation. The road of sterile vegetating, a state of dullness brought on by the biological rumination of days, cheating the memory by senile little pleasures in pushing checkers about. Is this the only alternative?"

Somewhere the wind rushed through a hallway. We were both shivering with either the cold or a fever, and we glanced at one another instinctively, without seeing each other's faces.

"Maybe by morning we'll forget this maundering at night," said Szafir. "And that will certainly be for the better. But I'll tell you one more thing. All of us are pushing this burden before us step by step, and we know more about it every day. Maybe at some time we'll know it to the end, or perhaps this will never be our lot. But I know one thing for sure: an overwhelming regret for that which is left behind us. And there are moments, certain times, when that regret becomes unbearable, and that's no doubt why from time to time those sicknesses of the social psyche occur, fits of hysteria and terror which seem a lasting paralysis to us, but which are only a temporary collapse of the heart. Did you know, unknown comrade, that the lake which the others already call a sea, and which they're flooding into the site of our valley, was designed by young engineers who come from these parts? It was they, because they knew the course of the river and the topography of the depths, who convinced the higher offices that it was essential?"

"So it's true that everybody will be resettled?"

"Yes, everybody."

"What time might it be?"

"Close to dawn. The cracks in the windows are getting white."

"They gave it to you properly, didn't they?"

Szafir coughed a while quietly, as though ashamed.

They're right, but it wasn't proper," he said at last. "Maybe my head's turned hard or I've turned to stone, no one can set human life back, but I know, I know very well, that something will remain after we're gone. Because we're men who have revolted, because we have taught them self-esteem. I'm sorry to talk like a retired propagandist. I'd never have dared by day, but by night and above all at a time like this, a man is bolder. So forgive me if I offend your ears, but I'll tell you once again that we've made people revolt and, what's most important, that which they bear in themselves can never be taken away from them by anybody."

"Look, whole societies were being born and died in the same bed. It fell to our lot to destroy plenty of houses and to build others, to change many creeds and almost to focus in our fate the fate of the nation."

"Well said, but it's too wide a formula for my case. I'm not much of a man, though I always tried to behave a little like a man. Perhaps because I moved about sluggishly, or didn't stand firm on my feet, sometimes I'd fall down and they'd grab me by the heels. This is my entire life story."

I could hear him rising with difficulty, rustling in the straw. He swayed uncertainly against the background of cracks already leaking a dull light.

"I already mentioned to you I had a talent for the violin. My father got drunk and fell into the river, so they sent me to work. Later, when I traveled to Spain, that Capri of our youth, a comrade who'd come back from Moscow urged me to enter a conservatory in France. There were opportunities, well-disposed people, and so on. But I traveled on and never got there."

He moved heavily toward the hallway, dragging his feet. But at one moment he stopped and said, hesitantly: "Maybe, if I had stayed in France, everything would have gone differently? . . . Maybe today I'd be a famous violinist, a virtuoso applauded by crowds of people?"

"Where are you going?"

"The rain is stopping."

He trundled into the hallway, shuffled awkwardly, and kept coughing with his laborious breath. Finally he called in an expressionless voice: "Come on. We're free."

When I went there, clinging to the walls, he pointed to the torn-out plank: "See that. We were freezing unnecessarily like two Lazaruses."

"It was nailed up before. I swear it."

"It doesn't matter. We can get out."

"Someone set us free."

"Maybe someone smashed out the plank. Maybe you didn't notice in the dark. It doesn't matter now."

He knelt down and on his knees, like a penitent, crawled through. We found ourselves on the porch. Rain was still falling, but not so heavily any more. The trees of the garden were standing in shallow water reflecting illuminated clouds.

"Dawn," he said. "Let's forget about last night."

"Yes, it'll soon be day," I replied.

And we eyed one another attentively, like people introducing themselves to each other.

I took a long time to wake up, struggling out of a heavy sleep in utmost torment. At first I saw only the window. Clutching a few streaks of blue, as though in a hand. All my bones and muscles ached, every inch of my body. My tongue was painful and rough.

Then I saw on the wall the winter landscape in sunlight and recalled my room, the season of the year, all the circumstances of my life. A mug with the remains of some greenish colored milk was standing on a chair woven out of blackened straw. I lifted it to my lips. The milk tasted of honey. I didn't know who had brought this drink, nor when.

Later I realized with surprise that I was lying, fully clothed and still in my tarpaulin raincoat, under an eiderdown quilt. I touched the stiff material. It was dry and felt warm.

Going out of the house, I directed my steps toward the river, which I vaguely recalled from somewhere as being stormy and terrible. A familiar sound brought me to a halt near the deserted house. I stood listening greedily. It was the clarinet of the unknown player on the far side of the river. And this music-making carved out of my memory a distant fragment of a table covered by a thread tablecloth and a livid, horribly livid bottle of soda pop, an old syphon with a lead top.

The naked garden was dry. A cold wind from the north was rolling through the trees, shuffling the leaves on the ground.

I went on further. And suddenly I saw the river below me, humble and quieter, but still flooding the meadows. The entire slope below me was covered with slime. All the bushes had bowed their tops toward the ground, in the direction of the town and in the direction the Sola flowed. A gray matting covered their branches, which resembled the hardened vegetation of a salt lake.

It looked as though a huge and heavy animal had trampled through the valley.

On the far side, machinery was again standing, snouts pointing down toward the water like giraffes at a water pool. Human crumbs were walking slowly among them. The voice of the clarinet was drowned out sometimes in the still great and hurried roaring of the river, which bore along fragments of property and twisted branches of trees as well as thick floating foam.

Their home still stood. A dark line on the wall, just above the stone foundations, marked the place up to which the water had reached. I didn't know whether they were still in there or whether they'd left their house earlier. The house was quiet, it lay heavily under the pointed streak of the red sorb.

Then I raised my head, and, as it turned out, just in time. The invisible jet was ploughing silently through the sky in a blue cavern between the clouds.

"Haven't seen a newspaper in ages," I said to myself.

I went back to the railroad, walking in an arrhythmic shortened step along the railroad ties, among which grew those weeds whose name I hadn't known up to now. I crumbled a woolly clump of gray stalks in my palms. Now I remembered that smell, the smell of wormwood.

They were greasing the points. They were at work not far from a new, temporary ramp made of pine beams soaked in creosote. They didn't even look up. So I didn't greet them, but set to work in silence.

"Just in time," said Count Pac, baring his teeth.

For the first time I thought that he wasn't a particularly handsome man.

"What for? I don't understand."

He eyed his hands in black gloves. Where I come from, young ladies of good family wore such gloves to the harvest festival.

"A celebration is being prepared, right, mister Jasiu?" and he looked obliquely at the partisan.

"Get away from me, or I'll tell you something spicy," muttered the provoked partisan.

The count straightened his fancy scarf around his neck: "An unusual day. Just look," and he pointed off to the side.

I glanced in that direction and caught sight of Miss Malvina, who was hastening toward the railroad shed carrying a large basket covered with a white napkin. Ildefons Korsak was scuttling after her, loaded with a crate from which the gleaming necks of bottles protruded.

"What sort of celebration?" I asked.

The count glanced at the partisan again: "How's that? Don't you know?"

"How can I?"

Pac crouched over the point mechanism. Thin smoke, veiling the railroad man's modest dwelling, was seeping out of the tin chimney pot.

"Is it a secret?" I asked.

Then Romus slowly straightened his back and spat several times, faintly; "Maybe we're going to say goodbye to you."

"To me?"

"People say you're leaving."

We gazed into one another's eyes. He bent carelessly at the hips, rocking a large grease-can, and spat nervously:

"As it is, you leave every morning. . . ."

Regina appeared in the door of the hut. She glanced at the sky, then splashed dirty water out of a washbowl.

"We're doing it for you," said Romus, indicating the can smeared with grease. "So it'll be softer for you to travel."

The partisan, on his knees, was gazing unthinkingly at that point on the horizon where the tracks ran together in a thicket of autumn dust. From there they ran on soaked in red clouds.

The railroad man unexpectedly limped up from somewhere and took a hammer out of the opening of a rusty rail hanging from a small post. He began ringing sonorously on the fire alarm. He did this with a kind of ceremonial pomp, much longer than usual. Then he tossed the hammer back to its place, and began tugging the tails of his navy-blue jacket, oddly crumpled and too tight. Only now did I notice that under this unusual attire he wore a striped shirt and huge red tie.

He coughed and called hoarsely, staring at the ground: "Please come and have something to eat and drink. Please don't stand on ceremony."

And he went into his hut first.

The table of unplaned planks was covered with a tablecloth. On it stood liter bottles marked with sealing wax, and also snacks, town produce from cans and jars, provided by Miss Regina.

The railroad man sat down stiffly beside her. Miss Malvina occupied a place on the left, with Ildefons Korsak on the right. We sat down on a long bench which swayed in all directions. An embarrassed silence fell.

Regina wore a fashionable white dress, no doubt brought back from her last journey. Her bright gleaming hair rested on her bare shoulders, the uneven curls moving every now and then over her large, strangely bright low-cut bosom. Count Pac groaned painfully and straightened himself on the bench so that we only kept our balance with difficulty. Then he stuck out his bluish lower lip and stared like a hungry horse at fresh clover.

"Well, yes," said the railroad man and began pouring vodka into our little glasses.

Regina straightened her hair-do with a sleepy gesture and with a sort of unnatural attention we watched her gesture, her dry hair full of electricity, her white hand, her shameless, hot armpit.

Count Pac again shifted on the bench.

"Sit still, God damn it," the partisan snarled.

"There's no room here, my legs are going to sleep," the count justified himself, without moving his greedy eyes.

The railroad man got up, smacked his lips quietly as though tasting something, then said: "Well, here's to us."

"See how forward he is," said Miss Malvina, discontentedly. "It ought not to pass in silence, without a word."

"Why talk unnecessarily?"

"A day like this," Miss Korsak was indignant. "Maybe it's all one to you. But she's young, she'll remember this moment to the end of her life. Let me tell you."

She rose, excited, with unhealthy flushes on her cheeks. The glass, filled to the brim with State liquor, trembled between her fingers: "According to old customs, I inform all those present and absent that those seated here — Miss Regina and Mr. Dobas . . ."

"My name's Debicki," said the railroad man, displeased.

"The old way is always more comfortable, it's an old habit . . . That those seated with us at this table, Miss Regina and Mr. Debicki are engaged. I beg the guests to drink the health of the young couple."

We rose from our seats. The glasses clanked loudly. Then the warmish liquor poured laboriously down our throats to the accompaniment of industrious gurgling.

We wanted to sit down again, but Miss Malvina protested: "What? Like Jews? I won't allow it. Mr. Debicki, you're a man, it's your turn first."

So the railroad man clumsily embraced the rich, buxom body of Regina, pulling her toward him as though she were a switch lever and gave his fiancée a smacking kiss in the vicinity of her nose.

We tried the snacks amidst an excited hubbub of talk. Count

Pac leaned confidingly to my ear: "Would you believe what she can do? She's nothing but sex, I tell you. I've spied on her more than once. She used to go down to the river when the weather was still warm. She lay on the bank in the sun and sun-bathed. Then she'd find warm molehills and roll herself all over in them. No shame at all, just like a mare. It gives a person the shivers just to think of it."

"Please pass the sprats, there's the jar," I said, uncertainly.

Count Pac gazed at me with his colorless eyes and shook his head.

"Oh goodness, what's the trouble?" Miss Korsak suddenly cried. "Mr. Krupa hasn't drunk a drop."

We all looked at the partisan who was sitting there with bent head: "My head aches," he said, aloofly.

"Come now, you're so sensitive," said Miss Malvina, with a sly smile. "His head aches over a glass of vodka. Don't sulk like a child. At a time like this . . ."

Korsak grabbed him in both hands while his sister began to force the rim of a glass between the partisan's clenched teeth. He struggled a moment, but he was ashamed to demonstrate openly, so he let the drink trickle into him. But he choked at one swallow and spattered vodka on Ildefons Korsak's knees.

"Oh you, you're like a bear with a sore head. That's why your little drink didn't go down well."

Romus was staring dully at the window: "Glowko is going," he said, softly.

But nobody paid any attention. So he stubbornly repeated: "Glowko's going home."

"Who? Where?" cried Miss Malvina. "Call him! Let him come and make merry with us!"

At the sight of the merrymakers pouring out of the shed, Sergeant Glowko stopped by the ditch. A grimace indicative of great moral tension appeared on his face.

"Mr. Glowko, please join us, please, your glass is waiting," Miss Malvina urged eagerly.

He tugged his leather straps and shifted from one foot to the other: "I'm just coming back from my beat. My wife's waiting at home."

"Your wife isn't a rabbit, she won't run away," Ildefons Korsak giggled, ambiguously.

"Please join, do, we're having a great celebration," Miss Malvina added.

Sergeant Glowko sighed painfully and looked around, in the direction of the township: "It's all very well for you, but I've a wife and children . . ."

"Children are an acquired taste," interrupted Ildefons Korsak. "Quiet with that dirty talk. Mr. Foreman, please join us for a minute."

Sergeant Glowko struggled with all his being with the temptation, fidgeting with his legs, which were muddy up to the knees: "I can't, you must excuse me, I can't. My wife, mister, she's upset, she don't have any sympathy. Maybe some other time."

"Tell the minx 'some other time,'" said the count. "Stop playing hard to get. Why these grimaces?"

"It's all very well for you to talk," Glowko defended himself mournfully. "Oh, what a life, what a life."

But, agitated by an ethical conflict, he didn't walk away.

He was seized by the arms and dragged, amidst merry shouting, to the table full of such treacherous attractions.

"But only for fifteen minutes, excuse me," the sergeant defended himself hypocritically. "I'll have one drink then go right home."

"One drink made a certain person's guts burst," said Pac, teasingly.

"Mr. Count, it isn't proper to talk like in a pigsty. You, a learned person," Miss Korsak was outraged.

"I'm no-not a co-co-count," he turned pale suddenly. "I'm not le-learned. I'm warning you for the la-last time."

We all sat down at the table again. The railroad man poured the vodka with deliberation. The sergeant listened eagerly to the agreeable sound, squinting anxiously at the window, where the township roofs glowed red.

"Well, here's to us," said the host.

We drank up, puffed, and Sergeant Glowko looked round the table more cheerfully.

"Maybe we should sing," said Miss Malvina. "Ildek, don't you know any songs for an occasion like this?"

"I'll sing, but only in Russian."

"Be quiet, accursed one. Always the same. And take his glass away from him, for he's feeble, poor man, the smell alone can turn him up."

Regina leaned back and rested her shoulders against the window sill, fanning herself with one hand. She gazed at her own breasts which did not fit into the white, girlish dress. Count Pac shivered all over: "It's hard to si-si-sit still, God knows," he whispered to me. "Impossible to go away any place on account of the rain. I haven't seen a woman for a week."

The partisan banged his prosthesis on the table, so that a slightly-salted pickle jumped up and was neatly caught in flight by Sergeant Glowko with two fingers.

"Don't throw your weight around, sit still like a human being," he snarled, looking wolfishly at his neighbor.

"Oh goodness, they're at it again. Eat and drink, my dears. Mr. Foreman, your glass is full."

The sergeant sighed, heartrendingly: "It's all very well for you," and he swallowed his vodka desperately at one gulp.

Already Regina's eyes were glassy. She raised a hand, gazed at her own white body, then kissed the warm bend in her elbow.

"Oh, the bitch," Count Pac whispered penetratingly.

Miss Malvina tinkled her glass: "I'll tell you something about singing. At home in the East, near Ejszyszki, there lived two brothers, Lonka and Sevus. Lonka, the older, was clever at music. He could play on any instrument, mister: polkas and mazurkas and tangos, he even knew some more serious pieces. When he picked up his accordion, even the most hard-hearted person would burst into tears. Oh, people liked him, that they did, no holiday, no celebration could do without him: 'Where's Lonka, bring Lonka, we invite Lonka,' nothing but Lonka, Lonka. When he came into a hut, it got brighter. He lived like a bird, in the service of the Lord God and of people. The younger, Sevus, he too played the concertina. He picked out things, mister, on the keys but God alone knew what it meant. Whether it was for laughing or crying. No tune, no cadences. He'd set about the dulcimer, and again it was horrid to hear. We all laughed at him, sometimes a person would say: 'Sevus, take your instrument, let's listen to your music.' And he, with a solemn face, like a priest, obeyed the request, fumbled with his clumsy fingers on the strings, until our ears hurt. Everyone giggled, he'd turn red, cross as the devil, play more and more feverishly; we were rolling on the floor, and he — if he didn't throw his concertina or dulcimer on the floor, he slammed the door. He had so much self-esteem. And one day, mister, he left for Poland, he was gone a long time. Until all at once someone said they were writing about him in the newspapers. He began sending money home, people were always writing postcards from far away, that Sevus was a great artist and was playing for people in towns, getting medals and making money. Once the rumor had it that he was coming to Ejszyszki, to his own parts and would give a concert. All of us, mister, rushed to town post haste, and Lonka took his accordion. We bought tickets, as dear as anything, we sat down in the hall and waited. A huge grand piano, like a platform, stood on a dais. Finally out comes Sevus, dressed in black and as pale as though he'd been sick. The people in front clapped and clapped, he bows time and again. Then he sits down on a stool, takes his measurements to that grand piano, adjusts his sleeves, frowns like he was going up for Holy Communion, then sir, he shuts his eyes and started fidgeting with his fingers over the keys. We think he's tuning up the instrument, we wait for what'll come next. Lonka holds his accordion on his knees, ready. But he don't do anything, he makes sounds in his own way. Finally he stopped, and here don't they just start clapping, don't they just start shouting. We stare at one another and can't make it out at all. It isn't proper just to sit there, so in the end we start clapping too. Then we go out onto the street and stand by the horses, and we don't know what to say. Lonka threw his accordion into the cart, and stands with his back to us. The town people come out of the hall, they praise Sevus, they nod their heads. Everyone knows they paid for their tickets, so they have to praise him. And we get into our carts without saying anything, and go home. Afterwards we never saw him again, mister. But in time we too started to praise him, for the newspapers kept writing about him. Even Lonka, when he was drunk, used to show a photo of Sevus and say he was his own brother. Yet everyone knew that Lonka was a talented and true artist, while Sevus was a caricature who didn't know how to play a single tune."

"Well, and what about it?" asked the partisan, somberly.

"I don't know," replied Miss Malvina. "That's how strange the world is."

The railroad man coughed: "Here's to us."

We drank up and splashed the dregs on the mud-blackened floor. The first drops of rain were rattling on the window pane. It suddenly got dark outside.

"Winter's coming," said Romus, in a thick voice.

Miss Malvina energetically straightened her jabot: "Why mourn, why think of tomorrow? Today is little Regina's festival; fill your glasses."

Regina put her chin in her fists and was gazing above my head at the wall stuck all over with newspapers, a wall full of cracks and rotten knots.

"For this wedding I'll give a feast like the world has never seen before," she said, lost in thought. "I'll sew myself a dress down to the ground with a train three yards long, we'll buy a Mass in the church, we'll buy all the lights, at the main altar and in all the naves, we'll buy a red carpet all the way through the church, we'll pay for the organ and for someone to play 'Ave Maria' on the violin. I'll give a wedding feast that will last five days, which will be enough for everybody. No girl ever had such a wedding, for sure none ever did, nor will. Everyone will hear about Regina, people will remember my wedding for years and years, won't they?"

"That they will, my child," said Miss Korsak hastily. "Eat and drink, all of you, don't be shy."

"Without champagne I cannot live," intoned Mr. Ildefons all at once, in Russian.

"Sssh, shame on you, silence!" Miss Malvina hissed, and with a nimble movement she caught her brother in a half nelson. "He's feeble, everything in his head is muddled up. Give me a coat, someone, I'll cover the poor wretch."

"What's that he was singing?" exclaimed the railroad man. "I never heard it before."

"There's many things you've never heard of, but you will," said the partisan, significantly.

"Krupa, I know you very well."

"D'you think she's marrying you for love?"

Miss Malvina laughed aloud hastily, but a trifle artificially: "Why bring in love, debauchery? They're serious people, it don't concern them. The young'uns can roll their eyes, sigh, and waste their time on taking walks and carrying on. But that's a sin for respectable people. Nothing good ever came out of love. Only scandal, lust, wantonness, and later tears and misery."

"And I've tried all the whore-houses from the Elbe to Port Arthur, aha," exclaimed Ildefons Korsak in a muffled voice, from under the railroad man's coat.

Miss Malvina hurled herself upon him with her entire weight, desperately: "Go to sleep, you monster, enough of that nonsensical chatter in front of other people. Please, my dears, eat and drink, Mr. Dobas, your glass is empty."

The partisan kicked the door, which flew open with a painful groan. A cold wind rushed in, dissolving the thick layers of tobacco smoke. Regina transferred her gaze to this crooked rectangle of the doorpost, in which our valley lay obliquely, the meadows covered with sludge from the flood, the river foaming and angry. Her make-up had already melted in the stuffiness of the crowded room, her gleaming hair had faded, she was staring the fixed gaze of an exhausted person: "I invite you all to my wedding. Every single one of you. It's going to be a real wedding. But the rest don't matter, does it?"

"That's the truth, my child, the truest truth," said Miss Korsak hastily. "Eat, drink and be merry, my dears."

Count Pac unexpectedly hiccupped into the fancy scarf at his chin: "Pardon," he muttered, and he stared around with eyes without irises.

He met my gaze, frowned and pondered over something. Then he showed me his teeth, which resembled fingernails yellowed by nicotine. Tiny streams of sweat were trickling down the little straw clumps of sparse hair on his cheeks: "You know," he said, "I'm not all that stupid, I have my own program," and he leaned over intimately toward me, upsetting a glass. I wanted to lean down and pick it up, but he wouldn't let me, he held my shoulder with his bony hand: "No need. Let it lie. You know, I served in the cadet corps before the war, a whole twelvemonth. Just imagine, on the day we were set free to civilian life, when we were collecting our things from the stores, someone clapped one hand to his forehead and he says: 'Mates, Kowalski never once stood guard.' You understand, in twelve months. Others had been on duty up to fifty times during that period, but not me, not one second. You see, what I want to say is that I never intruded myself, nobody noticed me. Maybe others were wittier, more charming, maybe they got the sympathy of their superiors earlier, maybe they got hold of a warmer blanket by it, but they also did guard duty, extra drill, various duties. You understand what I'm getting at: one has to stay in the middle, not among the best, nor among the worst either, but average. You follow me?" he whispered in a confiding tone.

"Yes."

"During the war too, I kept to the political average. Most of the nation neither fought at the front, nor hid in the forests, nor suffered in concentration camps. The ordinary majority stayed in their badly heated houses, ate frozen potatoes and dealt a little in the black market. I did the same. Nobody gave me a medal for what I did during the occupation, but nobody reproved me either. I didn't gain anything, but I didn't lose anything. See these hands," and he thrust his none-too-clean hands in front of my eyes, "they're all there, nothing's missing, though they don't have any souvenir rings from fighting colleagues. That's why I'm not pitiful, you can laugh at me if you want, please do, I can afford it."

"What are you whispering into his ear?" the partisan asked, hostilely.

They gazed intently at one another, heads swaying.

"Oh God," Sergeant Glowko groaned out. "It's all very well for you, but I have to go home. How shameful. Don't persuade me, good people, to take any more vodka."

"You've already drawn off yours," said Miss Malvina. "Nobody's forcing it on you."

"I can't bear it, excuse me, when a full glass is standing there. Let's drink up, good people, let's drink up. But what to?"

"To the happy couple," said the partisan in a voice not at all like his own, and he stretched a full mustard pot toward Regina. "Well, Regina, will you drink up?"

She awoke, wiped her mouth clumsily: "With you?"

"To our friendship, to everything."

"I know you very well, Krupa," the railroad man put in.

"You'll get to know me better. I've one piece of business with you, Regina. I'll remind you."

All of a sudden she dashed vodka into his eyes. He cried out, tried to leap up from the table, but I caught hold of him by his hands. He was blinking rapidly, weeping out the scalding fluid.

Count Pac unexpectedly seized him by the neck. He pressed the partisan's head to his own dry bosom: "You want to know what we're talking about? Want to know? I'm saying I'm a heavy sleeper. Scarcely do I put my head on the pillow, than I'm off. I sleep without dreams right through to morning. D'you know why?"

"No need, no need," Miss Korsak suddenly whispered. "What's all this for? Every man's fate is destined."

She uncertainly stroked Regina's elbow. Opaque tears were openly flowing down her cheeks.

"Light the lamp," said the railroad man.

"No need, better like this. Sometimes it's nice to sit a while in the dark," said the old lady, eagerly.

"I'll sew myself a white silk dress, I'll pin myrtle branches to the veil, let the band play all the time without stopping . . ."

"All right, my child, all right, we'll give a wedding everyone will remember."

Count Pac pressed the partisan's head more firmly: "But sleep doesn't come to you. Even if you do fall asleep, all sweaty, toward dawn, then horrible dreams come, and you waken with a shriek. D'you know why? Because you're sick, infected. You wanted to set the world right, make people happy. You swallowed any amount of these ideas, and they've eaten you up inside. Only have to touch you with one finger, and you all fall apart, like rot."

"Who are you talking to?" I asked, quietly.

"To you too. I didn't swallow pills like an old maid. I don't need to think about killing myself. I have a sound sleep. And who asked you, who needed your eagerness and zeal? Why did you put matters right by force, if no one asked you, you anxious repairman? What are you sobbing at me for, why do you shove your stump under my nose, why curse fate which you yourself chose against people?"

"Let go," said the partisan.

"He's suffocating the man!" shrieked Miss Malvina.

The railroad man leapt up and grabbed a hammer standing by the window. The count freed the partisan, and abruptly laughed soundlessly: "Can't a man joke? After all, this is an engagement party, isn't it, Miss Regina?"

He leaned across the table, took her moist hand gallantly and placed a ceremonial kiss upon it.

The sober Romus had been eyeing me insistently. The railroad man had just lit the lamp, and our secrets were revealed. Miss Korsak was whispering to Regina, the partisan leaned his head on the puddle-covered table, Sergeant Glowko was moving his lips soundlessly, tormented by ceaseless qualms of conscience, and Romus was eyeing me with impudent persistence.

"You kicked me, Romus."

He smiled sleepily, but his eyes remained fixed: "Me? You?"

"Yes, when the floods came."

"I don't know what you're talking about."

"Near the empty house. You kicked me and Szafir."

He was rubbing a dark roll of bread on the table with one hand: "Szafir has been sick in bed ten days," he said. "Very seriously ill."

"Romus, my head's reeling. What are you talking about?"

"I'm saying that Szafir doesn't leave his house. He's in a bad way."

I began rubbing my numbed forehead, urgently trying to remember something: "I must go to see him. There's something I absolutely must tell him, get me, Romus?"

"Don't go there. It's not allowed now."

Miss Malvina fidgetted on her stool: "Goodness, that quiet, it's nasty to listen to it. You men, come, sing a song or say something cheerful. Today's such a happy day."

We were sitting motionless in the sooty light of a small electric bulb. The wind scuffled around the walls, sometimes hurling a handful of damp leaves through the open door. Ildefons Korsak was showing some signs of life under the railroad man's coat by an alarming rumble of his stomach.

Sergeant Glowko pulled himself together and rose with a supreme effort: "Merci," he said. "It scares me to go home. Oh, what a life."

He stood uncertainly, as though expecting us to interfere, then moved staggeringly toward the door. After several attempts he finally got out into the dark, rainy night.

Everyone left in turn, and I too stepped into the cold darkness. I found the tracks and walked confidently toward home, dragging my right leg along the tracks.

But soon someone caught up with me. The hunched figure walked along for a time without a word.

"Romus?" I asked.

"No, it's me, the partisan. Can I come with you?"

"Please do. Awful night. The Sola is rising again."

"Uh-huh," he muttered, his thoughts somewhere else.

We trudged a long time, turning our faces away from the wind, which was blowing sharply, with icy rain. At last, just before reaching the township, the partisan unexpectedly stopped: "I've one question to ask you," he said.

"Well?"

I could feel him hesitate and reflect, as though he were arranging the words he wanted to say. Drops of rain drummed shamelessly on our bare heads. Cold streams trickled over our hair and under our collars. I flinched and wet my swollen, rough lips with my tongue.

"Do you believe I'm a Jew?"

I walked on. He walked after me, precisely in my tracks, waiting for an answer. I turned to the left, along the road that led home.

"Please answer," he said, eagerly.

I stopped abruptly. He halted half a pace in front of me.

"I'm a Jew too," I told him.

He laughed insincerely: "You're joking. But I'm asking you seriously."

"If you think about it, then you'll understand I'm not joking. I'm a Jew because I don't have my own country, because I wander from place to place, because nobody understands what I say. I'm a Jew because I can be crucified with impunity on any telegraph pole by the road."

He stood waiting for me to go on. Somewhere up above, beyond the monastery, the forest was roaring loftily. A burst of rain divided us abruptly. He turned away and walked off into the night along his own road.

"Justine," I said in an undertone.

Water was still dripping in through the leaky roof. A bare branch was caught in a crack between planks. I was scared of this semidarkness, of the ominous creaking of the empty house's ligaments.

"Justine?" I asked, through my weariness.

"Here I am. Here," she said.

Then I discerned the indistinct outline of a figure in the center of the huge room. She was standing with her head bowed, her left leg forward as though she were awaiting the first notes of a dance tune.

I went up to her, breathing desperately: "I ran all the way. I was in a great hurry. I had a bad dream."

"Do you sleep in the afternoon?"

"I can't get to sleep at night, so after lunch I'm sleepy, I'm dying of sleepiness."

"The strangest dreams come at that time of day."

"I had a bad dream. About you."

"I wasn't well. A cold."

"Were you walking about at night?"

"Your fault."

"Mine?"

"It's all your fault."

She raised her head and I caught sight of strange changes on her face. I tried to understand what had happened, but she anticipated me: "I've got myself up nicely, haven't I?"

She was wearing an unbuttoned jumper and a green, homemade skirt. I understood her intentions, contained in these clothes, and guessed her calculations.

"Shall we go?" she asked.

"Yes. I don't like this house now."

I drew aside the slimy planks and we went out on to the porch that was overgrown with the greenness of swollen moss. Smoke which smelled of pastoral poverty, warts and lichen filled the valley that had grown quiet before the early autumn dusk. The garden stood motionless in great puddles of water.

"An awful day for people with heart trouble," she whispered. "They're praying to live through the night."

We set off down a little path strewn with leaves.

"I don't recognize you at all," I said.

"There you are, then. But is that good or bad?"

"Different."

"I don't know anything about you either. I'm terribly curious. After all, you had one foot on the other side of the grave."

"Do you really want to know?"

She looked at me, taken aback, and started to sway her head in that peculiar manner of hers: "Well, no. I only said that."

I took her by the arm. I wanted to lead the way toward the right-hand branch leading to the railroad, away from their house. But she removed my hand: "No need," she said.

And we went along the hilltop, where, below us and within easy distance, stood their house garbed in the black, tousled vine. One of the windows was already pink with light.

"This is almost an engagement," I said.

"What?"

"I ran here to you straight from sleep."

"And what did you dream?"

"About you and a train."

"That's odd. After all, there are no trains here."

"But the first one will be here the day after tomorrow."

We stopped among the sparse pines on a sandy patch. Down below was the road which someone had once built, no one knew why; there was the alder clump deserted by autumn, the muddy fields and the Sola winding south. I spread my tarpaulin coat. We sat down under a buckthorn bush gleaming with drops of water. From here we gazed out, like birds in a nest, at this, our own section of the world.

"You know, I've never uttered a single superfluous word," I said, looking with embarrassment to the side, at the great stretch of the river near Podjelniaki. "I've saved them like a miser, I put them away as others put aside money for a rainy day."

I stopped. After a while she said, "Something smells strange here."

"It's the wild thyme. After the rain. You see, whatever I say turns out stupidly. It's easier for me to talk to you in the evening, when I can't sleep."

"I too had something I simply had to tell you."

"Won't you tell me now?"

"No. No need."

"Is that good or bad?"

She kept silent. On the far side of the river, in the Solec forest, a distant shot was fired, so deformed by the distance that it sounded like a stone falling from a height into water. The first light went on in the workmen's huts.

"Justine."

She glanced at me, then gazed attentively at my face, mouth, forehead. Finally our eyes met. I could sense that she wanted to say something, or rather I guessed that she wanted to convey something of unusual importance to me through this silence.

I embraced her with a commonplace gesture and she all at once stiffened. I began kissing her hair, the nape of her neck, her cold cheek, stealing toward her lips. They were compressed, unfriendly, smelling of the wind. With an enormous effort they resisted my exertions. At length they gave way, swelling with heat. We were now breathing the air with a single gasp.

I unfastened her jumper and plunged my hands into the warmth. Her body wasn't the body of a mature woman. It reminded me of delicate, fine spring grass. She tried to imprison my hands by pressing them to her fragile ribs with her elbows.

We parted our mouths for an instant, snatching fitfully for air like divers who, using the last of their strength, have emerged from the depths. She started to draw away from me, on her knees. But I seized her and wanted to turn her over on the cold raincoat.

"No," she stammered on my lips. "No . . ."

"Why not?"

"No."

"You don't understand me. Justine, I'll explain everything to you," my teeth rang painfully against hers.

"No."

And in this hot, stifling blackness I caught sight of the rigid, shameless face of the partisan. I pulled Justine to me abruptly, but she pushed me away with her knees, I tried to seize her in flight, I pressed my fingers into her wrists but she was already falling back into the sandy chasm. Losing balance, in this unexpected fright, we held onto one another with all our strength. Clinging thus we rolled down the cliff, ploughing a deep swath into the clean forest sand. I saw in turn her lips with the vestiges of lipstick and the low sky, flaking with dusk. Finally we came to a stop at the bottom, in the middle of the useless road, in a clump of silver wormwood.

I looked into her eyes, in which fear had gone out. Then we sat up, divided by the softened stalks of weeds. I saw her again as she had been before. Known for years, surely since childhood, yet always excitingly unknown.

"That's how it is with us. Breakneck," she said.

"You know, I like you."

"Yes, I know," she said.

"I see you don't have any doubts. What about you?"

"Me?" and she fell silent.

I reached out and began gathering grains of yellow sand from her hair that was fine as the spores of a dandelion. She caught sight of a scrap of moss on my neck. We brushed red pine needles, bits of peeled bark, and fragments of unknown weeds off ourselves. I smiled, she returned the smile, we looked at each other with contrarious attention in our eyes, and there was in this a sort of intimate familiarity, a hitherto unknown initiation.

Across the river, the clarinet resounded as usual and suddenly cut through the monotonous roar of the Sola. I stood up and gave her my hand. We climbed the cliff, plunging through sand that was friable as snow. I crawled on the forest turf, which prickled like stubble, reached down, put my arms around her and carried her, hot with exhaustion, to the damp buckthorn.

"The first train arrives the day after tomorrow. We'll take it and go as far away as we can from this neighborhood."

"Where to?"

"I've been lying. I have my own house, my own place. Will you come?"

"It's you who doesn't understand anything."

"Come the day after tomorrow, at a quarter of three, to the siding. That's where the train will stop."

She said nothing.

"I'm not promising you anything, but that's exactly why you probably won't regret taking the step. I want to take you to my own people."

"Is it good there? After all, you ran away."

"That's all unimportant. Now I know that it was nobody but you I was looking for here."

"And what do you promise me?"

"I'll make you a gift of the last remains of my feelings. And then I'll pass, do nothing but play checkers, listen to the radio, and warm my bones in the sun on a park bench."

"Do you think I need that?"

"I need it. I have to invest somewhere this little capital I've scraped together."

All of a sudden she smiled: "Maybe it would be worth risking."

"Justine, I'm talking seriously."

"Better not say anything. Look, how clammy the air is, what

strange stillness. As though we'd been covered by a chloroform mask. A terrible night is coming for people with heart trouble."

"Will you come?"

She leaned forward and kissed me on the lips. We both had parched lips, chapped by cold₀

"It hurts," she whispered.

"Very much?"

"No. I can bear it."

So I pulled her to me, on that squeaking tarpaulin coat. A bright drop fell on my hand. I was surprised it didn't sizzle on the heated skin.

"Why are your eyes open?" she asked.

"How do you know?"

"I can feel it."

I closed my eyelids. The pain on my lips was passing. We rocked together as once before in the empty house. Closer and closer, until we finally sank down gently under the thick branches of the buckthorn. She drew a breath with what was almost a cry and all at once opened her darkened eyes.

"No."

"I honestly don't understand anything."

"So much the better. You'll remember more often."

"I'd like you to be happy."

"Didn't anyone ever tell you you're an egoist?"

"I don't know what you have in mind," I said, uncertainly.

She was lying on her side, her back to me. It was as though she'd fallen asleep all at once in this moist twilight, like a tired child. I stroked her hair helplessly, touched her cool brow and then reached fearfully for her cheek. It was wet.

"Justine," I said hastily. "Justine, what's going on?"

I wanted to turn her over toward me, I reached for her slender neck, but she pressed her face into the navy blue raincoat and wouldn't let herself be moved.

I removed a ladybug which was wandering over her bare leg. "I don't know where I'm to blame," I said, quietly. "Maybe I shouldn't have spoken to you that time, when you were carrying the apples in the basket, maybe I shouldn't have wanted to reach that intimacy which would have given me the right to possess you. I don't know."

She pressed her hands to her lips, as though she wanted to warm them with her breath. A solitary bird flew crookedly over the valley. We could hear the heavy, sick beating of its wings.

"You see, I imagined you liked me, somehow. If I made a fool of myself, I apologize."

I heard my own feeble talk with bitterness. I was using shameless, naked words which turned rotten before they fell to the ground. Finally I stopped, imprisoned in helplessness.

> Lord, our God, hear our prayers!
> Thou with me, and I with Thee,
> Thou gavest me life
> Thou shalt be my end.

The distant moaning, effaced and indistinct, emerged from the river's roar and faded.

"You'll catch cold again," I whispered. "Get up, it's dark already?"

I helped her rise from the smelly rubber of our makeshift bedding. I turned her face to me. She gazed at me and I couldn't guess what she was thinking about.

"You have blood on your lips," I said in horror.

Then she looked down and I perceived her hand covered with redness. Some drops had already trickled between the bristly pine needles.

"What on earth have you done?" I asked, seeking with trembling hands for a handkerchief, which had got lost in my pockets.

I took her hand carefully, and she closed her eyes. Thick drops of blood was falling from the joint of her palm. In a sudden panic I tied the wound with the white handkerchief, looking in alarm at my own fingers, already smeared copiously with gore. Then I let her hand go. It fell powerless into a fold of her skirt. I could feel the coldness of blood on my fingers and was scared to wipe them in the wet moss.

We approached one another kneeling, embraced each other widely, cheeks together. I stretched out my hand with her blood far past her shoulders, over the cliff, over the alder thicket motionless in the dusk. I almost touched the river bank.

"Will you come?" I asked.

She moved her head, but I couldn't see her eyes.

"There's our place on the bank of the Sola. The water will flood it soon. We'll remember the bottom of this lake, well said?"

"Surely," she whispered.

"You smell of wormwood."

She turned her head abruptly: "I have to go," she said.

"How do you know what time it is?"

"I know."

She rose. I gazed at her hand, hanging beside her skirt. The white bandage was already red with blood.

"Will you come?" I asked.

"Mh."

I could no longer see her face in the growing darkness. It seemed to me that she was smiling, her head leaning back.

"Till we meet again," she said.

She walked away, to where their window was shining like a star in the encircling blackness of the valley.

"Justine!" I shouted.

She halted, then moved slowly to meet me. We stopped two paces from one another. She twisted her head like a bird, and was listening.

"I'll be waiting before three o'clock. Please remember."

A pine cone dropped dully somewhere in the dark. An owl hooted, then fell silent, alarmed by its own voice. And Justine was already walking without haste along the path leading to their house.

"Justine!" I called.

Again she turned toward me and again we met timidly among the wet bushes. I couldn't find the appropriate words to say it. I stood silent for a long time, and she waited patiently. A cloud of cold drops poured down from above.

"Well, nothing," I finally said, quietly. "Only please remember that I can't leave here by myself."

She stood a while longer, motionless. Then she turned away and went into the columnade of black trees. For a time I could see the swaying whiteness of my handkerchief on her hand. Then the terrifying quietness, which sick people fear so enormously, sucked her into itself.

I remained alone. I put my hand to my lips, the hand bearing her dried blood. I set off running toward the township, as once before, as in that other world.

In front of the house, in the center of the yard, an exuberant bonfire was crackling. I stretched out my hand and felt nothing. The gate had gone. So I cautiously stepped across the no longer existing fence and only then did I perceive Ildefons Korsak, who was shaking the railings of the fence, half dug out of the earth. A high pile of planks, blackened by the rain, was already lying not far from the hay shed.

"There's no fence," I said in amazement.

"No, there isn't," Mr. Ildefons agreed. "I took it down before nightfall."

Seeing my surprise, he wiped his hands on his trouser legs and straightened his whiskers. He looked rather like a fish with a stalk of dill in its jaws.

"We're getting ready, mister, gradually. God alone knows when they'll tell us to leave. Maybe in a month, maybe in a week, or maybe tomorrow. A fence is the most important thing. A person puts up his fence, and then he's on his own ground, his own master. We're taking the fence with us."

On the railings he'd dug up, yellow with fresh earth, Romus was lying, covered in deep shadow. He gazed sleepily at the red coals which blinked in the gray ashes.

"They'll drive you away too, Romus, to the town," I said in his direction.

He moved sluggishly, stretched out a hand with a blackened twig and poked the charcoal logs. Sparks flew up and took a long time to go out in the motionless mist.

"Nobody will scare me. I've agreed to go into service."

"With who?" I asked, rapidly.

He was silent, outlining something with the twig in the air that trembled above the bonfire.

"With people," he said finally.

"You could have gone to town like the others."

He held the stick at the height of my face and eyed me from under his lashes: "You're terrible curious."

"Surely it's no secret?"

He watched my uneasiness with a reluctant smile: "You go your way, mister, and we'll go ours."

"Who are you talking about?"

"You know who I'm talking about."

He cautiously turned over on his back and gazed into the night above him.

"Why talk with a fool?" said Ildefons Korsak. "Did anyone ever see such a bungler? All the livelong day he wanders along the river, in the alder thickets, in the forest, then he sits in front of Joseph Car's house and looks in the windows, like a rabbit staring at the sunset."

He set about a stubborn rail post again. He was working steadily, carefully, with groans. Someone was coming up out of the night. I could hear cautious footsteps, and then the trembling circle of light enfolded someone's muddied boots.

"You don't write any more?" I inquired.

He stopped his work, looked at me attentively, as though guessing my motive.

"You've lived so many years, you've seen so many countries, met so many people. Aren't you tempted to describe it all?"

"What for?" he replied, sternly. "True, I've seen a lot, but other people did too. I've known people, other people knew them too. Why describe what everyone knows and sees?"

"Don't you think it's worthwhile?"

"I remember, when I was still a child, a young gentleman came from Saint Petersburg. Up at the manor there was joy, mister, they gave away liquor to the people for nothing, any number of guests drove up, there was lights, music, rejoicing, but he shut himself up in a dark room and gave no sign of life. They would shout and beg, he — nothing. In the night someone bolder than the rest crept through the window and saw everything. Mister, what an uproar there was, they took him to town in a carriage with four horses, at a gallop. His family poured out money, for they were rich, that they were, well and the doctors saved him. He came a month later, pale, thin, not as handsome as before. Some said he'd failed an important examination, others that he'd fallen unhappily in love with a Russian princess. Nobody got at the truth, only he knew. But he didn't say anything. He used to walk about with a hunting dog, by himself. He'd smile for no reason, sometimes accost a person with incomprehensible words, sometimes he'd scare children without cause. And he lived like that, mister, unnecessarily long years, and people used to cross themselves at the sight of him. Sometimes I remember him and I wonder what's changed? Aren't there people like him today? Don't they scare people on muddy roads?"

Romus tossed another chip into the bonfire. It crackled sulfurously, and a tall tongue of flame rose above the coals. Then we caught sight of the partisan, who was nervously rubbing his arm on the tail of his top coat.

"Szafir has died," he said, without warning.

Ildefons Korsak nodded his head thoughtfully: "He was carrying it on his back. The dogs were afraid of him and everyone knows that the creatures are the first to sense it."

"He's lying alone in the house. People are afraid to go in. Glowko already telephoned to town."

"Why did he die?" I asked, with difficulty.

"Ach, they must have fed you on poppy seeds. He died because he died."

Romus leaned on one elbow and again began writing with his twig in the smoke of the bonfire.

"Sometimes, as I was passing by his windows, I'd hear a coughing, a coughing that made my hair stand on end. When other people were around he was embarrassed, he swallowed that cough of his, but when he was alone he didn't spare himself."

Ildefons Korsak sat down with a groan beside Romus. He whispered soundlessly and wiped his whiskers: "I wonder where they'll bury him?"

"It's all the same to him, it's out of his head now," said the partisan. "Who's that?"

"It's me." We recognized the voice of Count Pac.

"Everyone is gathering like sparrows round a horse's droppings," the partisan muttered. "Scared of the night?"

The count came into the bright circle of the bonfire, extricated a coal moss-covered with ash and, tossing it from hand to hand, lit a cigarette: "I forgot to buy matches," he said. "You, I see, are already for your journey?"

I thought he was speaking to Ildefons Korsak, but he gazed at me from above the glow of his cigarette.

"Yes, I'm leaving the day after tomorrow. But how did it happen?"

"In the usual way," said the partisan. "During the night, the wind smashed a window. Evidently he was suffocating, so he opened a window. An old woman saw it, she told Regina in the store, they both went up to the wall and started lamenting right away."

We were silent a long time, staring at the fire as it struggled capriciously in the logs. The heat nipped our cheeks. Romus yawned protractedly.

"Please tell me, honestly, quite frankly," I said quietly to the partisan, "whether you believe that Huniady lives here?"

"Who?" he asked, wrenched out of his meditations.

"Whether Huniady lives in the Solec forest?"

"Huniady?"

"Come, you know, we've spoken of him many times."

"I can't remember. So much nonsense has been talked all these years . . ."

"You served in his unit."

"I served in many brigades. I can't even name all my commanding officers."

"But Huniady? After all, there was such a man here."

"Maybe there was. But he must have gone away a long time

ago, or maybe they killed him. Mister, how much time has passed since the war. If it wasn't for this thing," and he stretched out his prosthesis, "I myself wouldn't believe I'd ever seen a war."

I touched the partisan's shoulder. He was gazing intently into the bonfire.

"He's here," I said.

Romus threw a stick into the fire. Sparks scattered again, and again they expired at our feet.

"But how do you know?" he asked, unexpectedly. "Maybe it was him that Harap carted dead into town? You walked a long way after him, you certainly recognized him."

"No. I don't know why I followed the cart."

"But that foreigner, the one who came with that other man? I was in the Solec forest with them. He knew the forest better than I do."

"Maybe he was looking for treasure in the German bunkers? After all, I've often heard it said that Hitler buried the gold of all the Jews in the world there."

The partisan choked in the smoke. He lifted his prosthesis to his mouth.

"Is that why he looked around your house later, and stuck a nail in the moss between the rafters?" Romus persisted.

No one answered him. Count Pac threw his cigarette end into the bonfire. Romus got up slowly and unexpectedly began spitting, time and again.

"Maybe you're Huniady?" he said suddenly.

They all gazed at me. I smiled uncertainly, I even wanted to laugh, but I could see their watchful, hostile eyes, and felt I was turning white for no reason.

"Romus, are you crazy?"

"Who knows what your business is?" he said, quietly.

Ildefons Korsak moved his greenish whiskers, for a time he attempted to form some words soundlessly, until he finally said: "Please leave. You won't find peace here. The water will swallow everything, the earth, and the forest, and the meadows and that noble burial mound, but it won't wash away human memory, nor that which is engraved in a man's heart, it won't melt . . ."

"You've been carried away by poetry like Grandpa Wernyhora," the partisan interrupted. "Maybe this gentleman came to rest, have a good time, laugh at other people's expense? Are there so few artful dodgers?"

"He started off with a fine trick," the count interposed sneeringly. "Have you all forgotten already?"

He bared his teeth and gazed at me with his colorless eyes.

"I'll tell you one thought, a very simple one, but it takes a man a long time to grasp it: life's like a card game — you have to help good luck along."

"I read that in some calendar," said the partisan. "And what have you, you son of a fallen class, gained from life?"

"The fact that I know everything about you, but you don't know anything about me."

And he gave the partisan his fist to sniff, clenched in a contemptuous gesture.

"Ach, you ought to be kicked in the ass." Krupa tugged at him, but at the same moment Ildefons Korsak separated them with his bony hand: "My dear gentlemen, there's death outside, and you, with all due respect, are squabbling like children."

Count Pac straightened the unfastened knot of the colorful scarf at his throat: "D'you know my coat of arms? Two dogs on a sh-shield: one is shitting, the o-other's growling."

A firebrand falling apart crackled. Despite ourselves, we glanced at the remains of the fire, dying out in white ash. Romus looked around furtively at the silent night.

"Bed time," said Ildefons Korsak, and he began stamping out the bonfire.

"He was a man without God," Romus's teeth clattered. "Such as he wander around the earth for ages."

The partisan hit his leather hand on his hip, straightening its fastening.

"You, fear the living, not the dead."

And he was the first to enter into the darkness. We could hear his cautious footsteps: he hit against some obstacle, loitered a little in the middle of the muddy road, and then started singing in an uncertain, strangely thin voice:

> A partisan's faith goes
> Along a path 'midst village huts.
> A pair of eyes shines at a window,
> And lips red as a rose . . .

A large truck drove up, with a canvas covering like that of a gipsy wagon. Six men wearing black garments obviously little worn, since they were tight and didn't fit their heavy, gnarled bodies, jumped out of the back. They landed right in the mud, one of them swearing juicily; then they went up to a boarding and here they carefully cleaned their boots on wisps of old grass. Finally they put out their cigarettes, a couple of them buttoned up their jackets. They entered the deserted garden and went up the wooden steps to the house.

I was standing not far away, gazing at the windows hung with dark bedspreads pulled off beds. I wanted to watch all this to the bitter end, before leaving and forgetting.

After some time two men ran hurriedly into the street. They crawled under the canvas of the truck and there their boots scuffled on the metal floor as they struggled with some object. Finally they tumbled out into the road a large oak coffin of good workmanship, polished, with white flounces at the head rest, too ample and beautiful for the dead man. They seized it expertly at both ends and, jumping over the puddles, went back into the house. A gust of wind hit them in the garden, so strong that they staggered. The first man's felt hat, big as a mushroom, fell off and rolled into the gooseberry bushes. So they placed the coffin on end and the victim hunted furiously for his lost headgear.

The day was really unusual. White clouds, like tropical boats, were rushing hastily south across a sky blue as the ocean. The frosty wind carried a smell of earth and the sap of vegetation awakening to life. It almost seemed as though the longed-for spring was arriving from the north after a severe winter.

I knew that people were watching at the windows of all the houses. That they were eyeing the truck, the coach of our times, that they were following the movements of the driver, who was walking to and fro beside his truck, trying to light a cigarette, protecting it by his hands from the wind.

Someone stopped behind me and sniffed ostentatiously. I knew it was Miss Malvina. Relinquishing any moral or ethical judgment of the day's event, she regarded it as her superior duty to take part in the mourning.

The door opened noisily, pushed clumsily from inside, and the men in black crossed the porch with the coffin on their shoulders. Cautiously they followed the path to the gate, where they struggled a while with the narrow passage, but after that the way was broad and straight, though full of mud. So they stepped along its edge, seeking the drier places, and the coffin on their shoulders shifted its headrest in wide semicircles. They carried it well, feet first, so that it saw this autumn road, these trees painfully crouching under the pressure of the north wind, which was bringing the false smells of spring from no one knew where.

We set off after them. Miss Malvina, humbly crouching against the wind, wrapped herself tightly in a large fringed kerchief, such as my mother used to wear, my mother who died because of me, though I never loved her. A flock of crows, pushed by a gust of wind, drifted toward the river, where the nasal voice of the clarinet resounded from time to time. Miss Malvina was quietly whispering prayers, assuredly those remembered from her own region, that country of legends and wonders, from her family settlement that was similar to our valley.

Near the last gardens, the funeral procession turned right, under the hill on which the monastery stood white. Harap, who was driving his cart to town, halted his horse, took his cap off and watched the procession dully, certainly surprised that they had done without his help, without the assistance of the man who drove the newborn to the township, and who drove away the dead.

Halfway up the slope, the men stopped and lowered the coffin. They rested, calculating with their eyes the distance that separated them from Szafir's last home. The coffin was standing in a clump of old weeds, nameless today, without color or smell. Alongside was a wild pear tree, as bristly as a mistletoe. Many wild pears, cut off by the early frosts, unnaturally sweet, lay in the grass. And even though the men were tired, not one of them picked up this winter fruit.

Later they changed places. The men on the left went round to the right, those on the right to the left. They bent over to the ground, their joints creaking. They raised Szafir high, for they had rested a little, and now he was pointing his legs at the sky, he seemed to be setting his heels firmly against that terrible blueness, as though he objected to this final journey. But they only adjusted themselves to the heavy, solid coffin, a coffin somewhat above the status and importance of the dead man's fate. Now they were moving on, now the coffin floated through the brown vegetation like an old perch.

The monks were standing on the white limestone wall. All but the awkward Father Gabriel, half monk and half farm laborer. They were motionlessly watching the coffin balancing below them. Then the vespers bell resounded, in a slow rhythm, with infrequent strokes, like an Orthodox church bell. Miss Malvina and I stopped at the pear tree, and we didn't know whether they were honoring the departed atheist or summoning to vespers.

Along the wall leaned the blocks of the stone Jewish tombstones. They were facing south and it looked as though they were drying up in the weary autumn sun.

The funeral procession passed them and approached a bed of

dwarf shrubs which marked the extent of the old forgotten cemetery. Only a few fresh bushes could be seen there above the graves of drowned people and murdered policemen.

Then, out of the undergrowth, the railroad man emerged, dragging his leg, with a shovel daubed with yellow earth. He showed them a pit near the cemetery edge, in a place that was steep and not shielded by anything. They took a few more steps and laid the coffin on a heap of rich, live earth.

I stopped at the end of the monastery wall. I was afraid to go up closer, I didn't want these newcomers to ask me questions, but at the same time I wanted to see everything, up to the end.

"See, mister, how terrible death is," whispered Miss Malvina.

"He didn't want any other, that's for sure."

"O my God, better not to be born," she sighed in terror.

"He'll gaze on this valley for years."

One of the men went up to the pit, stroked his hair and froze into immobility. After some time I guessed he was speaking, bidding farewell to his departed comrade. Then they turned the coffin around, feet facing the valley, and tied ropes under it. It swayed like a boat against the shore and slowly plunged into the golden pit. Each of them scattered a handful of earth, but I couldn't hear the ominous patter of earth on the coffin planks from where I was. The railroad man tossed in the first load of sand with his shovel. He and one of the men from the town quickly filled the pit.

Miss Malvina knelt down in the center of the path that was riddled by earthworms. She folded her hands piously and nodded in silence as she gazed toward the grave. Meanwhile they had made a low mound which they patted earnestly with their shovels, as though it were a quilt on the bed of a sleeping man.

Then they all stood around the grave. I could see their mouths open wide. I knew they were singing, and I knew what it was they were singing.

The bell stopped ringing. The wind rushed down toward the township and crushed trees around the houses. The township was gazing at us in terror with its blue windows.

"Now he knows everything," I told myself. Alarmingly, white balls of clouds were rolling along the edge of the hill. The men put their hats on and came out on the path. They began searching in their pockets for cigarettes. The sight surprised them too. Lighting matches in cupped hands, they gazed upward, above Szafir's grave.

"He drove us out, but he himself remained here," said Miss Malvina.

As I set out for the township, the monastery gate hinges groaned. I looked round: Father Gabriel was standing on the stone threshold, in shepherd's attire.

"Maybe you're coming to see us?" he asked with a knowing smile.

"No thanks. I know another way."

"I hear you're leaving?"

"Everybody is leaving. And the fathers?"

"Us? Already we haven't been here for a long time. We look from above at the township as though it were a far-off comet."

"You come down to us sometimes, Father."

"Yes, I alone. Because nature freed me first from all temptations. You haven't looked around our museum."

"No, I haven't."

"I understand. For us they're meteorites, but to you they're nothing of interest. What do you wish on your journey?"

"What do I wish? I don't know myself. My wishes are sacrilegious."

His face, cracked with many wrinkles, smiled, and he winked one eye: "In that case, I won't pry. I'll ring the bell for you some time, shall I?"

I'd gone halfway down the slope, when a sudden thought struck me. I turned back; the monk in his secular garb was still standing in the cherrywood frame of the gate.

"You know what, Father?" I shouted. "Please ring the bell for two people. At the morning Angelus, it must be the morning."

He nodded his head with a crooked smile, to let me know he understood and would carry out my request.

The wind was pouring dry leaves, which raced across the hard earth of the path. Some, seized by stronger gusts, flew across the township like mourning butterflies. I stopped once again: "I have a reason for leaving," I assured myself. "I alone."

And I started running toward the first houses of the settlement until I ran into a wire fence which greeted me with the creaking of an old mattress. Drinking in the cold air, in which I found the familiar smell of ozone, I looked back. The railroad man was sitting alone at the very top of the hill. He was grasping his knees and staring at the red earth underfoot.

"I alone," I repeated to myself.

All of a sudden I felt like shouting, like striking out with my fists at the sky cut across by the invisible carcass of the jet aircraft, like arousing this sleeping township.

"Congratulations. I congratulate you," said someone behind me.

I recoiled unpleasantly. The partisan was standing with knees bent, holding a fragile branch of chestnut in his hand.

"I congratulate you with all my heart," he said, stretching out his good hand.

I automatically pressed his hand, which was moist with sweat.

"I congratulate you and myself."

"What for?" I asked, uncertainly.

He closed his eyes, glassy with moisture, and jogged up and down: "That it wasn't us who were buried in the earth."

"You're the worse for drink."

"Oh fie, who drinks in the morning?" said he, shocked, and supporting himself more firmly against a tree. "What a suspicion," and he puffed sour breath in my face. "I'll reveal a secret to you. I know something better than vodka. I learned it in our first-aid post, you know, when this hand, you understand, why utter bad words, so it was then, primitive conditions, lack of medicines, you know how it was, and I was lying sick in the open bogs. There was a plant, with bitter fruit like unripe chestnuts, do you know it? Someone taught me how to make tea from these seeds, not too strong, just as it should be, for if you take too much, it's bad for you. So I pulled through, though it's not a habit or a narcotic, only a kind of medicine. There, near Podjelniaki, where the river's so wide, these bushes grow in the mud. Anyone drinking a little glass of this herb tea will be relaxed, kind, and not angry all day. It's a drink for forgetting."

"I'm leaving. I wanted to say goodbye."

He leaned back heavily against the chestnut tree trunk and bowed his muddled head: "Why do you mention that? Ah, you're a bitter, disappointed man. Be off quietly, and don't say anything."

He tried to raise his head, but the muscles of his neck refused to obey: "I'm leaving too. Don't let her think she's found her winning post. I'll wake them up some night and drive them out of their bed with fire."

Finally he straightened himself. He gazed at me with weary eyes: "I say that, but don't you believe me. See what sort of drink it is? I don't even feel angry now. But at night I toss and turn purely out of hatred. You think for sure that I loved her? Well, it was a passing fancy, I wanted to see what sort of woman she was. And she's a bitch, I tell you, a whore."

"Maybe we'll meet again some day," I said, politely.

"Who knows? I too know how to find my way. My colleagues are good guys. D'you think I've always screwed screws into railroad ties? Anyway, you know, you've got a round knowing eye, yet it has its own cunning. I know about you too, maybe we'll meet there, up above."

"Till we meet again."

"Till we meet again, if you're not a stool pigeon, if you haven't sold your own people, if you're not looking for a rope. Till we meet again."

I didn't walk away, but hesitated, and he understood:

"Well, be off, be off. I rounded it out, so it was nicer. And remember that drink. You'll know it easily, it has prickles like a green chestnut which hasn't yet burst."

I set off toward home, while he remained swaying under the tree, as though screwing his screw into the chestnut trunk. At the end of the street the men, giving one another a hand, were climbing into the back of the truck. The truck backed up in deep puddles and moved off, rocking deeply on its springs, toward the faroff town, marked on the horizon by glowing clouds of smoke.

Romus rushed away from the gate into Szafir's garden and ran crazily across the street without looking at me, then hid on the opposite side in someone else's garden. I knew quite well that he was standing behind a dense raspberry bush and eyeing me with brash attentiveness.

"Romus, I'm leaving," I said, not loudly.

He kept silent. I could discern the shape of his crouching body in the tangle of red stalks.

"Won't you say goodbye, Romus? We'll never meet again. After all, you were waiting for this day."

He couldn't stop himself from hastily spitting, but he kept a stubborn silence. So I went into our yard, oddly bare without the fence, equal segments of which were lying by the hayshed.

The pictures had already gone from the wall of my room, even the one with the winter sun auguring wind, with the rut of a path in the snow and the slender birch, that sentimental cypress of our neighborhood. Into my green canvas bag, on the very top, I placed my tarpaulin coat, unnecessary today, pulled the string and stood thus in the middle of the room. A sort of dread leaped at me from the window and seized my shoulders.

I put the bag down and went out on the veranda. A clothes line was swaying in the wind. I recognized the Korsaks' sheets, Mr. Il-defons' holiday shirt. They were preparing for the journey as for extreme unction.

I knocked at the door, provided with a bunch of dried flowers instead of a visiting card. No one answered. So I turned the handle and went in.

I'd never been here before. I didn't know this little room encrusted with hysterical, maidenly souvenirs. Ribbons, ornamental branches picked during a walk, withered flowers in bottles and behind a photograph was a straw hat and some holy image or other, its feet red with lipstick. And on a little table by the couch was the whole secret arsenal of female captivity, of female hope. A laboratory of forgery. The sanctuary of supreme deceit. Open jars of creams and ointments without lids, nail files and hairpins, curling irons and tweezers, pomades and false eyelashes, shampoos and medicines in little bottles with pink ribbons of prescriptions, pills for all manner of ailments and gleaming clippers, cigarette ends with blood-red tips and a stocking with a run in it.

I could hear the splash of water behind a flowery screen: "Good morning, Miss Regina. Am I interrupting?"

She ran out of her concealment, wearing a long robe, holding a mop of wet hair in both hands: "Oh, it's you," she said. "Excuse me for looking like this."

"I wanted to say goodbye to you. Especially to you."

She smiled, gazing at the floor: "My room is so untidy. It isn't allowed to reveal my secrets to men."

"But I already know the truths behind this fiction."

"You're making fun."

"No. On the contrary, I'm admiring."

"Too bad you won't be at my wedding."

She sat down on the couch and tossed a bundle of hair down her back with a movement of her head.

"So you've made up your mind?"

"Instead of a great love, a great wedding. That's good too."

"I'll write you. Will you both be staying here much longer?"

"I don't know. Probably we'll all have to leave before winter comes. Please be sure to write. I adore getting letters."

I shifted from one foot to the other. She raised her eyes and said, with a cheerless smile: "Who's to be envied in this world?"

"It will turn out all right," I said.

She made a gesture with one hand and said, with joking vigor: "Oh well, so what? It'll be all right, sure. But if it isn't, then that'll be good too."

She rose from the couch and came up to me: "I can see by your eyes you're hiding something up your sleeve. I wish you well. May everything come out well for you at least. Please sometimes remember poor, crazy Regina. Well, let's kiss; surely no one will cast a spell on me for that."

She embraced me in a womanly manner with her warm hands, kissed me for a long time on my mouth, within a hair's breadth of indecency.

"We already said goodbye once," she whispered.

"Maybe we'll meet again."

"Sure, like everyone. In Josephat's valley."

She turned her back. I knew she had taken a damp lock of bright hair between her teeth.

"Miss Regina . . ."

"Please don't say anything. Well, that's all. It happened, it's passed," and she suddenly grew quiet.

I went out on tiptoe, closing the door cautiously.

Miss Malvina was waiting on the veranda in her holiday dress, with the little jabot which emphasized the solemn feelings of the old maid. She came into my room after me and watched as I fastened my traveling bag for the second time.

"There's nothing like being solitary," she sighed at length. "Here today, gone tomorrow, not attached anywhere."

"Everything looks better on other people."

"Don't blaspheme, don't offend God, mister," she said, shocked. "You have a blessed life and you don't even know it. Healthy, not old, learned, just show me how many such can be counted up."

"But what do you know about me, miss?"

"I know that if they were to drive you to hard labor, from morning to night, so your eyes cloud over and you can't straighten your back, then the sun would shine brighter on you, the wind would be warmer, and life easier."

"Is that what everything ends in?"

"People are spoiled, mister, they're wanton as never before. And that's why the end of the world is coming, or if not, then we'll arrange it ourselves. Only think how many people would change their destiny for yours. But you threaten the sky and curse the world. Waste of words."

"Is that what you wanted to tell me on my departure?"

"Please don't get angry, don't remember me badly, but please think of what I've said."

"And what should I wish for you?"

"Me, me?" she took fright all of a sudden. "I'm old, I need

nothing. Fate doesn't have to add to what I have, as long as it don't take anything away."

"Goodbye, then. And thank you for everything."

I slung my bag over my shoulders. The chilly sun stood at the window in the dark branches of jasmine.

"Don't put yourself above heavenly power," the old lady whispered.

I went out into the street that led toward the railroad tracks. Above the rusty tracks I could already see the top of the shingled roof of the empty house. I could see the young oak thicket filled with a delicate dark blue on the other side of the river. I still had to go there, I had to shut that door before my long and uncertain journey.

He was kneeling amidst large, almost purple apples set out on straw. He was selecting the poorer ones marked with rot and putting them aside in a basket of spruce roots, which I knew well. He looked up, gazed a moment at the window, then said: "You keep leaving, but somehow you never do."

A half-open book was lying on the table by a lamp. I noticed a red ribbon between the thin pages.

"You're reading the Bible," I said.

He glanced at me with that smile of his, restricted to his lips alone: "You've a fine picture of me. A buffoon, well-read in the Bible. Nowadays even handbooks for cultural officials start with a quotation from the Old Testament. It's the most fashionable reading for atheists. A test of intelligence and superior taste. The hobby of aristocrats of the spirit. No, sir, Ive always respected the monuments of writing, but I read something else. The only thing that interests me is that which is in the range of my sight, my presence, my feelings."

"I've come to you without anger."

He rose and began wiping a huge, fine apple, like an overripe pumpkin, on his sleeve. There suddenly grew a brightness in the window, a slanting sunray fell into the room and settled like a cat on the table alongside the ruler with black marks of human teeth.

"An empty globe bursts no feebler than a globe with gunpowder in it. Maybe you'd like to try the apples? Please take some along on your journey."

I was standing motionless at the door.

"Are you looking for Justine? She went to Podjelniaki, you know, to the children there, surely I told you, to the orphanage."

"I wanted to see you before leaving. But now I'm sorry I came."

He turned to me and gazed somewhere to the side of my head,

at the gnarled planks of the door: "You came to see me, I remember. How can I help you? You see, somehow it's the way you look, so that everybody feels obliged to describe you, to define you, to give you good advice, teach you. You obviously ask for it, you lead people on."

He picked up the ruler and began striking it nervously against the seam of his trousers: "You're not looking for anything. Pride, unhealthy self-esteem pushes you on. You dress up your destiny in special meanings, ornament it with unrepeatable significance, you dress it up with a thrilling metaphor. You're trying to keep up appearances in the face of your own emptiness. Made hysterical by your lack of power, you're trying to make a royal robe for yourself out of the threads of life, to distinguish you from the crowd."

The sun on the table went out. The walls darkened and his face became invisible. He struck the ruler faster and faster. The sound reminded me of the beating of a terrified animal's heart.

"She lied to him about Podjelniaki," I said to myself quietly. "She's waiting for me at the siding."

And suddenly I was sorry for the hunched man, tense with vigilant hostility.

I took some steps forward and stretched out my hand: "Maybe you're right. If it's as you say it is, then surely I deserve sympathy more than the basest of the base."

He stiffened, outraged by my humility, which he evidently didn't trust.

"Won't you shake hands?"

He was silent. I saw he was hesitating.

"After all, you're richer than I am."

He touched my hand rapidly and then wiped his hand on his trousers for a long time.

"Too bad Justine isn't here. She likes you very much."

"Can't be helped. Maybe we'll meet again. Well said?"

I saw his cheek, outlined in light, suddenly twitch.

"Don't think badly of her," he said, quietly. "A person only knows as much as he knows about himself."

He paid no attention to my words.

"She's sick. She needs care."

I moved toward the door that was thickly inscribed with knots. Gray bunches of herbs were hanging over the frame.

"Please forget everything. That's best," he said, and I felt a violent uneasiness. I looked toward him from the threshold. He was standing crouched over the table, he placed the ruler tightly clutched in his palm on the pages of the open book. I couldn't see his face, it was covered in shadow, but I divined that the corners of his mouth, congealed with dried foam, were trembling spasmodically, that he was clenching his teeth with all his might, restraining the vibration that was intensifying within him.

I ran toward the siding without looking back. A group of people was standing by the railroad man's shed, but Justine was not among them. So I tossed my bag into a clump of old nettles and sat down on the bag, shielded by a bush. I gazed intently along the road running towards me along the tracks. I was waiting for Justine.

I listened to the voice of this valley. I could distinguish the groaning of the forest, the chattering of the river as it forced its way toward the town through its windings, I heard the rustle of grass and weeds whose names I had long since forgotten, I listened to the hiss of the wind and the deep silence of the earth.

My hands were trembling, my knees knocking, a biting chill crept under my coat and struck my muscles with numbness. The road in front of me was empty, completely empty, although I gazed as hard as I could. I looked into the bluish darkness between two lakes of forest, and waited for the figure of a girl to emerge from it.

"Such is the situation," I recalled Szafir's saying. "What's the situation? What does it signify?"

I pressed both hands to my temples, suffering like a speaker who's lost his train of thought. The moment of truth was approaching, while here I was in the alder bushes unprepared to receive it, and terrifyingly alone.

"The train's coming," said someone behind me.

"How do you know?"

"If you put your ear to the track, you can hear the wheels rumbling."

"But she isn't here."

"You must leave. That's why you came here," someone's stifled voice whispered.

Someone's hands took me under the armpits and lifted me from the bag. I was standing in a clump of still green yarrow.

"Is this you, Romus?" I asked.

"Yes. Please go to the platform. It stops here for only two minutes."

"But after all I can't leave alone."

"Oh, look, you can see the smoke."

He loaded my bag on my back and pushed me, not hard but

firmly. I made several steps toward the embankment. In fact, a net of dense smoke was forming over the forest.

"God, how cold it is," I said.

"North wind. Bringing snow. Please go on."

So, stooping under the bag like a smuggler coming back from a military excursion, I set off. I entered the wooden platform and it seemed to me that I was standing on a bridge, that I was watching an alien, unknown life from above. The train was approaching from Podjelniaki, pouring smoke and steam into the narrow ravine of the track, along which no one was walking. The locomotive stopped amidst silvery lamps with a ceremonial garland of spruce greenery. And immediately alongside, below, stood the inhabitants of the township. They had come to see how a person left this place for no reason.

"Where's this train going to?" I asked.

"People will tell you," said Count Pac, and he stroked his green hair, since he was sensitive to the presence of women.

"But poor man, he's turned pale, he can hardly stand on his feet," said Miss Malvina.

"He can't part with us, excuse me."

"He's one of those people who grumble all their lives. And they grumble in this manner a hundred years," cried the partisan.

"By tomorrow he'll be far away, in other places, with other people," sighed Regina.

The train was standing behind me. Someone helped me on to the step and threw my bag into the car. I could hear rapid spitting somewhere nearby, behind the wall of steam.

I wanted to look once more at these meadows with the extinct peat beds, at the river nestling to the hill with the oak thicket, so I looked up, and all of a sudden I caught sight of Justine. She was standing alone at the foot of the railroad embankment, her hands nervously twisted together.

"Justine!" I shouted, although she could see me, although she was staring at me with a fixed gaze.

"Justine! I'm waiting!"

But she shook her head.

All at once I woke up from my numbness. I jumped to the planks of the platform, then down to the ground. I rushed toward her, but she was already far away. She was running full speed, arms outstretched, towards the meadows and the river.

I stopped and saw her turn to the left as she rushed into an alder thicket. They were shouting something at me from behind, urging decisively. So I went back to the train, and leaned my head against the vibrating iron side. I could see them veiled every few moments in outbursts of steam. They were waiting for my departure.

Then the steam thinned out and again I caught sight of Justine in almost the same place as before. She was breathing quickly after the exhausting run, and was seeking me with wide open eyes in the windows of the car. Finally she caught sight of me standing on the platform and she shuddered, as though intending to take flight again.

Our eyes met. In her eyes was fear close to terror. Leaning forward, she was imploring me to stay where I was, not to pursue her. When I opened my mouth, she shook her head in a vigorous denial. So we stood thus, our gazes interlocked, vigilant, aware of every thought.

"God, why doesn't the train leave?" she cried at last.

From somewhere in the depths of steam, Romus' slow voice said: "The engine broke down. They're repairing it."

Indeed, someone was sneaking rapidly along the cars with a hammer in his hand. Noisy bangings resounded, a tongue of steam flowed, hissing, over the embankment and embraced the girl's legs. Slowly she sank into the whiteness, already immersed to her hips, then to her breast and to her shoulders. She clearly realized that she was being immersed, since she raised one hand violently, as though in a gesture to summon help or of farewell.

Then the train rocked backward and moved, its wheels rolling on the track I myself had laid. The engine whistled victoriously and the Solec forest answered with a hundredfold echo. The wheels rattled faster and faster over the joints in which were rooted spikes worked in by my hands.

I turned my face in the direction in which we were going, and stood with my back to the township and valley. I didn't want to see anything, I didn't long to remember anything. My gaze greeted the telegraph poles running by, just as everywhere else in the world. Down below somewhere the forgotten graves of Soviet soldiers slipped by, the last trace of this area.

Listening to the rattling of the train, I also listened at the same time to the wave of uneasiness arising within me.

"She's traveling in the next car," I suddenly whispered.

I turned and rushed along the swaying gangway to a door that opened and closed in time to the train's movement. I ran down the corridor, looking into the mostly empty compartments.

"She'll be in the next car, for sure."

Again the swaying gangplank of metal grating, again compartments in which a few travellers were gazing sleepily out of the window at the sad, autumn landscape, flooded by the light of the feeble sun. Banging against the walls of the corridor I ran persistently toward the end of the train.

"She is in the last car. She jumped aboard before the train gathered speed, now she's coming to meet me."

But beyond the last door, beyond the window bespattered with soot, all I could see was an unusually narrow triangle of tracks reaching with its peak to a sky swept clean of clouds and I realized that we were moving along a curved slope toward the town.

Only dry leaves were running after the train, but they too, after a brief chase, stayed in the end amidst the rusty tracks.

I recalled my bag. I went back to the familiar place. It was trembling on the very edge of the gangplank, already covered with a thick layer of soot. I could see how, in imperceptible movement, it was moving nearer and nearer to the edge, beyond which was an empty hole between the cars.

So I stood on two metal plates which kept rubbing against one another in some incomprehensible struggle and stared at that dun-coloured scrap of space, bounded by the edge of the car and the moving projections of the buffers. The ties, fleeing backwards and the spiky stones of gravel merged into one fluffy, soft whole giving off warmth. I gazed at this royal carpet, tempting with its comfort and rest, breathing a long journey, and I leaned over it slowly, as over a meadow in springtime, a meadow filled with the scents of grass, meadows, and fertile earth. Already I could feel underfoot the springy flexibility of rebellious stalks, already the wholesome chill of the peat bed dampness was permeating me, already I could hear the cry of birds greeting a new day that was pregnant with life.

Then all of a sudden I thought that now, in a moment, I would awaken, raise myself out of a stifling dream which comes to all of us one night or another, a dream full of specters and nightmares, fragments of passed and wasted experiences, imagined and never fulfilled, the dream of a distorted memory, a foreboding heated by fever, that I would scramble with the remains of my strength out of these seething depths to the edge of reality, and would get up to an ordinary, commonplace day, with its usual troubles, its everyday toil, its so well-known, familiar drudgery.

For a complete list of books available from Penguin in the United States, write to Dept. DG, Penguin Books, 299 Murray Hill Parkway, East Rutherford, New Jersey 07073.

For a complete list of books available from Penguin in Canada, write to Penguin Books Canada Limited, 2801 John Street, Markham, Ontario L3R 1B4.

If you live in the British Isles, write to Dept. EP, Penguin Books Ltd, Harmondsworth, Middlesex.